PRAISE FOR SU J. SOKOL

Praise for **_FIVE POINTS ON AN INVISIBLE LINE:_**

Told through five powerful points-of-view, this timely and provocative work of hopepunk weaves together activism, polyamory, political asylum and social justice into a near-future Montreal reimagined with grit and hope. A tender ode to resilience, family and radical love, Five Points offers a vivid portrait of a city—and world—on the brink, guided by a cast of memorable and distinct voices, each shimmering with optimism and empathy. A fierce and inspiring call-to-action.

CHRISTOPHER DIRADDO, AUTHOR
OF _THE FAMILY WAY._

FIVE POINTS ON AN
INVISIBLE LINE

FIVE POINTS ON AN INVISIBLE LINE

INVISIBLE LINE BOOK 2

SU J. SOKOL

FLAME ARROW PUBLISHING

ALSO BY SU J. SOKOL

Invisible Line (2014, 2025)

Run J Run (2019)

Zee (2020)

Five Points on an Invisible Line (Invisible Line #2)

Copyright © 2025 Su J. Sokol

Cover design by Damonza

Cover photo credit: **https://en.wikipedia.org/wiki/Pink_House_(Montreal)**

Printed in Canada

First Edition: 2025

Legal Deposit: 2025

Published by Flame Arrow Publishing

ISBN 978-1-990368-23-3 (Hardcover)

ISBN 978-1-990368-24-0 (Paperback)

ISBN 978-1-990368-22-6 (Ebook)

www.flamearrowpublishing.com

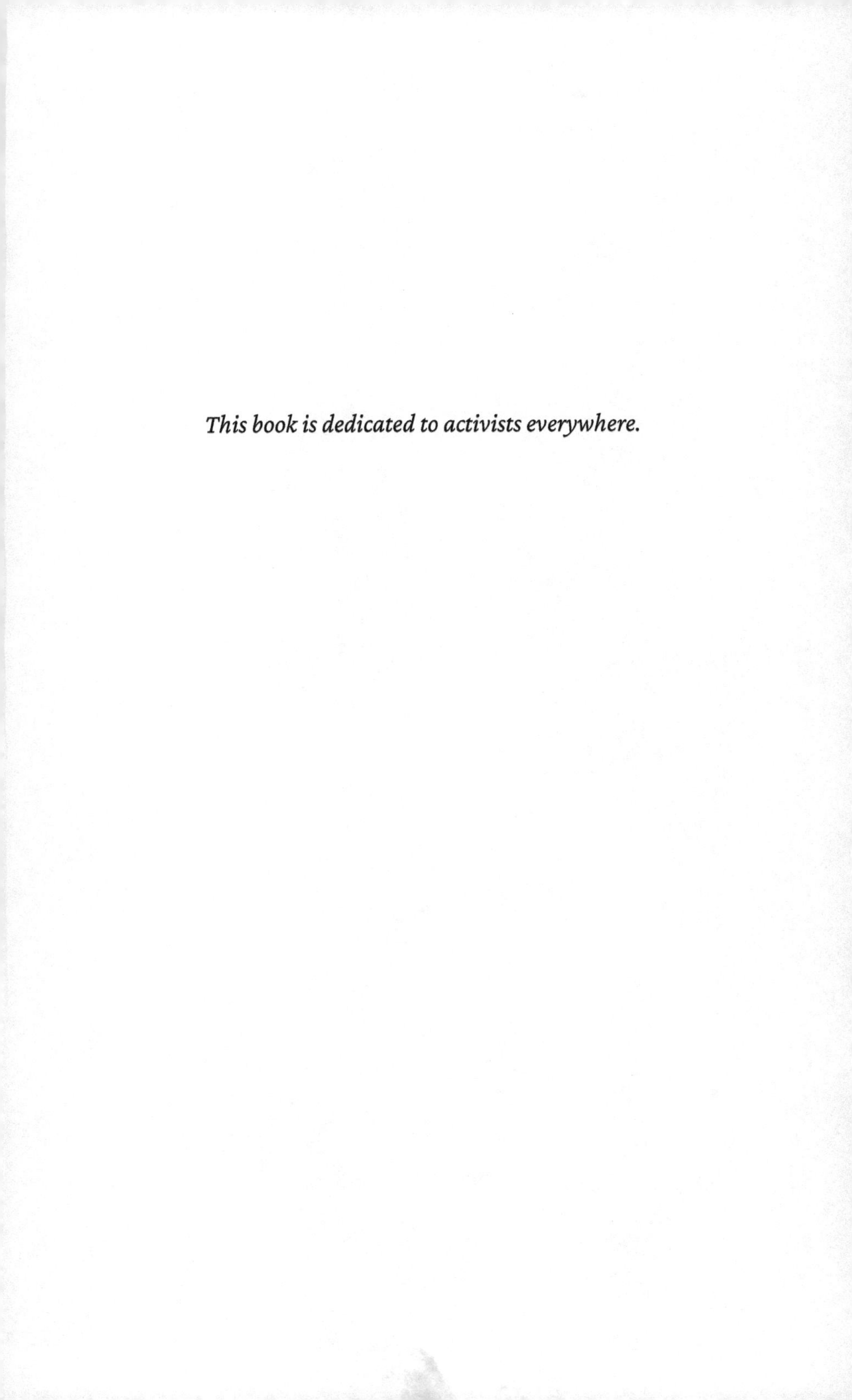

This book is dedicated to activists everywhere.

"The one thing we need more than hope is action. Once we start to act, hope is everywhere."

Greta Thunberg

AUTHOR'S NOTE ON CONTENT

Five Points on an Invisible Line is a work of hopepunk, exploring themes of solidarity, activism, love, and community. Hopepunk is also a genre that looks at marginalization and oppression, violence and struggle, and as such, often includes depictions of some darker experiences and realities. In this novel, some of these depictions include: police violence, PTSD, flashbacks to sexual assault, rape, torture, and suicidal ideation, child labour, and some fight scenes.

Along with these darker elements contained in the story, there are also comic, loving, and exciting moments, as well as scenes of pure joy. I intend for the reader to leave this tale with hope and a taste for continuing the fight for social justice.

Su J. Sokol

ACTION ONE: THE AIRPORT

CHAPTER 1
JANIE

I'm running with the kids on the high-speed lane of the moving walkway inside Tiohtià:ke/Montréal Airport. Beneath my winter jacket, lines of sweat trickle down from my armpits and between my breasts. Laek, meanwhile, sprints along effortlessly. Every so often, he shoots us an impatient look over his shoulder, though if he hadn't been on his wristpad when it was time to leave, we wouldn't be rushing right now.

Laek slows and I come even with him. "Let me carry the backpack, Janie."

"The backpack's not the problem," I tell him. "It's my short legs."

"Your legs are perfect," Laek says, and I can see he means it. His smile is sweet, not flirty—like he's simply stating a happy truth.

He takes my hand, which somehow makes it easier to pick up the pace. We zip past a moving loop of flat info-pics of tourist attractions like the Biodiversity Dome, parc du Mont-Royal, and Simon's favourite, the Musée de glace with its life-sized ice sculptures.

Hopping off the walkway at the international terminal, we're suddenly surrounded by travel ad holos. Giant red letters appear on a background of blue and white stripes: **CUBA, SI!** the ad seems to shout at us, and as we pass through, the sound of ocean waves fills our ears while the sweet scent of Cuban tobacco mixed with weed fills our nostrils.

"Hyper!" Simon cries, swinging his head from side to side to not miss anything.

"Stop acting like an ignorant regionalist," his sister says.

"Be nice, Siri," Laek scolds gently. "This is your brother's first time in a real airport."

The thing is, Siri's also never been to an airport and neither has Laek. I'm the only one of us who has. Though I was only four at the time, the memory of our family trip to see cousins in Montevideo is very clear in my mind today, down to the smell of the recycled air on the plane. Our visit was just before the X-Mass Attacks that disabled airports in ten major cities. Now, I find myself at the airport all the time, not as a passenger, but as a refugee lawyer. It's my way of paying it forward for all the good work our own lawyer did when we came as refugees from the United America three years ago.

"Wait till you see the arrivals area," I tell my family, leading them to the down escalators.

Before getting there, we have to run the gauntlet of fragrant food modules selling poutine, falafel, queue de castor, dragon bowls, and spicy noodle clouds.

"Mommy, can we get something?" Simon asks, looking to Siri for support.

"Simon and I could share," Siri offers, her eyes on the dragon bowls.

"We need to meet Philip," I remind the kids. "And we're late."

"I'm sure he'd like a queue de castor," Simon says hopefully.

"He probably would," Laek says smiling. "But first, help me find his arrival gate."

"Oui, Papa," Simon replies, running ahead to catch Laek's hand in his own. Simon at twelve still has the innocent, open heart of a young child, unembarrassed to gape at things and hold hands with his dad. It makes my own heart ache, for Simon is so much like Laek, or at least how Laek might have turned out had he actually been cared for in his childhood.

"Tabarnak!" cries Simon, the first to spot Philip's flight on the holo-board. "His plane's twenty-seven minutes late!"

"Watch your language!" Siri scolds.

"It's okay," I say. To me, "tabarnak" resonates less like a swear word and more like a quaint reference to the ancient Catholic mass. In any case, I'm relieved the plane is delayed, and my frustration at Laek for making us late dissipates like early morning fog in bright sunshine.

At Arrivals, I point out the huge ceiling screen showing images of airplanes arriving in real time, but transformed into light and sound art. Pulsating heat waves of purple and red emanate from the wings and noses of the planes, and the loud crescendo of a descending major scale sounds each time there's a landing. Simon's standing, mouth open, and even fifteen-year-old Siri's having trouble maintaining that well-practiced bored expression on her face.

We walk under the screen towards the arrival gate. The large space is busy, everyone rushing off in different directions. I turn to Laek, trying to gauge his state of mind.

"It's more crowded than I thought it'd be," Laek says in that flat voice he uses when he's suppressing an emotion.

"Yeah." Between the most recent pandemic, our politicians' constant stoking of xenophobic fears, and Québec's heavy carbon tax for air travel, international voyages are rare for ordinary people. Even more so than they were three years ago when we escaped New York by bicycle to seek political asylum in Québec. Laek's not wrong that today's airport crowds are unexpected, especially more than a week past the winter holidays.

"C'mon, this way," I say to the kids, who are still mesmerized by the ceiling screen.

Laek, meanwhile, is carefully checking out his surroundings without moving his head. He's one of those people who can achieve perfect stillness, and when he does move, it's with a graceful economy of motion that's something between beautiful and a little creepy. That he's doing this now tells me he's nervous, or at least wary. It might be our presence at an airport bringing back thoughts of his near-deportation, or memories of travel in general, which for Laek has always meant fleeing. Or perhaps it's just the prospect of seeing Philip again.

Of all of us, the stakes for this visit are highest for Laek. To Simon, Philip is his dad's best friend, the big, strong, gentle "Uncle" Phil who'd carry him on his shoulders even after Simon was no longer little; to Siri, he's the father she thinks she should've had—a solid, sensible man who loves sports as much as she does—instead of the damaged, unpredictable, too-young-and-too-attractive person who's her actual father. And to me? Up to now, Philip's simply been a good friend, a trusted confidant. I certainly can't claim he's ever been a rival, not when our goals have always been aligned in Laek's interest, in our mutual love for him. When the two of them parted that last night in Brooklyn, it was me who broke down first, though it was Laek who cried the hardest.

We move closer to the front of the waiting area. A little off to the right is a garderie and play area with puzzles and games where families can leave their kids for a short time.

"Whoa!" Simon says, staring at a giant 3-D math puzzle. "Can I try?"

"Sure," I tell him. "Siri, go with your brother."

She seems ready to argue but shrugs and follows him.

I turn back to Laek, who's sidling over to the left. He's tied his coat around his waist—he's only wearing a t-shirt despite the day's frigid temperatures. He's seemingly calm, but I know him too well. I lay my hand on his arm. It's rock hard. He's holding himself together so tightly that if I tapped him on the forehead, I imagine him cracking like the glaze on a piece of Raku pottery.

The flow into the arrivals area is only a trickle at first; then more passengers start coming through from behind the opaque barriers. The noise and hubbub suggest a planeload of people—perhaps Philip's plane? The holo-board indicates that it's landed, so I look for signs that the arriving passengers are from Paris.

"Do you think he'll be taken for French?" I ask Laek. It's seriously fucked-up that after two years of applications, Philip, a Puerto Rican New Yorker, only succeeded in obtaining a six-month visa to visit us by enrolling in a French-language program in Paris and arranging to do the winter semester in Montréal as a "Parisian" exchange student.

Laek shakes his head minutely—not an answer but a signal to talk about something else.

I listen carefully to the passengers' conversations. I have a good ear for accents, though my own New York-accented French sounds atrocious. The passengers seem Parisian to me.

"Don't worry, he'll be here soon," I say. "You know Philip. He's probably helping some senior citizen or family of twelve with their luggage."

Rather than laughing, or even responding, Laek turns very slightly to the left. I follow his gaze. The main thing in Laek's line of sight is the "Aide aux migrant·e·s" kiosk. A holo message offering help flashes in an alternating loop of a dozen different languages. Translation glasses hang over the side of the kiosk, which is lucky because whoever was working the booth seems to be on a break.

Laek faces forward again as a new wave of passengers begins streaming through. I look up at the holo-board; a plane from Tunis has also landed.

Minutes and more minutes pass and my excitement begins to morph into anxiety. I stand on my toes, craning my neck to see all around me, as though somehow Philip could just as easily appear behind or beside me as from the gates ahead of us. The passengers are coming in dribs and drabs now, mostly speaking Arabic, so probably from the other flight, yet Philip has still not appeared. I turn towards Laek, planning to murmur something reassuring, when I sense him go very still.

Philip is walking alone through the gate, about to reach the empty kiosk. The tension is back in Laek's body, but now it's the tension of keeping himself from springing forward. I release his arm, and he runs towards Philip, who's spotted us. If I had any residual question about how this reunion would make me feel, it's answered instantly and emphatically as my heart fills with joy.

I'm thinking how lucky it is that Philip's so large and solid. A smaller man, or one less strong, would be knocked over by the force and speed of Laek's body flying towards Philip's waiting embrace. Then I watch, horrified, while Laek, mid-flight, shoots his arms out to shove Philip hard against the chest. The momentum brings Philip down, Laek right on top of him. Less than a second later, the kiosk shatters, the concussive blast knocking me backwards. I watch pieces of metal and plastic rain down on Laek and Philip's prone bodies, the smoking remains of the kiosk a few short metres from where Philip had just been standing.

CHAPTER 2
LAEK

I smell plaster dust. Burning metal and polymers. My ears are ringing. I'm seized by an overpowering sense of déjà vu that makes me want to throw up my insides. To counter this, I concentrate on Philip's reassuring solidity beneath me. I press my hand against his chest. His heartbeat is strong but very fast.

Lifting my head slightly, I peer all around. If we were inside an analog watch and Philip's head were at twelve, then the kiosk where the bomb went off would be at ten. Siri and Simon are moving towards four. Still far away, good. Janie's closer, running frantically towards us. I signal to her with my eyes and chin. She gets it and stops. Changes direction to head off the kids. I don't want them in or near the clock face.

People are screaming, shouting. I think they are, anyway. I can't hear anything but the ringing in my ears. It's only been a few seconds since the blast, but we need to move. Cops will be here soon. I don't think anyone's dead—the blast was small— but I smell blood.

One last look to ensure that Janie and the kids are heading somewhere safer. She has them both firmly by the hand. Siri's resisting. Looking towards Philip and me. I catch her eye. Shake my head sharply. The room spins. When it stops, I see Siri look around once more before letting Janie drag her off.

Philip's trying to sit up. I put my mouth near his ear. "Fais comme moi," I tell him, hoping he'll get that I mean for him to follow my lead, including in language. "Comprends-tu?" I ask. My voice sounds raspy, but I can hear myself now. Philip nods. "Yeah, okay," he says in English, and in response to my sharp look, "Oui. D'accord."

I get up. Will the dizziness to pass. I help Philip to his feet, slide my hands over his chest and arms. He seems unhurt. Freaked out, though. I put on my coat to cover whatever's happened to my back, grab Philip's luggage, and lead him from the chaos.

We head right, away from the exits. Away from where everyone else is running. I studied a holo-map of the airport. Know exactly where I want to go. We mount the escalator. I take the steps two at a time, Philip right behind me. We're two thirds of the way up when the airport's security system kicks in.

ATTENTION À TOUS LES PASSAGERS ET PASSAGÈRES ! UN INCIDENT ...

I stop listening. Focus on what we need to do. Philip startles as the alarms begin to whine, the whole area flashing with emergency lighting. Green pulsating arrows appear in the air, pointing back down the escalator and towards the exits. Philip hesitates. I grab his arm, lead him towards the shopping concourse. He stumbles but lets me pull him along.

We walk against a growing tide of people running in the opposite direction. Some are dragging luggage or frantic children. A few shopkeepers are trying to lock doors, engage security barriers. Most are simply fleeing. There's shouting and screaming. Pushing and shoving. People stumbling. I hug the far right of the corridor. Keep Philip close beside me. A few people glance at us, confused that we're going the wrong way. Most ignore us, focused on their own safety.

The corridor seems longer than it should be. I pick up the pace. Philip awkwardly half-jogs beside me. "Don't run like that," I tell him. "Just lengthen your stride."

"Wait, Laek. Are you alright? Where are we going?" He sounds nervous, confused.

I lead us towards the end of the corridor. The map I found on the shadow-net indicated a secondary exit. Used mostly by airport staff. It's on the other side of the building from the Skyline and the shuttles to centre-ville. Once outside, we can cut a transversal path across the roadways. Eventually access a street leading to the old Dorval railway station. From there, we can catch a city bus home.

I sight the exit. Stop abruptly. My sneakers squeak in protest on the shiny floor.

"Merde," I whisper. The exit's blocked off. An imposing metal security gate standing between us and freedom.

"What's wrong?" Philip asks.

"We gotta go back down. Through whatever checkpoints they've set up."

"But we shouldn't have a problem. We're victims, not—"

"Philip," I say carefully, hand squeezing his shoulder. "Don't be stupid."

My voice sounds cold. He searches my eyes, and I hold his gaze, silent.

"Okay. Je te suis," he responds after a moment. I turn and Philip follows.

I lead us back down the corridor. Slip into a deserted gift shop. I grab a cheap tuque with the Habs emblem and a cartoon hockey player on it. Pull it over Philip's wavy hair, turning his head this way and that. Satisfied, I lead us to the exit, past the purchase scanners. The clerk's long gone. I pull some credits out of my pocket. Toss them onto the counter.

"What—" Philip begins.

"It's money, Philip. You know I don't pay by wrist chip."

"I mean, what. . . why aren't we getting the hell out of here like everyone else?"

"We are. After we pick up a couple of things."

"Laek, this is crazy."

"This way," I say, leading him out of the store and back along the concourse.

I move quickly towards a flower shop. Grab the most ostentatious bouquet I see—flowers of dark blue, metallic silver, tie-dyed amber—and thrust it into Philip's arms. He looks up at me, eyes questioning, worried.

"For Janie," I say. "You carry money?"

"No. . . I installed Interpay on my wrist chip."

I press my lips together. "We'll have to owe them, then. Let's go."

Philip hesitates, clearly uncomfortable, before following me to the escalator. I ride standing still, surveying the scene as we descend. "Dios mío," Philip whispers.

I remain silent. Medical teams are helping people with injuries. Other emergency personnel are cordoning off the area where the bomb went off. Capturing images on their wrist-pads. Taking samples. The bomb seems to have exploded in a mostly vertical path. There's a hole in the ceiling. Pieces of metal and plastic have rained down in a circle, but the circumference of damage is surprisingly small.

The escalator reaches the bottom. We follow the thinned-out crowd towards the exits. I set my face to look horrified rather than interested. What I feel, though, is blank. I try to make myself afraid. Or recapture the sudden anger I'd felt upstairs. I feel nothing at all. Not even alarm that the blankness has returned. Back again after two years of relatively good mental health.

We reach the first checkpoint. They're waving certain people left, towards the exits leading to the shuttle. Others are being sent right, towards a secured section of the airport. They're not checking wrist chips. Or pads. Too time-consuming. They'll want to evacuate as many people as possible, so they're using profiling. Two-parent families with children, older folx, female-presenting people, mostly all White, are being sent left. Young male-presenting people, women in hijabs, non-family groups—these people are being herded to the right.

I look outside. Wonder if Janie and the kids made it out. They should be okay. If I'd been with them, who knows? I get noticed for some reason. And if we'd added Philip to the mix, another man, a foreigner...

I look him over. Half Latine. Big. A football player's body with the face of an absent-minded professor, Janie likes to joke. But Philip can seem intimidating to people in authority. With the Habs hat and the flowers, I've made him look slightly ridiculous instead.

It's our turn. I smile at the guard. They smile back. Then shrug apologetically and motion us right. My expression doesn't change. I'm considering our narrowing array of options.

Someone from airport security takes Philip's luggage. They leave us the flowers.

We're put in a small, crowded room. I measure the space to be about eight by ten metres. We're all sitting on plasti-form chairs. They're made out of a milky white substance, and it looks like it's oozing. Alive. I shudder a little. Philip puts his arm around my shoulder.

"Are you okay?" he asks me.

"I'm cold," I answer. It feels about ten degrees in the room. But Philip would be thinking in Fahrenheit. Fifty degrees, then. I quickly convert the dimensions of the room from metres to feet. Divide the square footage by the number of people. Estimate the height of the ceiling to add to the calculation. I imagine the fraction that represents Philip's height to ceiling height. Then do the same with Janie's height. I busy myself looking for patterns in these numbers.

Nine people have been questioned and sent out. It's not clear whether they've been released or detained. I wonder who will do the next stage of questioning. The head of Airport Security? The Sûreté du Québec? National pride will cause them to wait before calling in the RCMP, let alone CSIA—Canada's version of the United America's Terror Squad. They'll call them eventually, though. I take slow, even breaths to keep from trembling.

Closing my eyes, I calculate the exact number of centimetres that Siri has grown from when she was twelve and newly arrived in Québec to her current age of fifteen. Use that to estimate Simon's height three years from now when he'll also be fifteen. How tall was I at fifteen? I was in prison then, back in the U. A. Not fully grown, smaller than most of the guards. I stop thinking. Go blank for an unknown period of time.

When I come back to myself, the room has grown quiet. I

notice that all the female-presenting people who'd been detained are gone. Not a good sign.

The sudden sound of the door opening turns every head in that direction. It's just another member of the airport security team. With sandwiches for their colleagues. They all dig into their meal, ignoring the rest of us. I conclude we're here for the long haul.

Did I miscalculate, sending Janie and the kids away? How should I have weighed the possibility of Philip and I detained against having Janie and the kids caught up in all this? Surely, they're safer without me. It always seems to come back to that.

And Philip? A single man is a bad demographic in a situation like this. Two can sometimes be a little better. Or a certain type of two.

I turn to Philip, place my hands on his shoulders and squeeze. *Fais comme moi, je t'en prie*, I imagine my hands saying. Then I kiss him full on the lips. He pulls away, his eyes darting around the room. I grab his face and do it again, speaking in an audible whisper about how much I want him. How I can't wait to get him home. People are watching us, some discreetly, others openly. "Get yourselves a room," I hear someone call out. Philip's expression seems to say, *Have you completely lost your mind?* But I keep right on, kissing and whispering, not oblivious to our audience, but playing to it. And especially to the airport security team.

One of the officers finally gets up, orders us to the interrogation booth.

"Show your ID," they bark.

I lift my arm to display my bracelet. The security agent scowls. Just because Québec lets us use bracelets instead of getting chipped doesn't mean law enforcement has to like it.

"J'suis allergique," I explain, my other wrist tight against my hip. "The chip implant makes me break out in a rash."

The officer scans my bracelet, grimaces, turns to Philip.

Philip scans his wrist chip. The agent seems surprised. "You were on the Paris flight," he notes. "I thought we'd passed you all through already. Tu as l'air d'un Tunisien."

Philip shrugs, a safe response, but the officer seems unsatisfied. "What took you so long?" they demand in French.

This is my question too, because by the time Philip came out, all the passengers on the flight from Paris seemed to have already come and gone. I turn to him, stare pointedly at the flowers. Philip notices, lifts up the bouquet, and grins sheepishly.

"Buying flowers for your lover while bombs go off? Pas fort."

I look down as though embarrassed, but in reality, I'm elated. They're going to let us go.

I take us home the long way. Around the back of the airport like I'd planned. We walk to Dorval to catch a local bus. We'll have to change buses at least once, twice if we want to avoid a long walk at the end, but I don't care. We both need some air.

Philip's face has always been easy to read. He wants badly to speak about what happened. To ask questions, to obtain explanations. So far, he's accepted my silence. My presumed authority over when and where a discussion about bombs in airports is safe. I quicken my pace to discourage idle conversation. He follows, hurrying to keep up.

On the bus ride home, I stand. Rub at the scar beneath my chip bracelet.

I ask Philip to ping Janie and tell her we're on our way home. When he's finished, I play the tour guide. Identify sights of interest. I talk without pausing, leaving no void Philip might be tempted to fill with questions I'm not ready to answer. Might never be ready to answer.

I show Philip where the main part of the airport used to be. Point out the Skyline in the distance that Janie and the kids took to get home. I talk to him about the domed greenhouse farms we begin to pass.

"What do they grow there?" Philip asks, falling back on his deeply ingrained good manners, but I can see he's troubled and would rather talk about what happened.

"Mostly Québec agricultural products. Melons. Courge ... I mean squash. Aubergine."

"Eggplants."

"Yeah, eggplants. Also non-traditional agriculture. The most popular are the bananas. They have some Latin name for the new strain. Most folx call them climate change bananas."

"Are they GMOs?"

"Not in the sense you mean. But still, there's lots of controversy. Each side of the debate claiming to champion the environment. And Québec's terres patrimoniales."

"Is it just agriculture?" Philip asks. "Fruits and vegetables, I mean?"

"No, they grow flowers too. Some experimental strains." Our eyes both go to the bouquet he's holding. "Yeah," I say. "Like these. Hideous, some of those flowers." I lapse into silence. My energy for pretending everything is normal is spent.

"Philip, mira," I say, switching to Spanish. "Why did it take you so long to come out after your plane landed? All the passengers on your flight were already gone."

He gazes down at his shoes, looking a little sheepish. "I was helping a family with their luggage. They had an elderly grandmother and four kids. The smallest looked about six, Kyla's age."

"Four kids *and* an elderly grandmother?"

"Yeah. No one was helping them, so. . ."

I start laughing.

"What's so funny?" Philip asks, a bit annoyed.

"Nothing. It's just that Janie was right."

"Janie's always right."

"Yeah." I lapse into silence again.

Philip looks around furtively before whispering, "Laek, I need to ask you something. How did you know—"

"I'm worried about Siri," I interrupt.

He switches gears immediately, a small crease forming between his brows. "What's the matter with Siri?"

"I think she's hiding something. She's been acting weird. Secret messages. Whispered conversations. And though she'd really been looking forward to your visit, at the last minute she told us she couldn't stay for the dinner we'd planned for you. Said she had a school project."

He relaxes again. "Maybe she's meeting a boy. Or a girl."

"She's into boys," I tell him. "But I don't think that's it. She wouldn't skip your welcome dinner for a boy. Siri's not like that."

"Yeah, she's a good kid. I don't think you need to worry about her."

"Says the man who had to rescue her after she crossed the border behind our backs. Because of a boy," I add, though I know I don't have to remind Philip of this incident from only two years back which ended in yet another wrenching goodbye between us.

Philip puts his hand on my shoulder. I flinch. He quickly removes it, frowning. Repeats that I shouldn't worry about Siri. That she was going through a rough time back then. I feel guilty, using his paternal affection for my daughter to distract him. To keep him from asking how I knew about the bomb.

But the truth is, I really am worried about Siri. I picture her now in the aftermath of the blast. As soon as I signalled her that we were alright, she'd checked out the scene. She hadn't seemed frightened or shocked. Instead, she surveyed the damage with the same professional interest that I, myself, had felt.

CHAPTER 3
PHILIP

"What the fuck, Laek!" Janie says, letting the hand she'd lifted towards his back drop.

Laek sits between Janie and me on the broad, butterscotch-coloured couch, the only piece of furniture in the apartment that doesn't look as though it were dragged home from a flea market. We're facing some kind of strange fireplace with small, rainbow-coloured flames. Three ceramic mugs of hot chocolate —mine and Laek's spiked with whiskey—rest on a low, narrow table that, though scarred, looks like it contains good marble. This could have been a cheerful, winter scene if not for the fact that Laek was bleeding beside me. I thrust my hand into my pocket and close on my chain of worry-rings, playing with them as I watch Janie chastise Laek.

"I'm sorry," he replies meekly.

It took us nearly half an hour to coax Laek out of his jacket. He said he was cold, but his real motive seemed to be keeping the kids from seeing his back. Simon was easily convinced to go to his room to work on an art project for school, but Siri was another story.

"Mommy, just make him go to the clinic!" she said, sounding exasperated.

"It's disrespectful to refer to your father in third person," I told her. "He's right here."

"Aren't you supposed to be meeting friends for a school project?" Janie asked Siri.

"But Daddy—" Siri objected.

"It's okay," Laek said. "Go to your meeting."

"It's not a meeting. It's just something for school."

"I know you're worried about your dad, chica," I said, trying to make up for coming down so hard on her a moment ago, "but your mom and I are here and your schoolwork's important. After you're back, you can tell me all about that hockey team of yours."

"Mostly, I've just gotten really good at skating backwards." Siri pulled her light brown hair into an elastic, showing off the high, wide cheekbones she inherited from Laek and that make her face so striking. "I still like baseball better, Uncle Philip."

I felt pleased, hearing her call me "uncle." After she left, I was still smiling—at least until Laek removed his jacket.

". . . the hell were you thinking, walking around with injuries like that?" Janie says now.

Laek's facing me, his back oriented towards Janie, so I try to stand up to see what injuries Janie's talking about. Laek puts his hands on my shoulders. "Please. Stay here."

I settle back and turn to Janie, wanting to diffuse the situation. "I know you're upset, but it was really my fault that—"

"What took so long?" she says, ignoring me. "Were you taking the scenic route? Hoping your wounds would go septic? Even Clara was worried. She pinged the house screen twice. Clara's the coordinator of École de la rue, where Laek works," she explains to me.

"I remember," I say.

Janie turns to Laek. "Well?"

"We were detained," Laek replies.

"We should have stuck together."

"So that you and the kids could be detained too?"

Janie stalks off towards the bathroom. "I need some supplies. Make sure he doesn't move," she says to me over her shoulder. And then to Laek, "Ping Clara."

Laek hesitates a moment, then lifts his wristband to his mouth and says, "Clara, audio."

A second later, a holo takes form in front of us. Clara's taller than I expected, with white, wavy hair and a tattoo of a bicycle on her neck. She looks like she's in her late fifties at most, though Laek told me she's over seventy.

"Chéri, are you alright?" she says to Laek. "I was worried."

"Pas besoin de t'inquiéter. I'm fine."

"Then why are you on audio only?" Clara has her hands on her hips.

"Um. Philip is here. We just got back and. . ." His gaze flicks to me, apologetic.

"Ah, I understand, darling. I look forward to meeting him in person." Now Clara's holo glances around the room, though with no video on our end, she can't see me. "We'll talk more about. . . what happened at the airport when I see you at work. Hugs to all of you."

While Laek was talking, I took the opportunity to stand so I could peer around at his injuries. The front of his t-shirt looks brand-new, white with a green bicycle emblazoned across the chest, but the back is charred, stained red and brown. Worse, it's studded with bits of plastic and metal, like an ugly piece of modern art featuring shrapnel. There's a weird pattern to it. . .

or lack of pattern. It triggers in me a strong wave of horror, a kind of trypophobia. The room tilts and I find myself fallen to one knee, supporting myself against the arm of the couch.

"Philip," I hear Janie say, her voice suddenly right beside me. I push myself to my feet. "Go turn up the fire," she says gently. "There's a control on the wall next to the fireplace."

"Sure. Okay. I can do that." My face heats with embarrassment.

I crouch in front of the fireplace and increase the power to the maximum. I'm rewarded with a whoosh and the welcome sounds of a crackling fire. The control panel includes a colour spectrum, like a palette on an art app, and I can also choose a pattern for the flames. I absorb myself in this task to block out the image of Laek's torn-up back, and I eventually settle on a bonfire-like flame of yellow and orange.

In the background is the sound of cutting and tearing—Janie going at Laek's shirt, I imagine. Laek is weirdly silent. After a few minutes, I look over at the two of them.

"Do you need help?" I ask.

Laek is now lying on the couch on his stomach, the back of his shirt torn open. Janie is dabbing at him with wet cotton balls and there's a strong antiseptic smell in the room. She tosses another blood-stained cotton ball into a garbage receptacle and grabs the tweezers. After a moment, she drops a sliver of something she removed from Laek's back into a small container. I listen to it clink.

"Can you find me a clean dish towel?" Janie asks without looking up.

I jump to my feet and head for the kitchen. As I check the cabinets for towels, I ask myself how I could have failed to notice that Laek was so badly injured. I review how he looked and moved while we walked along the concourse. He was fast, smooth, capable and decisive. He looked good, like he always does. In the interrogation room, he was quieter, but didn't seem to be in physical pain, and on the walk to the bus he was animated, obviously as relieved as I was to be out of there. After exiting the bus, he leaned on me a little, but I thought he was just tired, or being affectionate, or like me, a little shell-shocked from the experience. It's not every day that a bomb goes off right next to you, even if you hear about it on the news all the time.

I find some dish towels, choose the darkest-coloured one—less chance it will be ruined—and bring it to Janie. She presses it against Laek's back, just below a misshapen fragment of something that looks like a candle stub melted onto a tabletop. She touches the fragment carefully, pushing it slightly to one side. Laek sucks in a breath.

"Maybe Siri was right," I say. "We should take him to a clinic." Abashed, I realize that I just third-personned Laek as I'd chided Siri for doing earlier.

"No," he says firmly. "No clinic."

Janie doesn't look happy. "There's a motherfuckingly huge fragment just below your right shoulder blade. Can you feel it?"

"Yes," he answers, voice tight. "Can you get it out?"

"I could, but it might take a chunk of your flesh along with it. And I'm worried about infection. The clinic or a hospital would be a safer bet."

"Safer how?" Laek says, turning his head to try to face Janie. "Don't you think they'll be monitoring the hospitals and clinics? For certain types of injuries? Certain profiles?"

"I get that you don't want to be questioned but. . . what about Jabur?"

"Jabur?" I ask.

"A friend," Janie says. "He lives in the co-op, downstairs from us."

"Yeah. Alright." Laek lays his head back onto the couch and lets out a sigh.

"I'll go see if he's home," Janie says, practically running to the apartment door.

A few minutes later, she returns with a man carrying a black, rectangular bag. He has a hawkish nose and dark hair laced with silver and tied neatly in a ponytail.

"You must be the famous Philip," he says in a deep, rumbling French. He puts down the bag and grasps me by the shoulders, kissing my cheeks three times.

"I don't know what I'd be famous for," I say, embarrassed, but his remark makes me feel welcome for the first time since I landed in Montréal, bombs and interrogation not being the greeting I'd hoped for.

Jabur kneels beside Laek, placing a hand lightly on his neck while examining his injuries. "Can you walk to your room?" he asks. Laek nods. "Lean on me, habibi. Janie and Philip can wait for us out here."

I watch them until they disappear into the bedroom.

"He'll take good care of him, don't worry," Janie says, sitting down on the couch.

"He's a good doctor? He works at one of your. . . health clinics here?"

Janie pats the spot on the couch next to her, and when I've settled beside her, she continues. "Yes, he's a good doctor, but no, he doesn't work at a government clinic. He doesn't have recognized immigration status."

"So he's a refugee too?" I ask, angling my body towards hers.

"Sure he's a refugee, in the sense that he's seeking asylum, but he had to pass through the Union of Middle Eastern Nations, which is considered a safe third country. That means he can't claim asylum here."

"Can you help him appeal?" If any lawyer could help, Janie could.

"It's not appealable. His claim wasn't rejected, it was marked inadmissible, meaning Canada simply won't consider it. Because under our screwed-up laws, labelling certain favoured trading partners "safe" is more important than protecting people like Jabur, and needless to say, an un-statused person can't legally practice medicine."

"But he can here at the co-op?" I ask, not quite understanding how it all works.

"Yeah. We have a lot of people with precarious status living here, contributing however they can. That was our situation too, at first."

"I remember. But I thought you chose Montréal because it's a sanctuary city."

"Declaring yourself a sanctuary city and being one are two different things. It's a work-in-progress, but it's still safer than being back in the U. A. We have our mutual aid and support groups. And a government that isn't actively harassing us."

But people are planting bombs here too, I think to myself. I guess a naive part of me thought I could escape this kind of violence, that Montréal was somehow immune from the explosive hate reproducing itself all over the world. Janie seems to read my grim thoughts, or at least that I'm feeling grim, because she takes my hand.

"It's been a bit of a rough day, eh?"

I smile at the Canadian "eh" inserted into Janie's New York City-accented English and say, "I'd hoped for a big welcome, but hadn't expected fireworks." Janie's laugh at my feeble joke is full-throated.

We sit watching the fire. Janie asks me about Kyla, but quickly realizes that talking about my little daughter isn't going to cheer me up, not with her on the other side of the border.

"Can I make a holo-call to her?" I ask. It's been months since I've seen Kyla, and the aching emptiness in the middle of my chest feels like a black hole with teeth, eating away at me.

"Of course. Laek set up a secure connection."

She brings me into a small storage room just off the kitchen, not much bigger than a closet. The shelves are stocked with jars of pickled vegetables, grains, dried beans, and dried herbs. In the corner is a stool next to a mid-sized screen. Janie shows me how to log in, using her own biometrics to help me register the fingerprint of my left pinky for access. She leaves me to it, closing the door on her way out.

I enter Kyla's coordinates and wait as my request to connect passes through a scrambler and then a series of permissions: the server, the platform, and finally, the parental controls which only allow a set list of contacts to call my daughter's screen.

"Papi!" Kyla jumps up and down, her dark brown corkscrew curls bouncing with her.

"Mija!" I respond, my heart immediately feeling lighter. "Step back so I can see all of you."

She skips away from the screen and spins around, ending with a flourish. "Now you!"

I back up towards the door and spin around like she did, only more awkwardly.

"Papi, where are you? Are you hiding in a closet?"

I laugh. "This is just where the special screen for calling you is. How was school today?"

"I didn't go. Mama said there were nasty germs in my class. She didn't want me to get sick and bring it home to my baby brother. Papi, are you in… *Kwabec*?"

"That's right, Québec," I say, pronouncing it slowly for her.

"Is Simon there? Can I talk to him?"

I smile. Kyla worships Siri but adores Simon. "He's studying in his room."

Kyla pushes out her bottom lip in a pout.

"Maybe next time," I say. "Do you want to hear about my plane ride?"

"Yes!"

"Well, after we took off, I looked down through the window and everything was so tiny, it reminded me of the miniature city you and I built together."

"Mama made me turn it back into a dollhouse."

"That's alright," I say, and try to convince myself that it is. "Then we were in the fluffiest clouds I've ever seen. They were like the colour of the snow in Montréal. And even though the trip was five hours, when we got here, it was exactly the same time as when we left."

Her dark eyes grow wide. "Because you were in another time! Are you in my time now?"

"Yes, mija, I'm in your time zone now."

"And you're on the same side of the ocean with New York too, right?"

"That's right. Good on you for knowing your geography."

"Can I come to *K-bec* too and see Siri and Simon and Uncle Laek and Aunt Janie?"

"I would like that more than anything. But we have to get permission first."

"Because of the border?"

"Yes, mija, because of the border."

"I hate the border!" she says, stamping her foot.

Before I can tell her that I hate it too and maybe stamp my own foot, I hear my ex's voice in the background. "Kyla, come watch your brother!" She sounds annoyed, as usual.

"I have to go, Papi," Kyla whispers.

"It's alright. Tell your mother I'll call again on Friday, okay *mijita?*"

"Okay, papito," she says, half affectionate and half teasing in a way that seems far too mature for a seven-year-old. "I miss you," she says, and then the screen goes black.

I miss you too, I whisper back. I stare at the emptiness for a few more minutes, going over what Kyla said, how she looked, intent on memorizing every detail. When I'm finished, I take a moment to tuck in my shirt and rub the wetness from my eyes before leaving the storage room. Janie looks up as I come into living room to slump back down beside her.

"Everything okay with Kyla?" she asks.

I nod and she gives me a sad, knowing smile. Then she leans against me. I wrap my arm around her. The top of her curly head barely reaches my shoulder. I'd forgotten how short she was—something that tends to happen when not in her actual, physical presence. Janie has a huge personality, a huge intellect, a huge heart. She's like a tiny race car with a giant motor. Except she hates cars.

"I've never seen a fire like this," I say to break the silence.

"It was invented here in Québec. The flame is less like fire-light and more like sunlight. It helps with seasonal affective disorder and. . . depression." She gives me a significant look.

"I guess your family's lucky to have one?" I respond, raising my eyebrows.

"Yeah. We actually have a prescription, so it was a lot less expensive."

"And does it work?" I ask, not ready to directly voice my real concern.

"It seems somewhat helpful. But it's more effective when used in conjunction with therapy and meds. And I'm not talking about self-medicating." She sighs.

Though Janie has answered my unasked question about

how Laek is doing pretty thoroughly, I'm not quite ready to let it drop.

"He was. . . strange at the airport, Janie."

"Laek can be strange."

"Not his usual strange. He was, cómo explicar?" I turn to face her. "Kind of. . . scary?"

"The world has been a bit scary lately," Janie says, sitting up. "Every day, new neo-fascist groups seem to sprout up. Or crawl out from under rocks."

"New neo-fascist groups?"

"You know, neo-nazi, white supremacist, ultra-nationalist, genderist—"

"I get it, Janie. I was just making a joke about how 'new' and 'neo' mean the same thing."

"Oh."

"You laughed at my other stupid joke," I remind her.

"Yeah, you're right. It's my fault for encouraging you."

We both laugh. She slips her arm around my waist and I feel almost happy.

"It's so good you're here, Philip. I've missed you. And Laek's been on cloud nine since your visa was finally approved, though I don't think he totally believed it until he saw you at the airport. And then. . ." Janie sighs again. "Being so close to a bomb explosion would be traumatic for anyone. But for Laek, with his history. . ."

I nod as Janie tries to normalize or explain Laek's behaviour at the airport, telling me that though his bouts with PTSD have lessened, he's been under a lot of stress lately and not sleeping enough. And I do feel somewhat reassured. Janie's so solid, so grounded and convincing. And the flames are bright and soothing. But the Laek I observed at the airport didn't seem the least bit tired. He was sharp, hyper-alert, and somehow, he knew that a bomb was about to explode when no one else did.

***

Later, after Dr. Jabur is gone and Janie has checked on Laek, she looks me up and down.

"You look tired. Simon and I are going to run some errands. We'll be gone a while. Go lie down with Laek. The two of you can nap or whatever while I'm gone."

"You must be tired too, Janie. Maybe you should lie down with Laek."

Janie raises her eyebrows slightly and smiles. "Another time."

My face grows warm. "If you're sure." I quickly add, "A nap would be great."

After Janie and Simon are gone, I slip into the bedroom and shut the door behind me. Laek is lying on his stomach, the blankets around his waist, his back bare. It looks much better than before, the cuts and burns covered in a paste a bit darker than his natural skin colour. There's a used-up tube of artificial skin sitting on the bedside table, a brand I've never seen.

Laek seems to be asleep. I lie down beside him and he doesn't stir. In fact, it seems like he's barely breathing, which is making me nervous. I look at him again. His eyes are still closed, the edges of his eyelids almost violet, his eyelashes long and dark. He's so beautiful.

Maybe I should check his pulse. I reach my hand towards his neck like I saw Dr. Jabur do but stop myself. I don't want to wake him. I pull the blanket carefully up over his back instead and try to relax. After a few moments, I turn to check on him again.

"What?" Laek says without opening his eyes.

"Nothing, sorry. Go back to sleep." I continue to lie stiffly beside him.

"How can I sleep when you keep looking at me?"

I turn to face him. "How do you know I'm looking at you when your eyes are closed?"

"I can feel it."

Like you could feel the bomb that was about to explode? I almost say, but swallow my response. "Sorry," I say instead. "I just wanted to make sure you were okay."

"I'm fine," he says, opening his eyes and climbing on top of me. He lowers his face towards mine. I close my own eyes, to better concentrate on how it feels when our lips finally touch, a contact that's soft but firm, exploring, insistent. I open my mouth, let his tongue slip inside. I feel a rush of heat and my arms move to pull him more tightly against me. I stop, afraid of touching his back, of hurting him.

"Laek," I say. "Maybe this isn't a good idea."

"Are you worried about Janie?" he asks.

I think about that last night in Brooklyn, when Laek made clear that he knew I was in love with him. During our talk, he suggested that Janie could help me to also come to Montréal someday. *Janie?* I said, surprised he'd suggest her to facilitate such a thing. *Yeah, Janie,* Laek replied, adding with his deadpan humour, *You remember her. My partner? The lawyer? The one who said, 'Why don't you guys go into the bedroom where you can have some privacy?'*

And Janie had done just as promised, working tirelessly to secure my visas and permits, though we still haven't figured out how I can stay permanently, let alone bring Kyla here.

Laek waits patiently, face poised above mine. I want to smooth the hair away from his face, then pull his mouth towards my mouth again, but I resist.

"No, I'm not worried about Janie," I tell him now, and this is mostly true.

"Then what?"

"It's just that. . . I've waited so long to. . . and I finally get here and. . . todo se va al garete. And I don't really know what I think I'm doing here."

"I thought you were here to be with me. To be with us," Laek says.

"Do you really think I went through all that. . . that I crossed the border just so I could fuck you?" I watch Laek's expression, worried I'd gone too far, but he's trying not to smile.

"There are worse reasons to cross a border," he quips.

"Mira, Laek. Just a few hours ago a bomb went off next to us. You were hurt and didn't tell me. And then you put your tongue in my mouth in front of the border patrol—"

"They were only airport security." He lowers his head to my shoulder.

"Laek! You're not listening! I'm in a new country, I don't know how long I can stay and when I'm going to see my little girl again, and this bomb goes off and. . . you seemed to know there was a bomb and I don't know how." There, I said it.

"Okay. Okay," Laek says in a soothing voice. "I get it. But Philip. . ."

Laek's luminous grey eyes stare right into me, affirming our intimate connection, and I think he's going to finally open up to me. "Yeah?" I say softly.

"Will you just hold me?"

"Sure," I reply, not sure if I'm disappointed or relieved that he's both sidestepped my question and accepted that we're not going to have sex right now.

He falls asleep again lying on top of me. It's exactly the position we were in when the bomb exploded. Laek shielded me with his own body, protected me as I hadn't been able to do for him, neither here nor in New York. Not even when the cops had beaten him to within an inch of his life. And now, I can't even wrap my arms around him for fear of hurting him.

A wave of intense, frustrated emotion seizes me, and I squeeze my hands into fists. After a moment, I relax them and circle my left arm gently around his hips. With my right hand, I cup the back of his head. Until I learn more, this gesture of protection is the best I can do.

CHAPTER 4
SIRI

Once on the street, I unlock my trottinette with my wristpad. It unfolds in one smooth motion. I kick hard with the ice claws on my sneakers and soon I'm speeding along rue Ottawa. The icy streets and sidewalks are white-grey like the sky, but in between are bright colours from murals, holos, and rooftop trees and greenhouses. The cold wind passes through my tuque and chills my ears, but I don't mind. Being outside makes me feel alive and calm, and going fast makes what happened at the airport this morning feel more far away.

I turn south towards the canal and push my trot even faster, though I left myself plenty of time so I wouldn't be late. People who are late are engaged in self-centring behaviour. But another part of me is annoyed about letting my parents shoo me out of the apartment—like I'd never seen someone hurt before. Like I'd never seen *Daddy* hurt before.

Though I guess it's just as well I left early since I have things to do before my meeting. Yeah, meeting. It's creepy how Daddy called it that when I told them I was just getting together with friends. He always seems to know things a normal person shouldn't. Like about that bomb. I wonder if the antifa youth action group I'm trying to join knew about it too.

I stop at my favourite boulangerie. No holos, just a retro wooden entrance with a real door harp that plays when you push it open. I like new tech but get why people think low-tech is pretty. The bakery is warm and the smells are thick and good. It's like I can take little tastes of the pastries without even buying them. The checkout is personned—someone with red-dyed hair and violet lips. I buy two croissants and two hot-pressed sandwiches, stuffing it all into my backpack. I leave the store, mount my trot, and turn southwest towards the canal again.

The street is mostly industrial and kind of monochrome, except for the old red-brick buildings across the canal. Other-wise it's snow, clouds, and steel-coloured water; there are even some grey and white gulls flying overhead. Are they lost? Shouldn't they have flown south or something by now?

Just before the Écluses St-Gabriel, I look to see if Robin—or Robin Hood, as they're called—is around. Tangled bushes stick out of the ground, covered in fluffy snow. The footbridge a few metres away is empty. Robin is nowhere in sight.

Disappointed, I head for the other place I can usually find them. I'd hoped to talk to them about the youth group and whether they think it makes sense for me to try to join. I mean, they're pretty radical and Montréal's not as bad as New York; maybe a group like Jeune Vanguard isn't necessary. On the other hand, things are getting worse all over. We need to be bold and strong and meet the right-wing boneheads blow for blow.

Robin would have something helpful to say, I'm sure. They live on the street and have seen a lot; plus they're around my age and, like me, into rad politics. I set a good pace so the sandwich I bought for them doesn't get too cold. I know that Mommy thinks it's hopeless, trying to help Robin and every other unhoused person in the city by myself. It's not that she disapproves exactly, she just doesn't think it changes anything, not in the way things need to change to create a more just and equitable society. Fair, I guess.

The problem is, Mommy's head's still stuck in New York, where giving to every person you see who's in need would clean you out. Mommy told me it's like emptying a child-sized pail of water onto the desert sands. Afterwards, the sands are still dry as ever and you have no more water left. But what I'd like to tell her is that we're not in New York anymore. And Robin and the others aren't sand; they're people.

I fold up my trot near métro Charlevoix where Robin some-times hangs out. Maid Marian, the collie who's Robin's companion dog, is tied up at the bike rack near the social housing building. I rush over, then stop short. Robin's not there. Instead, there's some tall person near Maid Marian. They're watching the building, their face in profile. They look about Daddy's age—thirty-something—but with blue eyes and blond hair. Handsome, if you like that tough, Aryan look, which I personally don't. Then they turn and I back away a step.

The whole right side of their face is ruined. It's burned or... I'm not sure, deformed in some way. Maid Marian notices me and barks her hello. I see her bowl by the bike rack and Robin's bag behind the bowl—a hockey bag, filled not with hockey equipment but clothes, blankets, other stuff. Where's Robin? Did that person, who's now turned their back to me, steal their things? Slow down, I tell myself. Maid Marian isn't agitated, so she probably knows them. I decide to go; if I don't leave now, I'm gonna be late.

I take the green line train, then change at Lionel-Groulx for the orange. At Laurier, I change again, for the purple line going north. The train's across the platform, so I make a dash for it with my trottinette across my back, slipping through the doors just as they're closing. My stop is UbiTrans-de Gaspé, only two stations away, but at the last minute, I decide to get off one stop earlier, at Bernard, to make sure no one's following me.

The sidewalks are full of people milling around, coming in and out of cafés, friperies, vape joints, and virtual travel salons. I take to the street, weaving around traffic until I get to the part of Bernard that's closed to large motorized vehicles. Here, the street is filled with fat-tired snow bikes, electric skateboards and one or two of the new hoverplanks.

At the end of Bernard, I glance to my left at a row of broken-down warehouse buildings. Across the railroad tracks is an ugly condo development. I wonder where my interview will be. I look around carefully before sending the agreed message via a shadow-net app I already downloaded. Though I'm two minutes early, I get a response right away:

> walk over to rue du Laos and stand across the
> street from the old pub

I follow the instructions. Across from Brasserie Agent Orange, I get another message.

> behind you are railroad tracks walk about five
> metres further north you'll see a hole in the
> fence go through it and cross

I fold up my trot. I have to duck down to get through the hole. There's an "Accès Interdit" sign. I ignore it but look up and down the tracks to make sure a train isn't coming before darting across. As soon as I've done that, my wristpad signals me again.

go through the tunnel to téluq u someone will
find you.

I walk through, then cross rue des Carrières. There's no one around except two old folx holding hands and a younger person taking crates out of a truck. The younger person turns in my direction and beckons me over. I watch the fingers of their left hand move like they're playing the piano: one-four-two-four. That's the right pattern, so I go over to them. They hoist a big crate into my arms and point me to the side entrance of the school building. Then they return to work, ignoring me.

When I get to the building, the door opens. As soon as I'm through it, someone pushes on my back to guide me down a hallway. I know better than to turn around. We stop at an elevator whose door is already open. I'm shoved into the corner of the elevator. I don't like the rough treatment I'm getting but suck it up. It's my choice to be here.

After a short time, the elevator pings and the person turns me around and pushes me outside. Without thinking, I look up to see what floor we're on. My companion gives me what feels like an angry shove. We go down a long, empty hallway to a stairwell. I'm guided down a flight of stairs and through another hallway. It's tiring, carrying both the heavy crate and my trottinette. I'm about to ask how much farther it is when we get to a room. The door is opened and I'm pushed inside.

"Place your wristpad in the box," a weirdly high-pitched voice says. "You can put the crate in the corner."

I put it down gratefully, along with my trot, then stow my wristpad inside a small, heavy-looking box of matte greyish-black metal. I assume it's a greybox, to block signals. As I'm doing that, I hear the click of the door locking. I straighten up and turn. There are three people in the room, all wearing loose black pants, too-big jackets, and dark face masks with holes for the eyes and nose. Over each of their mouths is this weird, oval thing that's strapped on.

"*Seet* down," another voice says. It sounds distorted. Oh! The oval thing's a voicemod.

I look the three of them over. The person with the distorted voice—the one who brought me here—is slim and tall. I can tell they're muscular, even through the jacket. The second one is a few centimetres shorter than me but wider at the shoulders and hips. They haven't spoken yet. The last one is big, with a round stomach and thick, powerful-looking arms and legs.

"Do you have a wrist chip?" the big one with the high-pitched voice asks. It sounds like they've sucked some helium.

"Her parents probably wouldn't let her get chipped yet. Right, little Siri?" the one with the distorted voice says. I shouldn't make assumptions, but I'm almost sure they're a guy.

"No chip," I say, annoyed that Distorted Voice is right. My parents' attitude about this is ridiculous. I'm almost sixteen!

"Put out your hands," the big one with the helium voice says.

I do what they say, holding my hands palms up. The shorter one passes a black disc over my hands and wrists then points to a small table. It's the only furniture in the room. There's a single chair on one side of the table and three on the other side, interrogation-style.

"T'as lu nos documents?" the short one asks. Their voice sounds syncopated, like the off-beat music that my mom likes to play sometimes.

"Yes, I read everything," I answer in French. "And triple-deleted it afterwards."

"But you didn't follow all our instructions, did you?"

Distorted Voice says, switching to French now. "You didn't get off at the right station de métro."

I tell them that I didn't think that part was important, answering in the language of the question, as I always do. So far it seems that the shorter one with the syncopated voice is francophone and the big one with the high-pitched helium voice is anglophone. I'm not sure about Distorted Voice. Allophone maybe? They keep going back and forth between French and English, and both languages seem accented, though it's hard to tell with the voicemod.

"If you're gonna be one of us, you need to adopt principles of collective discipline," Distorted Voice says.

"I will! I mean, I'm sorry." Had I blown it already?

"Let's talk about your reasons for wanting to join," Helium says.

I relax, feeling more confident. I not only read what they sent me, but a whole bunch of texts on topics like the history of antifa, bloc noir, rear guard, vanguard and youth guard, shock troops, and anarchist anti-oppression organizing. I launch into my speech, explaining my inspirations, philosophies, rationales. It's easy; I'm good at this. I guess having a mother who's an activist lawyer and a father who's been involved in rad politics since he was a teenager is an advantage, even if I don't always agree with my parents. It also helps that everything I'm saying about my beliefs is totally true. I'm hoping they can tell.

As I talk, I watch the faces of my three black-clothed, masked interviewers, wondering who they are, wondering if I know them and if they're much older than me. Then I force myself to stop because what I'm doing is self-centring and dangerous. My potential comrades' security is more important than my idle curiosity.

They're nodding a lot to what I'm saying, so I guess the

interview's going well. Then they ask me about doxing. I gather my thoughts before talking.

"Doxing is an essential activity for calling out racists, islamophobes, nazis, homophobes—any violent person of the extrême droite. People deserve to know who's living in their communities or part of the police or teaching in their schools." Syncopated is listening carefully and Helium nods in agreement. I decide it's important to be totally honest. "At the same time, doxing has been used against good people too. Trans folx, feminists and queers folx, antifa activists. It's put their lives in jeopardy 'cause doxing can do that. We need to. . . to reflect when we dox someone. To make sure it's definitely the right thing to do."

Distorted slams their hand against the table.

"Grow up, Siri! That slippery slope thinking is for weaklings. For people who aren't clear-thinking. You can't join us if you're anti-doxing."

"I'm not! I didn't say that! I just think we need to be careful—"

"To look at both sides? You learn that from your mommy the lawyer?"

It was creepy the way the voicemod distorted the word "mommy," making it sound dirty. It's also creepy how familiar this dude—yeah dude!—seems. Who is he?

"Enough," Syncopated says. "We can discuss *Applicant Z*'s answers later," they say, emphasizing that they're not using my real name like Distorted Dude keeps doing. "We need to cover one last topic—the use of force and violence. What are your thoughts, Z?"

"I believe in the diversity of tactics principle," I say firmly. I'm careful to not sound weak-minded this time. Plus, I'm sure about what I think in this case. "Look, not everyone can do violence, or is comfortable with it. Like my father, for example."

"Your father," Distorted Dude says, standing and shoving his chair back. Syncopated looks up, like they're surprised. Distorted shakes his head and crosses his arms over his chest.

"Go on," Helium says. "How do you feel about using this tactic?"

"Someone has to be willing and capable to meet violence with violence. Otherwise, it won't be safe for those who can't."

"And you believe you are? Capable, I mean?" Syncopated says, glancing at Distorted.

"Yes," I say, as confidently as I can.

At the end of the interview, Syncopated asks me if I have any questions or final comments. I nod. "I was at the airport today," I begin. Distorted, who'd been looking down, jerks his head towards me. The other two also seem more attentive. I want to ask them if they know who's responsible for the bomb. I'm secretly hoping that whatever they say will also help me figure out how Daddy knew about it—but this is an inappropriate personal motive.

In the end, I don't ask them anything, just tell them that I looked the bomb site over carefully, using what I had learned from a manual about on-scene observations. I conclude by saying that I hope I can be of use.

Syncopated thanks me on behalf of their comrades. I'm given my wristpad back by Helium. Distorted Dude leads me back downstairs, taking me a different way this time. When we get to a door that leads outside, Distorted Dude blocks my exit.

"Excuse me," I tell him. He stays put. I say, "I need to go home."

When he still doesn't move, I get frustrated, thinking about all the hostile questions, the smirks and little remarks. What's his problem? I ask him to get out of my way one more time, and when he doesn't budge, I push him aside, hard. He tries to push me back, but this time I don't have a big crate in my hands and, anticipating his move, I pivot. He then grabs both of my shoulders and pushes me hard against the wall. The strap holding the trottinette across my back snaps, and with it, my temper. I grab my trot as it slips to the ground and I swing it at Distorted Dude. He moves his arm to block the blow.

"Aii!" he cries out, the voicemod drawing out the sound creepily. He pulls the mod off and says in his normal voice. "Osti de câlice de tabarnak, Siri, I think you broke my arm!"

All at once, I realize who this dude is.

CHAPTER 5
SIMON

After school, Aiza and I stand on the métro platform while I work on my portrait of her. Her face shape looks right—long and narrow with a small chin—and her nose and lips seem the right size and shape too. Maybe I got the eyes wrong? Somehow, she's more beautiful in real life.

"Je peux le voir?" Aiza asks.

"I'll show you later." I answer her in French, the language of school. At home, I speak English with my mother, French with my father, and Franglais with Siri. Outside of school, Aiza and I sometimes speak Babble, which we invented by combining all those languages plus Arabic, Hebrew, Gola and Swahili, plus some words we made up. Ever since Uncle Philip arrived, I've also gotten to practice my Spanish. Maybe I can convince the government to let him stay if I learn Spanish fluently and show them what a great teacher he is.

"Have you finished my portrait yet?" I ask her.

"Almost," she says.

Our ligne verte train pulls into the station. Even if you can't read words, you'd know it was a green line train because of the green line painted on it. If you're visually impaired but can hear, you can listen for the train music, a song called "La Grenouille verte peut sauter." Plus, when it pulls in, the platform vibrates under your feet in a special pattern to tell people that the green train is here. Sometimes there are even green holographic frogs hopping around inside.

Back when we lived in New York City, my sister taught me to always pay attention on the subway. I look around the train and notice two senior citizens sitting next to each other. They're wearing identical silver jumpers and worn-out black boots with real laces; on their heads are tuques—one in orange and one in purple. Their faces are wrinkled as old figs and one of them is bald. The other holds a small dog who looks very intelligent.

"Qu'est-ce que tu regardes?" Aiza asks me.

"Those two people. Do you want to play the game?" I ask, to hide my embarrassment at getting distracted by them instead of being alert to my whole environment. If I'd been more alert at the airport, maybe I would have spotted the bomb and Daddy wouldn't have gotten hurt.

"Okay," she says. "You go first."

I think for a minute, then begin my story about the two humans and the dog I've been watching. "They're from Tanzania. They're best friends, no, they're brothers—no wait! They're actually a brother and a sister. They worked at a zoo in their home country and were caught liberating the animals. The government was after them so they had to escape. They managed to smuggle out the dog, whose name is. . . Winnie. She was the star of a Tanzanian circus act."

"Pas mal," Aiza says. "But here's my story. You're right, they are a man and a woman, but they're actually lovers. They come from the Midwestern Drylands of the United America, and they're wanted by their government because they're first cousins and not allowed to marry each other. The dog is named Winnie like you said, but she was the one who helped them escape—by creating a diversion at the border. Winnie chased the border guard's cat, giving the lovers time to run across the distortion field and escape."

I think about my story and hers, trying to decide who won the game. The trick is to come up with the one that's the most realistic and also the most fantastical. Both our stories have good fantastical parts, but Aiza's has more realistic bits than mine does, like being from the Midwestern Drylands where, in real life, lots of different types of people aren't allowed to get married. The problem with my story is that I don't know if in the real here and now they still have zoos in Tanzania. On the other hand, the escape across the border Aiza told about isn't realistic. I mean, a border guard would never bring their companion animal to work. The border's no place for innocent creatures.

I don't blame Aiza for not knowing how these things work. I mean, she was born here, and though her parents were refugees like us, she told me they won't talk about what happened. I remember escaping across the border very well. Sometimes, it seems like another life, but other times—like right now—it feels like just yesterday. I don't remember being scared, but I guess that's because I didn't know what was going on. I thought we were just on an adventure.

"Are you coming?" Aiza says, pulling on my arm to get me off the train before the doors close. Once again, I wasn't paying attention to the here and now.

"You win," I finally say, but Aiza is already halfway up the stairs.

I follow her from the subway towards our apartment building, my stomach grumbling. It's been hours since I've eaten and I had to skip dessert because the cafeteria cookies had eggs in them, which are stolen from chickens.

"Is your father home?" I ask. Aiza's dad makes the best after-school snacks.

"No. He has another job interview. And my mom's doing a shift at Le Détour."

"We can go to my place. Maybe one of my parents left us cookies."

She doesn't answer but I can tell she feels worried about something. My mom has been trying to teach me to read non-verbal signals, but I'm not always sure if I'm doing it right.

"Will your sister be home?" she finally asks.

"I'm not sure," I answer. "Why?"

"I want us to have some privacy."

"For what?"

Aiza stops smiling and she shakes her head a little. Her face looks like that when I don't understand what she's thinking, even though it's not fair for her to expect me to read her mind.

"We need privacy to work on our portraits."

"Oh," I say, though I'm still not sure I get it exactly.

Inside our building, I use my wristpad to call for the elevator. The security in our co-op is very good. I'm glad. If Daddy hadn't explained all its details to me, I'd probably still be having nightmares like the ones that started after he got beat up by those cops back in New York.

We take the elevator to the very top of the building. Mommy calls our apartment "the penthouse" with her jokey voice, I guess because the apartment isn't luxurious at all, though we do have three bedrooms, which makes us very lucky. The other reason we're lucky is because we live right below the roof gardens, where the whole family works as part of our social contribution to the co-op. Most important of all, if the United American government ever comes to try to find Daddy, we can all escape to the roof. Mommy said I don't need to think about that kind of thing anymore, but I can't help it, especially after the airport bomb.

"Siri!" I call out as I open our apartment door. "Is anyone home?" No one answers.

I lead Aiza into the kitchen, where we find two covered plates and a bowl of fruit. I lift one of the covers and find crudités with hummus. Under the second cover are cookies. Yes! I press my wristpad against the screen on the refrigerator. It logs me in and shows me where everyone else in the family is. Mommy is near the Old Port, which means that one of her clients probably has a refugee hearing. Siri is at her school in Pointe-St-Charles. Oh yeah, she has basketball practice. Now Philip shows up on the screen too. His signal ended at the university, at UQAM, so he's either taking a class in French or giving one in Spanish. Daddy, as usual, is off the grid, but I think it's one of his nights when he's home for supper.

"We have the place to ourselves. Where do you want to work?" I ask Aiza as I stuff a cookie into my mouth.

"Can we use Siri's room?" She looks first at the cookies, then at the veggies, finally grabbing a cookie like me.

"We could, but she may be mad when she gets home."

"It's better than working out here." Aiza uses a napkin to brush crumbs off her chin.

"Why don't we just work in my room?" I suggest.

"But that's where your Uncle Philip is staying."

"Not anymore," I tell Aiza. "I got my room back this weekend."

"Oh! That's great, Simon. You don't have to share with your sister anymore."

"Yeah." Truthfully, I like sharing a room with Siri like we did in New York.

The two of us settle onto my bed, facing each other, she at

the head and me at the foot. I open up my most recent portrait of Aiza. I'm thinking about how I could make her eyes look more sparkly when I hear her asking me a question.

"Sorry, what did you say?" I ask.

"Since you have your room back, where's your Uncle Philip staying?"

"He's staying in my parents' room."

I look at Aiza to see what highlight colour to add to her black braids. She's squinting at me and her nose looks like it's smelling something it doesn't like. I've seen this expression before. It usually means she's confused or surprised, but in a bad way.

"What's the matter?" I put my screen down.

"Nothing. It just seems weird that your Uncle Philip is sleeping in your parents' room."

"What's weird about it?"

"Don't your parents need their privacy? Like for. . ." and now she lowers her voice to a whisper, ". . . sex? I mean, if they're all sharing one room. . ."

I hadn't thought about this. I don't like to think about my parents—or anyone—having sex, even though I know they do that sometimes. I mean, they had to have done it at least twice for Siri and me to be born. But Mommy is already thirty-eight years old. She's done having babies. I know this for a fact because when I was younger and asked her for a baby sib, she explained about the two-parent/two-child rule.

"Well, my parents' bed is pretty big," I tell Aiza. "And my dad works a lot at night, so maybe it's just so my mom doesn't get lonely or nervous when he's not here." That's how I feel without Siri sleeping on the top of the bunk bed like she did when we were younger.

"Simon, it sounds to me like your Uncle Philip might be having sex with your maman."

Aiza seems upset, and I can't figure out why since she seems to like the idea of sex and romance. I mean, she's always having her stories be about that. Then I remember her story about the cousins who couldn't get married.

"You know that Philip isn't really my uncle, right?" I say to her. "He isn't the actual brother of either of my parents. He's like your Tanty Cora who's your maman's best friend. So you don't have to worry about the incest taboo we learned about in school."

"I know that, Simon! I'm not worried about incest, I'm worried about polygamy." Aiza is speaking in that voice she uses to explain things to me, as though I were a little kid and I hadn't learned all the same words that she had in our sex ed and social mores class. It's annoying. "And polygamy is illegal, and also—" she continues, but I cut her off.

"It's not polygamy!" I now feel not just annoyed but unhappy to still be talking about sex and, on top of that, to hear Aiza say that my parents might be breaking the law. "First of all, my parents aren't actually married, and Philip is divorced, so they can't be doing polygamy. I mean, is having... sex with more than one person illegal too?" I make this sound like a rhetorical question even though I'm not actually sure of the answer.

"No, but I don't like the idea of two men sharing a woman. It's... unfeminist."

"My mom would never be unfeminist! If she's... fooking around with Daddy and with Philip, it's because she wants to." I use the word in Babble that means having sex, just to show Aiza that I can handle this conversation, that I'm as grown up as she is. Aiza doesn't seem to be convinced by what I'm saying, so I tell her one more thing, using my most confident voice. "Plus, it's way more likely that it's Daddy and Philip who are fooking around together."

I'm pretty sure that what I just said is true. Daddy and Philip were always hugging and putting their arms around each other back in New York, but Mommy and Philip just kissed cheeks. Hugging seems closer to sex than little cheek-kisses do.

Fortunately, Aiza has finally stopped arguing. I look at her face to try to see what she's thinking now, but even though I use all of the tricks I've been taught for getting social cues, I can't tell if what I said has reassured her at all.

CHAPTER 6
JANIE

"Alors," Pierre-Ryan says, green eyes twinkling, "When did you first decide that you were going to faire l'amour with our Philippe?"

I let out a surprised chuckle, remembering the first time I sat in this office, not as a colleague but as a client. His solid wooden desk inspired confidence, and the homey floral-patterned chairs encouraged trust, but I still wondered whether this unprepossessing person could actually help us obtain refugee protection. In the end, it was his frankness that finally won me over. I told him everything during that first meeting, and I don't hesitate to do the same now.

"It was just after you told us we'd finally been granted permanent residency," I answer. "Laek and I were euphoric, of course, and I wanted the kids to be just as happy. I thought if they knew they didn't have to completely cut ties with their old friends, it would reassure them, Siri especially. So I made up this game where each of us gets to organize a party and choose one special guest to invite from New York."

"Et puis?"

"Well, after the kids took their turns, I jumped in to say I'd invite Philip. You should have seen the confused looks on their faces! They think of Philip as their father's friend, not mine, but Laek just gave me this sexy smile and asked me what kind of party I had in mind."

"And what kind of party did you have in mind?"

"Honestly, I'm not sure I'd thought it all the way through. I mean, since Laek already knew I was okay with him having a romantic/sexual relationship with Philip, maybe this was my way of expressing my interest in getting in on the action. And I was happy he seemed into it, but I hadn't taken it too seriously, seeing as how we might never have the opportunity."

"Au final, was it a good party?" P.R. asks, cheeks even redder than usual.

"Laek wasn't home; he was working one of his night shifts, scouring the streets in some of the rougher neighbourhoods for kids who might need shelter. I was feeling anxious, thinking about the airport bombing."

P.R. tilts his head, waiting. I could tell him about Philip's reassuring solidity, the soft patch of hair on his broad chest, his thick, strong arms, my surprise at lovemaking that was gentle, almost tentative, yet ultimately very thorough. Or I could tell him about the kind of connection that comes from three years of exchanging heartfelt messages with someone who loves and understands Laek as I do and who's also one of the last ties to my city of birth. Or I could tell him that, for a change, I simply decided to take something for myself without overthinking it. Instead, I just shrug.

"But Janie, why do you seem upset? Was he a bad lover?"

I laugh. "No, not at all. But it's not how it was supposed to happen."

"What do you mean?"

"We were supposed to be together, all three of us. And if

not. . ." Now I feel my own face growing warm, though talking about sex with my friends doesn't usually embarrass me. "If anything, it's Laek and Philip who should've gone first. That's how I imagined it would happen."

"It is surprising. From what you told me, our Philippe has been madly in love with Laek for a long time. Has Laek refused him?"

"No, it's kind of the other way around. I don't get it, and it worries me."

"Écoute," Pierre-Ryan says. "You worry too much." His voice has lost its playful tone as he turns concerned eyes on me. "Things will work out as they should. And why would Philippe not want to first make love with a beautiful, intelligent woman such as yourself?"

"Thank you, but I remember when Laek and I first met you, in this very office, and it wasn't me you were staring at. Even you couldn't keep your eyes off him."

He turns an even deeper shade of red. "It was not like that, Janie. I was watching Laek because I was afraid for him. He seemed very vulnerable. . . très innocent."

"It's true he brings out the protective side of people. Philip's like that too with him and. . ." I shrug again. "So am I."

"Yet in reality, perhaps Laek does not need our protection. After all, he has lived all these difficult things, and he has come through. . . well, if not undamaged, he has survived and is still strong. Do you sense that Laek is jealous that you have been with Philippe first?"

"No, he seems honestly pleased that Philip and I became intimate this quickly. I think Laek is surprised, though. And confused, like I am."

"And when you don't understand something, it worries you."

I sigh. "Well, yeah."

"Janie, taking care of Laek and Philippe's relationship is not your responsibility. But if it makes you feel any better, consider this: the first physical contact Philippe had with Laek upon arriving in Montréal was being pushed to the ground as a bomb went off nearby. Franchement, that would be traumatizing for anyone."

"Truth."

"And has Laek told Philippe how he knew about the bomb? Has he told you?"

I don't answer, deciding suddenly it's time to get back to work. Not that I wouldn't share this information with Pierre-Ryan, the person who spent countless hours preparing our case for the peanuts a Legal Aid mandate pays only to have Laek blow it all by giving damaging, previously undiscussed testimony. Laek hadn't planned to do that, of course, or even consciously recalled the incident in question until that moment in the hearing. In the same way, I'm not sure Laek consciously knows what tipped him off about the bomb. In any case, I trust him—both to figure it out and share it with us when he's ready.

"Right again. It's not my job to choreograph Laek and Philip's relationship. But it is my job to figure out how Philip can stay here permanently, should he decide he wants to. So I'm gonna get back to that research before my 10 a.m. rendez-vous."

"D'accord," P.R. says. "Ping me if you have any new ideas."

Three hours and four clients later, I'm no closer to an answer for Philip than I was before. Pierre-Ryan and I have gone through the limited possibilities for obtaining permanent residency a dozen times at least, but I make myself review them all again.

Number one: Philip makes a refugee claim as we did. The problem is, as far as I know, he hasn't been the victim of any special mistreatment and does not seriously fear for his life. It's true he's been dragged in and interrogated a few times by federal cops because of his connection to Laek and, although Philip has not said this directly, I have the impression he was roughed up some. The same could be said, though, for countless other people in the U.A. who are, for instance, racialized, Muslim, or, like Philip, Latine, especially since the Border Conflicts.

Unfortunately, as a teacher, Philip also doesn't qualify for a special immigration visa available to "Desirable Professionals." These visas seem to be exclusively issued to climate scientists, aeronautic engineers, and cyber-security experts.

The most obvious solution would be to apply for a "family solidarity" visa, but the tricky part is figuring out which one of us would claim to be Philip's partner, since neither Canada nor Québec recognize polyamorous unions. And whichever one of us made this claim would have to convincingly cast the other one aside. The idea of even pretending to end my union with Laek makes my heart ache.

I decide to do some more research into exceptional renewal of a student visa. This may be a good stopgap measure since Philip hasn't figured out yet what he's going to do about Kyla—another seemingly insurmountable problem because Philip is too good a parent to ever abandon his daughter, and too good a person to take her away from her mother. I admire this about him at the same time that it frustrates me. Kyla would be much better off with Philip than with Dana, whose mean-spirited new husband is totally uninterested in raising someone else's child. Plus, Montréal is a much safer place to raise a kid, especially one who's dark-skinned.

I put aside the research to review my notes for a client's deportation hearing tomorrow. I'm deep into it when my wristpad sounds. For a moment I'm confused. It's not the tone

I'm using to alert me to text messages or holo chat requests. I recognize it immediately, though—it's the beginning notes to Aaron Copeland's twentieth century "Fanfare for the Common Man," the first musical code ever used on the Montréal metro system. I researched this because, as a musician, I'd been interested in learning how songs had come to be attached to different train lines, and—

I remember now. I chose this combination of notes for the shadow-net app Laek persuaded me to install for sensitive communications. I lunge for my wristpad bracelet on the far corner of my desk, knocking it to the ground, and by the time I reach it, the melody sounding on my wristpad has transposed itself up a third and then a fifth from the original key, adding a note of panic to a musical sequence that already sounds like a call to battle.

I slip the wristpad on and quickly open the message using my iris scan. All I see is a jumble of symbols. Laek's encrypted the message. I run out of my office into the circular reception area we share with three other lawyers. I find my spare bike bag in the closet and search for the decryptor, which Laek insists I keep somewhere separate from my wristpad.

Pierre-Ryan's office door is open. He looks up in inquiry as I frantically toss items out of my bag. I find my "court shoes," an air pump for my bike, a pair of holo-blockers, clean underwear, a mask, contraceptives, an ear pod, a snack bar—items that seem reasonable enough to carry around when viewed individually, but which suggest an anxiety disorder when all lined up on the ground before me.

I finally find the decryptor and run back to my office. I press it against the message, enter my regular passcode and then a second passcode which I miraculously remember. The font changes to a rich cerulean blue with a comic book font that's the signature style of the app but seems wildly inappropriate in view of the words of Laek's message:

Clara est morte.

I look up. Pierre-Ryan is standing in my doorway. "Qu'est-ce qui se passe?" he asks.

"Ferme la porte." Once he's shut the door, I tell him. "Laek says Clara's dead."

"Clara. . . Clara Bazinet? The directrice of École de la rue?"

"Yeah, Laek's boss," I say as I type my response and encrypt it.

Are you sure? What happened? Are you okay?

The response from Laek is slow in coming. Finally, I read:

Ils l'ont tuée.

My head jerks up.

"What?" Pierre-Ryan asks. "What did Laek say?"

"That Clara was murdered."

Pierre-Ryan brings his thumb to his wrist chip and soon he's reading something in the air only he can see. Meanwhile, I'm typing furiously:

What do you mean? Who killed her? And once again: Are you okay?

"I found a reportage," P.R. tells me. "It says she died in a bike accident late last night."

"Oh my God. But why is Laek saying they killed her?" I wonder out loud.

"They?" Pierre-Ryan inquires.

I shake my head and type another message to Laek.

> Please answer, Laek. You're scaring me. I need to see you. Use Face à Face.

My wristpad sings out the next three notes of Fanfare to the Common Man, signalling the end of our text session. A long moment later, a full-size holographic image of Laek—that is, an oddly disguised version of Laek—stands before me.

Laek's holo is transparent, almost smokey, and uses a colour wheel that only includes blacks and greys. His clothing is ragged, knees poking through holes in his pants, a torn black hoodie on top—not the way he actually dressed this morning. Laek's image is not only wearing the sweatshirt hood but a veil covers his face from forehead to chin, with holes cut out for his eyes and mouth. Even with his face covered like this, I would recognize him in an instant from his bony knees, the shape of his torso, his posture.

"Voice only, no holo," Laek says. "Someone might come in. I don't want you seen."

"P.R. is in my office," I tell him in audio-only mode.

He nods his acquiescence.

"What happened, Laek?" I ask. "Why do you say that Clara was killed?"

"Something's going on, Janie."

"What? What do you mean?"

Laek doesn't answer. His holo projection is wavering. His hands go to his face. I realize that he's crying. As he rubs at his eyes with the heels of his hands, strips of the veil are torn away, and to my horror, chunks of his face along with it. The code for the veil and his face must be attached, a quick, slapped-together attempt at sending an incognito image.

"Sweetheart, P.R. says Clara was killed in a bike accident."

Laek stops swiping at his eyes, but his whole body seems to quake.

"No. She's cycled forever, knew the city's bike lanes like the back of her hand."

"Laek, even at seventy-two, she wasn't always the most cautious cyclist."

"It was no accident," he says. The holograph stops wavering, and Laek lifts his head. He's suddenly frighteningly still. He releases his clenched fists and his fingers open like grey petals falling from his wrists. "She must have found something out. And they killed her."

The holo dissipates all at once.

Pierre-Ryan and I are both silent for a long moment. I meet his eyes.

"You should go to him," he says.

So much for not worrying about Laek.

CHAPTER 7
LAEK

Stephan Cloutier's eyes are an unforgiving blue. Early sixties, maybe. Square-chinned and clean-shaven. In good shape for a man his age. Vain, though: he's holding his stomach in. And his grin shows too much tooth on the right side, making it appear clownish. Or feral.

It's been eight days since Clara Bazinet died. Was killed. Maybe that's why I'm studying Cloutier, our new director, as though he's an enemy. I force my muscles to relax. My face to smile. My body language to be more welcoming. He walks over to our group. Stands too close to me. My instinctive aversion to him is reinforced: he has the body language of a predator.

"How long have you been at the school?" he asks, grinning wolfishly. His French is from another generation, tagged by rolling r's and an upper-class cadence.

"Three years," I tell him, using a sing-song patois to try to cover my immigrant roots.

"I thought you seemed older than the other boys," he continues in French. "It's never too late to make something of your life. Come to my office later and—"

Some of the students in my group start to snicker. Pascal, newer to the school, is still trying to prove himself through jokes and disruptive behaviour. "Ouais," he says. "If you study hard, maybe you can be a teacher when you grow up!" He bumps fists with Rafi and Jayden, then doubles over with laughter.

Robin frowns at Pascal. "Laek is our teacher," they say to Cloutier.

I watch Cloutier's reaction. He's one of those people who pales rather than flushes when embarrassed. Or angry. And the anger on his face is so raw, Pascal steps back a pace. I hold my ground. Force all emotion from my own face.

"Let me introduce you to the others, Monsieur," I say, trying to soothe wounded feelings.

"No need," he answers. "I can find my own way. This is my school now, after all."

I excuse myself, trying to ignore the menace in his words and tone.

The summons comes after teaching my late afternoon history class. I finger-comb my hair. Tuck in my shirt. Walk down the hallway, towards what used to be Clara's office. I brace myself for seeing Cloutier at Clara's desk. He's not there. Her old office is oddly empty of all signs of life. A worker I've never met is painting the purple walls white. What happened to Clara's art? Her paper books and mementos? Most urgently, I wonder who has her contacts and files, carefully amassed during her fifty years as an activist.

I continue down the hall. My friend Chloë, our music therapist, is walking towards me. I ask her where Cloutier is.

"In the old conference room," she tells me.

"Ça va, toi?" I ask. She's holding her jacket tightly around her. Her face paler than usual.

"Be careful," she tells me, then continues down the hall.

Unusually, the conference room door is closed. I rap on it. After a moment, I hear "Entrez!" I walk in.

The room's been transformed. It's now an outsized private office. The conference table is gone. In its place, a small round table. Five carved chairs. On the right side of the room, a leather couch. New. On the left side of the room is a broad desk. Topped with glass. He sits behind it. His chair is huge. Oxblood red. Also leather. The whole room stinks of it. The student art that used to hang from the walls is gone. Replaced by placid landscapes. Some portraits, maybe Cloutier's ancestors. And a case, filled with objects, historical or military. Is that an actual rifle on the upper shelf?

He doesn't invite me to sit so I remain standing. He's peering at his screen. Reading whatever's on it carefully. I wait him out. He finally looks up.

"Do you find it amusing? Posing as a student?"

"That's not—"

"Mais oui! Tu es un poseur! Everything about you is a pose. Your clothes. Your long hair. The three earrings in your left ear. Those wrist tattoos. Are you trying to cover your chip?"

"I'm not chipped," I tell him. Regret it immediately. It's none of his business.

He laughs. As though he knows he's caught me.

"I'm sorry about this morning," I try. "My students, they—"

"You can't hope to control a group of homeless youth with that approach. Pretending to be one of them. You must show them a good example. Discipline. Hard work. Cleanliness."

I'm tempted to tell him I shower every day. Or more seriously, that I was once a street kid myself. Instead I practice my active listening skills. Hoping his anger and embarrassment will run their course. Or be satisfied by my humble pose as I allow him to lecture me.

What's he even doing here? I've done my research. Know he's not an educator. Up till now, he ran a large family foundation. Donations to private universities. The arts. International charity conglomerates with a religious angle. He's rich, powerful. Notoriously controlling. Devoid of any social justice background. He certainly doesn't need the job.

And why did the board hire him, moving, uncharacteristically, at light-speed? Sure, his foundation's money could keep our org running a long time. We could've waited, though. Hired an interim direction team. Consulted the union. But everyone's reeling from Clara's death.

When Cloutier's done with his speech, he stands. Walks around his giant desk. Moves too close to me again. He claps my shoulder. Like all is forgiven. I smile, face feeling tight. He squeezes my arm in an overly familiar way and I resist the urge to tell him to get his fucking hands off me.

He finally releases his grip, which has slid down to my bicep. I leave his office. I'm covered in sweat. I head to my office. Change my mind. I have an hour break before the night shift, so I go downstairs to the shower facilities. Take some fresh clothes from my locker and shuck the old ones off. Step into the shower, my second today. I turn the water on as hot as I can stand it. Hoping it will wash his touch from me. Instead it merely mingles with the hot tears on my face as I imagine my mentor Clara's broken body on the road.

It's after supper the next day. I'm sitting on the couch with Janie and Philip. I give the two of them a minute to scan the document I've projected in the air in front of us. The fireplace is crackling behind it. Making the text look like it's on fire. I wish it were.

"The new director didn't wait long, did he?" Janie says, shaking her head.

"Do you even own five button-down shirts?" Philip asks. "If not, I could give you some of mine."

"I have three," I tell him. "A white one with a frayed cuff. A black one. But that's silk. And a purple one. A colour he'll probably outlaw."

"I love your purple shirt!" Simon calls out from the kitchen where he's sitting at the table doing his homework.

"You would!" Siri responds, running water and the clanking of silverware in the background.

"We could buy you a couple of new shirts," Janie says. "Our budget would stand it."

"You're also gonna need a haircut," Philip says, still reading the part of Cloutier's document related to dress and comportement of teachers.

"I'm more worried about the sections related to the kids."

Philip's eyes scan down a little further. "Yeah, I see what you mean," he says. "Making students address teachers as 'Monsieur' and 'Madame.' Requiring punitive responses for rule-breaking, no matter how mild. Doesn't show much trust for students. Or for teachers."

"He's giving the students a dress code too? Shelterless kids?" Janie says, reading ahead. "And they've genderized it too!" she continues, sounding even more outraged. "Boys are forbidden to wear earrings. And girls can only wear them if they're no bigger than a toonie!"

"Wait a second!" Siri says, coming into the living room, dish rag in hand. "What are they gonna do about enby students? Say they can only wear one earring?"

Simon follows Siri into the living room. "I like when people wear one earring. Asymmetry is cool!"

"It's discrimination, Simon. Don't they teach you anything at your weird school?"

"C'mere," I say to Simon, who's looking wounded from Siri's usual tough love. I pull him onto my lap, wrap my arms around him, and kiss the top of his mop of dark hair. This would make a typical twelve-year-old embarrassed, but Simon isn't typical.

Simon spots the new puzzle I found at the barter shop and slides out of my embrace.

"He's been hired to fill the shoes of a beloved director of many years and has no experience," Philip says. "He's probably just nervous."

I swallow my frustration. Philip loves structure, rules. Sometimes I think it makes him too comfortable with authority.

"It's arrogant, though," Janie says for me. "He should be watching and learning, not making changes before under-standing the context. Why was someone with no teaching and no social services background hired in the first place?"

"You're right, Janie," Philip says apologetically.

I berate myself. Philip is unfailingly fair. And he doesn't know everything that happened. But if I told him about the creepster vibe I got from Cloutier when he touched me, Philip'd probably go to my workplace and beat the crap out of him, director or not. Which wouldn't be a good idea for a long list of reasons, including that maybe I'm being paranoid. I know that I struggle with my mental health. I can't always trust my instincts. But then again, I was right about the bomb.

"So what do you want to do, Laek?" Janie asks. "Go along with it for now, or resist?"

"I don't know," I tell her. "I hate going along with bullshit. But I need to choose my battles. I'm more worried about him messing with the curriculum than with my wardrobe."

Philip frowns. "Bad leadership at a school can be. . . dangerous. And—" He trails off, seeming lost in thought. I'm about to ask him if everything's okay back at our old school. Then Janie smiles and I know she's come up with a devious plan.

"Why don't you let me give you a haircut," she says. "I'll make sure it complies, yet. . ."

"I'd forgotten you know how to cut hair," Philip says.

"I'm out of here," Siri says. "I don't want Mommy to get any ideas about using those scissors on me. C'mon, Simon, we can play a screen game."

"Did you both do your homework?" I ask.

"Yeah," Siri says. "I did it at school before basketball practice."

"Simon?" I ask.

"Yes," he says, but his eyes dart to the side, like he's hiding something.

Janie and I share a look. "All of it?" she asks Simon.

"Well, I needed to work on a new drawing first, so. . ."

"I'll tell you what, Simon," I say, "if you can finish the rest of your homework in the next twenty minutes, you can still play a screen game, but no rushing through it, okay? And Siri, I want you to check that Simon's finished his work before you agree to play with him. Got it?"

"Oui, Papa," Simon answers as Siri answers, "Got it."

Janie nods her approval and the two of them disappear towards their rooms. Some minutes later, I'm sitting on the floor, a soft towel draped around my neck and torso. Janie's on the couch just behind me, her legs on either side of my shoulders, the height differential giving her good access to my head. Three wineglasses sit on the table, burgundy liquid at different heights. My glass is half full.

We chat about inconsequential things. I enjoy listening to

the two of them talk. Janie has a surprisingly low speaking voice and Philip's is very low. Their voices are soothing after listening all day to the loud, higher pitches of my students.

Janie's fingers are in my hair. Snipping here. Gently pushing strands aside there. The micro-edges of Philip's new razor buzz softly against my skull. It's also soothing, like the electromagnetic therapy I get for the pain in my ribs. Janie cutting my hair is a surprisingly sensual experience. I feel the beginning of a hard-on. Then my eyes start to close. I force them open. Falling asleep with sharp edges near your throat doesn't seem like a good idea.

"That looks like it feels good," Philip says.

"Mmm," I say. "If you're really good in bed, maybe Janie'll give you a haircut too."

I glance over at Philip. He looks like he's been slapped. I feel tears spring to my eyes, like I'd slapped myself. Why did I say that?

Janie laughs, a low throaty sound. "I predict there'll be lots of haircuts in our future."

Philip hesitates a beat, then laughs too, and I join them. Give Philip a sidelong glance. He's smiling. I sigh and lean against Janie's knee. I decide not to open my mouth for the rest of the evening. But talking's the only thing keeping me awake. I feel my eyes begin to close once again. Blink myself awake.

"It's alright, sweetheart," Janie says. "You can fall asleep."

"Don't worry. I'll watch your back," Philip says. "And those scissors of Janie's."

I shut my eyes. At first, I stay half-awake, listening to them slip between English and French, Philip's Parisian accent making his voice sound even lower. They speak a little Spanish too, something Janie rarely does. As I grow sleepier, their voices go from sense to nonsense to a comforting babble of soft multilingual background sounds. Then silence.

I'm on my bike, moving along empty streets. I'm looking for my friends, my family, but everyone's gone. The absence of others fills me with a visceral panic. I realize I'm utterly alone. Everyone dead and somehow I'm to blame. I stand on my pedals, pumping as fast as I can, hoping to come across someone, anyone.

Suddenly, out of nowhere, the police car.

My fear shoots up another level. I break, skid, turn. The cop car is still in front of me. I pivot, pivot again. My bike is gone. I try to run. My legs won't respond. The cop is bearing down on me, closer, closer. He's huge. Square-shaped. Grey like granite. He grabs me. Throws me against his car. Burning metal against my forehead. The phaser stick hard against the back of my neck. His hot breath in my ear, his hands on my body. I can't scream or he'll find Janie too. And Philip. My body is pain. I try to move, to jerk away from him, from his stick, from his hands.

I wake up, heart frantically beating, half-risen from the couch.

"It's okay. Easy does it."

Philip's voice. His hands are on my shoulders. It seems very late. The fire's low, the apartment quiet. I let my head fall back, onto his thigh. His hands rather than Janie's slip through my hair. I take some moments to enjoy the feeling before carefully sitting up again.

"Sorry," I say, "I was having a nightmare."

"It seemed like a bad one. Do you want to tell me about it?" he asks.

"No," I say, too quickly.

"Alright," he says, eyes bright in the firelight.

"It's just. . . the details are already gone." I hate hurting his feelings again, but hearing about my dream is not going to help either of us. "It feels late," I say, changing the topic. "What are you still doing out here?"

"You were leaning on me and I didn't want to wake you."

"Thanks," I say, scratching at some bits of hair sticking to my neck. I bring my hand up to the side of my head. The skin feels new there, delicate. "How'd the haircut come out?"

"Go take a look," Philip responds.

He follows me into the bathroom. I look in the mirror. Turn my head sideways. Janie's cut the sides short, but at an artful cant, like the rings of Saturn. My hair's longer in the front, just above the eyebrows. Angled back from my ears. It's all totally regulation, but also totally rad. On the left side, she's managed to shave a beautiful calligraphic "L" for Laek. I laugh with pleasure. "C'est beau, non?" I say to Philip. Though she's made me look too young.

"Formidable," Philip responds. "Janie could be a coiffeuse instead of a lawyer."

"Yeah, but then who'd figure out how to get you immigration status?"

"Yeah," he answers, but sounds troubled.

"I'm glad you're here, Philip," I say, putting my hand on his shoulder.

"I'm glad to be here too," he answers, sounding pleased now.

But even as I'm congratulating myself for finally saying the right thing, I wonder how we'll find a way to keep him here, safe from the phantoms in my dream.

CHAPTER 8
SIRI

"Cinq minutes de plus," my teacher, Monsieur Guillaume, says.

My classmates bend over their screens, some looking panicked. I finished my historical essay on the Quiet Revolution ten minutes ago, so I sneak another look at the unexpected message from the group I'd tried to join last month, hoping *we* might start a revolution.

Fucking Gabriel! Why does he always have to ruin everything?

Because of him, I'd had to say no to joining Jeune Vanguard —there's no way I'll be in a group that includes him, even if they are doing great stuff instead of just endlessly talking. I didn't tell them why, but it looks like they figured it out 'cause now they're sending me an apology for the "aggressive and inappropriate behaviour of one of our members." Good, but their apology doesn't change the fact that fucking Gabriel is in their group.

I see my teacher coming towards me. He peers over my shoulder to scan my essay.

"Très bien," he says, nodding and smiling. He tells me

about an interactive holo-walkthrough that might interest me that had originally been at the Musée Pointe-à-Callière before most of the Old Port flooded.

Monsieur Guillaume means well, but he lives too much in the past.

"Merci," I tell him, asking him to ping the link to my school screen. He smiles like I've made his day, then tells me I can start my homework. I decide to take a final look at the game theory project my math group just finished. We're supposed to present today in class, and if it's good enough, we might be given a spot in the provincial math and tech fair in the spring.

With a brush of my thumb, I open the project doc and see the familiar text and graphics just before the whole screen gets hyper bright and whites out. I close and reopen the doc. The text's been replaced by strings of meaningless code, and the interactive graphics are still and flat like they've been run over by a truck.

Merde, merde, merde! I run a few diagnostics but all I get is "file can't be read" and "data corrupted." Could another group have sabotaged our project? That makes no sense. I'm friends with practically everyone in my class.

I hard-restart my school screen, tapping impatiently on the desktop as I wait for the reboot. Everything's the same: Quiet Revolution essay fine, math project garbage. I have a weird thought and check the time stamp of the message from Jeune Vanguard that asked if I'd be willing to meet for a "conciliation and restorative justice session" with fucking Gabriel. Huh, I was right. I received it *after* arriving at school. How did they manage to get it through our school building's fire wall?

For the next ten minutes, I try to debug the file but get nowhere. After class, I run down the hall and find Maneesh, who's leaning against the holo message board outside the cafeteria.

"Checke cette merde-là," I tell xir, flashing the sad remains of our school project.

"Tabarnoushe!" xe says, as close to cursing as Maneesh ever gets.

Maneesh checks xir own school screen. Xe flips open the project file and I see the same scrambled text and squashed graphics.

"What will we do?" Maneesh asks, looking at me with xir beautiful, puppy-dog eyes.

I sigh. I'd hoped it was just my screen, or if not, that Maneesh might have some ideas for fixing the problem. I like the way my friends look to me for leadership, but it's kind of intense that Maneesh didn't even ask what diagnostics I'd run or anything. On the other hand, I would've been insulted if xe'd suggested obvious debugging strategies I'd already tried.

"Je sais pas," I tell xir. "I might be able to figure it out with some of the tools I can access at home, but the presentation's this afternoon."

"There's another problem," Maneesh says. "Julie has a stomach ache. She wanted to go home this morning, but I got her to stay. I didn't think we'd be able to do it—"

Maneesh stops talking as xe notices the look on my face.

"Right," Maneesh says. "We should tell her to go home. It will increase the probability that the teacher will let us postpone the presentation."

"Plus, she said she's not feeling well. Pragmatism *and* empathy."

"You're right. I'll find Julie," Maneesh offers. "We have the same class next period."

"Sounds like a plan."

Maneesh walks off, confident that I've solved our problem, but I'm still feeling the weight of it. The best we can hope is that we'll have until Thursday to either fix this glitch or redo, practically from scratch, a project that took the three of us nearly two weeks to complete.

It's during Ethics, my second-to-last class of the day, that the thought creeps into my head: a group that can ping a message through my school's firewall might also have the technical expertise to debug and repair our game theory project. Plus, Gabriel does owe me another apology. I decide that a conciliation and restorative justice session with fucking Gabriel might be a good idea after all.

"Come help with the cooking," my mom says when I get home.

I join her in the kitchen. "Can't Simon? I have a meeting tonight. I need to get ready."

"There's nothing on the schedule about a meeting. You know the rules. All extra-curriculars need to be logged onto the family calendar."

"I know, but it was kind of last minute."

"What about your homework?" she asks, taking a knife from the drawer.

"This is a homework meeting. I need some help with the game theory project."

"I thought you were presenting it today."

"Yeah, but it got postponed, which is lucky 'cause it turns out it needs debugging."

Mommy sighs. "I still need help with dinner."

"Isn't it Daddy's turn to make supper?"

"There's apparently some crisis with the roof garden—the air vents, I think. Daddy's up there trying to fix it. He said he'd be down in time to cook but. . ." Mommy shrugs and smiles as though to say, "You know Daddy." Sometimes I think she lets him get away with too much. Though if Daddy does his makeup meal this weekend, it'll probably mean chocolate chip pancakes for all of us.

My mom hands me two onions from the panier. Kitchen duty isn't a terrible price to pay if she lets me go to the meeting without any more hassle, but onions make my eyes tear. I cut off the strands of beardy roots at one end and peel off the outer skin, which is still covered with bits of dirt from the greenhouse garden.

"Can I ask you something?" I say, wiping my right eye with my sleeve. "Do you think it's ethically correct to. . . to not forgive someone for something they apologized for?"

"That depends," Mommy answers as she peels some purple garlic. "How bad was the thing the person did? And did they try to make up for it?"

"Yeah," I use my other sleeve to wipe both eyes. "But what they did was pretty bad."

"How bad?"

"Not like murdering someone," I say, "but pretty bad." I sniff. My eyes are so teary that I can hardly see.

"Come here," Mommy says, pulling me closer to the sink. She turns on the water and tells me to lean over so that I'm close to the spray. "Running water will help."

"Isn't that against the municipal water conservation law?" I say, snuffling and rubbing my eyes. I sound like I'm literally sobbing over the idea of wasting water.

"We have our own water recycling system in the building," Mommy reminds me. "Listen, Siri. Sometimes people do things that break our hearts. We try to use our brains to decide how to respond, but you can't separate thinking and feeling so easily, and besides, ignoring your heart is rarely a good idea."

She rubs my back as though I were really crying and not just tearing up because of onions. The whole conversation suddenly seems over-the-top and embarrassing.

When I can see again, I reach for another onion, but my mom takes it from my hands.

"I can finish!" I say, more sharply than I mean to.

"I know, sweetheart," she answers, handing me a pile of carrots. "But you're great at cutting root vegetables. I admire how thin you're able to slice things."

At supper, I'm too geared up to eat much. I keep thinking about Gabriel, and what the conciliation session tonight might be like. I know what restorative justice is—it helps that my mom's a community lawyer—but I've never been part of a process like that myself.

What can I ask Gabriel to do that could make things more right? One thing's for sure, I'm going to demand that he get my school project fixed, whether he fixes it himself or finds someone else in the group who has the skills to do it. How many math assignments did I do for him when we were both in the Classe d'accueil as new migrants learning French? How many times did I share my lunch with him and whatever little money I had? I thought he was so cool with his muscles and holo-tattoos and the way he called me "little Siri from Brooklyn." I was only twelve. And he was fifteen and knew I liked him.

I find I'm sitting with my arms folded over my chest. I can't stop thinking now about that afternoon in the basement just before my thirteenth birthday. It's not like Gabriel raped me or anything, but he touched me where he shouldn't have. I'd said no and he didn't listen, and suddenly his muscles were scary instead of cool.

"Eat some carrot ginger soup," my mother says. "You could use an auto-immune boost."

That day with Gabriel, when I went home, my mother was making a creamy white sauce. She made me taste it before realizing I was upset. I haven't liked eating anything with a white sauce since. But the carrot soup is orange and thin—not quite enough carrots for the five of us—so I lift my spoon and eat some of it. It's good, so I eat some more. Plus, I don't want her to think anything's up and ask me more questions. That afternoon, she sensed that something had happened and got most of the details out of me. And then she told Daddy.

I smile. I'm not twelve years old anymore and can take care of myself. I don't want or need my parents telling me what to do and getting all in my business—Daddy especially. I glance sideways at him. Philip has his hand on his shoulder and is telling him about some funny thing a student in his Spanish class said. Mommy and Simon are both laughing, but I've missed the joke. Daddy smiles slightly but then looks away from Philip and towards me. I quickly turn my attention back to my soup bowl.

I don't know what Daddy said or did to Gabriel that night, but Gabriel wouldn't look me in the eye for at least a month afterwards. He didn't seem sorry, he just seemed scared—like pissing-your-pants scared. But how could he be afraid of Daddy? Daddy would never hurt anyone. He's never hit or even shouted at me or Simon. He once made us all stop in the middle of a bike path so he could rescue a caterpillar. And one time, I saw a man who was crazy from drugs hit Daddy in the face. Daddy not only didn't hit him back, he half-carried the man to a street clinic where he could receive treatment. So what could he have done to make Gabriel too freaked out to even look at me?

Gabriel made me afraid and Daddy made him afraid. Is that restorative justice? It didn't feel restorative. It felt awful because, to tell the truth, I still wanted Gabriel to be my friend.

And if he wasn't my friend anymore, I wanted it to be because I decided he didn't deserve to be my friend, not because he was scared of my father.

"Is that okay, Siri?" I hear Simon say.

"What? Sorry, I missed what you said."

"Mommy told me the graphics in your project got all buggy. I could help, if you wanted. I'm good at debugging graphics."

"Thanks, maybe," I say. "But I'm meeting with some friends tonight who might be able to help me fix it."

This isn't really a lie. If all goes well, the people I'm meeting with tonight will become my comrades. And as for Gabriel, even if I haven't seen him in two years, even if I almost broke his arm with my trottinette a few weeks ago, once upon a time, he had been my friend.

There are only four of us at the meeting, which takes place in a small common room at Concordia College. Along with me and Gabriel, there's a comrade from the group who calls themself Anaïs, and a person named Adrienne-Marie from another group. I'm nervous, which pisses me off, and that helps me be angry instead, which I prefer.

Gabriel has his arm in a sling which takes some of the edge off my anger. He hesitates, then jumps into an apology that sounds rehearsed:

"I'm here to tell you that I am very sorry for everything, Siri."

"Everything?" I say.

"Yeah, I mean not just for pushing you at the. . . interview, but what I did three years ago. Siri and I went to high school together for a while," he continues, turning to Adrienne-Marie.

"I touched her without her permission. There are no excuses for my behaviour and I fully own it," he finishes, now turning back to me. But he doesn't quite meet my eyes.

I nod, glad to hear this more unconditional apology, better than the one he made back then when he couldn't stop saying that it was because he liked me and knew I liked him back. At the same time, this apology sounds kind of like a formula, words other people have put in his mouth. I feel unsatisfied.

"Can you elaborate more?" Adrienne-Marie says, like she senses how I'm feeling. When he doesn't respond right away, she adds, "Maybe there's more to say about the incidents?"

"We talked about it back then and I even gave Siri a gift to make up for it. Not something corny like flowers but a real plant. And I can give her more presents—reparations—if she wants." This sounds more like Gabriel—a bit frustrated and clueless, trying to look good and not really understanding why his half-assed apology afterwards didn't erase what happened. "Also, I was only fifteen then," he adds.

"That's how old Siri is now," Anaïs says, and I can't help smiling at them.

"Siri," Adrienne-Marie says. "Would you like to speak about how you experienced Gabriel's violence towards you?"

I think about all the things I'd been planning to say. How he was my best friend. How the fact that I had a crush on him made his behaviour morally worse, not more justified. How unsafe I felt, how angry, how confused and ashamed even though I didn't do anything wrong. At least he didn't mention that we were both stoned.

Thinking about it, I realize that I don't want to say any of those things right now. I don't want to go back to that time when I was so young and hurt and powerless. Instead I ask, "What about how hostile you were to me at the interview, how you tried to shove me around?"

"I already said I was sorry for that." He touches his arm and frowns.

"But why did you act that way? We haven't seen each other in forever."

"I just needed to be sure that you were tough enough now, to do the kind of work we do. I mean, when I knew you before. . ."

"You mean when I was twelve?" I stare him down and he looks away.

Adrienne-Marie seems like a really calm and serious person, but I notice a corner of her mouth curling up. Anaïs, meanwhile, looks disgusted with Gabriel, even kind of shocked.

I wait to see if Gabriel's gonna mention how we dated later that year, when I was still stupid enough to think I could reform him. And how I finally broke up with him not because of my parents' disapproval, not even because of how our relationship took me away from my other friends, but because I never felt one hundred percent safe and I was tired of feeling that way.

Instead of mentioning that history and admitting he felt rejected by me, he just shrugs and says, "Maybe girls are more mature than boys."

That's when I decide to let go of the past, along with any expectations about changing Gabriel. Instead, I'll focus on my future, my future with Jeune Vanguard—because I've decided I'm not going to let fucking Gabriel keep me from joining this group. But one last thing first before finishing this meeting. I tell Gabriel about my math project and the help I need to repair it.

CHAPTER 9
PHILIP

After over a month of both taking a class and teaching a class at UQÀM, I'm still feeling disoriented. Maybe Janie also took a wrong turn and is running late. She likes to say she's directionally impaired, her way of embracing a tendency to get lost, but I can't help thinking there's something convoluted about how this building is organized. The initials for the pavilions don't exactly correspond to their names, and you can't pass from one section to another unless you're on a certain floor. It seems like a terrible setup if you need to escape a shooter.

I finally find the right elevator and locate "Chanteur des voyelles," the café that's reputed to be the best on campus. When I arrive, Janie's already there.

I lean over to kiss her on both cheeks, but she kisses me directly on the lips instead. I feel warm to the pit of my stomach; then I think about Laek and feel a little bad.

"Do you want anything?" I ask.

"I already got myself a tisane and a croissant," she answers, gesturing to the table.

I return balancing a mate latte and a bowl of bean and

synth-meat chili on a tray. I sit beside Janie not only because it puts me physically closer to her, but also because it gives me a view of the fairy lights on rue Saint-Denis.

"So how's your day going?" Janie asks.

"Good. They promoted me to a more advanced French course and my new teacher's from Madagascar, so her accent's easy to understand. The class I'm giving went well too. It's great to be teaching again." I take a spoon of the chili. It's good-tasting but not nearly spicy enough.

"Do you think you'll try to continue teaching Spanish if... if you end up going back?"

"No," I say firmly, thinking to leave it at that, but Janie has a way of getting me to talk. "I could probably get a position at a private school, even with the new laws, but teaching Spanish to a bunch of rich, privileged White kids while Latine workers can be fired or detained as suspected 'border terrorists' for speaking Spanish... I just can't stomach it, Janie."

"What about teaching French at your old high school? You're already good enough to do that in the United America," she remarks.

"Well, that bar's pretty low. But no, I don't want to go back to my school. It's been hard enough without Laek there, pretending nothing's wrong. No one even dares to talk about him!"

"They're scared. The alternative schools are being targeted. Their jobs are at risk."

"I just want someone to acknowledge what happened. Not only that he's gone but why he had to flee. I feel so... alone sometimes."

Janie's expression is filled with empathy. It makes me uncomfortable, like I'm feeling too sorry for myself. I shovel some chili into my mouth, using that as an excuse to look away.

"Hey," Janie says, and places her hand on mine. "Have you spoken to Laek about this?"

"He knows the political context and fucking oughta know how much I've missed him."

"Of course he does, but I mean what happened to you. The gun thing."

"No," I say, trying to push away images of running students, of broken glass and screaming, of blood. "There's nothing to tell. Nothing actually happened."

"Philip—"

"No!" I say, louder than I'd intended. A few heads turn. "Excusez-moi," I say, ducking my head in embarrassment. "I'm sorry, Janie. I get. . . I get angry sometimes."

"I've seen you angry, so it's good you've managed to keep yourself out of trouble."

"Verdad," I say.

"Are you still enjoying Montréal?"

"It's great here. You can leave your bags on the backs of your chairs, use wrist bracelets instead of chips, wave your arms around without someone cloning your ID. Montrealers are so relaxed compared to New Yorkers and Parisians. Vibrant yet laid back—an unusual combo."

"So do you want to try to stay?" she asks.

"Being with you and Laek. . . there's nothing I want more. But. . ." I imagine Kyla and I living on opposite sides of the border, her growing up without me there. I press the heels of my hands against my eyes. "Even if you could find a way to get me permanent residency, which seems pretty unlikely, there's Kyla. How could I leave her behind?"

"What if I could get her here too?" Janie leans forward, hands flat against the table.

"Dana would never let her go. If only to spite me."

"I could try to win full custody for you. There are ways. If I could prove—"

I put my spoon down. "No. I won't do that to Dana."

"She'd do it to you."

"I'm not her. Could you really try to take her child away, Janie? As a woman?"

Janie gives me a hard look. "My loyalty is to my values; I don't give a shit about outmoded notions of gender treason. Dana is a terrible parent."

"She loves Kyla just like I do."

Janie opens her mouth to argue, but I hope she'll just drop it. Sometimes Janie's ferociously protective side can make her a little harsh, but it's why she's such a good lawyer for the underdog. It's remarkable how much I've come to know Janie during these past three years apart and how the Laek I thought I knew has become a mysterious near-stranger.

"How'd you manage to beat me here?" I ask, not wanting to think about all that.

"I used a mapping app."

"But this school's greyboxed, right? Doesn't that mean location-enabled devices won't work inside the building? I tried their holo-directions, which are frankly terrible."

"That's why I used Laek's shadow-net app. Why didn't you? You have it too."

"I'm not using any of Laek's fucking. . ." I take a deep breath, focusing my gaze on the blueish trees. "I choose not to use any of Laek's tech. For the last three years, I used nothing but. What did that get me?"

"Not arrested? Us not found, extradited?"

I shrug, not wanting to fight with Janie about this.

"Look, I get that you're frustrated that Laek's been vague about. . . the airport," Janie says, taking what seems like a wide segue we both know is not.

"Doesn't he trust me?"

"Of course he trusts you. He just needs more time."

"I've been patient. Haven't I been patient?"

"When a person's seen a lot of violence, that can make them careful. Even distant. But Philip. . ." She takes my hand in hers. I look down at my empty bowl. She squeezes, insistent. Her hand is so small in mine. Like a child's hand. But her grip isn't a child's grip. She moves her fingernail over the ridges of my knuckle. I shiver and meet her eyes.

"Do you love him, Philip? Do you still love him?"

"Yes," I say, trying to swallow the lump in my throat. "Very much."

She smiles, and it makes her face seem to glow. "Alright, then," she says, standing. "I have to go back to work. Laek's off today, so maybe the two of you can talk. He'll probably be up on the roof, working in the garden. Give him a kiss for me."

I find Laek on the roof, just like Janie said he'd be. He's not working in the garden though, he's vaping weed. A thick veil of purplish smoke hovers around him as he sits against the parapet, motionless as a statue. His pose is something between artful and relaxed: right knee folded up, the other splayed to the side, chin lifted to the heavens exposing his bare throat as he stares, mesmerized, at a sky filled with low-hanging white clouds. I have an urge to reach through the smoke and take him in my arms, give him that kiss from Janie; the other part of me wants to pull the vape out of his hand and kick his drugged-out ass.

"Hey," he calls out without turning his head, just as I'm about to leave him to his habit.

"Hey yourself. Janie told me you'd be working in the garden."

"I am. Was. Just taking a little break. Testing the product." His voice sounds hoarse.

"You use weed a lot?"

"When I'm using, I use a lot. When I'm not, I don't at all."

He laughs, though I can't see what's funny.

"What does your doctor say about that?" I ask. "I've heard weed isn't good for. . . for people who experience depression."

"Depends on the type. Anyhow, I don't take it for depression. I take it for pain."

"Oh," I say, the mild rebuke feeling worse for the gentle tone in which it was delivered. "So the pain in your ribs is still pretty bad?" I picture Laek in that hospital bed three years ago, going through morphine withdrawal after the cops broke seven of his ribs.

Laek takes another hit from the vape. "Right now I'm feeling no pain."

"I guess not. Otherwise you'd know that you were freezing your ass off out here."

"So come here and warm it up," Laek says.

I stay where I am. "What about the gardening?"

"I finished putting in the rest of the winter garlic. Now I'm dealing with the cannabis."

"By testing the product," I say.

"Micro-dosing, yeah. You know much about plants, farming?"

"Not really," I tell him.

"Well, growing cannabis is complicated. You have to regulate the light. First by providing lots of it. Eighteen or even twenty-four hours a day. I installed special lamps. In the beginning, it's all leaves, green stuff. To get it to flower, to make the part you smoke, the next step is to limit the light. Then the buds begin to grow. You with me?"

I nod. This is the most information about anything Laek has given me since I arrived.

"Okay. After the plants start budding, you check to see which are male and which are female. You know why?" Laek asks.

I shake my head.

"Because you need to kill all the males."

"That seems harsh," I tell him. He doesn't laugh like I expect him to.

"Only female plants are valuable. And if you don't kill the males, they'll pollinate the females."

"And this is bad why?"

"Because then all the plant's energy will go into making seeds instead of flowers. What you want, what the growers of cannabis want, is to have the females horny all the time, making lots of flowers with the hope of being pollinated, but never being pollinated."

"That's—"

"Horrible. Yes," Laek finishes, staring straight at me, looking unhappy.

I sigh, remembering my promise to Janie to try to talk to Laek.

"I think you're angry at me," I finally say. "Could it be that you feel a little jealous?"

"Why would I be jealous?"

"Because I'm sleeping with Janie?"

"So am I," Laek answers, seeming genuinely puzzled.

"But you're having to share her—"

"Okay, now you're making me angry. Janie's not a thing. A thing you share. She's a human being. Making her own ethical choices about who she's sexually intimate with."

Though he claims to be angry, his face is as smooth as glass. I'd rather have him shout at me, plus I'm so frustrated with how non-communicative he's been. "Mira, Laek, don't sit there and lie to me. At least admit you're pissed off or. . . or something."

"I'm not angry," he says softly. "And not jealous either. Envious, maybe, but not of you. Like I said, you're not getting anything I'm not getting. Janie is, though. She's getting you."

That feeling of rebuke again, of guilt. But I'm not having any of it.

"Well maybe there's a reason for that," I say. "Maybe after three years of being apart with almost no messages from you, I'm feeling a bit distant."

"What about the holos I sent you?"

"Holos?" I say, playing dumb.

"You know. The guy. In the black mask."

"The naked guy you mean? I thought that was holo-spam. Pornography."

"It was supposed to look like porn. So they wouldn't suspect anything. I thought you'd find it amusing."

"Amusing," I say slowly, as though I'm testing the idea out. "You've always had a strange sense of humour. But I would've preferred a few words letting me know you were okay. Maybe even asking how I was doing. A silent, naked man wearing a black mask and carrying a knife was less than reassuring."

"That was the knife you gave me! To tell you I was looking after myself."

"It could just as easily have meant that you were thinking of slitting your throat."

He ducks his head, and I see I've struck a nerve, his face an eloquent mix of pain and guilt. When did we get so good at hurting each other?

"Laek," I say, a little more gently. "If you wanted me to

know what you were thinking, you could have added a speech bubble, or even had that... that sexy holo say a few words."

"It wasn't safe," he insists. "I couldn't risk it."

"But Janie wrote to me regularly. She shared her news and kept up with mine, even if everything was coded, encrypted, and camouflaged to death. She helped me not feel so abandoned. Is it any wonder I feel a stronger connection to her now?"

"What Janie did was risky. But at least she followed my precautions." Laek watches me carefully, lips a thin line. There's something about his face that tells me the effects of the cannabis have worn off. "How about you, Philip? Did you follow my security protocols?"

"Yes," I say, not meeting his eyes. "I followed your goddamned protocols."

"And what about my other instructions? Did you keep your head down? I get the feeling there's something you're not telling me."

"There's plenty you're not telling me."

Laek's face tightens, and for a moment, I fear I've gone too far. Then his expression smooths, and the moment is gone. I feel desperate to do this conversation over again, to say something that will bring back the natural intimacy we used to have. I could open up, tell him what happened at school like Janie wants me to. Or I could simply admit that of course I knew that the holo was of him, how I replayed it over and over again, even masturbating to it when I was feeling particularly desperate and lonely. If I did that, though, he'd know I didn't destroy it after viewing, as the warning accompanying the image had instructed.

I remain silent. Though I don't really want to fight with him, I'm not prepared to back down either. I decide the safest thing is to change the subject again.

"The smoke from the weed. . . it was purple. What makes it that colour?"

"It's spliced with blueberry. Gives it a sweet flavour too."

"Really?" I say.

"Nah, I'm just fucking with you."

And with that, Laek stands up in one smooth motion and walks away from me. I watch him stride purposefully towards the greenhouse on the other side of the roof, vape in one hand and the knife I gave him gripped hard in the other.

CHAPTER 10
SIMON

"Dépêche-toi! We're going to lose her!" I shout to Aiza.

I round the corner at rue Charlevoix, but Aiza calls after me.

"Wait, Simon. Maybe spying on Siri is a bad idea. I want to visit the art installations."

"Me too, but after we figure out where Siri's secret meeting is."

Aiza doesn't answer. She's kicking at a little lump of icy snow and peeking nervously into parc St-Gabriel, but there's no one near us except an old person walking with their companion dog.

"Aiza, qu'est-ce qu'il y a?" I ask, wishing she'd stop kicking at the snow. It's already almost all melted!

"I just think we should respect Siri's privacy."

"She's my sib. We have to look after each other. Maybe she's fallen in love with another boy who's trying to get her to do something dangerous."

"If she's with a boy, she'll be even madder if she finds out we're following her."

And there it is again. That quick look into the park. Her foot kicking the snow.

"Aiza, are you scared of Siri?"

"Of course I'm scared of Siri! Elle fait peur! She's tall and strong and isn't afraid of anything. And she has a bad temper. I was there when she said she'd cut you up into little pieces and add you to the stew she was making if you touched her things again."

"She didn't mean that literally! My family doesn't even eat meat."

"Franchement, Simon, I know she wasn't really going to eat you! But that doesn't mean she won't. . . beat us up or something."

"Siri would never hurt us. Plus, she told me she likes you."

"She did?" Aiza says, smiling with her eyebrows high up—a happy-surprised face.

"Yeah. She said you were good for me. Whatever that's supposed to mean."

Aiza's smile grows even huger. "D'accord. We'll keep following her."

We start walking again, in the direction of the railway tracks. I look all around, but don't see anyone on a trottinette. I sigh. "She's way ahead of us now. We'll never find her."

"Si! If we can figure out where she was going, we can just go there too. That's easier than trying to sneak up on her."

"But how could we figure that out?" I ask. The sun had been behind a cloud but now it slips out again, lighting up the railway bridge. On the street below the bridge, purple ice-melting crystals sparkle and glow. I take an image with my wristpad.

"By looking at all the clues," Aiza says. "The message you saw on her screen said that the meeting was at. . ."

"Le bâtiment numérique. But what does that mean?"

"I don't know," Aiza says. "How do you meet in a digital building? Plus, Siri took the métro and her trottinette, so she was going someplace in meatspace."

"I don't like that expression," I tell her. "Anyhow, maybe we should go to the art exposition now and think about it more. Meetings are two hours, at least at the co-op, so as long as we figure out where it is before then, we can hide and see who comes out the building."

"D'accord. The installation is right here in Grand Trunk Park. Maybe we'll see some elephants!" Aiza says.

"Grand Trunk has nothing to do with elephants. It's the name of the old railway line."

"I know. I'm joking, Simon."

At the installation, there's a welcome booth decorated with fairy lights and holo snowflakes. Aiza picks out two pairs of exhibition glasses from a greybox and hands one to me.

"Whoa, Simon! I can't believe it. My joke turned out to be true!"

I put on my glasses and I'm suddenly looking up at a life-sized elephant. The elephant is huge, with legs like trees, wrinkled skin, beautiful kind eyes, and enormous ears that look like they could flap and the elephant would take off into the sky. The elephant's pretty realistic-looking, except for being coloured neon-pink. There's a caption which says, "The Pink Elephant in the Room." The elephant's trunk points us to the entry.

At the entry are places to put your feet, or your wheels if you're using a mobility device. As soon as we do this, the sidewalk starts moving, like at the airport. The exhibit space that our glasses show us is way bigger than it could possibly be in the here-and-now. We move down a "street," passing building fronts that seem to lean over us. All around us are tons of ugly car pieces, and each is attached to a pipe sucking up something from the earth. Further along, factories pop up in the background, spitting out layers of dirty smoke.

"Regarde!" Aiza says.

I turn to where she's looking and see huge industrial farms. There are holos of cows and pigs and sheep, all walking sadly with their heads down, some being herded into short, ugly buildings and others into small trucks that look like the prison vans in New York that cops use during demos. I look away because it makes my heart hurt. Instead, I check out the scene close to us, and that's when I see the other animals.

There are butterflies and bees and bats flying around, wolves and bears and cougars and buffalo running down the street, salmon and turtles swimming around in a fountain. It's beautiful and surreal, like in a fantasy screenshow about utopia. Right in the middle of it all, there's another elephant. When we get closer, I see that the elephant is staring at us, not with kind eyes like the other one, but with sad, angry eyes that follow us. And now I notice that all the animals have stopped prowling around and are watching us too, looking mad and sad and. . . and scary, especially the extinct ones. We both walk faster, trying to get to the end of the exhibit, but we can't escape their eyes. Finally, we get to the exit, where a small monkey is waving goodbye while holding a sign which says, "Seventh-wave Extinction."

I take off the glasses, placing them in the box outside the exhibit. Aiza is still wearing hers, staring off at something I can't see. I think there are tears in her eyes. I feel unhappy too.

A little while later, we're walking on rue Wellington, quiet in our own thoughts.

"That was good art," Aiza finally says. "But it was sad."

"I think good art is supposed to make you feel emotions. And sadness is an emotion."

Aiza nods, still looking unhappy, and even though I know

it's okay to feel sad, I don't like seeing her this way. "Hey, you know what?" I say. "Even when art is sad, if it's very good, it can also feel happy, 'cause good art makes you think about beauty. And it's like that beauty somehow. . . gets mixed up in the sadness and makes the sadness almost happy. Do you know what I mean?"

"Yes," Aiza says. "But happy isn't exactly the right word. It needs a stronger word. Like joyous. Or. . . exultant."

"Exultant," I say slowly. "Yeah, that's perfect, Aiza!"

Aiza takes my hand. "I think we should tell everyone who's a member of Protecteurs de la planète about this exhibit."

"Or maybe we should tell everyone who *isn't* a member yet. Maybe it would make them want to join the Peeps and fight for our planet and all of the animals who live here!"

Aiza smiles now and squeezes my hand tight, "When you grow up, you're going to be a great organizer. Like your maman and papa! Or like Andressa!"

"I could never be like Andressa. She's not even grown up yet and she invented the Peeps. I bet she's one of the most famous environmental activists in the whole world!"

"I want to be just like her," Aiza says.

"Me too."

We walk along the tracks until the road turns east, taking us away from them. We end up on a quiet street that curves like a snake. It's starting to get dark and I can smell the suppers that people are cooking in the pastel-coloured buildings we're passing. At the corner is a skinny strip of park sloping up to above the railway tracks. We climb it and watch as the sky goes dark and the buildings get bright.

I turn away from the buildings because I'd rather see natural beauty right now. I'm still thinking of those poor animals. Tracked and killed by hunters, or murdered by animal-farmers—or just by too much concrete and pollution.

My eyes search for bright snow instead. I see a big patch of unmelted whiteness near a bush. I get a little closer and see that there's a trottinette track right in the middle of it!

"Look!" I shout to Aiza, pointing to the mark in the snow. There are more of them in the mud further down the hill. Aiza runs ahead of me and kneels beside a smear of mud. "I think this may be from Siri's trottinette too!" she says. "I can use my magnifying app to find more."

We follow more wheel prints that take us towards rue de Sébastopol.

"I remember this street," Aiza says. "My maman took me here to see the murals. They show the history of the neighbourhood. And afterwards, we went to. . . Simon! I think I know where Siri's meeting is!"

"Where?" I ask her.

"Bâtiment Sept'art! Maman told me about it. How the community fought the city and the developers and won, and how it became an artists' collective. There are always new exhibitions from all over the world. And there's a digital version of the whole building—a bâtiment numérique! *C'est ça*, Simon! Siri's meeting has to be at Bâtiment Sept'art!"

I run to catch up to Aiza as she rushes ahead towards the next street.

"The bâtiment is just past this street," she calls out. "But first, come see this."

She activates something with her wristpad and a warm, orange light begins to glow inside the five-sided glass cage on the top of a lamppost. The lamppost looks like it's wearing a black pointy hat but made of iron. Suddenly the street is filled with holos of people wearing strange clothing and speaking different languages.

"Who are they?" I ask.

"Ancestors," she answers, reverently.

I follow Aiza as she moves through the crowd of holos, weaving between a short person with a weird cap and someone who looks pregnant. Aiza gives the pregnant person a lot of space like they were real. I'm starting to get nervous about missing Siri, so I pass Aiza, plowing right through the holos. I feel rude because the holos are hyper-realistic, with very human expressions on their faces. I close my eyes; it bothers me less that way. I walk a few paces and then open my eyes. I close them again and walk some more. Once I'm used to walking with my eyes closed, I walk faster. I hit something solid, bounce, and land on my butt.

"Simon!" Aiza cries, sounding nervous.

I open my eyes. The holos have evaporated, leaving the street empty. Almost empty. Someone is standing above me, someone tall and strong-looking. One side of the person's face has smooth, pale skin, clear blue eyes, and shiny blond hair. It's perfect, like the kind of face you see on screen stars or superheroes. The other side of the face is all jaggy lines and red patches of skin; the hair on that side is patchy too, with only half an eyebrow.

With those eyes staring right at me, I can't move; I can't even look away.

"Simon, run!" Aiza says, and it's as if her words free me from a magical paralysis spell.

I jump to my feet and run as fast as I can away from the two-faced human.

CHAPTER 11
LAEK

"Papa, t'as oublié! You're supposed to help me with my project after school."

Simon and I are in the foyer of the apartment getting ready to leave for the day. Everyone else is already gone.

"I didn't forget, love." I hand him his tuque. "Something came up. Maybe Mommy can help you instead."

"She's busy too. There's an emergency meeting of the Guild of Refugee Lawyers. You didn't write on the kitchen screen who your meeting was with."

"Siri could help with your project," I say, avoiding his eyes. "Or even better, ask Philip."

"Does Uncle Philip know anything about the effect of non-ionizing radiation on birds?"

"You'd be surprised how many things he knows but hasn't told us about," I answer.

Simon brightens, missing my tone. "Okay, Papa. I'll ask him after school. But don't forget about taking me to the bird park on Sunday. Maybe Uncle Philip will want to come."

"Maybe," I say, this time in a neutral tone, then lean over to kiss the top of Simon's head. "Go on. Aiza's waiting for you."

I watch him run down the hallway to the elevator. After he gets on, I double back. Mount the stairs to the roof. Step outside and lift my head to the sky. Snowflakes gently stroke my cheeks and melt on my eyelashes as I listen to Simon's words drift up through the air vent. "It's snowing again! Yay!" I hear, followed by Aiza's murmured response.

Attached to the back of the ventilation pipe is a metal box, flush to the parapet. Inside is a round greybox. I open it with my fingerprint, feel for the tiny chip in the diamond-shaped recess, and hide it in my knee patch.

It's getting late, so I grab my bike from under the overhang. Ride it along the edge beside the parapet then straight down the gardening chute, braking hard as I spill out onto the ruelle behind our building. I bike along the back alley; take a left onto rue Shannon. The road opens up just as the sun comes out from behind a cloud, igniting the snow with a zillion sparkles of light. Sharp joy spreads through my limbs. I accelerate. The speed and my wheel studs minimize but don't eliminate the skids and sideways motion. I grin hard, revelling in the physical challenge, my bike and I one unified creature on the hard-packed snow.

Rue Shannon takes me to the bike path Janie calls "The Yellow Brick Road." Its surface is clean of snow. I picture the teams of stationary bikers who power the generator that heats the path from below. I promise myself to take an extra turn pedalling this week in gratitude for the late-season, much-needed snowfall. I eventually get to parc de Mont-Royal. I pedal still faster, a welcome heat in my thighs as I climb. It's not the quickest route to work, but it's the most beautiful, and by the time I exit the park to mix with the traffic going north and east, I feel good.

Arriving at École de la rue, I have just enough time before the staff meeting to stash my bike and change my clothes. I fly down the stairs two at a time. The locker room smells musty. A stark contrast to the fresh smell of snow. Our newly "renovated" meeting room—what used to be our lunchroom—will smell of the cheap paint job and the new industrial carpeting. And of Cloutier's aftershave. A little joy drains out of me.

I use my wristpad to open my locker. Exchange my grey jeans and comfortable sweater for dark bamboo slacks and a white shirt with filaments on the cuffs and collar. Replace my calf-high biker's boots with plain shoes of dyed hemp. I check my appearance in the bathroom mirror. My haircut still looks fresh, the three simple studs in my left ear a statement without being a shout. I wear no other adornment aside from my wristpad bracelet which covers the tattoo underneath. I hope I've found the right balance—plain enough to escape Cloutier's attention but without completely crushing my sense of self. As a kid, everything I wore was chosen for me, ill-fitting and worn. Now, though I still wear castoffs, they're stylish castoffs, carefully selected from clothing exchanges and *friperies* across the city.

I check the time. Still a little early. Too much of a risk I'll find myself alone with Cloutier. My visceral reaction to this possibility reminds me of earlier injuries to my body and psyche by men who get off on power. I push away these sensory memories, the odours, the intimacy of that violence. Focus instead on thoughts of my family. The family I'm hiding things from. The family I've, once again, somehow put in danger. What if I lose them? Lose Philip?

A blank interval.

I find myself sitting on the tiled floor beneath the sink, covered in sweat. My wristpad tells me I've lost six entire minutes. I jump to my feet. Stare at the mirror again. My twin stares back at me, indifferent. I steel myself and dive into that indifference. Change places with my shadow. I leave behind this morning's hard-edged joy; the tactile comfort of my soft, worn clothes; the pleasure of my own body, damaged but strong. This buys me the right to also shed the pain, the fear, the despair. I'm blank and empty and there's a certain strength in that. I bound up the stairs. Though I'll be a little late for the meeting, at least I'm prepared for it.

"Sobriety, punctuality. . ." Cloutier is saying as I slip into the room. I aim myself at the other side of the table from him, but he calls my name. Motions to the chair on his right. I hesitate a fraction of a second. Pull out the chair and sit down.

"I was speaking of the values that our school represents. And how anyone who wishes to keep working here must live those values."

"Je m'excuse," I say with unfeigned sincerity. I am, after all, four minutes late.

"Je te pardonne. You're young. There's still time to learn some discipline."

He lays his hand on my shoulder but it's nothing to me. My shoulder's an insensate collection of bone and muscle and flesh; the hairy, knuckled hand resting on it is without weight or consequence. I meet his eye and he smiles at me. Is it possible for a smile to be both patronizing and lascivious? I smile back sweetly, but maybe there's something else in my smile too because he falters and quickly removes his hand.

Cloutier recovers his poise and continues where he left off, voice and posture communicating a desire to appear gracious yet unyielding. I scan the meeting's agenda. Certain items aren't there. Items that Chloë and I had raised—like the sharp increase in the number of kids who are missing from our classes. I look around the table. Chloë's missing too.

My mind races. Was there something she'd mentioned? We've been talking less since I refused to accept the results of our internal investigation into Clara's death. But still, she'd have told me if she couldn't come today. Staff meetings under Clara Bazinet were important, but under Cloutier's reign, absences are not tolerated. Something with her girlfriend maybe? But they broke up five weeks ago. An emergency with her family in Gaspésie?

Cloutier is pointing out figures on a holo-graph he's projected above the table.

"Non-recurrent funding," he's explaining, "is as unreliable as seasonal labour. This is one reason I've decided not to apply for renewals of our more. . . unstable funding sources," he concludes. "But luckily, my family's foundation has agreed to make up the difference, fully committing itself to supporting our organization."

And controlling it, I think to myself.

"Our next order of business is the re-orientation of our pedagogical goals. We need a curriculum that supports the success of each of our students by giving them the skills they need to compete in the job market. Science, technology, language and history, for those who are capable. More targeted job training programs for those who are not."

"But. . ." I glance around the table. A few of my colleagues look down. Some gaze at Cloutier, submissive smiles pasted on their faces. Daniel-Lin shakes his head slightly, as though in warning. I hesitate but decide not to back down. "Shouldn't a full liberal arts education be offered to everyone? And certain subjects are even more essential for our students. Like Gender and Sexuality Studies. Critical Thinking. The arts."

"Art therapy. Art appreciation. How is this going to get

them off the streets and contributing to the economy?" Cloutier's expression radiates disapproval.

I look around for support. Feel the loss of two outspoken colleagues who recently left, Nadège for a new post and Jean-Paul for a parental leave he told me would be permanent.

"Studies show that an arts curriculum improves performance in the core subjects," I say in a neutral tone, inviting discussion.

"That's true—" Marla, our math teacher, begins, but Cloutier cuts her off.

"Laek, I think you're out of your depth."

"Chloë has put together all the studies. Where. . . where is Chloë?" I blurt out.

No one speaks, but I can sense the heightened attention, the feeling of both relief that the question's been asked, and dread as we wait for Cloutier's answer.

"Chloë's not well," he states. "She will be on leave for an indefinite period. Some of you will therefore need to take on extra responsibilities as we move forward with our restructuring. Don't worry, you will be given the opportunity to retrain. If you are interested in this option, please sign up for a one-to-one meeting at my office...."

***

It's near dark. I slow to a near stop at the intersection, activating the blinker on my wristpad. I turn, moving fast but in control. Always in control. I don't understand why Janie and Philip think I'm reckless. I'm very careful with my body. I eat a healthy, plant-based diet. Drink lots of water, using the best filtration systems that you can buy or trade for. Wear a breathing mask on low air quality days. Exercise, sleep when I can. Get sun in the winter.

It's true I've sometimes had to put myself in physical danger. It was always for a reason, though, the benefits carefully weighed. Like at the airport. Once again, my chest constricts, thinking about what might happen if we can't keep Philip here.

I pull into the ruelle next to a nondescript building and lock up my bike. The storefront houses a craft shop. Inside, I stroll between aisles, eyes scanning the shelves of brightly coloured plastics, flexible wires, recycled textiles. My hand dives into a bin of glass beads. They feel cool against my fingers as I sift through them. I choose a handful of different sizes and colours. Think about braiding them into my hair. Remember my hair's too short now, so add a couple of wires to make bracelets for Siri and Simon.

When the storefront's empty, I go up to pay. Rana's working the cash himself today. He refuses both money and barter, claiming I overpaid last time. I argue a little, then acquiesce, squeezing his shoulder in thanks. He steps aside, allowing me to slip into the back room.

I push aside a crate blocking the trap door. Open it using this week's code and go down the stairs. Delia is at the inner reception area to the Garderie Mariposa Daycare. Dressed with impeccable style as usual with earrings of shiny foil hanging to her shoulders.

"¡Ay mano! I haven't seen you in a while."

"Lo siento, Delia. It's been crazy at home."

"Everything okay with tu broki?"

I shrug and smile, not really wanting to talk about Philip.

"We can chat later," she says, switching to French. "You want to go straight down?"

"I can help with the kids before going to the communication room. Who's working?"

"Nathalie. Ahmar's on break." She unlocks the door with her wristpad.

I emerge into a narrow hall. The walls are the colour of grass, peppered with magenta flowers with tiny faces, red cardinals in flight. And everywhere, butterflies. 2-D images on the walls, holographic ones fluttering around the limited space. Butterflies are beautiful, can pass over false borders, pollinate plants. Here, they're a security system.

I wait for my identity to be verified. The door to the children's room opens. "Laek!" Nathalie says, a baby in her arms. "J'suis contente de te voir."

"It's good to see you too. Désolé. It's been a while. How can I help?"

"If you could stay with these two. . . I need to contact some folx."

"Is there a situation?" I ask.

"You remember Ariel," she says, indicating a pre-schooler carefully building with a pile of flexible 3-D shapes. Ariel doesn't look up but I can sense xir focus on our conversation. "I don't think you've met Ariel's baby sib," Nathalie continues. "Iel s'appelle Sol." She gazes down at the chubby baby sleeping in her arms. "We just learned that their papa agreed to voluntary removal to the U.A. for the level-three farmworkers' citizenship lottery."

I keep my face carefully neutral despite this news that their father just agreed to five years of what's basically slave labour. Followed by a gamble whose most likely result will be deportation to whatever hell he was escaping from in the first place.

"And their maman?" I ask hopefully.

"We're trying to locate her."

I remember the news on the réseau's link this morning. "Was she staying at Sainte—"

"Oui, c'est ça," Nathalie says in a calm voice.

My heart sinks. She passes me the baby and I ease the child's warm, moist weight onto my left shoulder. Begin a soothing, rocking motion. The sleeping baby doesn't stir. The rocking is more for me. Ariel finally looks up from the pile of shapes. I carefully lower myself onto the floor next to xir. Hold the baby tightly against my chest.

"Can I help you build?" I ask in French, one of three languages xe can already speak.

"Oui," xe answers softly. I reach for a shape with my free hand.

Two hours later, I'm in the sub-basement sitting in the Centre's greybox room. I take out Philip's knife, the one he gave me before I left New York. The knife I jokingly said while hospitalized that I should use to slit my throat. Maybe not a joke. Philip, at least, wasn't laughing. But he gave me the knife anyway. To show his trust. To be worthy of that trust, there's not much I wouldn't do.

I use the tip of the knife to make a small slit in my wrist. Some blood oozes out. I take the diamond-shaped chip from my knee patch and place it inside the slit. Spray the wound with artificial skin. Wait for it to dry.

Al arranged for the creation of this hacked version of my chip for my sixteenth birthday. Using it as a wrist chip will ensure a response from him. So many times, I've been tempted to throw the chip into the river. The East River. Le fleuve Saint-Laurent. Any river.

I sit in the corner of the room hugging my knees. Almost three years since I last contacted my old "mentor." We needed him then. I promised myself I'd never need him again.

The artificial skin is dry and tight across my wrist. It's time.

Using the chip, I choose a new avatar, a grey unicorn. I'm not an artist like my son, but I do notice details. I tweak the image, change its proportions to more closely resemble mine. I work on the eyes, making them as almond-shaped as my own. Bright with anger. Or unshed tears. The horn is bone-white. Tipped with red. And on the unicorn's torn-up back, shrapnel protrudes, blood dripping down his heaving sides.

Satisfied, I tag it with my biometrics and flick my finger, sending my unicorn galloping through the room's south wall and across Québec's virtual southern border.

I wait. Five minutes. Ten minutes. Thirty-five. I'm not worried. Al may not be alone. And when he is, he'll answer. And even if he doesn't, that's a kind of answer too. Answers are what I need right now. What my family needs.

Eyes closed, I rest my head against the corner. I'm not sure of the moment when sleep takes me. Or if I'm truly asleep. I find myself wandering the Midwestern Drylands again. This time I have my magna skates, though you can't skate on sand. Since I know I'm dreaming, I use my skates to fly instead. The flying fills me with a heady joy. Too late, I realize my mistake. I've left myself vulnerable, the joy opening me again to pain. I fall to the sand, sinking with my skates, lower and lower into the ground. Hot sand fills my mouth and nose until I can't breathe.

I jerk awake, my eyes opening to a dread sight. A man of death, his face a skull of radioactive green. His body is stooped but imposing. He wears camouflage pants, blood-stained knives of various sizes hanging from his belt. A nineteenth century bandolier crosses his narrow chest. Incongruously, he carries six worn shopping bags filled with the kinds of things a person who is unhoused might carry. A nice touch. Al has finally answered my call.

I yawn and stretch, signalling boredom. Across the border,

in some unknown place, my unicorn avatar does the same. The skull face turns in my direction.

"You're looking well. Though the blood and shrapnel is a little on-the-nose. Let alone the unicorn."

Skull-man speaks these words with an upper-class British accent and the pacing of a screenshow villain. Which is to say, nothing like Al's real voice. But I'd recognize his word choices and the way he arranges them anywhere. I compose my response:

"Skip the pleasantries. I have only one question. Was he the target?"

"Which "he" are we talking about?"

"You fucking know who I'm asking you about. Answer me or don't answer me."

"A question for a question. Are you sleeping with him yet?"

"Jealous? You always were a dirty old man."

"You know I never touched you."

"And you know you wanted to."

"Yes? No? Help me out, unicorn boy, what's the right answer?"

"That was. A reminder that I can't trust anything you say."

"Then why go to this trouble to contact me?"

"You promised you'd help keep my family safe. Naive of me to think you might keep that promise."

"I've kept my promise. It's you who's failing your family, worrying about HIM when you should be worried about HER. That group she's in is putting her at risk. Do you know what she's involved in at the moment?"

"I know exactly what my daughter's up to. My group has our eye on—"

"I'm not talking about your daughter. I'm talking about Janie."

I cut the connection, a cold shock taking my breath away. The shock is quickly replaced by fury. He broke our anonymity code, our most cardinal safety rule. Fucking Al whose own real name I have never and will never know. I grab Philip's knife and lunge at the afterimage of Al's holo, the skull mouth frozen in the shape of Janie's name. The holo dissipates as my knife passes through it harmlessly, still thirsting for blood. I turn it on myself, making a long slash across my wrist. I hold the wrist out from my body. Watch the blood flow from it like it's somebody else's. Watch until my heart begins to slow its panicked rhythm. Watch as the blood slows too.

I use my tongue and teeth to extract the chip from my wrist. I consider swallowing it. Letting it drown in the acid river of my stomach. Instead, I spit it out onto the ground.

CHAPTER 12
JANIE

What wakes me is the screech and sigh of the stairwell door closing. Though the noise isn't loud, my hearing is acute, especially at night, and the stairwell is only two metres from the entrance to our apartment.

Laek enters the bedroom silently, but my eyes are open now and the streetlight outside our window casts a faint glow through the curtains. I watch him slip off his clothes and fold them with efficient gestures that seem almost frictionless. I could watch him peel an orange and still marvel at his quiet grace. Philip, a solid presence just beside me, doesn't even stir. A heavy sleeper, he'll surely miss Laek's middle-of-the night entry. I think about feigning sleep—Laek obviously doesn't want to disturb anyone—but except when necessary in the courtroom, I'm not much good at pretence.

Not bothering with pyjamas (maybe because the dresser he shares with Philip also squeaks), Laek slips into bed nude. I turn towards him, placing my hands on his chest. His skin is uncharacteristically cold, his nipples hard like dried lentils. He's trembling slightly, and I sense it's not from the temperature. I pull him against me and he presses his face into the space between my shoulder and my neck.

He takes a long, shuddering breath and lets it out. "Sorry to wake you," he whispers.

"It's okay," I whisper back. In truth, everything wakes me: being too cold or too hot, someone shifting in the bed, one of the kids talking in their sleep. . . or Laek not home at 4 a.m., on a day he isn't scheduled to do a night shift. "I couldn't sleep anyway," I finish.

With the gentlest of touches, Laek outlines my face with his thumb. "Janie," he breathes in a long exhalation, like it's a whole thought instead of just my name. A wave of emotion composed partly of lust and partly of anger hits me low in the stomach; I'm not sure if I want to fuck him or throttle him. God, how I wish I had time for either of those things, but the earlier I begin my preparations, the more likely the action my group has planned will come off safely.

I take a moment to pull my emotions together. "You okay?" I ask. "I was worried."

"You shouldn't—" he begins, then stops himself. "I'm sorry," he says instead.

I wait to see if he'll say more. He turns onto his back and stretches, a hand going to his ribs which must be aching terribly with all the hours he's been up and about. When he sees me watching, he straightens his arm like a child caught in the act. Philip, on the other side of me, also rolls onto his back, his gentle snore followed by a sigh.

"Could we talk about it later?" Laek asks softly.

"That's fine." For now it's enough that he didn't try to tell me, stupidly, that I shouldn't worry about him; that he didn't attempt to pretend nothing bad had happened while crawling into bed near morning in a fragile, obviously fucked-up state. So instead of pushing him to talk, I take him in my arms, sensing his gratitude in the way the muscles in his arms relax and his body sinks into my embrace. Eyes half closed, Laek rubs his lips gently against mine, slipping his tongue into my mouth. I slide my hands down his smooth back to his narrow hips to cup his ass in my hands, my insides flowing like hot, melted butterscotch. I really don't have time for this.

"I gotta get up, sweetheart, to go to the airport," I say.

He releases me immediately. "A deportation?" he asks in a whisper.

"Yeah." This is not precisely untrue.

"You don't always have to be there," Laek says, his empathy almost undoing my resolve to keep my group's plans a secret from him for now. I try to convince myself it's not because he'll tell me it's too dangerous and that maybe he's right. Instead, I focus on how he chose not to share his plans with me last night either and that frankly, it's safer this way: if ever we're questioned by the authorities, we can honestly say that we don't know what the other one is up to. But keeping things from people I love is hard for me.

"It's not one of my clients," I tell him, carefully choosing what information to share. "It's just. . . I promised I'd go, and even if I can't help, at least I can bear witness."

He looks unhappy but nods his head in understanding. I climb over him to gather the clothes I'd laid out the night before. Laek watches me for a moment, then turns onto his side. A breath later, he stretches onto his back, then turns onto his other side, bringing his knees to his chest, and I wonder how much pain he's in and how much of it is physical. Fetal position is generally not a great sign when it comes to one's mental state. By the time I leave the room, he's fast asleep, curled in a tight ball in the middle of the bed where I'd been lying. At least he can benefit from my body heat still lingering in the sheets.

When I return to the bedroom after I'm showered and dressed to grab my wristpad, Laek is still curled up, but Philip has thrown an arm and a leg over him, and even as I watch, the tight ball Laek's made of himself begins to relax. I smile and relax a little too, an idea beginning to form in the back of my mind.

Half an hour later, I'm in Verdun. Pierre-Ryan answers my knock immediately.

"Oh my God, Janie, you cycled in this weather! Your cheeks are raw." He waves me into his kitchen like a mother hen. "Have some tea."

I join him at the small, round table. He's placed a steaming mug on a doily, probably his grandmother's. "Why's the tea orange?" I take a sip. "And why does it taste like poison?"

"It's curcuma. Good for the immune system. And a natural remedy for treating cancer."

"I don't have cancer." I put the cup down.

"Dieu merci! It also helps with diabetes—"

"I don't—"

"And irritable bowels. I know you get nervous."

"Okay, time to change the subject. We need to do my hair."

I get up and walk towards his bathroom, trying to swallow all my saliva in order to get the taste of the tea out of my mouth. P.R. follows closely behind.

"Ferme les yeux," he orders once I'm in front of the mirror.

Eyes closed, I listen to the wet, misty sound of the spray pump, feel his polylatex-gloved hands pushing and tugging at my curls.

"I still don't understand why you don't simply use a wig," he says.

"Plausible deniability. Plus, wasn't the fact that my hair is similar to Andressa's one of the reasons I was chosen to do this?"

"You weren't chosen. You volunteered."

"Yeah, but—"

"Don't talk. It might get into your mouth."

"It couldn't taste worse than the tea."

P.R.'s only response is to tug a little harder at my hair.

"Okay, you can open your eyes now," he finally says. "It's a quick dry formula."

In the mirror, my new mop of grass-green curls looks about right. My reddish cheeks should help too, since they make me appear younger, though even normally people often mistake me for a child—at least from behind—because of how short I am.

"She's fourteen, right?" I ask, remembering that she's even younger than Siri.

"Yes. Which reminds me. She's not so, euh, developed as you are."

"Yeah, I brought a chest binder. A friend lent it to me. It's a bit loose for me, so should just do the trick." Pierre-Ryan stands rooted to the bathroom floor. "Well, if you want to watch. . ." I say and begin to remove my sweater. He turns a shade of red I'm sure is even deeper than my own wind-darkened cheeks and flees the bathroom.

A few minutes later, I'm ready to go. I pull the tuque over my newly dyed curls, covering them completely. I can't feel the tiny receiver embedded in the earflaps and I say a little prayer it will be undetectable to the authorities as well. My comrades will be transmitting the coded instructions at 19.5 kilo hertz, an auditory frequency that's too high for most adults to hear, yet below the threshold of any security devices aimed at blocking ultrasonic weapons. It'll be audible to children and teenagers though, and hopefully, to me. For once, my unusually sensitive ears might prove useful.

"Where's the suitcase?" I ask.

"Right here." P.R. pulls a battered silver valise out of the closet. "It's identical to the one Andressa has, only yours has straps."

I examine the bag, finding the recess where the straps have been added, pull them out, and slip my arms into them. The valise now resembles a large, shiny backpack.

"Your ukulele is inside. Please be careful, Janie," P.R. adds, his expression serious.

"I will, mon cher ami." I put my hands on his shoulders, reaching up to kiss both his cheeks. "At least they can't deport me. I have you to thank for that."

***

The bike ride to the airport takes about an hour. The sweat under my armpits and in the small of my back is cooling me down, making me shiver. Pushing myself those last two kilometres was the right call though, because my timing is perfect. As I lock up, the first Skyline of the day slides into the elevated station. I mix with the crowd, as though I'd just gotten off too. Inside the airport, I shove my thermo-mittens into my jeans' pockets. The jeans are orange, like the ones Andressa's supposed to have on today, and I'm also sporting the red hemp high-tops she's made so popular by wearing them in all weather during the eco-actions she's led.

Already, members of the Insurrection Band are beginning to coalesce. I watch them from the corner of my eye as I smile and greet the airport workers I know. Most smile back, some calling me Maître Wolfe or just Janie. With all the time I've spent at the airport as a refugee lawyer, I've gotten on friendly terms with many of the people who work here—not only clerks and porters but security staff. I try not to think about how I'm about to blow all that social capital, at least with my buddies at security.

As though an invisible conductor had lifted their baton, band members take out their instruments and begin to tune or test them. There are snare drums, sousaphones, clarinets, fiddles, and saxes; bass drums, flutes, and cymbals. There's even a hurdy-gurdy. The instruments are decorated with ribbons and holo-stickers and all manner of shiny things, but the masks the musicians pull over their faces are even more glitzy.

Historically, Québec has had a love-hate relationship with face coverings, at times passing laws to make them illegal in order to fuck with anarchists and persecute Muslims; at other times they've been obligatory to discourage the spread of one pandemic or another. Throughout it all, though, masks that are seen as festive or sexy are generally tolerated. And it doesn't hurt that many members of our anarcho-punk band enjoy wearing daring clothing. Band members of all genders show off their cleavage, muscles, nipple rings, luminescent tattoos, tight pants, short skirts, and loose, flowing robes decorated with lace or topped with wings.

I feel plain in my jeans and sneakers; even my new green curls are covered up by a hat, at least for now. I take a small wind synthesizer from the inside pocket of my coat and try a quick trill. It's not my preferred instrument, but I play it well enough.

We jump into our first song. It's a neo-trad Québec protest piece from the Carré Rouge era, popularized, it's said, by a nude cycling manif. I join in on my synthesizer with sharp piercing notes at key moments or little embellishments during the quieter parts. When the song is done, we segue directly into "Bella Ciao".

Our band begins to slowly move past the tear-shaped biometric check-in modules and closer to the security zone that feeds passengers to the departure gates. Security is watching and listening, not pleased but not particularly wary either. They've grown used to us. The musical flash mob has become a regular thing at deportations; we use it to protest, to gently disrupt, to tell the people being thrown out like unwanted garbage that we're on their side. And, as I told Laek, we also come to bear witness. Today, though, we hope to do more than that.

There's no sign yet of Andressa Marques. If Simon knew I was involved in trying to rescue Andressa from deportation and smuggle her to a safe house, I'd gain a shit load of parental respect points. As fervent animal rights activists, Simon and Aiza are both loyal members of Andressa's Protecteurs de la planète aka Peeps, who are not only fighting the dirty energy industry, but exposing the ruthlessness of the telecom monopoly whose Gen 9 tech is suspected of killing birds.

I move to the middle of our growing mob of musicians and toss my head from side to side. The band immediately breaks into a more contemporary piece by the Maghrebian post-grrrl band Saida Menebhi, followed in quick succession by a #Ana-Zeda song from an earlier decade that uses harmonized ululation. Raising my left arm a few centimetres, palm flat to the ground, I wiggle my fingers in time with the music. Some people with suitcases stop to listen; a few begin clapping to the beat and or dancing.

Although everything's going as planned, my stomach and bowels feel like they're also doing a little dance. What if I missed the signal somehow and the deportation already happened? My stomach cramps and I wonder if Pierre-Ryan's curcuma tea is also a laxative. I am going to strangle P.R.—right after I strangle Laek for keeping me up half the night with anxiety.

I refocus on the music, deciding it's time to introduce some New Orleans marching band tunes. I signal for "Carnival of Eris," and then we glide from New Orleans to New York with "Joyous Bridges," the favourite of an obscure Brooklyn anarchist band I credit with saving Laek's life. The music's upbeat and reassuring and I need this.

We're playing "Canarsie Cacophonic Capitalism" when I hear a sound, scratchy and high, like a fork making bad contact with a knife. The signal's repeated, sending literal shivers down my spine. I play a sustained piercing note on my synthesizer and the band breaks immediately into HK & Les Saltimbanks' "On lâche rien."

I don't see Andressa yet, but I trust my comrades, so I start moving towards the outer edge of the security zone, in the direction I was told will intersect with Andressa's path. I wiggle the fingers of my right hand in syncopated counterbeat. Phase three begins. The dancers' movements become more frenetic as someone posing as a traveller bends to open her valise. Out of the corner of my eye I notice an airport security agent put a hand to their ear; another one shifts position slightly. It's about to go down.

Everything starts moving faster. Two agents of Canada Border Enforcement enter the area. I don't know them, but there's something else that feels unfamiliar, at least with one of them. Is it their gun? CBE agents carry semi-automatic pistols but theirs looks more like a phaser weapon. Strange because phasers—whether guns or sticks—aren't carried by government law enforcement in Canada. Before I can think it through, I lift up my wind synthesizer, and some dozen comrades reach into their pockets and toss handfuls of glitter, confetti, and purple fluorescent ice-melting crystals into the air to make a snowstorm of sparkle.

SDF, chômeurs, ouvriers

Paysans, immigrés sans papier

Ils ont voulu nous diviser...

I see her. Her head of grass-green curls matches my own, and she's pulling a silver suitcase that's the twin of the one I'm wearing on my back. Two uniformed Gardiens Commissionnés with their familiar blue and orange badges walk on either side of her. They're unarmed but tough and unfriendly-looking. One, large with a blond ponytail pulled tightly back from their face, holds the wrist of Andressa's free hand. It looks narrow and frail in the private cop's meaty fist. A CBE agent steps ahead, the other slips behind. I make my way towards them.

Ils nous parlaient d'égalité

Et comme des cons on les a crus...

I'm about seven metres away from Andressa when she sees me. She appears calm, almost flat in her affect. I've seen that with Laek, so I know that Andressa's either very practiced at staying cool or she's losing her shit entirely. I signal the dancers, and they begin to make a large, loose circle around me, Andressa, and her two guards-for-hire. We hadn't planned on both the CBE and private security agents, but we can improvise. Other musicians dance smaller circles around the two Border agents.

Mais on s'est bien fait baiser...

The circles begin to tighten; I can see the beginnings of alarm in the eyes of the private guards. The one that isn't holding Andressa begins to shout; the words are lost as cymbals crash and bass drums boom. The music reaches a feverish pitch.

On lâche rien ! On lâche rien ! On lâche rien, on lâche rien !

I've already pulled my mask over my nose and mouth as

another boom sounds and the area fills with black, acrid smoke. The two cops-for-hire begin to cough. A second smoke bomb goes off, and in the growing chaos, I slip off my backpack and remove my cap, freeing my green curls. The blond guard releases Andressa and doubles over in a coughing fit. Camouflaged by the thick smoke, I lunge for the girl, pull my hat over her hair, and grab her shoulders to spin us around 180 degrees until we've switched places. As the silver backpack slides from my back to become a silver suitcase, I take one last breath before pulling off my face-covering and handing it to Andressa. She's spirited away by two masked sousaphone players.

The pony-tailed guard recovers first. Handkerchief over their face, they wrap their other arm around my chest and I let myself be dragged away, coughing, as the members of my band choke and shout and begin to flee the scene. I watch as airport security arrives wearing uniform masks and orders everyone to clear the area or be arrested. As we turn the corner, they're kicking their way through tinsel and glitter, uninterested in pursuing the retreating band members.

I allow myself a small smile. It was almost too easy, and even as I'm having this thought, I try to stop myself. It's bad luck, kina hora, a way of drawing the attention of the Evil Eye. I think instead about how much time to give it until I let them see that they grabbed the wrong person. The longer I wait, the closer Andressa will be to safety, but the worse things are likely to go for me.

Some minutes later, we're walking down a long corridor towards a secured section of the airport when the blond cop-for-hire looks at me and does a double take. I'd been coughing and rubbing my eyes almost constantly, so this is likely the first time they've gotten a good look at me. The guard addresses one of the CBE agents in French, who interrupts saying, "Speak English."

I'm surprised by this exchange but need to try to take control of the conversation.

"Where are you taking me?" I say. "Am I being charged with something?"

"Shut up," the CBE agent says without breaking stride. They're large, with a square jaw. I try to place the accent. An anglophone, obviously, but not a Montrealer nor an Ontarian. Western Canada, maybe? The accent sounds a little Californian with the way they pronounce their a's and o's. I'm still puzzling this out when we arrive at a heavy-looking door with a tinted glass transom.

"Leave us here," the same agent says, dismissing the private security. As the two of them walk off, the pony-tailed guard glances over their shoulder looking worried.

The square-chinned agent motions me inside. The other one stays outside the door. Once in the room, the agent takes my bag but doesn't try to open it. I look around. The room is small. In the corner is a metal desk, a glow lamp on top of it, either old or defective because it keeps flickering. Two white polymer chairs sit beside it. I look up at the agent, who's towering over me, and decide to remain standing.

"Why are you holding me? I think you've made some kind of mistake."

"There's no mistake, Andressa," the agent says.

"I'm not Andressa. Scan my wristpad. I'm a second-tier naturalized citizen of Canada."

"Maybe you stole the wristpad. It's why we. . . why some jurisdictions require wrist chips. But if you're really not Andressa, tell us where your friends have taken her."

Something seems off but exhausted from lack of sleep and the stress of pulling off a complicated action, I can't figure it out. "Which friends?" I say. "I have a lot of friends."

"You've also made some powerful enemies. You're a

terrorist and a border criminal, about to be deported. Where are your friends now?"

"You know very well I'm not Andressa."

The agent takes a step towards me, pushes me against the wall, right hand trying to cup my breast, still partially flattened under the chest binder.

"So you're just gonna full-out grope me? Is that your default MO? Pathetic," I say, with all the contempt I feel.

The agent flushes, and even knowing how stupid it is to provoke any kind of cop when I'm alone with them in a small, closed room, I can't help feeling a moment of triumph.

"No, we'll have plenty of time for that later," the agent says. Before I can react, they punch me hard in the stomach. I double over, the air knocked out of me. They pull me back to a standing position and lean over to push their face close to mine. "You must think we're very stupid. We know exactly who you are. Your little show may have made us miss the first plane, but don't worry, there's another flight leaving soon, with a stop-over at the good ol' United America. Have you ever been there, *Andressa*?"

My eyes are at almost level with the badge on the agent's uniform. I stare at it and understanding dawns. The gun, the accent, and now the insignia. It's all not quite right. There's the familiar crown of Canada Border Enforcement, but the blue colour is a tad too bright and on the shield, instead of a Canada goose, there's an eagle.

I feel a hard tug on my arm; the agent lets go of me. I drop to my knees, stomach hollow, hand gripping my own bare wrist where my wristpad had just been.

I throw up, curcuma-scented vomit spewing all over the agent's shiny black shoes.

CHAPTER 13
JANIE

"Release her now and maybe I won't demand moral damages from the Protectrice for mistreatment of a Canadian citizen and résidente du Québec." Pierre-Ryan's words—officious, over-confident—are music to my ears. I'd just about given up hope that anyone would find me.

"She's a border criminal," is the reply. "With no chip or wristpad to prove her identity."

"This is Janie Wolfe, my law partner," P.R. repeats.

"So you say," the agent responds.

"We can simply perform a genetic identification test."

"Do you have an injunction? No? Then we have a plane to catch." The agent smirks.

"There are other ways to establish identity. Madame Wolfe is a musician. *Par contre*, since the famous Earth Day songfest action, everyone knows that Andressa Marques, the young woman you pretend to have before you, cannot hold a tune."

"That's *carry* a tune," I say, unable to turn off my internal "autocorrect," though speaking English awkwardly is something I've seen P.R. do to get anglos to let their guard down.

"Pick up your instrument, Janie," P.R. orders. I'm not sure whether the dirty look he gives me is feigned or not.

"This is ridiculous," the agent says, and I can't disagree. Does P.R. really believe he can get away with proving my identity by having me play a song?

Nevertheless, I trust P.R., so I unzip the silver luggage bag and take out my ukulele. It seems heavier than it should be, and I hear something rattle inside. I slip my hand below the strings and into the sound hole. My hand closes on a familiar shape. I pull out a wristpad. Not my wristpad, which was stolen from me by the agent, but a different one. I don't know where it came from or how it got inside my ukulele, but I have a suspicion, so I play along.

"My wristpad! It must have fallen inside when I was preparing for our gig."

The guard tries to grab the wristpad from my hands, but I step back, and P.R. puts himself between us.

"How do I know she didn't steal that wristpad?" the guard asks.

"Steal a wristpad that has her own biometrics on it?"

"You haven't proven that," the guard says, hands on his hips.

"We don't have to. Before, it may have been Janie's burden to prove her identity, but with her wrist chip recovered, the burden has shifted to you to prove it's not hers. We can contact a judge right now, if you wish. I have a written motion already prepared on my screen. Or you can scan it, even do a deep verification, but I assure you, all the biometrics will match."

The guard's face reddens, but I'm confident we've won when their shoulders slump.

"*On y va*, Janie. We're done here," P.R. says.

I make my way to the door, and P.R. follows behind me.

"This isn't over," the guard shouts as we leave.

A short time later, we're driving too fast in Pierre-Ryan's car, my bike in his trunk.

"I have some questions. And slow the fuck down," I say.

He eases his foot off the pedal and sets the car to autonomous. "Yes?"

"First of all, how did you find me?"

"It wasn't easy. The authorities refused to collaborate. Luckily, one of the workers who cleans the planes. . . What is the English euphemism for that job?"

"Aircraft groomer," I say.

"They heard me asking about you and being hit with a wall of stones."

"Being stonewalled." I give P.R. a glance to see if he's messing with me again, but his face is impassive.

"The aircraft groomer told me they'd seen you this morning. So I knew you'd made it here. Since you didn't contact me as promised, I decided you must still be in the airport. I searched everywhere, even in the annex where they hold the people they plan to deport. I made a scene, banging on the doors, and finally, a Gardien came out and led me to your room."

"What did the guard look like?"

"Tall. Châtain hair. Held in a ponytail."

"Could the hair have been dirty blond rather than light brown?"

"The Gardien's hair was clean, Janie. Since they are much taller than you, you were probably too far down to see it clearly."

I glance at P.R. again. This time he can't keep the mirth off of his face. Yeah, he's messing with me, those faux English errors all for my benefit. I laugh for longer than his little joke merits, then just sit there smiling, happy to have pulled this off, to be free, and thinking about the guard, to have found both kindness and moral courage where I'd least expected it. A plane rises in the sky above the highway and I sober up; that guard was still ready to deport the real Andressa. Plus, I have one more question and I'm fairly certain I won't like the answer.

"So tell me how one of Laek's hacked wristpads found its way into my ukulele."

Pierre-Ryan sighs. "I was concerned. It seemed like a good precaution."

"This was not your precaution. You didn't contact Laek to see if he had a spare-fucking-wristpad lying around. Did you even know he keeps spares?"

"I am not naive, Janie. I know Laek's history and have long suspected that his identity chip is altered. That being the case, it is not hard to imagine he could have access to spares."

"P.R., you know what I'm asking. Did you contact Laek or did he contact you?"

Another pause. "He contacted me. But Janie—"

"When? When did he contact you?"

"He came by. Early this morning, at around three. He gave me the wristpad then."

Three o'clock in the morning, a little before Laek came home and slipped into bed with me, needy and shivering. And seemingly innocent. "And you told him everything?"

"I don't break confidentiality. And Laek didn't ask."

"But he knew somehow."

P.R. takes manual control of the car to switch into a faster lane. When he's done, he turns to me. "We didn't speak about it. He simply gave me the wristpad and asked that I put it where you would find it, if need be. It was me who chose to place it in your ukulele."

I hesitate, frustrated by uncertainty. "But he must have known. Why else. . ."

"Janie, I don't know. As your skillful cross-examination has revealed, Laek woke me at three in the morning with his delivery, then you came at around five. What this demonstrates is I have not had much sleep, certainly not enough to figure out what our master covert operator knew or didn't know at a given moment."

"You should have told me about Laek's visit when I saw you this morning."

"I didn't want you to be distracted."

"I'm a professional," I say through gritted teeth.

"Of course," he says gently. "But when it comes to Laek—"

"Let me out right here," I say abruptly.

"Janie, don't be—"

"Now, P.R. I need some air."

Pierre-Ryan pulls his car over. "Janie, you shouldn't be angry. I care deeply about both of you and don't wish to take sides. But remember this: it is with you that I've chosen to spend every working day. Please, let me take you home."

Pierre-Ryan looks so worried and upset, I almost relent. But in the end, I realize it's neither his problem nor his solution. I know what I need to do; I knew it already when I left Laek this morning—which seems like days ago—curled up in the middle of the bed.

"Ne t'inquiète pas trop, mon ami. You're not the one I'm angry with."

Before he can begin to plead Laek's case too, I jump out of the car to retrieve my bike.

CHAPTER 14
PHILIP

"But when is Mommy coming back?" Simon asks for the second time.

"I don't know exactly," Laek says. "But. . . I'm sure she's safe."

"I know that, Papa. I was just hoping that she could meet us at the bird park."

Simon sits across from me at the kitchen table. He digs into the chocolate-banana crêpe as soon as Laek serves it to him. Nothing in his face or body language betrays any anxiety about his mother's safety. He truly seems to only be worried about the visit to this bird park.

Looking at Laek, someone might think he's also unconcerned about Janie's whereabouts—but they'd be wrong. He's leaning casually against the kitchen counter, waiting to flip the last of the crêpes he's cooking for our breakfast. He seems relaxed enough to melt into the flooring. But meanwhile, his left thumb keeps worrying the seams on the knee patch of his jeans, searching for loose threads that aren't there.

"She's staying with some friends outside the city for a few days," I tell Simon.

If I hadn't been watching Laek out of the corner of my eye, I might have missed how his left hand suddenly stilled before he covered it up by reaching for the frying pan. Now Laek is all buoyant energy. He slides the last crêpe onto my plate with panache, though this will be my third, leaving only one for himself, already turning cold. He flops onto his chair, gulps down a glass of water, and looks around the table with a wide, careless smile that communicates a profound sense of relief. Didn't he know that Janie was with friends? That she'd decided to take a few days away from everything?

"But you can still come, right, Uncle Philip?" Simon asks.

"I wouldn't miss it for the world, mijo," I say.

Laek responds with a smile that's even brighter than Simon's. Throwing his right arm around my shoulder, he stuffs a mouthful of dripping crêpe into his mouth with his other hand. "This is going to be great," he says, squeezing and pounding my shoulder. He places a sloppy kiss on my forehead, leaving my skin sticky with maple syrup. Then he considerately licks it clean, the heat from his tongue making my whole body flush.

We ride in single file along the canal, Simon between us on the bike path. Laek says we're riding east, but my chip tells me we're going due north. Janie warned me long ago that Montréal has its own, idiosyncratic way of reckoning direction, but this is the first time I've checked it against my compass app.

The water is to our right, and across the canal stand old

brick factory buildings, now residences, topped with green-houses. On our left, we pass a jumbled mix of structures made of coloured glass, fronted by narrow parks, free bike stands, food markets setting up for the day, and info kiosks. I keep turning back to the canal. I watch the water change from clear to green to steel grey with flashes of white. Simon also has his face turned towards the canal. Laek does not, though he points out things on both sides of our path.

"See the Farine Five Roses?" he shouts over his left shoulder. "They used to make flour there but now it's a gay bar. Up ahead of us is a spa and a bathhouse. And a wetwear lab."

"What's that building up ahead that looks like it's made of toy blocks?" I ask.

"It's called Habitat 67. Built for a World's Fair from last century—but it started out as a McGill architectural student's thesis project. It's social housing now."

I smile, thinking about what it would have been like to live in a time when there were World's Fairs and children as well as adults travelled from different corners of the globe, filled with wonder. I don't know what I find stranger: the idea of ordinary people fearlessly visiting different countries just for fun, or how wonder was so easily manufactured.

The canal slowly widens into a river as we enter the Vieux Port area, and our path widens with it. It's now divided into three sections, with designated lanes for foot traffic; for cyclists; and for scooters, grav boards, and magna skates. It's a warm, sunny morning—though just yesterday it was freezing cold—and the area's already filling up with people wearing shorts and riding all sorts of vehicles. It's like we've jumped from winter straight into summer, though tomorrow it might snow again. Supposedly, March can be like that in Montréal.

At the Bassin de l'Horloge, apparently named for an old

clock tower, we turn left onto rue Berri. Laek says we'll follow it to avenue Algonquin and continue north, a route that will take us from the fleuve St-Laurent all the way to the rivière des Prairies. Simon is safe and comfortable here in our protected bike lane, speeding up to say something to Laek, or slowing down to share some factoid with me, usually about birds, as excited as a puppy running back and forth between family members.

Simon looks over his shoulder and I prepare myself for another fun fact about blue jays. Instead, when we're practically side by side, he says, "We'll bring Kyla here." He's caught me off guard and I try to smile, but my face must show my despair because Simon quickly adds, "Don't worry, Uncle Philip, my parents will figure something out."

I slow, purposely falling behind, unable to frame a suitable response. Against my will, I imagine Kyla here, on the bike she's just learned to ride, or maybe on a miniature version of Siri's scooter. A flood of images follows, as though the first one were a gateway drug: Simon holding Kyla's hand as he walks her to school. Siri teaching her to skate. Warm summer days picnicking in parc du Mont-Royal. Warm winter evenings in front of the fireplace. And even warmer nights, all year round, in bed with Laek and Janie.

Almost sick with want, I try to block out these images, to save myself from the inevitable disappointment, because if Janie had found a viable plan to keep me here, let alone to allow me to send for Kyla, she would've told me. She's not like Laek, who's always withholding information, protecting me he thinks, as though I weren't a grown-ass man, older than he is; as though I wasn't someone who's made bad choices and suffered the consequences, and who, like him, has secrets.

"You okay back there?" Laek calls out.

I give him the "thumbs up" and try to concentrate on the present, but it's no good. I can't live in the moment, the way he does. If I believed in prayer, I'd get down on my knees right here and now and pray for a future together. If I could bargain with fate, there are few things I wouldn't give to make those earlier images, that imagined life, real.

My heart squeezes painfully in my chest when I think of how quickly the time is passing. In a few months, my visa will expire and I'll be back in that dark place where I'm not enveloped by this beautiful family and their quirky, loving community. Siri and Simon will grow up without their "Uncle" Philip. Janie's vibrant body, her sharp wit, will be rendered into dead, electronic communication. And worst of all—I will admit this to myself—is that I won't ever hear Laek's voice, see his sweet smile, hold him in my arms. What the hell am I doing, keeping him at a distance? Am I punishing him or punishing myself? Maybe it's just self-preservation, because the closer we get, the more it's gonna hurt when we're pulled apart again, the border, and Laek's protective silence, between us once more.

Simon interrupts my gloomy contemplations. "Wait till you see this!" he shouts over his shoulder, standing up on his pedals. I notice a steep rise up ahead and do likewise. All of the motorized traffic goes left, and those on skates or boards or scooters, along with some on bicycles, go right; the rest of us—all cyclists—mount the slope into some kind of a tunnel.

"Where are we going?" I ask, but the tunnel has swallowed any reply.

Inside, it's black as night. I feel unbalanced, unable to see ahead of me on the path. Are we still going uphill? Yes, my legs tell me. An instant later, the path is illuminated by pink and purple bricks of light. "What's up ahead?" I call out.

"A light at the end of the tunnel!" Simon answers with the

confidence of a prophet, and I marvel at how he vacillates from one moment to the next between clueless and uncanny.

Now multi-coloured images of cyclists in glow-paint fill the walls.

"Go, go, go!" Simon yells, as the cyclists in the mural fly by me as though they're in motion, like pre-screen animation.

"Woohoo!" Laek shouts and the echo prolongs his cry of joy. I find myself whooping with him, an ecstatic abandonment as I fly down the hill and through the tunnel at their heels. Fuck pessimism, fuck despair. My time here isn't over yet and I refuse to give up.

We emerge from the tunnel to glide onto avenue Algonquin. I notice that fewer buildings here have roof gardens, let alone solar paneling, but I guess not everyone lives off-grid like Laek and Janie and their neighbours. After less than half an hour more of riding, it seems like we've left the city. We're on a raised, two-lane path; the road passes below on either side of us, and next to the road are small fields containing gardens. Not much is growing—just some green shoots emerging from the snow melt. On our right, multi-family buildings have given way to homes that look like they were built on stilts and resemble nothing so much as bird houses. A couple of people pass us on grav boards, and two teenagers on magna skates and holding sticks chase a rubber ring in the air while a third teenager flies it remotely.

Soon after, I see signs for Autoroute Papineau. Laek, far ahead of us, doubles back.

"We turn off just ahead," he says.

"But Papa, my map says that we should cross the highway and keep going to the entrance to the park. See?" Simon presses on his oversized wristpad to emit a holo map.

"I have a different map." Laek points to his head. "Showing a shortcut to the bird park."

"Did a little birdie tell you about it?" Simon says, a playful smile on his face. There's no cliché or wordplay Simon can resist.

We veer left, following a path so narrow that only someone who knew about it could find it. Beside our path, tall, yellowed grass pokes out from between the remaining clumps of snow. As we ride, the rivière des Prairies becomes visible just ahead; not long after, the path turns right, leading to a narrow finger of land that crosses the water. I'm grateful for the stone walls on either side of the path. They seem sturdy and are covered with brightly coloured murals.

We're about two thirds of the way across the causeway to the island which holds the bird sanctuary when we come upon a group of three people busy painting a continuation of the wall murals. Laek stops to greet them and Simon and I stop behind him.

"Hola!" Laek says before continuing in French. "Meet my son, Simon. He's an artist. Simon, these are some friends of mine who are also artists."

"Buenos días," Simon says shyly.

"Bonjour, Simon," one of them responds.

"He looks just like you, Laek, except for the curls," says a short, round person with green skin. I don't know if it's a body tattoo, some strange illness, or a new kind of sunscreen.

"And who's this?" another one asks, pointing their bearded chin at me. This one's hair is in long, black dreads. They're wearing an artist's one-piece, and they're even bigger than I am.

"C'est mon chum," Laek answers with a smile, using that word "chum" which here can signify anything from a buddy to a lover.

"Et ta blonde?" asks the green-skinned one.

Laek's smile slips a little. "Staying with friends for a few days." He glances at me as though seeking confirmation. I nod in what I hope is a reassuring way.

"That's probably a good idea," the bearded artist says. "After the airport action."

"Go Peeps!" says the last artist—a thin person with pale skin and an expressionless face.

"Yeah, go Peeps!" Simon responds enthusiastically.

"We're doing a bird mural," the expressionless artist says, as though "Go Peeps" were a password and Simon has now been inducted. "Would you like to help?"

"We're on a mission, actually," Simon says, looking torn. "To the bird sanctuary."

"It won't take long," the green-skinned one says. "Laek told us you're good at drawing blue jays. We're drawing one in flight, and the wing details are tricky. If you're willing to help, I can bring you to the sanctuary where your dads are when you're done."

"I would love to paint a blue jay! But. . ." Simon looks to Laek, whose face is unreadable. He then turns to me but I'm not sure what I'm supposed to say. Plus, I'm still running the words "your dads" through my head.

"Well," I finally say, when no one steps up. "It's really up to you, Simon, but it sounds like they could use your help doing something you're good at. And we can scout out the best place to watch the birds while we're waiting for you."

"Okay, I'll do it." Simon says, sounding relieved.

We ride the rest of the way across the causeway and to the back entrance of the sanctuary.

"We can leave our bikes here," Laek says to me, motioning towards a thicket.

"How will we lock them up? There's nothing but brambles."

"They're raspberry canes."

"Okay, but I still don't see how we're going to lock our bikes to them."

"We're not. No one's coming here to steal our bikes. But if you're worried, we can lock them together." I wheel my bike over to Laek's. "Not that way," he says. "Sixty-nine them. Wheel to handlebars, handlebars to wheel."

I don't know if he's just fucking with me or if this is really the best way to lock two bicycles together, but I do as he says. Meanwhile, Laek inspects the fence, kicking at the icy, wet leaves that have accumulated at the bottom. Eventually, a person-sized gap that seems to have been dug out on purpose is revealed. Laek uses it to slip under the fence gracefully.

"Why are we sneaking into a public bird sanctuary?" I ask him. "I'm not comfortable with this."

Laek ignores me, so I follow him in, my belt almost getting caught on the bottom of the fence. Laek walks along the back perimeter of the park, head lifted to the sky. I try to spot exotic birds—though aside from pigeons, most birds would seem exotic to me. I notice a small, pretty bird high in a tree.

"What's that yellow one?" I ask, pointing.

"A finch. Over there are a couple of swallows," Laek says, indicating with his chin.

After a few minutes, I say, "I thought there'd be more different kinds of birds."

Laek doesn't answer. He's very intent on his examination of the sky, though he keeps looking at the fence rather than towards the middle of the park.

"There," he finally says, grabbing my arm and pointing, this time with his finger.

I peer in the direction he indicates, but don't see anything.

I'm surprised, because my eyes are pretty good, so I move closer to Laek, to try to see from his point of view. I scan the sky, the fence, the trees, for any kind of movement or bright colour. Nothing.

"I don't see the bird you mean," I finally say.

"Not a bird, Phil. The answer to your question. Both your questions."

I shake my head, not understanding. Laek grasps my shoulders, turning me slightly to the left. "See that structure just beyond the fence? Like a tree missing its bottom branches?"

"Yeah."

"Look at the top. The small metal cage."

I see the thing he means. It looks like a weird, oversized birdcage. I don't understand why you'd have something like that just outside a bird sanctuary. I'm about to ask him about it when part of the structure is suddenly engulfed in a bright blueish-white light; there's a sizzling noise that gets louder, followed by a loud pop. A shower of sparks falls towards the ground, extinguishing while they're still airborne. I back up a step, startled, and stumble into Laek. I spin around as he lowers what looks like a phaser handgun to his side.

"What the fuck!" I say.

"Yeah, the thing I zapped is part of a wireless transmission facility—a WTF."

"No, I mean what the fuck are you doing with a phaser gun?"

"Could you please keep your voice down," Laek says calmly.

"Laek, what-the-actual-fuck!" I hiss at him, gesturing to the gun-like device in his hand.

"It's not a phaser gun."

"Looks like one to me."

"Are guns something you know a lot about?" he asks.

I don't answer him, feeling like I've fallen into a trap. Well, if he wants to ask me about how I've learned about guns since he left New York, let him ask me.

"It's a conducted energy device," he finally says. "Not designed to cause harm to people."

"So you just used it to shoot out a. . . what is it, a 9G tower?"

"Yeah. And a transponder. The former's killing small animal life. The latter combines with chip tech to track and spy on us. Two birds, one stone."

"That's. . . a very tasteless metaphor," I finally say, but Laek's already walked off and found his second target.

He stands stock still, his left arm pointing the phaser gun —I don't know what else to call it—at the target. He squeezes, but his arm lifts at the last second, and he misses. I have an urge to stand behind him, help him level the shot, but I stay where I am, a coldness in the pit of my stomach. He tries again and this time hits it. He moves down the row of trees.

"What will Simon think?" I say when I've caught up to him.

"We'll be done by the time my friend brings Simon. In any case, I'm doing this for him. You helped Simon with the research. Remember? The effect of non-ionizing radiation on birds?"

Laek finds another one, also just outside the park's boundaries. He aims, steadying his left hand with his right, and shoots. Sizzle, pop, cascade of sparks. He checks his wristpad and heads off in another direction. I hustle to catch up with him.

"I don't think this is what Simon had in mind," I say.

"Simon used to play this Animal Rescue game as a little kid. Got so obsessed, he'd wake up at 3 a.m. to play behind our backs. You play screen games much as a kid?"

First the question about guns and now one about screen games. Either Laek knows about what happened or he's made some impressive intuitive leaps. I ignore his question.

"Mira, Laek, if Simon sees you with that phaser gun—"

"It's not—"

"I remember how traumatized he was after you were hurt so badly by the cops. With a phaser weapon. For him to see his father with one, or something that looks like one. . ."

"That's why he's not here with us. What are you so agitated about? We both know that you're no pacifist."

He's right, I'm not a pacifist, but he's playing some kind of game with me and I don't like it. I cross my arms over my chest and walk off in another direction to look for birds, leaving Laek to perform without an audience.

Around half an hour later, I begin to circle back. I've seen a bunch of birds, including some big ones—cormorants or herons or something—but I'm tired of being alone. And yeah, I'm worried about Simon. And about Laek.

Back where we started, I see Laek a little ways off, standing by a copse of trees across the field from where we first entered the park. He motions me over. As soon as I get to him, he takes my arm and pulls me into the trees.

"There," he says, pointing. "The last one. I don't think I can make the shot. There're some branches in the way. Could you manage it?" he asks, offering me the gun.

My hand itches to reach for it, but another part of me feels a deep aversion to it.

"If these things are dangerous to birds, why put them near a bird sanctuary?" I ask.

"Because for this tech to perform the way they want it to perform, they need a fuckload of towers. And they gotta go somewhere. And birds can't vote."

"But aren't there zoning laws or something about where they can put the towers?"

"Sure. Peeps organized die-ins and other actions. So now towers are prohibited in animal-protection zones. They've decided to interpret that to mean that they can put them up just outside the fence. As though birds—or radiation—can't slip over artificial borders."

Laek is looking at me expectantly, so I take the gun from his hands. I examine the device, check the charges. Laek tells me which part of the tower I need to zap to short it out. It's not a very big target, but I know I can hit it. I take aim, begin to squeeze the trigger. Laek, standing just behind me, leans forward, his breath warm.

"Ready Shooter One," he whispers.

I drop the gun like it was on fire and turn away from him, conscious of my rapidly beating heart and the sweat dampening my palms and my armpits.

When I look up again, Simon is running towards us, something cradled in his hands. He's crying and I see that the thing he's cradling is red. I think of blood, fear sharpening my senses. No, not blood but a bird. A bright red bird.

Laek rushes to Simon. He cups his right hand gently over the bird and wraps his left arm around Simon. It takes me a moment to notice the green-skinned artist, almost blending into the natural background.

"What kind of bird is it? I mean, *was* it," I say to the artist.

"A cardinal. The bright red ones are the males. They're more beautiful, but also more vulnerable to radiation. We found him on our way in. Simon wanted to save the poor soul, but it was too late."

Simon lets out a pitiful wail and Laek pulls him in close. Soon, Laek is crying too, sobs wracking his body as he holds Simon. I swallow hard, close to tears myself. I imagine wrapping my arms around the two of them and take a step in that direction. Then I remember the gun. Anger and frustration dry my tears, my fingers twitch.

Simon's face is pressed against Laek's chest, so I pick the gun up.

I make the shot.

CHAPTER 15
JANIE AND LAEK

JANIE

I stay away for eight days.

On the first day, I report my wristpad stolen and wait for the Régie de la sécurité des données et de la localisation to do a signal search. Unsurprisingly, they don't find it, which means the chip's been removed from Canadian jurisdiction or that it's been destroyed. Or greyboxed. In any case, I tell myself not to worry because the new chip I order will be legally registered and the stolen one, if used, would come up as counterfeit. At least theoretically. I don't know how the technology works except that it is tied to the wearer's biometrics.

I don't go out much. The roomshare where I'm crashing is in a converted office building just south of the wetlands of Sainte-Anne-de-Bellevue. Of the five comrades who live there, two work nights, and one has a live-in job and only needs a place on the weekends. There's one night, though, when everyone is home, so the six of us sleep side-by-side on floor mats sharing four pillows and five blankets. They're apologetic but I actually enjoy the close but undemanding camaraderie.

For the first few days, I worry about Andressa, but after learning she's up north, safe outside the settler government's jurisdiction, I return to worrying about Philip's future instead. As I've already done repeatedly, I consider the different scenarios. I do more legal research, still uncertain about my idea. Putting the research aside, I engage my comrades in discussions on everything from family and social theory to relationship dynamics to utopian migration policies. I decide to stick to my plan, despite a niggling doubt.

Every day, I contact P.R. at the office via a secure communication hub. Through him, I receive eleven messages from Simon at random times and on random subjects (all of which I return); two messages a day regularly from Philip (which I return only once a day); and three messages from Siri (and I return all of them and send an extra message in between). From Laek, I receive only one message and it's on day seven. It says, "Please come home." I decide to return that message in person.

I arrive at the co-op in the early afternoon, timing it so that the kids and Philip are still in school. Laek is waiting for me just outside the apartment door. He seems uncertain, ill at ease in a way I've not often seen. He leans forward to kiss me, his eyes moving to the hallway as though he fears I've been followed. I take his hand and lead him into the apartment, closing the door behind us.

We settle onto the couch and only then do I think to remove my coat. I have a flash of memory, of Laek returning from the airport with Philip, sitting on this same couch and refusing to remove his jacket. Was that really almost three months ago?

"Janie, Janie," he says, touching my face gently. "Are you okay?"

He runs his hands up and down my body. I don't know if he's assuring himself that I'm really here or checking for broken bones.

"Laek, stop, I'm fine," I say, removing his hands.

"Did they hurt you?" he asks.

"Did who hurt me?" During my time at the roomshare and my long bike ride home, my anger had diminished, but with Laek asking me these questions, treating me like I'm some precious thing instead of an equal partner in our life's work, I feel it boil up again.

"Did you know all along what I was doing?" I ask him. Laek looks down at his lap, shakes his head minutely. "You were at P.R.'s that morning. If he didn't tell you, who did?"

"No one. I just obtained some. . . tertiary information. And put it together."

"What information? And who from?"

"I. . . I'm sorry, Janie. I shouldn't have. But I was scared," He meets my eyes but then looks away again.

"Shouldn't have what?" I respond, raising my voice a little. "Seriously, Laek, I'm getting a bit tired of your evasions. Just tell me what you did."

He bites his lower lip.

"Laek!" I grab him by his arms and shake him. "What. Did. You. Do?"

LAEK

"I contacted Al." I say it quickly. Like pulling a bandaid off a wound.

"You did what?"

"I needed to know about the airport. I thought—"

"You contacted fucking Al!" Janie's cheeks redden like two exclamation points.

"I know you think he's dangerous. He is. But it was important."

"You promised me!" Janie says. She releases my arms and I once again feel the absence of her hands on my body. Suddenly, whatever it was I was afraid of, whatever I thought Al could help me with, is nothing compared to the fear of losing Janie.

"Please. Listen to me. If it wasn't for Al, I'd be dead. Siri would still be on the other side of the border. I did it for us. For Phil. I needed to know—"

"And you thought he'd tell you whatever it was you needed to know?"

"I thought I could learn something. From how he responded."

"And did you? Tell me what you learned," Janie says, her voice unnaturally calm.

"He warned me that you were involved in something dangerous. Janie, when you were being held, were there any. . . I mean, could the U. A. have been involved?"

"Could Al have been involved?" she counters.

"I—"

"Was it also Al who told you about the bomb in the airport?" she pursues.

I shrug and Janie looks away from me. I want her hot anger. I want her to shout at me. To shake me again. To punish me with her sharp fingers and her sharper words. Because maybe then, she'll be able to forgive me.

"I get it. I misjudged." I let my tone become heated, going on the offensive. "But what were you thinking, planning an action like that at the airport? And using bombs of all things."

"Smoke bombs."

"But the optics—" I remember standing in the bird sanctuary holding something that looked like a phaser gun. I allow the full weight of this hypocrisy to settle onto my shoulders.

"Laek, I know you don't mean what you're saying." The effort she's putting into keeping her voice calm shows in the tightness of her jaw. "You have nothing but contempt for those who refuse to distinguish between real violence and things like tactical vandalism. And I know you couldn't possibly justify berating me just because you were scared for my safety. Not when the shoe is on the other foot all the fucking time. So tell me what's really bothering you."

"Philip's visa's running down," I say quickly. "And I think there's something he's not telling us." I try to let the deep truth of my words show on my face, hoping that admitting to this one worry will satisfy her, without me having to give voice to the others.

"Did you ask him? Have you had a real conversation with him since he's arrived?"

"If we can find a way to keep him here, there'll be plenty of time for conversation."

"You mean if *I* can find a way to keep him here." Janie's voice has an edge of bitterness.

"I know you're doing your best. But you realize it too. Philip isn't safe in the U.A."

Janie's eyes flick to mine. She nods her head, but it doesn't feel like agreement.

"I've been working on that problem," she says, sounding

calm and resigned. "It's why I've come to a decision. The days I was gone showed me that I need to. . . move out."

I open my mouth. Close it. A coldness seizes my throat. It spreads to the pit of my stomach and from my stomach to my balls. I feel like I can't breathe, though my heart is beating painfully in my chest.

Janie's leaving me.

You promised me. I taste these words on my lips. Did I speak them aloud? I have no right. They're Janie's words. She just said them to me when I told her I'd contacted Al. And her own promise that she'd never leave me, when she was just nineteen and me sixteen, was one she never should have made. And I never should have accepted. Every family I've ever had was destroyed. All my old comrades, my former family, dead. All but Al. Was it me who sent them to their deaths?

Janie's still talking. I can see her lips move. Her hands gesture to help shape her words. But I can't hear what she's saying. *You promised me. You promised me.* These are the words that fill my ears. I concentrate harder. I think Janie's talking about Phil. Is he going with her? That would be best. They can keep each other safe. Is she taking the kids too? They'll be better off with her. But I think losing them too may kill me.

I wonder what it feels like to die. Does your body go numb, or does pain follow you all the way to death? I'm so cold. I shove my hands under my armpits and let myself go completely blank. This way I won't feel anything.

JANIE

". . . I thought it all through and I need to move out," I repeat.

Laek's expression is unreadable. Blank. Even his hands, usually so eloquent, have stilled.

"Only temporarily," I quickly add. This amendment has

about as much impact on Laek's affect as a dragonfly dipping its tail into a large, smooth pond.

"Listen, it's part of the plan I've come up with to find a way for Philip to stay. No other option will work but sponsorship, partner sponsorship. Therefore, there are only two choices: I declare him as my partner or you do. Laek? Are you listening?"

He turns his head a fraction of an inch in my direction, as though he's heard a small sound but isn't sure it's worth investigating. I grab his hands to get his full attention.

"I've thought about this a lot and it should be you. It's closer to the truth and more credible. For one thing, I don't think people would believe I'd leave you for another man. But you leaving me for a man is another thing. It adds an element of. . . of desperation, almost like a refugee claim. Officials here know that the U.A. has become more socially reactionary, while Canada, and Montréal especially, is very queer-friendly. That will win Philip sympathy. Especially if I'm seen to be understanding and supportive."

He doesn't react. I'm starting to worry, so I line up my other arguments.

"It would be good for the two of you. You'd have a chance to get close again without me in the way. You've had a rough start; you haven't really talked frankly and there are too many secrets between you. You can repair that damage, begin again. And I'd come back, of course, when enough time had passed. Maybe after Philip has sent for Kyla. . ." I trail off, realizing I haven't figured out yet how Philip's daughter can join us too. Well, one thing at a time.

Laek pulls his hands from mine, slides a little further away from me on the couch. He's way too calm and that, more than anything, tells me how badly I've miscalculated.

"Laek, talk to me. Tell me what you're thinking."

"You promised me," he whispers, but it's as though he's talking to himself.

"It would only be temporary," I insist again. Laek doesn't respond. I reach for his hands and he lets me hold them, but he's indifferent to the contact, as though his hands belong to someone else. And when I gaze into his eyes, there's nobody's home. Here I am, talking about leaving, but he's already gone.

CHAPTER 16
PHILIP AND JANIE

PHILIP

I pause just outside the apartment door, unsure if I should knock or use my keys. I've been letting myself in since the second week of my arrival, encouraged by both Laek and Janie to get over my natural inclination to politely knock, but now that Janie's back, my fear of bursting in at an inopportune moment has returned. It's weird that I feel more careful about boundaries around Janie than around Laek when it's with her that I've actually "been intimate"—though in my imagination, I've had sex with Laek about a thousand times.

I rap on the door and wait. When there's no immediate response, I press my ear against the cool grey metal, but all is silent. I knock again. This time, I hear someone approach. I picture Laek or Janie peering at me through the one-way screen and stand a little straighter. The door finally opens.

"Philip!" Janie says. "Don't you have class now? And keys to the apartment?"

"Sorry. Should I come back later?" I can see over Janie's

head into the living room. Laek is sitting on the couch, his back to me, but he doesn't turn around.

"No, no, of course not. Come in." Janie gives me a hug, arms around my waist while her curly head presses briefly against my solar plexus. I hug her back, hard, an unexpected wave of desire rolling over me, but after a moment, she pushes me away and motions me to follow her.

As we walk through the living room and into the kitchen, I call out, "Hey, Laek!" raising my hand in greeting. Laek ignores me.

"What's with him?" I ask Janie, who's busy preparing some kind of tea.

"I could have sworn you had class now," she repeats, ignoring my question.

"I do, but it's the French class I'm taking, not the Spanish class I'm teaching. So I decided I could skip it when I heard you were back."

"How'd you know I was back?"

"From Laek. He left word on my UQÀM message board. It was sweet of him. He knew I'd be anxious to see you. We've both missed you a lot, Janie, and were worried too, Laek especially."

"How could you tell he was worried?"

"Well, you know, that way he has of moving his body when he's anxious—very smooth and careful. Like a dancer with a bomb strapped to his chest."

Janie lets out a snort of laughter as she pours a concoction of milky, boiling water filled with herbs and branches through a strainer. The kitchen is steamy with the aroma of citrus, coconut, and spice, and something else, almost grassy.

"Why didn't he say hello just now?" I ask her. "Is he mad at me?"

She shakes her head. "No, it's not that."

"Then what?"

"You described it pretty well yourself. It's more like there's a bomb strapped to his heart and he's afraid of the explosion, so he's moved away a little. Away from himself."

"I'm not following you. Did something happen?"

"Yeah. I had an idea. A very stupid one, as it turns out." She sniffs the hot liquid and, with a satisfied nod, lifts the strainer and brings it to the sink.

"What idea?" I ask her, as she grabs a large, oddly bulbous, mug.

"Let's talk later. I think the tea's steeped enough. Grab the pot, okay? It's for Laek."

"Okay, but I don't see how tea and lemon is going to help if he. . . if he's having a psychic break or something," I say, trying to be nonchalant about it, but my hand is moving towards my pocket where I keep my chain of worry-rings.

"This is a cannabis tea, medicinal. It's a powerful indica dominant hybrid. That lemony smell? It's limonene, which helps with stress. The spicy smell is another terpene—caryophyllene. It's good for anxiety and depression," she says matter-of-factly.

"You and Laek know an awful lot about pot. Maybe you should start a business."

"You're funny," she says, smiling slightly. "Don't you know how we get by so well in this building, with so many of us off the grid? We have the highest grade cannabis on the island of Montréal, and our garlic ain't half bad either. C'mon, help me get Laek to drink this."

I hesitate in the entranceway, uncertain. Janie turns to me.

"Don't worry. I'm going to tell you what happened. I'm not like Laek, with his. . . elegant evasions. But I need you to be patient. Can you manage that?"

"I can be whatever you need me to be, Janie, but it would

help if you at least gave me some idea of what's wrong with him." I'm still standing in the entranceway, reluctant to leave the kitchen and join Laek in the living room until I know more.

"He's dissociating, something he does at moments of stress, though most people can't tell. This is just more severe than usual. At least I think that's what's going on. I've already left messages for a couple of the therapists in the building, and for Jabur. We have a lot of talent and resources in this co-op. Nurses, doctors, farmers, social workers, teachers, specialists in cybersecurity—"

"Refugee lawyers," I add, hoping to make her smile, but instead she frowns.

She squares her shoulders and walks into the living room. I follow her, then sit down on the couch beside Laek, putting my hand on his shoulder. He leans towards me a little and I wrap my arm around him. Janie's frown curves into an almost-smile.

JANIE

Thank God Philip's here, I think to myself as I watch a little of the tension drain from Laek's body. I should actually be thanking Laek, who had the foresight to contact him. Though it wasn't foresight, it was simple kindness, a trait that comes so naturally to Laek, I often take it for granted. Especially when I'm angry at him for other. . . personality traits.

I fill the teacup halfway so it'll cool faster and I blow on it too, watching Laek from the corner of my eye. My anger is cooling along with the tea, but that tight core of frustration lodged inside my chest feels like it might be there for the long haul.

"Drink some of this," I say, offering him my grandmother's favourite teacup—gourd-shaped, and painted with leaves and vines.

Laek makes no move to drink.

"Laek, please, take a sip," I say, feeling that frustration grow.

"Let me," Philip says gently.

He takes the mug from my hands and, without any attempt to coax or cajole Laek to drink, simply guides the rim towards his lips. Laek takes a sip of the tea, then a larger swallow. Philip waits, then pushes the cup once again towards Laek's mouth. Laek swallows and swallows again until the mug is empty. His body movements are still tightly controlled but he seems slightly more present.

"Should I pour more tea, Janie?" Philip asks.

"I don't know. Maybe." I wonder if I should've let it seep for longer, or if I got the blend wrong, and if the risks of giving him too much outweigh the risks of this fugue state he's in.

"Well, how much is he supposed to have?" Beneath Philip's usual calm unflappability, I sense his near-panic at seeing Laek in such a strange and fragile state.

"I said I don't know!" I snap. "I'm not his fucking doctor!"

"I'm sorry." Philip looks miserable. "You knew all that stuff about terpenes and so forth, so I thought—"

"No, I'm sorry. I just. . . I'm stressed."

The crease between his brows smooths. "I can imagine," he says, voice gentle with empathy. "But it'll be okay. It's gonna be okay, Laek," Philip repeats, this time speaking directly to Laek while squeezing his shoulder. He releases Laek's shoulder and reaches for my hand. I let him give it a squeeze too.

"I am worried," I tell him. "I've seen him this bad before, but only once or twice."

"You also seem angry," Philip observes. "And I can't help noticing that you were also angry that first night, when we got back from the airport. Laek was hurt. And now he's hurt again, hurt in his mind, and you're angry again."

"Are you saying I'm angry when he's hurt, when he's not well? That makes no sense."

"Maybe it does in a way. The day of the bombing, Laek chose a roundabout route to get home even though he was injured and even though he should have known you'd be worried. And maybe you don't like it when someone you love doesn't seem to care about their own body."

"And maybe you should give up teaching languages and go into pop psychology."

"But this time it's Laek who's been worried about you, not even sleeping he was so worried, but now you're back, gracias a dios." Philip directs his words to Laek again. "Janie's back. Now everything's gonna be alright."

I look down, feeling guilty, but beneath that guilt, I still feel angry, trapped, and that makes me feel even guiltier. Which makes me angry again. When I finally lift my head, Laek's gaze is focused, intent.

"I release you from your promise," he says quietly.

Philip looks from Laek to me, then tugs at his earlobe, a thing I've seen him do when he's at a loss. I also feel rattled, less about what Laek's said than by his affectless, chilling delivery.

"I release you," Laek repeats, louder but no less toneless, "from all oaths or bonds made knowingly or unknowingly...."

I shiver as Laek, an avowed atheist, repeats words from an ancient religion, not his own. It's a prayer I shared with him from my childhood, a childhood so different from his own lonely, difficult one. My eyes tear up. I remember my grandfather, a cantor, his gorgeous, resonant voice as he sung words like these at the Kol Nidre service for our chavurah community.

May those of my vows that come between my soul and myself

Be no longer deemed as vows, my oaths as oaths, nor my bonds as
binding.
Be they all null and void;
And release me from them.

"I'll be right back," I say, sprinting to the entranceway for my luggage, ignoring both Philip's bewildered expression and Laek's flat, hopeless stare. I pull my ukulele out of the bag and return to the couch with it, moved by emotion and instinct rather than logic.

I begin strumming immediately, not bothering to tune. I trust in my memory of this prayer, its haunting melody, in the ability of my fingers to find the notes as I sing:

The oaths that I made, the vows I've kept,
Come from my heart, made new and clean-swept.
Blessed is the pleasure of choosing freely.

For rededication to my soul's path
This is the question I must ask:
Have I erred against life either knowingly or unknowingly?

Have I blocked my ears to the cries of living creatures?
Closed my eyes to the Earth's desolation?
Remained silent in the face of oppression?
Sat passively by while others run to fling open the doors of the
prisons?
Locked my mind against acknowledging injustice?
Refused to accept my role and responsibility?

The healing of the world is the work of all.
Release me from my vows so that I might embrace them freely,
The borderless beauty of our souls in community.

Laek is blinking furiously, his Adam's apple bobbing in his throat.

"Thank you for releasing me." I put down my ukulele to stroke his beautiful hands. "But I'm where I want to be. Now you. Release yourself from whatever promises you made to Al."

Laek's body is taut with the effort of either holding something tightly within it or perhaps simply with holding himself together. I take his hands in mine and he shivers, and I can both see and feel the moment when he finally lets go and the tightness in his body loosens. A sob escapes his throat, raw and full of pain. I lock eyes with him.

"Vows are important," I say, squeezing his hands, "but not all of them should be kept. At every new moment, you need to choose what's right. Your promise to never contact Al again—" Another tremor passes through Laek's body causing his hands to jerk in my grip. I hold fast to them. "I'm not angry that you broke your promise," I continue. "I'm angry that you felt you needed to. That after all that's happened, you still don't realize what he did to you."

He begins to truly weep then, building with the violence of a storm that's been brewing too long. His body spasms and his cries pierce my heart even as I experience relief that the pressure's finally being released, that those dark clouds might eventually be replaced with sunshine.

"He took me in when I was a. . .a. . .alone," he stutters, voice thick with tears, syncopated with hiccups. "T. . .t. . .taught me everything I know about resistance. Got me out of prison. S. . .saved me again when I tried to. . . when I hurt myself."

I swallow, trying not to cry myself. I think about what Al did to Laek, and the power of my anger overpowers my sadness. "Sweetheart, he used you." I say. "You were a four-teen-year-old runaway. Fourteen! And instead of protecting you, he took your pain, your trauma, your. . . your talents and your ideals, but worst of all—and it's this I'll never forgive him for—he took your incredible capacity for love and loyalty and he weaponized it. He made you a tool and even now, after all this time, it's still how you see yourself, your value. How do you think that makes me feel? Makes Philip feel? And what kind of model is that for your children?"

With every sentence, Laek sobs harder, and by the time I'm done, he's folded his legs against his chest and buried his face in his knees. Philip puts his arms around Laek to soothe him, looking at me a little askance. I pick up the ukulele and play another melody from my childhood, my tradition, a song whose tune I remember but whose words I've forgotten, so I sing variations of "ai yai yai" and "bim bim bum" as Philip holds onto Laek, stroking his hair.

I continue to play, choosing the old songs, the saddest melodies, the ones I love most, and with each song I play, Laek's sobs renew. It's like he'd greyboxed his own emotions, and my music is the frequency that's finally found its way through.

"It's okay, it's okay," Philip murmurs, and finally, "Don't cry. Please don't cry."

I pause in my singing. "Don't tell him that. He needs to cry."

"Yeah, alright," Philip says, his voice low and hoarse, and I realize he's also near tears. I put down my instrument and stretch my arms around both him and Laek. Soon all three of us are crying, hands grasping hands, faces pressed against each other's shoulder and chests. How we must look! And thinking this, I remember that the kids will be home soon.

PHILIP

Janie has cleaned up her tea things, replied to messages from both Dr. Jabur and one of the therapists in the co-op, and prepared a snack for the kids, all the while recounting what she'd said to Laek about moving out. Her logic is flawless, yet it somehow doesn't make her idea any less utterly wrong. Laek sits beside me, listening attentively, as though he's also hearing this for the first time.

As she speaks, Janie treats Laek to small affectionate touches—on his cheek, his knee—and his body responds to these touches like a desert plant to rain. Laek did, in fact, grow up in the Midwestern Drylands, though I don't know much more about his childhood.

"Next time you have a plan for saving me," I say, "Maybe run it by me first?"

Janie looks abashed but Laek laughs like this is the funniest thing he's ever heard.

"And that goes for you too," I add, turning to Laek.

Laek laughs harder and I wonder if he's on the edge of hysteria. "He's got a point, Janie," he says. "But your plan, unlike my airport rescue, was thought-out. Great socio-legal analysis. We... we could do it if necessary. If you wanted to go that route, Phil," he finishes quietly.

"I'm not comfortable with it," I say quickly. "Janie shouldn't leave because of me."

"No, I'll try to think of something else," Janie says. "I would frankly have a lot of trouble going through with it. Not just for the obvious reasons but because it feels dishonest."

My face must show my surprise because Janie shakes her head and smiles at me. "I know people think lawyers are good liars. And it's true, I'm capable of playing with truth to protect my client, to make it more likely that a just or at least juster result is reached, but I hate it. Even though I know the system's broken, totally stacked against marginalized groups, I always want to walk that line of telling as much truth as power can stand to hear."

"I respect that," I tell her. "I think we could all stand to hear a bit more truth."

Now it's Laek's turn to look abashed. "I'm going to try to do better with that," he says in a subdued tone, his eyes soft with regret, chin firm with determination. I'm reminded of what an enigma Laek can be. Sometimes his face is like a mask, his thoughts as impenetrable as titanium. But sometimes all his emotions are right there on the surface.

Despite the fact that things are back on kilter for the moment, Janie still seems troubled. I tell her to come sit down. Laek moves over and she settles into the space between the two of us. Laek rests his head on the top of her head and I take her hand. Janie lets out a contented sigh. Then the sound of the door opening makes the two of them lift their heads at once.

Simon walks in. Janie sighs again, but this time her sigh seems less contented and more tired. Nevertheless, she springs to her feet to greet him.

"Mommy!" he cries. "You're home!"

"I missed you, my sweetheart!" Simon bends over a little to accept his mother's hug.

"Why did you stay away so long?" he asks. "We had to go to the bird sanctuary without you. Maybe you could've saved the cardinal who died. It was so sad. Papa and I both cried. Uncle Philip didn't, but I could tell he was sad too."

I'm suddenly struck by how many people depend on Janie, and for so many different things. She's shouldering way more than her fair share. "Your mom's not a doctor, mijo."

"But Mommy can do practically anything! Or anything that

doesn't need tallness," Simon amends, winking, and for a moment, he looks just like Laek.

"I'm sorry. I needed a little time away," Janie says.

"We all need a break sometimes," Laek says. "Maybe we should take Mommy off the work wheel for a while. I wouldn't mind taking on some extra cooking and cleaning."

"Papa, your eyes are red. Have you been using cannabis? Or were you crying?"

"I. . . maybe a little of both." Laek flees into the kitchen. He returns with a plate of cookies and a platter of seaweed crackers with that spicy nut cheese Simon likes. I catch his eye to see if he's alright and he gives me a weak smile.

"Or maybe we should go on vacation!" Simon exclaims. "A real vacation, with a hotel room and a long train ride and everything! That's what Mommy really needs!"

"I don't know about that," Janie says, but she's smiling.

"Actually," I add, "I'd love to see more of the province before. . . my visa runs out."

Laek and Janie share an identical pained look. I feel bad for putting it like that.

"But where would we go?" Janie asks.

"How about Percé?" Laek says after a moment. "I have a friend there. Chloë. We haven't spoken much since she left the job. It would be good to see her face to face."

Is there anywhere that Laek doesn't have a friend?

"Yay, they have Gannett birds there!" Simon enthuses. "And Rocher Percé!"

"Is that the huge, pierced rock with the natural arch? I'd love to see that," I say.

Laek turns to Janie. "What do you think?"

"It's tempting. Aside from visiting the Laurentides, we've barely left Montréal since we moved here. It's probably expensive, though, paying for train tickets and hotel rooms."

"How far is it?" I ask Janie. "Would we need travel documents?"

"That's only required up north," Janie says. "In the regions, your visa is enough."

"Well, don't worry about the money. I have a little extra put aside. I've been saving a lot, living here with you. And eating your food," I add, grabbing a couple of the cookies.

"I don't know," Janie says around a mouth full of cheese and crackers.

"We could go next month," Laek says, still looking a bit pale. "In April, when Philip's semester is over. Pierre-Ryan will cover for you, Janie. And the collective will redistribute tasks. You're always saying that you're no good to anyone if you don't look after yourself. And a vacation, with a long train ride, quiet walks. . . it's perfect for talking. For sharing secrets." He shifts his eyes to me. I nod once.

"So what do you say, Janie?" I ask.

"Okay. Yeah. Let's do it."

"Yay!" Simon says, cookie in one hand, a cracker loaded with cheese in the other. Just then, the door rattles again and Siri walks in, trottinette hanging over her shoulder. "Have a cookie to celebrate!" Simon says in lieu of a greeting.

"What's going on?" she asks.

"We're going on a vacation!" Simon proclaims joyfully.

ACTION TWO: THE BUILDING

CHAPTER 17
SIRI

The last time my parents announced that we were going on vacation, what they meant was that we were sneaking across the border to ask for asylum. If things had gone as planned, I'd have never seen any of my friends again. My parents don't realize it, but what they did ended my childhood. So yeah, hearing last night that we're "going on vacation" with Daddy looking like he was recovering from some new trauma was kind of triggering.

Leaning into my turn onto rue Lajeunesse, I pedal through the lake the street has become after four solid days of rain. Sometimes I feel like the whole island of Montréal is going to sink into the water and disappear.

I check my map. The rain's making the holo image wavy, so I close it before I get motion sick. I have the route memorized anyway—I'm just nervous about being late. This will be my first time at Jeune Vanguard's regular monthly meeting, and I'll finally be assigned to a subcommittee. I hope it'll be Tactical Action or Security, though they usually choose older comrades for that. But if I can earn their trust. . . which won't happen if my parents' stupid vacation conflicts with the April actions I've been hearing about. Fuck it, if that happens, they can just go on "vacation" without me this time.

The rain begins to let up. I tap the left side of my helmet and say, "Playlists." They appear in the air in front of me; flashing in the periphery is a holo ad for a newer version of the music app my helmet is using. I blink my eyes three times fast to make the ad disappear.

"Style: angry. Order: rando," I say. If there were a music filter like, "Play me songs my parents would never listen to," that's the one I'd choose.

I pedal hard up the hill, pushing past my frustration with my parents, who still don't seem to realize that I'm old enough to take care of myself. Like how they're always getting on my case about wearing a helmet. Sure, at the speeds I go on my bike and my trot, it's definitely safer, but if I forget it sometimes, what's the big deal? I don't need Mommy's nagging or Daddy's big sad eyes as he lectures me about respecting my own body. He should talk!

Uncle Philip's response was to install this music system into my helmet. I guess you could call it a bribe—or even manipulation—but if you know you're being manipulated and go along with it for your own reasons, is it still manipulation?

Just ahead, a car stopped at the corner begins to move. I pedal through the stop sign with it, using it to shield me from the traffic. As I clear the intersection, a driver waiting to cross on the perpendicular street honks at me for the extra half second I cost them. "Waaah, waaah," it goes, sounding like a spoiled toddler. I ignore it. Spoiled brats shouldn't get attention.

I'm early, so when I see a small park not far from my destination, I decide to ride in and out of it a few times, just like the way Uncle Philip made me bike back and forth across the border, part of the complicated plan for getting me back to Montréal safely. That night, I finally learned what the government goons did to Daddy when he was the same age I am now. This not only took away my innocence, but any moral right to be angry with him for making us leave our home forever.

But I am still so angry.

I slip into the ruelle just behind the social housing building where we're meeting. Hidden alleyways are like the city's buried treasure. This one has sparkly blue fairy lights looping around fences and hanging from balconies, and the backs of the sheds are covered in glow-paint murals. With the sun setting, it looks magical. I lock up my bike and walk to the building's entrance, exactly on time.

In the common room are two long tables surrounded by cheap plasti-form chairs. I count fifteen people, sixteen including me, and they all look older than I am, though no one looks thirty or anything. Everyone's wearing masks or scarves on their faces. I purposely came in unmasked as a way of showing trust, but now I fumble for my own scarf, embarrassed, like in those nightmares when you're in front of the class and suddenly realize you're naked.

Someone comes around to collect our wristpads. I dump mine into the greybox, used to this routine. Those with chips are given grey matte wrist bands to cover them. I wish I were chipped. All my apps would be so seamless then! Soon I'll be sixteen and have the right to the surgery whether my parents like it or not.

We go around the room to do check-in and intros, like at co-op meetings. Here, everyone's supposed to give their nom de guerre, though we can change it each meeting. We start with the person just to my right, moving around counterclockwise so that I'll go last.

"I'm Comrade X, he/him, of the regional coordinating and intel committees." He's wearing a torn one-piece jumpsuit and expensive-looking wraparound glasses. I'm not sure if they're medically prescribed or just an accessory.

The tall comrade beside him says, "I'm Goldman, but you can call me Em. My pronouns are xe and xir, and I'm in a liminal state of mind."

There are a few laughs, but a little forced, like this is an old joke.

The next person introduces themself as "Oiseau Noir," and they do resemble a bird in how they turn their head with sudden, fast movements.

As we continue to go around the table, I concentrate on memorizing the rest of the noms de guerre of the others—Anaïs from the Conciliation meeting, Harriet, Myriam, QS, Ari and Ali, or maybe it was Ali and Ari—and then I space out while practicing in my head what I'm gonna say when it's my turn. I immediately feel guilty for failing to do respectful listening, and a little panicked that I might have missed something important. At least I'm fully focused again when the person I knew as "Syncopated Voice" at my original interview introduces herself as Marie-Max or "M.M.," and I manage to pay attention to everyone else, including Gabriel, who has the nerve to introduce himself by his regular name.

I thought a lot about the name I'd use tonight, remembering the stories my mom made up about a bicycling family who go on exciting voyages. Eventually, I figured out that she used these stories to tell us, without telling us, that if one day we'd have to leave our life in Brooklyn, she hoped we'd see it as an adventure. In the stories was a mother named "Stardust," a father called "Ocean," a boy named "Panther," and the big sister was "Dandelion." I wasn't sure I liked being named for a weedy flower, but Daddy told me to look up the name's origin. I learned it meant lion's tooth, which made me feel better.

Still, the good thing about a nom de guerre is that you choose it—not your parents, not anyone else. I wanted a name that represents the traits I hope to embody, like courage, ethical thinking, love, and loyalty. That's why I decided on the hero from that old Greek play we read in school this year.

When it's finally my turn, all eyes are on me.

"My name is Antigone, pronoun 'she,' and no assigned committee since this is my first general meeting. Though I hope—" I hear the door and turn my head to see that someone new is joining us. They push away a thick lock of blue hair hanging over their right eye. Familiarity followed by surprise makes me swallow my words.

"And I'm Robin Hood, pronouns they and them, member of the security committee. All's clear," they say, and then smiling at me, "Welcome, Antigone. Glad you could join us."

As the meeting continues, my eyes keep sneaking peeks at Robin, who I haven't seen since before that day when the man with the scarred face was near their stuff. I'm happy Robin's here, that I have a real friend in this group instead of only my "frenemy" Gabriel, but I'm also kind of shocked. I shouldn't be. Robin's obsessed with rad politics—it's almost all we talked about when I'd come by—and our views are similar, so of course we'd be interested in the same group. Had I unconsciously othered Robin, labelling them an "unhoused person," who couldn't join an org or do other "normal" things?

"Les Darkes Femmes is having their Spring Equinox Night Walk on Saturday," Anaïs, who's facilitating the meeting, says. "They need two comrades to do security. Volunteers?"

My hand shoots up. So do Robin's, Gabriel's and Harriet's.

"We need to send experienced comrades," Gabriel says, not looking at me.

"It's true there was some trouble last year," Anaïs says. "Thunder Alliance showed up with some genderist identitarian boneheads from Brossard."

"The Darkes Femmes are going to want female-identified people and enbies. Not cis men, Gabriel," Robin says, smiling apologetically. "So maybe Harriet and me? Sorry, Antigone, I have to agree that this shouldn't be a first assignment for anyone."

That's the other thing that seems weird about Robin at this meeting. I think of them as being my age, but somehow, they seem older here. I hope we'll get to work together soon, but I guess not at the Night Walk. I shrug and smile. At least Gabriel can't go either.

Planning for the April action is the last item on the agenda. By the time we get to it, I've learned several new acronyms, memorized all my comrades' names, and volunteered to do work for the pop-ed committee, the auto-financement committee, and the media committee. My most interesting assignment will be to go through a bunch of old digital photos with an image recognition app and match them to other photos of known fashes. It's drudge work, but closer to security or tactical than the other tasks.

"So for the April action," Anaïs says, "there are several components. Em?"

Em stands, activating a holo map. "The first component will take place between rue Les Roches and Place Enchantée, the two official-unofficial border crossings." Xe uses a handheld laser pointer. "It'll be a standard demo: images, chanting, music. . . you know the drill.

"Component two is direct confrontation, with comrades moving towards the border cops' instalments to tease, taunt, and disrupt." Em looks around and when there are no questions, continues. "Component three will be to penetrate the area where they've erected the trailers to detain refugee-seekers crossing by way of the United America."

"So the first two components are only distractions," Myriam says.

"No," Anaïs responds. "All three components are distractions."

"For component four," M.M. finishes.

I look around the table. People are nodding, not saying anything, except for Ari who whispers into Ali's ear. I raise my hand. "What's component four?"

"Need to know only," Comrade X says.

"He means that only the comrades involved will learn the whole plan," M.M. explains.

I understand perfectly what "need to know" means but hide my impatience. I want to find out how I can get involved in the fourth component. It sounds like the most important one.

"Okay," I say, "But how will it be decided who participates in which parts of the action? Are there, like, qualifications or something?"

"Well, for the first two components," Em replies, "we can just self-select based on who prefers singing and chanting or who prefers taunting and disruption." A few people look at each other and laugh, clearly knowing who prefers what. "For component three," Em continues, "We only need a couple of people, maybe folx who can pass as medical personnel or journalists."

Ali raises his hand, which has a cool tattoo of a thorny rose on it. "I could pose as a nurse. I'm actually studying nursing."

"Me too," Ari says. "I mean, I'm not studying nursing but I could pose as a journalist."

The eye-rolling I notice makes me wish I understood the group's social dynamics, though if I had to guess, it's probably that Ali and Ari want to do everything together and always agree with each other. In any case, there are no objections, so we start forming work groups for the first three components. Harriet and QS have contacts at all the student unions and have already reserved e-buses to leave from UQÀM, Concordia, Université de Montréal, and Turtle Island U. Other comrades step forward to do communication blitzes at the cégeps. I volunteer to hit some of the high schools. Gabriel snorts but Harriet and QS seem to appreciate the offer.

"So that leaves component four," Anaïs says. "As we decided last meeting, M.M. and I will be coordinating, but two other comrades will be needed to actually execute the plan."

"For this component, we need comrades with a good memory, a good sense of orientation, and a capacity to improvise," M.M. adds.

This is no time for modesty, so I raise my hand. "I'm good at all those things."

"I'm worried that your immigrant status could put you in danger. Comrade Antigone wasn't born here," Robin explains, turning to me with an apologetic smile.

"That's true," I say, feeling a little weird that my immigration status has come up. And also that Robin's questioning my participation. "But I have second-tier citizenship. Not the highest, I know, but. . ." I think of the word my mother would use. "Not precarious either."

"I didn't realize you weren't from Canada, Comrade Antigone," M.M. says. "What languages do you speak?" she asks, lifting her eyebrows.

"Aside from English and French? I'm from New York, so I also speak Spanish."

I see M.M. and Anaïs share a look across the table, but Gabriel sees it too.

"If you need a Spanish speaker, I should do it," he says. "It's my native tongue."

Anaïs and M.M. exchange another look. M.M. turns to Gabriel.

"Do you think you're well-adapted for this action? You tend to have a hot head."

"But Siri—" Gabriel starts.

"Antigone," M.M. corrects with a stern look.

"Antigone's inexperienced," Gabriel says. "And I doubt she really speaks Spanish."

"Of course Gabriel's Spanish is better," I say, trying to ignore the fact that he just called me a liar. "But you said you needed two people. I've been speaking Spanish since I was little."

"Then why didn't you speak Spanish with me in school?" Gabriel pushes away from the table and stands, looking furious. It's true I never spoke Spanish to him when we were in high school, even though he told me how he and his mom and sister managed to escape to Canada from Venezuela after his father was killed. It happened during the United America's proxy coup in his country and I got the feeling Gabriel thought I shared some blame for what happened, just because my family's from the U.A.

"I didn't think you wanted me to. People can be weird about language. You remember how I wouldn't speak French at first. And my dad refused to speak English."

"You're always talking about your father. No one fucking cares," Gabriel shouts.

"Hey, *calme-toi* the fuck down!" Anaïs says in a firm, even voice.

Gabriel sits back down. Everyone around the table gets very quiet.

After a moment, M.M. speaks. "We have a... dilemma here. Antigone— if you are to be involved in the action, it needs to be with a more experienced comrade. But can you and Gabriel collaborate? Put aside your... your chicanes?"

"Absolutely," I respond.

"I'm a professional," Gabriel says. "But I don't know about her."

I know he's just trying to bait me, so I smile and answer in my best puertorriqueño accent, "Esto es un mamey. Yo lo puedo hacer."

"What does that mean?" Anaïs asks.

"It'll be no problem. Easy-peasy," I reply.

"And what does easy-peasy mean?" M.M. asks.

"It has to do with peas. About how easy it is to make pea soup."

"Really?" Anaïs asks.

"No," I admit with a smile. "I'm just improvising."

A bunch of people laugh and I can sense their relief—and approval.

"Okay, Antigone," M.M. says. "We'll give you a try. Mais écoute, if something isn't going well, we may decide to pull you out, c'est bon?"

"C'est bon," I say.

"And you, Gabriel," Anaïs adds, "Try to act like the professional you are."

The meeting's adjourned a few minutes later, but six of us— me, Gabriel, Anaïs, M.M., Comrade X, and Robin—stay longer. Anaïs offers me a cookie and I munch on it while they tell me that the April actions on the twenty-second are a kind of warm-up for the much larger May Day actions planned for the following month. The twenty-second falls on a Friday, the exact day my parents want to leave on vacation. So either I convince them to wait until after, or they go without me. Planning the rest of the actions' details are left for our next strategy session. I say good night, rushing out to leave before they change their minds.

I'm two blocks away when I realize I forgot my helmet. I stop, unsure what to do. If I go back, it'll make me look totally irresponsible. Why would they trust me with a tricky assignment if I can't even remember my own bike gear? On the other hand, if I don't go back, I won't just look irresponsible, I'll *be* irresponsible. I turn my bike around.

The door to the back is locked now, but I luck out. An older resident is leaving the building, carrying what looks like a heavy platter with a long baguette tucked under one arm. They're having some trouble manoeuvring out the door so I hold it open for them, then slip inside. The meeting room is down the ramp and to the left. I listen carefully, hoping that everyone is gone and I can grab my helmet without being seen. I'm almost at the turn when I hear voices. I creep forward to listen.

". . . Do you know who her parents are?" It's Anaïs's voice. I stop in my tracks. "Her mother's the refugee lawyer who took the hit for Andressa and helped her escape. And her father. . . her father's the one they call Ocean. He's been involved in hard core stuff since he was just a kid himself. So maybe like father, like daughter."

"Why do they call him Ocean?" I hear Comrade X ask.

"There's no one with a network as deep and wide as his. No one on our side, anyways."

"You think you know what side he's on?" Gabriel hisses. "Well you don't. He's fucking crazy. And he's probably not even Siri's real father."

I clench my fists, ready to sprint around the corner and end this conversation, but then Comrade X asks Gabriel what he means by that. My curiosity freezes me mid-step.

"He's too young. Have you met him? I have. Plus. . . he prefers men."

"Are you some kind of homophobe?" Anaïs asks, sounding disgusted.

"No. It's just something I heard. The point is, he's not who he pretends to be and he. . . he can't be trusted. And neither can Siri. Antigone. Whatever. Plus, she grew up soft. As soon as things get. . . get hard, she'll run the other way."

I've heard more than enough. I turn the corner and walk towards them. The clinical part of my brain notes that Robin notices me first—I didn't even realize that Robin was there!—but I ignore everyone and head straight for Gabriel. Before he even has time to open his mouth, I'm standing right in front of him, my face millimetres from his.

"Shut the fuck up," I say. "You don't get to talk about my family. And if you ever again even say my father's name, I'll put my fist down your throat."

There's a moment of total silence. It's Anaïs who breaks it.

"Antigone, I don't know how much you heard but. . . we're very sorry. That whole conversation was inappropriate."

M.M. chimes in with, "Je m'excuse," while Comrade X mumbles, "Désolé."

Robin is frowning and won't meet my eye. "I'm also sorry," they say, though they didn't participate in the conversation as far as I know. Everyone's now looking at Gabriel. He swallows and takes a step back from me before speaking. "Sorry. . . Antigone," he says.

I find myself thinking about the name Ocean, this name that my father is supposedly known by. Did he pick that nom de guerre himself or is it just a weird coincidence? And what about my mother? Does she know that the name she used for

Daddy in her bicycling family bedtime stories is the same name strangers now call him? Something about that makes me feel even more naked than when I walked into the meeting without my face covering.

"Don't call me Antigone. I have a new name now," I say, my face feeling hot. "It's Dandelion." There's the beginning of a smirk on Gabriel's face. I close the distance between us. "And it means lion's tooth."

CHAPTER 18
SIMON AND LAEK

SIMON

"Keep going. All the way to the front of the bike box," Daddy says. "Ça va, Aiza?" he adds as he passes on the left, biking between us and the traffic on rue Ontario.

"Ça va!" Aiza answers, but I add, "Papa, we're not little kids. We know how to bike safely in the street with cars."

"I know. The question is if they know how to drive safely in the street with cyclists."

Daddy winks at the two of us. Aiza giggles. She's always laughing at Daddy's jokes. At least she's having fun. I hope she still thinks it's fun when we get to Daddy's job. Last year for career day, I got to visit her mom's pottery studio and it was hyper! I mean, getting to miss school to do art is one thing; missing school just to spend the day at a different school is another.

After locking up our bikes up at École de la rue, my dad brings us to a secret door on the side of the building on rue St-Christophe. We follow him downstairs to the locker room.

"I'm going to change into my work shoes. You can put your jackets in my locker."

Daddy takes off his high boots with the silver toes and switches them for plain black shoes. I think his boots are much nicer, but maybe they're not allowed in his school. We stuff our jackets into the locker.

"What about your backpacks? Do you want to hold onto them?" he asks.

"We might need our screens," I say. "To take notes and pics for our report."

"You can bring your screens with you. But no taking photos without asking permission."

"We won't," we both say at once.

"And stick close. Aiza's parents will be mad at me if I lose her." Daddy smiles and Aiza laughs again. "Okay, last thing, anyone need to use the bathroom?"

"Papa!" I say. "We're not little kids!"

"In that case, wait here for me. I need to pee," Daddy says.

Aiza giggles louder than ever.

* * *

The classes at École de la rue aren't anything like the classes at our school. For one thing, the kids are all different ages and there are way less of them—though Daddy mentions that there are a lot of kids missing. Also, they don't sit in rows like Aiza and I have to do in class. Some of them sit at tables and others just roam around the room, going from different screens and set-ups that Daddy calls "work stations."

We follow my dad around from station to station. He looks over what everyone's doing. Sometimes he asks questions or gives advice; other times he just nods or smiles. There's one kid who's just staring into space, but instead of yelling at them,

Daddy takes the kid to a corner of the room with a comfy-looking chair, gives them a screen and ear pods, and pats them on the shoulder before moving on to the next kid.

After he's checked on everyone, Daddy brings us to the front of the room and claps his hands three times. "Écoutez, listen up," he says. Most of the kids stop what they're doing, but a boy named Pascal is jumping around, so Daddy claps again twice, this time more loudly. Everyone gets totally silent and Pascal sits down.

"I want to introduce our visitors, Aiza and Simon. Please treat them kindly."

"Are they new students, Laek?" a kid whose name I don't know asks in English. I've heard at least four different languages in class so far, which makes me wonder what their language rules are. I also wonder if we should call my dad "Laek" for today.

"No, just visiting. They may have questions for you. And if there's an artistic part to your project, you can ask them to help. They're student artists."

The whispering starts up again. Daddy claps his hand just once, but hyper loud. "Last time," he says, and now he isn't smiling. The whispering stops, but Daddy waits a few extra seconds, maybe to make sure the quiet will last.

"Thank you for your attention. Just a reminder that you have twenty more minutes to work on your own projects. After that, I'm going to give a short presentation in honour of our visitors on the influence of art on historical revolutionary movements. Okay, back to work everyone. History, like the revolution, waits for no one."

And now my dad is smiling again. It's like the sun has come out from behind the clouds.

We're walking down the hall after a lunch of spicy noodles and red bean sorbet when an older kid with floppy blue hair stops my dad.

"Laek, can I talk to you?" they say.

"Could it wait?" my dad asks, looking over at us for a second.

"It's about. . . the job readiness program, and—"

"Hi, Robin," a kid who's walking by us says.

"Yeah, okay. Let's go to my office." Daddy turns to us. "Listen you two, this shouldn't take long. Wait here for me. I'll be right back."

The blue-haired kid follows Daddy down the hall. We wait in the hallway, watching the students who walk by. They're laughing and whispering, shoving each other or messing around. No one's getting bullied, at least as far as I can tell.

"Stop fidgeting," Aiza says.

"I'm bored."

"Your papa will be back in a minute."

"It feels like a million minutes already," I complain.

"It's been less than five minutes, je t'assure," Aisha responds.

"Let's take some pics while we wait." I take out my screen.

"Your father told us not to take unauthorized photos." She folds her arms across her chest.

"We can photograph the murals and artwork and stuff."

"This mural behind us *is* pretty hyper," she says, looking over her shoulder.

"Yeah, all the kids are painted exactly life-sized. We can play with perspective."

We both take out our school screens. Aiza moves a few steps back, takes some shots, then changes her angle. I take a series of images while moving closer, then further, from the wall. A few kids walk by while I'm doing that, but I can edit them out later if my dad makes me.

"Stand in front of the mural," I say to Aiza. "Like you're part of it."

Aiza does as I ask. Some kids stop to watch us.

"Now wave your arms around or something," I say.

"Qu'est-ce que vous faites?" It's a kid we saw in Daddy's class—Pascal, if I'm remembering his name right, the one who kept jumping out of his seat.

"Taking pics and vids," I answer in French.

"Take a photo of me!" Pascal demands.

"Mon p—, I mean, Laek said we can't. No unauthorized photos."

"I'm authorizing you," Pascal tells me. Then he does a handstand. I can't resist capturing it on my screen. With his legs still in the air, he starts walking on his hands. Some other kids start horsing around too. Aiza and I both take a bunch of photos and videos. I think about how we can create a multi-media collage. Swap the kids' heads for. . . for closeup shots of the history cubes I took photos of in my dad's class.

I aim my wrist screen at the ceiling, the mural again, then the opposite wall. I look for Pascal, but he's gone. I lower my screen and see that all the kids have disappeared down the hall. They've been replaced by one tall man in a blueish-grey suit and what looks like fake hair.

"What do you think you're doing?" he says to us.

He's not shouting, so I answer him calmly. "Taking photos for our school report."

"And who gave you permission to take photos on this property?"

"Laek," I say, but Aiza interrupts me.

"Monsieur Laek is Simon's father. It's career day. I'm sorry if—"

"And who are you, young lady?" He talks in an old-fashioned way and seems strict.

"I'm Simon's friend. Monsieur Laek said I had permission to come along."

"Mais oui, but you shouldn't be standing here in the hallway. I'm surprised that Laek left you here alone. Come with me to my office. We'll wait for him there."

We follow him to a room down the hall. It's way bigger than my dad's office or my mom's or Pierre-Ryan's or even the one that Clara Bazinet, the old director of the school who died and was Daddy's good friend, used to have. His desk is huge too and looks like it's made out of a dead tree. And there's a big table too, where a lot of people could sit together. I also notice the artwork on the walls. There's so much of it, it's like we're in a mini-museum.

"I could give you a tour, if you'd like," he offers as I look at the artwork.

"Merci, Monsieur Cloutier," I say, realizing who he must be.

He smiles—maybe he's happy I know his name—and puts his hand on my shoulder.

"So, the two of you like to take pictures," he says.

"Oui," I tell him. "We're artists."

"Students," Aiza says, who's still standing near the door.

"Maybe I can take your photographs," he says with a big smile.

"D'accord," I tell him to be polite, though I don't really like getting my picture taken.

"Non, merci," Aiza says at the same time, though she usually does like being photographed. I look at her. Her eyes seem like they want to warn me about something.

Monsieur Cloutier keeps his arm around my shoulder and

leads me to a large painting of two children with blue mountains behind them.

"Monsieur, could you take us to. . . to Simon's father's office?" Aiza asks. "He's probably worried about us."

"If he were worried about you, perhaps he shouldn't have left you alone."

I don't like him saying that, as if my father did something wrong. I suddenly remember that Daddy doesn't like his boss.

"Maybe we should go," I say. "I know where my dad's office is."

I try to pull away from Monsieur Cloutier, but he doesn't let go of my shoulder. It's then that I notice the trophy case behind his desk, and that there's a gun on one of its glass shelves. My heart starts beating faster, but just as I'm about to panic, there's a sharp knock on the door. Before Monsieur Cloutier even has time to say, "Entrez," my father walks in.

"Simon, Aiza, come here immediately!" he says.

We both run to his side.

"Je m'excuse," he says. "I hope they didn't disturb you."

"Pas du tout," Monsieur Cloutier responds, and suddenly his smile doesn't look so nice.

As my father leads us out of the office, I notice a photograph on Monsieur Cloutier's desk. It's of a beautiful man with blond hair. He looks a lot like Monsieur Cloutier except much younger and I wonder if it's a photo of him but from a long time ago—from when his hair was real and his smile was too.

LAEK

"Wait outside," I tell Simon and Aiza. "And this time, don't go anywhere."

"Papa. . ." Simon starts, clearly unhappy to be left alone again.

"It won't be long," I say. "I just need a word with Monsieur Cloutier."

Simon gazes up at me. Looking troubled and confused. And a little frightened. It's not an expression I like to see on his face. On any child's face. A wave of anger rises in me. I push it back, not yet ready to ride it.

I re-enter Cloutier's office. Close the door behind me. Cloutier's standing by one of his paintings. I keep myself from lunging at him by counting to myself.

"Did the children leave something behind?" he asks, a self-satisfied smile on his face.

I breathe. Take a few steps towards him. Stop. "Their sense of safety?" I reply.

"I have no idea what you mean, Laek." The smile hasn't left his face.

I advance a few more steps.

"Your boy's a lot like you," Cloutier continues. "Charmingly innocent."

"I'm far from innocent," I say in a level tone.

"Naive, then." He shrugs, as though it's all the same to him.

"Don't imagine you know me. Or what I'm capable of," I say softly.

"Are you threatening me?" He puts his hands on his hips.

I don't respond. Simply close the space between us. He backs off a pace.

"You should be careful," I say. "About the lines you choose to cross."

"I think you should leave," he says.

"We have business, first. You never responded to my message about the kids who've been missing from my class."

"Homeless youth disappear. They're usually runaways to begin with." He shrugs again.

"That's why it's important that they feel safe here." I wait a beat. "But you understand this. Why else would you have gone to such trouble to get this position, at an organization that serves vulnerable youth? Though it pays far less than your other endeavours."

My last words have caught his attention. I watch his face pale as mild fear for his physical safety is replaced by fear of a different sort. Confirmation? Though he can't be sure if I'm referring to the foundation he uses as a cover for his political activities or his connections to that so-called youth employment initiative.

"I'm sorry if I made the children uncomfortable," Cloutier says, watching me carefully. "Would you tell them I'm sorry and that they're welcome to visit any time? Accompanied by you, of course," he quickly adds. "Will you tell them that for me?"

"I will not," I say, "But I appreciate the gesture."

I turn and leave the office. I'm calmer now. And when the children look up at me with trust and affection in their eyes, I give them my most reassuring smile.

SIMON

"Do you think your papa is mad at us?" Aiza asks.

We're laying on our stomachs across my bed, looking at the photos we took earlier.

"I don't think so. He's making our favourite for supper: peanut butter banana crêpes."

"But his face looked very angry when he found us in Monsieur Cloutier's office."

I use my holo dial on the photo of Aiza in front of the mural. If I do this right, I can make it look like Aiza's inside the wall with the painted-on kids.

"Why do you think your papa went back inside, Simon?"

I shrug.

"When he came out, he looked. . . his face looked less angry and more content."

"You look at my dad's face an awful lot." I stop working on the photo to turn to Aiza. "Do you have a crush on him?"

"No, of course not!" She frowns at me and her voice sounds annoyed.

"I'm only asking because I know he has problems with crushes. In school, I mean, with students. I've heard him talk about it with my mom and with Uncle Philip."

"He is very handsome. And hyper nice." She sighs and looks down at her lap for a second before sitting up very straight. "But he's a grownup. And your father. It would be. . . inappropriate for me to have a crush on him. Besides, I'd rather have a. . . a romantic relationship with someone my own age. Who shares my interests. Wouldn't you?"

"I. . . I haven't really thought about it," I say.

"You know, you're very handsome too, Simon."

"Thank you," I say. Aiza seems to be waiting for me to say something else, so I add, "So are you. That's why I love drawing and photographing you."

Aiza smiles, which makes her dark eyes look even more beautiful. I feel myself smiling back. Aiza touches the side of my face, leans forward and. . . and kisses me! I pull away.

"Sorry," she says. "I. . . I like you and. . . I thought that you liked me back."

"I do like you, but. . ." I swallow hard, not sure what to say.

"Don't worry, Simon. It's okay if you're not interested in me."

"Of course I'm interested in you! You're my best friend."

"I mean interested in kissing me. But you're not, right?"

I shake my head, wanting to get back to working on the portrait.

"Is there another girl you're interested in?"

"No. I'm not interested in doing. . . stuff like that with any girls."

"Oh. Oh!" She smacks her forehead. "Je suis tellement bête! You're into boys, not girls!"

"No," I say. "That's not it."

"Then what?" When I don't respond, she adds, "Don't be embarrassed. There's nothing wrong with being gay."

"I know that!"

"Then why won't you admit—"

"Can we go back to working on our projects?"

"With you ignoring me and refusing to talk to me? I might as well go home."

I don't know what to say. I want her to stay but I don't want to talk about kissing. She seems mad but she should've asked before she kissed me. I'm the one who should be mad. And why isn't being best friends enough for her? Why does it have to get all messy, like in one of her romance stories? I guess if Aiza wants to go home, I shouldn't try to stop her.

"Alright," I say. "See you tomorrow?"

Now Aiza looks sad. I wish there was something I could do to make her happy again. I smell the crêpes cooking in the kitchen and my stomach growls.

"Do you at least want to take a peanut butter banana crêpe home with you?"

CHAPTER 19
SIRI AND JANIE

SIRI

I use my elbows to pull myself under the bushes. The ground is squishy and damp and the bushes scratch my cheeks. I scoot forward to see across the road better, but Gabriel says, "Close enough!" and I stop where I am. It's like his mouth is right in my ear. Hyper intimate. But it's not really. He's at another stand of bushes about twenty metres away.

"I need to see!" I tell him.

"But not be seen. Or be heard either. Subvocalize, Siri. I thought you'd practiced!"

"I did. I did," I repeat, this time without voicing it. I touch the small sensory e-patches on my throat and jaw to make sure they're in place. "Can you still hear me?"

"Loud and clear."

"Maybe I should use the stealth cloak. Then I could—"

"The cloak's for emergencies. You use it long enough, they might spot us."

"It's not a meta-material, just optical camouflage. An e-mag detector won't find it."

"This is why I didn't want to work with you," he snaps. "You think you're so smart, studying up on all that science but forgetting basic rules like always using two different forms of security. Even if you have to use the cloak, you still keep your head down!"

I resist the urge to tell him that as tactical leader of this operation, he oughta know how the technology we're using works instead of relying on someone three years younger than he is to do all his homework. Again.

"So how am I supposed to surveil the building from behind the bushes?" I ask.

"Wait. Your eyes will adjust, like in the dark. After a few minutes, if you still can't see, push the branches apart a little instead of sticking your whole fucking head out."

I feel myself flush. It's like he's trying to piss me off. Well, I won't let him. Besides, maybe I do need to be more patient, something I'm starting to think I'm not so good at. I take a deep breath, then another. It smells cold and fresh, like melted snow and pine and mud. Like spring. Spring makes me think of baseball. I wonder what my comrades would think if they knew I played ball. Not exactly a typical anarchist pastime, but I can't help loving the sport any more than I can help loving the greasy pizza I used to eat as a little kid in Brooklyn.

There! Gabriel was actually right. I can make out the building now, including the small metal door facing the fenced-in yard. I raise my eyes to the roof where skinny exhaust pipes curl around each other like nests of snakes. But something's wrong with the building's shape. It's some kind of polygon, but every time I try to count the sides, I get confused, like trying to trace a Möbius strip.

I rub my eyes against the backs of my hands, careful not to

get mud in them, then peer across the road again. I follow the line of the building to the left, then the right. That's it. There's something wrong with the right side. I focus on the four points at each corner of the wall, but it's like there's a fifth point, pulling the wall out of alignment or into a different shape. It's also kind of blurry. Is it a distortion field?

"More likely a shielding device," Gabriel's voice replies, though I hadn't meant to voice my ideas. I have to stop accidentally moving my lips if I don't want the e-patches to broadcast all my thoughts to Gabriel. "It's probably like our cloak," he continues. "Only way bigger."

"How do you know that?" I ask. I saw a distortion field once, when my family first crossed the border. At the time, I thought it was just the rain that made it so hard to see into Québec. I was a kid then, naive, a kid who thought she was on a biking vacation with her family.

"If it were a distortion field, we could still see through it, just not very well."

So maybe he has learned to do his homework since he left high school.

"The part of the building that's near the border is the cloaked part," I say.

"Hmm-k," I hear through my ear pod.

"Maybe the building stretches all the way across the border. Like that famous library?"

"Enough talking. Just watch the yard for when the workers come out. I'll watch the guards, the road, and any vehicles that pass."

"For how long?"

"Tired already, Little Siri?" I don't respond. I won't be baited. "Until we see what we came here to see, however many hours that takes," he finally answers.

I settle in for a long wait, hoping for a chance to show some initiative.

JANIE

I'm cycling on rue de Bellechasse near the park, maybe five minutes from my office, when a change in the breeze brings the scent of grass and mud with it. A memory flashes: Prospect Park, Brooklyn in the spring, the kids in their baseball jerseys, Siri among them. I can picture it so clearly: her teammates laughing and roughhousing and tossing the ball back and forth, the red soil of the field already staining the knees of their new, white baseball pants.

So many hours I'd spent in the park watching Siri play ball. Every year, there were fewer girls on the team, many switching to all-female softball, soccer or basketball leagues. Siri, though she played other sports too, never left baseball, her first love, but the changed gender demographics affected her style of play, forcing her to prove herself over and over again.

The first time I saw her get hit by a fastball, my stomach dropped like I was riding the Coney Island Astro-Cyclone. I held myself back from running into the batter's box, knowing she'd never forgive me for embarrassing her. Also, I was pretty sure she'd let herself get hit—her reflexes were more than fast enough to have avoided the pitch if she'd wanted to. Afterwards, I'd asked her about it and I've never forgotten her reply: "Sometimes you have to take a hit for the team, Mommy," she'd said, and there'd been steel in her eyes.

Ahead and to my right is a large, red-bricked school building surrounded by muddy fields. Kids in dark sports leggings and school hoodies jog around the track; others stand in groups, vaping or just messing around. Despite the normality of the scene, I feel uneasy, my breakfast a churning mass just below my diaphragm.

The source of my nervousness isn't hard to pinpoint. I know what Siri's doing this morning, have known about her group's plans for a few days. Laek and I decided not to interfere, a decision that was harder for him than for me, but we both knew it was the only ethical choice. Still, I kept hoping the plan would change or Siri would be replaced by a more experienced comrade—or anyone, more experienced or not. Such hopes are selfish, not at all *solidaire*. Would it be better if someone else's child got into trouble, got hurt?

Past the park is a two-way street, liberally painted with yellow symbols for cyclists and motorists. I try to concentrate on the workday ahead of me. No hearing, thankfully, just some research and correspondence. If my family can get through this day intact, we can have a well-earned break from the recent drama. An actual vacation! I pedal faster, figuring the sooner I start the workday, the sooner it will be over.

The road is gritty under my tires. Though most of the purple snow-melting crystals have been swept up against the curb to be sucked up by the auto-vacuums, some bits have blown across the bike path. On top of that, there's more motorized traffic than usual, the construction on the parallel street forcing drivers onto this one. A truck roars by, though trucks shouldn't even be on this road. I stick my middle finger out, using it to point towards the throughway it should be driving on, then pull my helmet visor lower over my eyes.

I arrive at the part of my ride that I like the least, where the bike path is neither separated from traffic by a safety barrier nor raised up above the street. Instead, the path's been shoved between the car traffic on the left and the parking spots on the right. And now another fucking truck is coming up behind me. I take a quick glance over my shoulder and it's then that I hear the car door opening just ahead of me. It sounds like a gun being cocked.

Too close to brake without injury, my instincts are to swerve, the muscles of my arms already tensing to jerk my handlebars to the left. But the truck. It's coming up fast, too fast to stop itself from crushing a cyclist who's wandered into its path.

"Take the hit, Mommy," I hear my daughter's voice say.

So I do.

SIRI

One second I'm watching a bright orange butterfly lazily flapping its wings to fly over the fence; the next second everything past the fence has gone blurry. If I hadn't seen the butterfly to begin with, I wouldn't have recognized it as the dull, orange blob making patterns in the air above the yard. And now other blobs are filling the yard—people-shaped blobs. They're streaming out from the small metal door I can't see anymore but whose location I remember. It must be the workers, or prisoners if our suspicions are correct, on the first of the two yard breaks our intel told us to expect.

"Gabriel," I subvocalize.

"I see them," he answers.

"Maybe I should—"

"No. Just count them. Do your job, Siri. Don't take unnecessary risks."

I do as he says, trying to count the number of human-shaped forms. My eyes strain to pierce the distortion barrier, trying to see faces, heights, colouring, anything. I count forty-five of them; the second time, I count forty-eight. I try again, concentrating on their movements so I don't miss or double-count anyone. This time I count forty-eight again and the same a third time. I record the number, then concentrate on what else I can notice about them.

They do seem like teenagers. There's something about the exaggerated way they slump against the fence that reminds me of the kids at my own high school during recess.

I record whatever I can in the cryptonotes of my wristpad, guessing at shirt colours, hair shapes and lengths, whatever stuff I think I can describe. The ones near the fence are easier to see, the distortion effect thinner there. It's easier to hear them too. I can't make out their words, but the rhythm or something makes it sound like a lot of them are speaking Spanish. It's like how you can guess whether a person's speaking French or English even when you're too far away to listen in on the actual conversation.

If I could only get closer. . . but without warning, the shapes start moving away from the fence and back towards the building. The ten-minute break is over, and there won't be another until eleven. Three more hours stuck under this bush with no guarantee we'll get better intel the next time they come out.

JANIE

Sound and colour whirl together like a loud, red vortex, my body flung into its centre, where the soundtrack to my life has had the volume turned way up. I bounce, am flung out again, and the vortex goes silent to allow other sounds in. The first thing I hear—or think I hear—is the tune that was playing in my head all last night when I couldn't sleep; then little by little, the street noise returns: bicycle bells, car horns, conversation, shouts of children from the nearby park.

"Madame, madame!" someone says. "Are you hurt?"

I sit up slowly, bending my knees and stretching them out

again. I run each hand over the opposite arm. I don't think I have any broken bones, but my head hurts. That fucking earworm is way too loud.

"Je signale le 911," a pedestrian says, bringing their wrist to their mouth.

"Non, non, s'il vous plaît," I beg. "C'est bon. It's just that horrible song."

Now the pedestrian looks confused as well as concerned.

I remove my helmet carefully. There's a crack shaped like a small lightning bolt going up the middle, and the polymer visor is completely crushed. Shit, that helmet cost me like half a month's income. Well, better my helmet than my head.

I try to stand but totter a little. Someone grabs my right arm, someone wearing a smooth, round helmet of white and blue. My heartbeat accelerates, years of facing riot cops conditioning my reaction. But no, the person at my arm is just a cyclist like me, though with unfortunate taste in helmets. They look around forty, their silver bangs blunt-cut over large eyes framed by blue eyelashes. They're leaning on a four-legged cane covered with sparkly stars, and beside them is a blue, arm-powered recumbent bike.

"Merci," I say and my eyes go to my own bicycle, laying injured on its side. I reach for it.

"Let me," the helmeted cyclist says, righting the bicycle for me. "The wheel is bent," they say, giving it a once over. "It's fixable, mais ça va vous coûter cher."

I gaze for the first time at the driver who doored me—slightly stooped in their business-wear, with thinning hair and a pale complexion. They're wringing their hands, head turning this way and that as though looking for an escape.

"I hope you're okay, Madame, but. . ." the driver begins and I'm already primed to jump down their throat. A badly placed "but" can do that, as in the phrase, "I'm not racist, but...."

"But you were coming up the street so fast, I didn't see you," they finish.

My new cyclist friend comes to my rescue. "The street is straight as the part in Premier Ministre Therioux's hair. You can see someone coming for over a kilometre."

"Bicycles never follow the law! They're always going through stops and—"

I picture bicycles, riderless, rolling around the city, having their way with it. I giggle.

"You're bleeding," the cyclist says.

I put a hand to my forehead. It comes away bloody.

"J'appelle une ambulance," that same pedestrian from before insists.

I shake my head no, which I realize is a mistake when everything starts spinning.

"Would you prefer your own family doctor?" the cyclist asks.

"Yes," I say, this time without moving my head at all.

"But we should call La Societé de l'assurance automobile. A new wheel will cost you."

This time it's the driver who begs. "Please, no. My insurance will go through the roof!"

"I hear they've added an extra penalty for dooring," the cyclist adds.

"Let me pay." The driver wrings their hands. "How much will a wheel cost? Five hundred? Seven hundred?"

"Your axle looks a bit bent too," my new friend remarks. "And your helmet's toast."

"Give me your codes. I'll beam you two thousand. And you should probably lie down," the driver adds, looking a bit remorseful for the first time during our exchange.

"With the axle—" the cyclist pursues.

"It's okay," I say. "I know a cycling co-op that will give me a good deal."

The driver and I exchange codes and they quickly beam me the credits. "I. . . I'll be more careful in the future," they say.

"We can all afford to be more careful," I say, feeling generous, and they look relieved.

"Okay, show's over," I say to the remaining rubberneckers, who walk off. I turn to the cyclist. "Thanks for your help. My name's Janie, she/her."

"Cat, she/her. Of Co-op Villeray Nord." She extends her hand.

"I'm from Co-op Griffintown B," I say, folding in my fingers for a fist-bump instead.

Cat grins. "I thought you might be part of the network."

"How could you tell?" I ask.

"Cheap clothes, nice bike," she says. I laugh. "Do you want me to help you get home? You could have a concussion."

"Nah, I doubt it. It's a good helmet. Except for the visor I added on, which managed to cut my forehead. Next time I'll use sunglasses." I take my bike from her. "Anyway, I don't work far from here, and my work partner's a mother hen. He'll take good care of me."

We exchange coordinates and Cat bikes off in the other direction. A few minutes later, I arrive at my office, half dragging and half pushing my bike.

"Janie!" Pierre-Ryan says. "Qu'est-ce qui s'est passé? You look terrible!"

"You should see the other guy," I say.

"This is no joking matter. Allez, let's clean you up in the bathroom."

"The last time we were in the bathroom together, you dyed my hair green."

"At your request. And you remember where that led."

He takes out the first aid kit, rummages around for supplies. I tell him what happened, sitting still for his ministrations for as long as I can stand it.

"Stop fussing," I finally say. He continues dabbing at my cut with some orange liquid. "Is that curcuma?" I add.

"You should let me take you home. I can order us a car from Commun-taxi."

"A car's what got me into this mess. No, seriously P.R., I'd rather work than go home. It'll take my mind off my worries."

"What about my worries? Sitting here waiting while you. . . plante ta face."

"What? Do you mean face-plant?" I see the smile in the corner of his mouth. "Stop trying to make me laugh. It hurts my head to laugh."

"Alright, but tell me what's worrying you so much you ride into a door. Is it Laek?"

"No. I mean, sure, but that's more or less a constant. It's actually Siri."

"What's going on?" he asks, putting the first aid kit away.

I hesitate, wondering how much to say. "She's. . . involved in something that's going down this morning. An action. I'm not supposed to know about it, but I do. And I had this premonition when I woke up that something bad was going to happen."

"Something bad did happen. You got doored and probably have a concussion."

"Stop already! I don't have a concussion!" I stand to walk back to my office.

"You told me that music was playing inside your head." P.R. follows me there.

I turn to face him. "Music is always playing inside my head. I'm a musician."

"Did you lose consciousness? Do you have memory loss?" he asks, eyebrows raised.

Rather than installing myself behind my desk, I perch on the corner of it. "No. I remember exactly what I was thinking right before I was doored. About a particular baseball game, where I learned something about my daughter. Don't laugh, P.R., but I think it was a sign. A sign that I need to find Siri and make sure she's okay."

"I would never laugh at your. . . good instincts, Janie. But why must everything fall to your shoulders? Won't you at least let me help?" He raises his hands, palms open in a plea.

"You could help, maybe," I say. "How did you get to work today?"

"On my e-moto."

"It's pretty fast, isn't it? And stealthy."

"Do you want me to take you somewhere?" he asks cautiously.

"No. I want to borrow it."

"Janie, you've already gotten into one accident today."

"If I find Siri and need to take her somewhere. . . there's no room for three on that seat."

"Your helmet is broken and my motorcycle helmet is too big for your head," P.R. grumbles, scowling fiercely. It's the same scowl he wears when he's about to lose in court.

"With all the swelling from the concussion you think I have, it should fit just fine."

SIRI

Exactly on time, the little door opens and the yard begins to fill with people again. They're teenagers, I'm sure of it. As sure as I am that the owners are doing every nasty thing we suspect to our sisters and brothers imprisoned in that sweatshop. If only we had some proof!

I take the "cloak" out of the zippered pocket of my utility jacket and unfold it. The material is hyper-thin, lightweight and elastic. I place it over one of my hands and watch as the cloak reflects back the colour of the brown soil under my palm, making my hand seem to disappear. I pull the cloak onto my head, like a hood, then squirm and twist until I've worked it down my back. I place my heels into the foot pockets and my arms and hands into sleeves that end in mittens. The cloak tightens around me, snug and secure.

I snake out one arm, then the other, followed by my head. It's weird not being able to see my own body. I glance towards the bushes where Gabriel is hiding, remembering how he lectured me about not sticking my head out. He hasn't noticed anything so I crawl on hands and knees to where the grass meets the road.

"You see them, Siri?" Gabriel's voice says in my ear.

"Yep," I subvocalize. And I'm going to get a closer look, I think without saying.

I step onto the road. A brief flicker as the grass reflected by the cloak turns into dark grey glassphalt. I dart across, not worried about traffic. The road is marked "private" with woods on either side of it, and I haven't seen a single vehicle. I guess you need privacy when you've basically kidnapped teenaged refugees and runaways to work in your microchip factory.

I run full out from the road to the fence. Two people are speaking Spanish right beside it. They're still blurry, but I can see their faces a little.

"Hermanes," I whisper. "No me miren. Estoy aquí para ayudar. Let me help."

They both freeze; the one who's closer rotates their head

slowly like they're stretching their neck. "Where are you, Siri?" Gabriel's voice says in my ear. "You won't be able to see me," I continue in Spanish, ignoring Gabriel. I struggle for the right words. "I'm wearing una capa... un dispositivo de camuflaje."

"What the hell, Siri! Get back here!"

"Qué quieres?" the taller one asks, sounding suspicious.

"I want to help," I repeat. "If you tell me your names and..."

"It's not safe to talk to ghosts," the taller one says, using the phrase, "blanquita fantasme." They won't turn or address me directly, but they haven't walked away either.

"If we had some names of the people who are here, plus the name of someone you know on the outside, maybe we could—"

"We're fine," the taller kid says firmly, staring at the fence. "Six more months and—"

"Hector, they've already lied to us many times. First it was six months, then a year; they said they'd get us protective gear, that we wouldn't have to work so many hours."

"If you don't get your ass back here, I'm coming after you," Gabriel says in my ear.

"Por favor," I say to the two of them, feeling desperate. "In a few minutes, they'll make you go back inside." I hesitate, then decide to go all in. "I belong to a youth action group that's trying to help. My name's Siri. I'm fifteen. How old are you?"

The smaller kid leans forward and whispers, "I'm fourteen.... My name is Mia Garcia Sanchez."

"Mia!" the other one hisses.

"Is that your brother?" I ask.

"Yes. He's sixteen. We have a great aunt who lives in Ottawa," Mia continues, pronouncing it like the Algonquin word *adawe* it was taken from.

"What's your aunt's name?" I ask. Hector has walked away.

"Luisa Sanchez Aguilar."

"Can you bring me someone else? The more names the better."

As Mia's form moves out into the yard, I repeat in subvocalization the names of Mia, Hector and Luisa. "You got that?" I ask Gabriel.

"Yeah. You have three minutes. Then you come back and we're out of here."

"D'accord," I say.

Mia returns with two others. The first is Nizar Hussein, fifteen, and he has a younger brother named Mahmoud, who's only nine, in Montréal. He tells me they were separated. He doesn't know the name of Mahmoud's foster parents and is crazy with worry for him.

I subvocalize all the names for Gabriel's benefit.

"Okay, got it. That's it, Siri, come back now," he says.

"There's one more, it'll only take a minute," I tell him.

Gabriel starts to argue with me, so I pull the bud out of my ear. Mia's second friend reminds me of Simon a little, the way they keep hopping back and forth from foot to foot like they can't keep still.

"Mon nom est Pascal Bourque, il/he, and I don't have anyone on the outside."

"Your parents?"

"One is dead. The other said I'm dead to her."

"Another relative? A friend? No? Is there anyone outside who you trust?"

Pascal jerks his head suddenly. I notice that the yard is now almost empty of people and that guards are streaming out the side door of the building. Mia tugs Pascal's arm.

"¡Corre!" she says, talking to Pascal, but I know she's telling me to run too.

Pascal releases the fence. "Tell my teacher. Laek. Don't know his last name."

Suddenly, everything goes hyper bright as a high-pitched sound seems to shoot a bolt of electricity through my head. I slap my pod back into my ear, unsure if this will help but wanting Gabriel's voice there again. I see Pascal and Mia run for the door, hands over their ears, and I can finally perceive the full shape of the building, long and monstrous, the right side flashing between laser bright and dark as night. I'm running, already halfway across the street, when I realize the same thing is happening to my arms and legs: visible, invisible, then visible again. I dive behind the bushes, roll myself into a ball, my neck prickling, waiting to be grabbed.

I hear Gabriel's voice. "Right here, fuckers!" he yells. "Try to catch me!"

I lift my head a little. Gabriel is running up the private road, northwards, where it will eventually intersect with chemin St-Bernard. If he gets that far, he'll be on a public road, at least, and he's fast, much faster than the two guards chasing him. Hope makes me spring to my feet. I run diagonally towards the strip of woods we'd come through when we hiked our way from the main *manif*. Then I see one of the guards speak into his wrist chip, and soon after, hear the artificial hum of an e-car.

Gabriel takes a quick look over his shoulder, then dives into the ditch by the side of the road. "Siri... split up..." I hear, his voice breathless in my ear. "Go left... kk... left..."

The car has already passed without seeing me, in pursuit of Gabriel, so I must be fully invisible again. I strain my eyes to follow Gabriel's progress. All I can see is the movement of an occasional tree branch as he makes his way through the woods. Soon, the woods swallow him up, and he's as invisible as if he were wearing a cloak. I do as Gabriel said and dash into the woods on the opposite side from where he went. A tiny spark inside my chest burns with excitement. We got what we came for! But then a wave of fear for Gabriel sweeps over me. It puts out the spark like an ocean wave would put out a candle.

CHAPTER 20

JANIE, SIRI, LAEK

JANIE

I'm zooming along on P.R.'s e-moto, halfway across the Jacques-Cartier Bridge, when I realize I don't know where I'm going and I don't have a plan. Of the two problems, the first is the more worrisome. I'm capable of improvising, but I couldn't navigate myself out of a parking lot. I use my wristpad to contact Laek.

"Siri?" he answers before it even pings.

"I'm on my way to find her. Only. . . I don't know where she is."

There's a pause. "You have an app. You can track her."

"No I don't."

"Yeah, you do," he insists. "I installed it myself. When I got everyone new wristpads. It's a crypto app. Looks like a compass?"

"I thought that was a compass."

"It is. Go into settings. There's a function called 'F'. Choose it. In addition to the four cardinal directions, you'll see SO and SE. Activate SO and it will point you to Siri."

"SO? Those aren't Siri's initials." I don't know why I'm asking about such trivialities. Maybe information control calms me in a situation that's so, well, out-of-control.

"The 'O' stands for ouest. Because she's left-handed. If north is up, where your head is, your left hand would point—"

"Yeah, I get it now. And Simon's right-handed, so Est, SE." I descend from the bridge into Longueuil and begin the ridiculously long loop the highway does before letting you go south, towards the border.

"But Janie, did you hear from her? Did Siri contact you?"

"No." Laek doesn't respond, and in his silence, I can hear his fear. It fills the space between us, as though he were right beside me. "Don't worry, I'll find her," I say.

He doesn't answer "I know you will," but that's okay. I'm glad he won't lie to me, even by simply mouthing the meaningless phrases people say in moments like these.

"I love you," he says instead.

"I love you too," I reply. At least we have this truth between us.

I cut the connection and speed up. It's a straight run down to the border, about an hour's ride, giving me a long time to consider everything that could have gone wrong. I haven't been near the border since we crossed it by bike three years ago seeking asylum, and the closer I get, the more anxious I feel. At the same time, thinking of Siri possibly in trouble, I can't get there fast enough. I'm careful to stick to the speed limit, though; getting stopped by the cops is the last thing I need.

The city has long disappeared behind me. The highway I'm on is hemmed in by a seemingly endless line of giant box stores and soulless industrial parks. I focus on the vacation we've planned, imagining us walking together under the sun, surrounded by rocks and people, the air smelling of the sea. *Hang on, Siri, I'm on my way,* I whisper, trying to magically project my thoughts to her.

At rue Bogton, my app indicates that I should take a right, which takes me away from the official border crossing. Bogton is quiet, almost empty; I follow it to the animal sanctuary that used to be a zoo, then turn left onto rue Les Roches, a narrow, two-way country road which, once past the farms and open fields, becomes thick with trees on both sides. I think of those asylum seekers who've made their way through the woods, entering Québec via Roxham or Les Roches to avoid the official crossing at Lacolle.

My app is telling me I'm close now, the flashing blue stick figure that represents my daughter less than a kilometre away. I search the road as I move along it, but don't spot her, and when I check my app again, it shows that I've passed her. I turn around and ride back the way I came. The same thing happens; I've passed her again somehow. It's like one of those night-mares where, no matter what you do, your goal evades you.

I slowly backtrack. This time I keep my eyes on my wristpad and see the moment my blue dot and Siri's stick figure change places. I stop and get off the moto. Staring into the trees, I will the stick figure to become corporeal, for Siri to appear. A light breeze whispers through the branches, teasing my ears, which strain for any sound that could be Siri walking in the woods. I take a deep breath through my nose, as though to sniff my daughter out. She's in there somewhere, I know it. I exhale, and with a grunt, push the moto into the woods.

It's slow going, shoving an e-moto through undergrowth, even a sleek, light one like P.R.'s. A couple of dozen metres in, where it won't be easily seen, I prop it up with its heavy stand, double-lock it, and continue on foot.

The ground is damp and springy and smells like good

compost. I check my wristpad again and set off in a southeasterly direction. After a few moments, I have to correct my course. A dozen metres later, I've somehow gone astray again. I decide to keep my eye on the compass, as I did before. A branch smacks me in the forehead. It hurts, but I ignore it. There's a patch of ground near a tree that's clear of rocks and seems almost pressed down, like someone was lying on it, and it lines up with the icon of Siri on my app. Could she have been here earlier? The figure on my app is flashing. Is it supposed to do that?

I move closer. There's something about this patch of ground. . . it's almost surreal, the dirt and moss and mulch like an image of itself. Lying just beside it, near the tree, is something shaped like a root but made of a synthetic material. Maybe a strap torn from a backpack? It looks worn, but the ends aren't frayed; instead, the material cuts off in a weirdly unnatural way. Then I recognize the strap. It's from Siri's trottinette. My neck feels like there are insects with sharp little pincers walking all over it.

"Siri," I breathe and she sits up, like a sleepy child emerging from under her blankets, except the blankets are invisible and she's appearing from nowhere. Her hand clutches a cloak; the other holds the strap of her trottinette, which has also suddenly appeared.

"Mommy!" she says, and then, "You're bleeding."

She bursts into tears.

SIRI

The whole time we're riding on Pierre-Ryan's moto, Mommy talks, yelling over the wind and the drone of the motor as I hang on to her waist and try not to imagine those cops-for-hire finding Gabriel in the woods and dragging him off somewhere. She tells me about her bike accident, about Cat the cyclist from Co-op Villeray Nord, about why she dislikes driving, which she finds both boring and stressful. I don't say anything, even when she drives too fast and even when she takes two wrong turns before finding her way to the college campus at Saint-Lambert. It's only when we're parked in the faculty lot that I finally blurt out: "How did you know?"

She hesitates. "Daddy told me about your action a few days ago."

I squirm a little, thinking about the lie I told her about sleeping over at Maneesh's place because xe was having relationship problems. Well, the part about xir relationship problems was true, but the sleepover was so my parents wouldn't catch me sneaking out early this morning.

"How did Daddy find out?"

"You know Daddy. He has his sources."

"No, I don't know Daddy, or his sources." I kick at a bit of grass that's come through a crack in the pavement near where the moto's parked, angry now instead of guilty. "We're a secret group! With a strong culture of security!"

"Sweetheart," Mommy says quietly, "Maybe you should keep your voice down."

"There's no one fucking here in this fucking ugly parking lot."

Mommy sighs. "Daddy had inside information. From a contact in your group."

"A spy," I say, furious.

"No, a friend." She reaches out to me. I move away to find something else to kick, but there's nothing. "Siri, listen, it's not a betrayal. The more senior members of your group—they know all about it."

I take a minute to process that. "So in other words, we're just your little puppets."

"No! Not at all. Your group is completely independent, making your own decisions, and it's important for it to stay that way. If you decide to do something that's. . . of dubious legality, the penalties are less serious because of the Youth Offender Community Justice Act. But if they thought there were adults in the background, telling you what to do, the legal consequences would be much worse. Not to mention the ethical issues that would raise. So we're careful not to exert any influence over your decisions."

"Except for Daddy's spy."

"Daddy's contact is performing a necessary function. Our groups need to be independent but also coordinated. It wouldn't make sense for us to work at cross purposes or. . . waste resources by duplicating efforts. Daddy's well-placed to act as a bridge. He plays that role well. He's a bridge between lots of different groups and actors."

I remember Anaïs, Comrade X, and the others, how they all knew Daddy. Suddenly my anger drains out of me and I'm just very tired. "But they call him Ocean!" I say, clinging to a last bit of outrage. "Like in your stories! It's such a creepy coincidence."

Mommy smiles now. "There's a saying: there's no such thing as coincidence."

"What do you mean?"

"When I made up those bedtime stories about the bicycling family, I chose names that were like. . . a code for each of us. I was Stardust because, well, when I was little, I wanted to travel to the stars. And for Daddy, I picked Ocean, in part because his name is sometimes pronounced 'lake' and, well, for other reasons. The things I did to try to get you to go to sleep! You'll understand one day if you ever decide to have kids."

"You mean if I even get to have kids before your generation destroys the world."

Mommy looks sad, and I feel bad. It wasn't people like her who messed things up.

"Tell me the rest," I say, but I still can't look at her. I watch the road instead, in case anyone followed us.

"Okay. When we first got here, Daddy had to lay low, for safety reasons, but it was hard for him. He's very. . . social, so he began developing new contacts, new networks. He would give me intel to pass on to my groups. I told them I had a source named Ocean. So it's because of me that he's called by the same name as in your bedtime stories."

I'm almost disappointed. Even though it was creepy that they were calling him Ocean, it also felt a little magical. Mommy puts her hand on my shoulder.

"Listen, Siri, even if I don't believe in coincidence, I do believe in, I don't know, magical connections. Because here's the thing—even though we were worried about you, we decided not to interfere. But I had a premonition this morning. That's why I came."

"What kind of premonition?" I ask.

"I was thinking about baseball—"

"Baseball? Really?" I turn to her. Should I tell her that I was thinking of baseball too?

"Yeah, and suddenly I knew I needed to find you. Something went wrong, didn't it?"

I shrug, unwilling to say.

"It's okay, you don't have to tell me. But are you alright?"

"Yes."

"And. . . your teammates?"

"This isn't actually baseball, Mommy." But maybe it's not such a bad comparison because what I did was let my team down. I wasn't supposed to be the one deciding the plays. Maybe I'm too used to being the pitcher. I saw an opening and I took it, and it put Gabriel in danger. I swallow hard, my stomach feeling like it does when I get motion sick.

"Do you need to report? Check in?" she asks.

"I did already. When I was in the woods. But my. . . partner hadn't checked in yet. And they told me not to look for him."

"Do you want to contact them again? There's a place where you can send a secure message. A professor at the college is a friend."

"Of Daddy's?"

"Of mine and P.R.'s. Meanwhile, I'll call P.R. so he can pick up his moto. And I should tell Daddy and Philip where we are. Maybe Philip can change our tickets so we can leave on our trip from the train station here instead of going all the way back to Montréal."

We go inside. Mommy's professor friend meets us at the security station. Her name is Cygne and she's tall and bony with long, wispy white hair and bright blue eyes. I let her take me to the elliptical privacy booth and I make contact. I repeat the coded information I already gave in the woods. I don't know who I'm talking to—probably M.M. or Anaïs—I can't be sure with the voicemod they're using, but I have no trouble making out their words. Even so, I ask them to repeat the part about how Player One—Gabriel—still hasn't checked in.

LAEK

We've been assigned to the train car that has "group and family" seating. Three seats facing three others. I catch Janie's eye. Point with my chin. She takes the front-facing window seat. Siri climbs in next to her. I take the outside seat. Our daughter safely between us.

"I call the other window seat!" Simon says, climbing into the seat opposite his mother. He looks up at Philip. "Or maybe you should sit there, Uncle Philip. You're the guest."

I shoot Philip a look. He says, "That's okay, mijo. I can see over your head."

Philip moves to take the seat next to Simon but I grab his wrist. Tug him to the outside seat instead. Better defensive position. I put the large shopping bag between them.

"You two can be in charge of the snacks," I say.

"Hyper!" Simon reaches in to grab a chocolate banana oat muffin. "Want one, Siri?"

"I'm not hungry," she says.

Janie puts her arm around Siri. I long to do the same, but my arms need to be free. Just in case. I note the exits at the front of the car. Turn my head to measure the distance to those behind us. The car's about half-full. There's a couple with twins sitting with two older adults. Across the aisle from them, a family of four with a small dog. Behind them, a group of six retirees laughing. They're taking images with their wristpads. I examine the rest of the passengers. None seem to be paying us any special interest. Still, I remain vigilant.

A conductor who favours her left leg—Anselma, she/her—checks our tickets. Philip displays the wristpad I gave him and the conductor scans it with her mini-wand. It blips five times, once for each of our tickets. She moves on.

Janie looks out the window. Philip looks at me. Siri looks straight ahead at the seat across from her as though it holds the secrets of the universe. Simon's attention is on the bag of snacks.

"You promised us stories," he says, fishing out a container of spicy olives.

Janie glances at me. I shake my head. She turns her gaze to Philip.

"Um, okay. I'll start," he says. "You already know I was born in New York and that my grandparents on my father's side are from Puerto Rico. But I don't think I ever mentioned that my mom's parents are from Massachusetts and that my grandmother was Acadian."

"No, you didn't," Janie says, echoing my thoughts.

"Now I know why you're good at Spanish *and* French." Simon looks thoughtful for a moment. "I learned in school about la déportation des Acadiens. The government should let you live here since they threw your ancestors out back then. And Kyla too."

There's a moment of painful silence. Janie looks guilty, as though Philip's lack of prospects for immigration status were her fault. As for Philip, every time his daughter's name is mentioned, he winces a little, like from a chronic pain he'd forgotten for a moment.

Philip forces a smile and says, "There's a lot of things the government should do to make up for what they did back then, and not just to the Acadians."

"You mean the First Nations, Inuit, and Métis."

Philip musses Simon's hair. "Yes. Do you want to hear about my grandma now?"

Simon nods.

"Okay, so when she was in college, she left school and ran off to Mardi Gras. To find her roots, you could say. She joined a krewe, learned to play the glockenspiel, and stayed in New Orleans for seven months. When she returned to her college in Waltham, Massachusetts, she changed her major to music. End of story."

"Hyper!" Simon says. "She ran away from home for her art."

"Don't get any ideas, mijo," Philip says. "Your family isn't forcing you to study something you're not interested in, which was her situation."

"What were they making her study?"

"Economics, I think. Or maybe engineering."

"Or maybe electronics. Or something else that starts with an E," Simon says.

Philip laughs. Siri's grim expression doesn't change. Janie raises her eyebrows at me, but I shake my head again.

"My turn, I guess," she says. "Like Philip, my parents were born in New York, but my mother's side of the family has roots in South America."

"Argentinian Jews, right?" Philip says.

"They were from Uruguay, actually," I correct him.

"Montevideo," Janie confirms. "But I had a great uncle who lived in Luscano for a time."

"Luscano!" Simon exclaims, and even Siri turns her eyes towards her mother before resuming her staring contest with the seat. She still hasn't eaten a thing.

"So he was part of El Movimiento de la Gran Comuna?" Philip asks.

"We read about that," Simon chimes in. "In that epic poem by Siré."

"Yeah, but the story I want to tell you is about how he met the love of his life, Daniel."

Janie's story-telling talent has captured everyone's attention. Even mine, though I've heard the tale before. I pull my attention away. I need to focus on other things. Like making sure Siri's safe; that we're all safe. And deciding how long to wait before sending someone in on an extraction mission if Gabriel's really been taken.

I check my wristpad. There's no message. And if there was,

I would have felt it since I've set it to burn. It lies tight against my wrist. Cool. Waiting. Useless.

When Janie is finished, Simon asks me if I have a story from my childhood.

Is there a story I could tell? Something funny? Harmless but true?

After a moment, Janie says, "Let's give Daddy more time to think of one."

Philip holds my gaze a moment before looking away. Disappointed. Maybe angry.

"I have an idea," Janie says. "Philip, have you ever played two truths and a lie?"

"Everyone says three things and you have to figure out which is the lie?" he asks, eyebrows raised.

"Exactly. Simon, do you want to go first?" Janie asks.

Simon nods with enthusiasm. "Yes! Umm, okay. I got one. My favourite colour is red. My favourite colour is turquoise. My favourite colour is orange."

Siri gives her brother a disgusted glance. "You're not playing right! A person can only have one favourite colour, so two of those statements must be lies."

"Who says? I always have two favourite colours."

"Why does he have to be so weird!" Siri says, rolling her eyes.

"Siri, be nice," Janie tells her. "Don't take out how you're feeling on your brother. Anyway, I know the answer. Your favourite colour is not red. At least not this week."

"How'd you guess?" Simon asks. "Your turn, Uncle Philip."

"Excuse me," I say. Everyone turns. "I need to. . . I won't be long."

I stand. Turn towards the back of the car. Philip has started his two truths and a lie, about crushes he had in high school. I feel his eyes on my back as I walk down the corridor. When I reach the toilets, I peer over my shoulder. Philip's facing Simon now, explaining something. I exit the car and enter the gangway connection. Remain there in the vestibule. Through the thick glass, I watch my family.

The vape pen is in the front pocket of my jeans. I take it out and fill my lungs. Exhale. Repeat. Repeat again. After a few minutes, the conductor finally arrives, raps on the glass. I press on the button that opens the door.

"Je suis désolée mais. . . there's no smoking or vaping between the cars."

"I have a medical prescription," I tell her with a slight smile.

"I understand, but we have a place for that. Upstairs," she says pointing. "Next to the observation area. I could show you—"

"I'd rather not be so far from my family, my daughter. . ." I bite my lower lip. "Excuse me. I'm just in a lot of pain right now. Maybe you understand?" I say, indicating her leg.

"I didn't think it was obvious." Her hand goes automatically to her left hip.

"It's not, I'm just observant. And I know what pain looks like. Do you want some?"

"Non, merci. I have a patch." She looks me over and seems to come to a decision. "How much time do you need?"

"Dix minutes. Even five would be helpful."

"I'll make sure no one comes back here for ten minutes. How far are you going?"

"Percé," I tell her.

"That's a long way. Maybe you'll be able to sleep through some of it."

"I hope so," I answer.

As soon as she's gone, I use my wristpad to open communication with my contact. Two seconds later, I feel the burn on my wrist. I send a one-word inquiry.

> News?

> no. we sent another team to where the second player was found. nothing.

> Could he have been picked up?

> our contacts say no

> What's the consensus?

> that it's too soon. more danger extracting the tooth than waiting to see if it heals on its own

> Infection may be more of a risk than blood loss.

> this tooth often aches then it turns out to be a false alarm. you've said so yourself

I don't answer. Lift my vape pen to my lips, concentrating on that instead. Under my feet, I feel the movable plates of the metal floor shift. The walls accordion as we go into a long, steep turn. I press my face against the glass of the door again. Philip's frustrated. I can read his body language from here. Can only imagine how completely Janie's kicking his ass. At parties, she never loses this game. I smile. Phil has a competitive streak. Endearing, since it's so at odds with his generous nature. But maybe why he loved those screen games so much as a kid.

The smile slips from my face. How I yearn to be back in my seat. Surrounded by my family. But a decision needs to be made. Maybe Gabriel's just laying low. It's what I might have done when I was younger. Or maybe his radio silence is a way of getting attention. Or punishing Siri. I don't like Gabriel.

Don't trust him. But there's also a not insignificant possibility that he's in danger. My wristpad burns. They want to know how I vote.

I can't see Siri's face, but her body language is also clear. She's drooping. Head in hands. I play with the vape pen. Sigh and return it to my pocket.

> I vote to extract if no news in 24 hrs. But I won't block consensus.

I reenter the car, stopping to use the toilet, then return to my seat.

"How do you do that?" Philip's saying to Janie as I sit back down. He's more amazed than frustrated now. "You beat me four rounds in a row!"

"People have what's called 'tells'—facial expressions, body language, tone of voice. Sometimes, I don't know what tipped me off. I guess it's my superpower." Janie grins, pleased.

"It's pretty impressive."

"It does come in handy at court. Though knowing when someone's lying doesn't mean I know what the truth is. And it doesn't work for everybody," she finishes, turning to me.

"So Daddy's too much of a liar even for you," Siri says, shooting me an angry look.

Her words sting, but I can't be angry with Siri for feeling that way.

"No, you've misunderstood me. Your father's the most honest person I know. But he's good at controlling his body, suppressing his emotions. That means he could get away with lying if he wanted. But he refuses to. At most, he'll withhold information."

"That's just as bad," Siri says.

"Maybe not," Philip replies, surprising me.

My eyes fill, but I push the tears away. It occurs to me that maybe Siri's right, that I just lied again, lied about how I'm feeling. I try to bring the tears back, but it's too late.

I rest my hand on Philip's knee, put my other arm around Siri. Janie looks worn out. The events of the day finally catching up with her. She tilts her head and I nod. Then I turn to Siri.

"I do have a story."

I take a deep breath and begin.

CHAPTER 21
LAEK

"I never met my grandfolx. My only parent was Alis, my mother."

My hands now rest on my own lap. I gaze at a point just to the left of Philip's right ear.

"It was just me and my mom until I was around eight. Driving from state to state in the Midwestern Drylands. My mom picking up work in different places."

"That's when you first learned about borders, right?" Simon pipes up. "You told me you used to look for the dark lines between each state, like on a map, only they weren't there."

I force myself to look at my son. To smile. "That's right, love. The lines were invisible, but also very real. Some states set up blockades. Wouldn't let you in if you were sick. Or didn't have a job waiting for you."

Simon's own smile looks tremulous, confusion and sadness tugging at its corners.

"I remember it as a happy time, though," I say gently. "We

were free. We had each other. We played games. My mother danced, sang me songs. She... she had a beautiful voice."

"So does Mommy," Simon says, his smile steady now. "And Uncle Philip too."

"Yeah, they do." Janie and Philip are watching me closely. Siri doesn't look my way, but I can tell she's listening.

"How did you go to school if you were always moving around?" Simon asks.

"I didn't. My mom taught me herself."

"But then how did she go to work? And who watched you when she was working?"

"I looked after myself. Or she'd leave me at the library or some other secure place. It was at a library where I began to discover my love of history. But that was much later."

"But how—"

"Simon," Janie says. "Let Daddy tell his story."

Simon subsides, and I take a deep breath. In truth, Simon's questions don't bother me. It's figuring out how much truth to tell that's hard. At our refugee hearing, I said too much. And it nearly got me deported as a security risk.

"Like I said, we were happy. Even though our life wasn't always easy. But one day I got sick. People around us were sick all the time. Eyes permanently red and itchy. Dry coughs. Open sores. The land was. . . blighted. From climate change, the weather experiments, the bio warfare labs. But I don't remember ever having been sick before. My mother panicked."

I remember the dust dancing in the air, making patterns. I thought it was trying to tell me something, an urgent truth about the unity of life and—

"Papa? Aren't you going to tell us what happened next?" Simon's voice, a little hesitant, a little impatient, brings me back to the present.

"Sorry, love. When I got sick, my mother decided to go back to the place where I was born. The Community, she called it."

I take another deep breath and shift in my seat, my knees knocking against Philip's.

"They had medicines there, clean water and food. I got well. And I liked the place at first. People remembered Alis, made a big fuss over her. And over me. And there were other kids to play with, a school, beds.

"But it wasn't. . . a good place. I learned that later." I pause, thinking about what I could say. "There were very strict rules. Not just about what you should do but. . . but who you should be. And not be. I wasn't good at following those rules.

"My mom wasn't happy either. I could tell. She stopped singing. She. . . I felt guilty. I knew she'd decided to leave The Community after I was born, and now here she was, back again. All because of me, because I got sick."

I turn to Siri now.

"Lots of times, kids think things are their fault that aren't. Or they blame their parents for events outside their control. I did both. Blamed myself. Blamed my mom. I couldn't understand why we didn't just leave. At that age, I didn't appreciate the power they had over her. You see, they were a cult, protected by the U.A. government for their own reasons. Do you know what a cult is?" I ask Simon.

"A religion?" Simon responds.

"Not just a religion," Siri says. "A cult is hyper-extremist. They have this one powerful leader, usually a dude, and he gets to have sex with everyone."

"TMI!" Simon says, hands over ears.

I want to correct Siri, but in this case at least, she's not wrong. Instead, I tell Simon, "We were a farming community, actually. It's where I learned to take care of plants."

"In the Midwestern Drylands?" Philip says, sounding skeptical.

"We lived off-grid, under a dome," I explain.

"Wait a sec," Philip says. "You mean you were a domie?"

"Some people called us—them—that. But they called themselves The Community."

"I can't believe you never told me that! I mean. . ." Philip stops, visibly composes himself, and continues. "That must have been. . . weird. I remember when they closed the place down. After your leader was implicated in the government's weather experiments scandal. I saw him on the news when I was in college. Scarily charismatic. What ever happened to him?"

"I don't know," I say. Does Philip realize this man was probably my biological father?

"What happened to you and your mom?" Simon asks with concern in his voice. "Did she go to jail?"

"No. What Uncle Philip said, that was all later. We were gone by then. I mean. . ." I sigh. Simon won't take this well. "My mom died, love. She got sick and died. And I ran away."

What I don't mention is that I ran away before she died. I'll carry that guilt alone.

"It's okay, Papa," Simon says. "I already knew you didn't have a parent anymore."

He stretches out his hand to me. My eyes fill, but not because my mother is dead. What hurts my heart is that this world is too cruel for a kid like Simon. After a moment, I let go of his hand. It's an awkward, diagonal reach for him and I don't think I'll be able to hold myself together with my child trying to wrap his smaller hand around my larger one.

"I was fourteen when I ran," I continue after a moment. "I headed west. My goal was San Francisco. It was just after Fisherman's Wharf disappeared under the sea, but before Yerba Buena had to relocate inland. I'd heard there was good community there. I needed that. I guess I understand my mom better now. Why she went back. It wasn't just because I was sick. She wanted to belong somewhere. Wanted me to belong too. But I didn't. Not there."

"Dios! The Pacific Coast's a good, long way from the Drylands. And you, just a kid."

"I managed. I hitchhiked, sometimes caught long rides."

"But how did you live?" Philip insists. "Where did you get credits, food?"

"I managed." I look Philip straight in the eye now. He catches on and shuts up.

But it's too late. "Did you get jobs, Papa, like your maman did?" he asks innocently.

"Yes."

"What kind of work did you do?"

"Whatever people would pay me for," I say, instantly regretting this formulation.

"I want to hear about your route," Philip says quickly.

"Well, that's where the libraries come in." I turn to Simon. Smile. "I followed a route that took me through places with libraries. I knew I could find refuge there. Like when I was little. At the libraries, there were books, maps, databases, other research tools. And people whose job it was to share knowledge. It's there I first started reading history. Not just the official histories that are taught at schools and shown on our screens. I read people's histories, workers' histories, Indigenous histories, Black histories, herstories, queerstories, tales of rebellion, abolition and struggle. It was at a library that I found the group I later joined."

"What was the group called, Papa?"

"They didn't have a name. Or rather, they had a lot of

names, because they were a network of groups. Or cells, as they used to be called."

"Was it a youth group?" Siri leans forward, no longer hiding the fact that she's listening.

"No. We were mixed. There were a few of us still in our teens but most were in their twenties or thirties or older. Our liaison was a middle-aged man—"

Janie shoots me a look, but she needn't worry. I won't be mentioning Al's name.

"Anyway, except for also being off the grid, this group was the polar opposite of the place I left. Instead of isolating themselves and shunning outsiders, they were engaged with the world, passionate about justice. Ready to put themselves on the line for social change. They offered me acceptance, support, camaraderie, love." *And lots of sex*, I think but don't say. My family doesn't need to know I was promiscuous as fuck as a teenager.

"We were totally egalitarian. They listened to my ideas even though I was young. And kindly but thoroughly tore them apart when they made no sense." I laugh. Then remember how it all ended, and the laugh dies in my throat.

"They were my family. And they were good to me. For the short time I had them."

I stop. It's like I've arrived at the edge of a ravine.

"What happened, Papa? Did they. . . did they all die?" Simon asks softly.

"I don't really know. I came home one day. The cops were there. The Terror Squad."

"The Terror Squad?" Simon's eyes are wide.

"What they called themselves was the Anti-Terrorist Squad," Janie tells the kids. "But our name was more accurate. Their reputation was bad enough that they were supposedly disbanded, but it's not really true. They're simply more clandestine now, continuing their dirty work from deep within the state's public/private enforcement industry."

"But back then, they operated openly," I say, taking up the thread. "Used a strategy of fear and repression. My group... we were on a list. They took us. Separated us. I was... questioned. For a long time. It went very badly."

I pause. During this quiet, even Simon dares not ask any questions.

"I don't know what happened to any of them. I never saw them again." None of them but Al. How did he escape? How was my own release eventually secured?

"I was released some months later. Another cell made contact with me. They became my new family. Until they were also taken. I was away from the safe house when it happened. I'd gone to get some compost from a nearby community garden." I wrap my arms around my chest, like I'm trying to hold my bones together. "When I got back, the house was empty. There were signs of struggle. I blamed myself. I wanted to—"

I swallow my words. I'd forgotten for a moment who my audience was. My fingertips stretch towards my scarred wrists. I curl my hands into fists instead. Thoughts begin to fragment, pulling my mind from my body. Broken brick. Shattered glass. Iron-rich blood in the soil...

The train takes a curve, rocking us gently in its embrace. I remember that I'm somewhere relatively safe. With people I love. A family who needs me, who needs me to keep my shit together. I bite the inside of my cheek, hoping the pain will ground me.

"I blamed myself. Both times the Terror Squad arrived, I was outside the safe house at the critical moment. It was... too lucky, and I didn't understand it. Still don't. The thing is, I don't believe in coincidence."

Janie and Siri share a quick look, their identical rosebud lips almost smiling.

"And just like when I was younger, with my mother, I also thought about blaming the people close to me. I was convinced we'd been denounced. A spy, or a government operative planted in our group. It might've even been true."

I think about Al, how he'd sent me on an errand that afternoon, right before my first group was arrested. I know Janie's thinking of him too. Her lips have gone from a rosebud to a thick hard line. Whether or not he was playing both sides, I understand why Janie hates Al on principle for using me so hard when I was a teenager. But Al was more of a father to me than the man whose genes I carry.

I look at Siri, really look at her. Maybe I didn't have a father but she does, and she deserves as much wisdom as I can scrape together from my own fucked-up experiences.

"But listen, Siri. When they send people to infiltrate us, they're causing direct harm. But the worse harm is when this tactic makes us suspect one another. That erosion of trust is like a slow poison. Killing us from the inside. We need to resist it. Sure, it's necessary to have good security protocols, to listen to our heads and our guts when something seems off. But we also have to follow our hearts. To trust our comrades. Otherwise, we're doing our enemies' work for them, turning something that could be strong and unified into a handful of painful splinters."

Janie's face is flushed with emotion. She reaches across Siri's lap to take my hand.

"So I try to have trust in others. And trust in myself too. We all make mistakes. And when we do, it's best to acknowledge and learn from them, not wallow in guilt. Guilt, like paranoia, is essentially an egocentric emotion. Also, remember that if someone swings a club at you and you duck and it hits someone else, that's not your fault. It's the fault of the person swinging the club."

"But what if you—" Siri suddenly looks at her wristpad.

Simultaneously, I realize that the warm, almost burning sensation against my wrist isn't the ghost-pain of an old, self-inflicted injury, but rather, a signal that a message has come in on my own wristpad.

"Siri," Janie says. "Can't your friends wait? Daddy's still telling his story."

"It's fine, I'm done," I say.

I glance at the message and see they've decided to go with my recommendation to send someone to extract Gabriel. My reaction is strongly ambivalent: uneasy that I pushed for this against my own instincts but elated to have some good news I can share with Siri. Because yes, I plan to break with strict protocol and tell her.

"Which of your friends is it?" Philip asks Siri. "You seem happy to hear from them."

"It's not—I mean it's from Gabriel. I was worried about him."

"Gabriel?" Simon says. "I thought you hated him."

"Sometimes. But I'm glad he's safe. Pass me a muffin," she adds.

Flooded with relief, I'm composing my own message inside my head: No need to send a surgeon. The tooth has fallen out on its own. I stand, intending to go between the cars again.

"Where are you going, Papa?" Simon asks. "You should have a muffin too. You haven't eaten anything yet!"

I look down into Simon's sweet face, creased with worry for me, and sit back down.

"Sure, a muffin sounds great."

The message can wait.

CHAPTER 22
PHILIP AND LAEK

PHILIP

"The causeway's in the other direction," I tell Laek. "Is this one of your shortcuts?"

"It's the scenic route," he replies, grinning. "What's the matter, tired already?"

"Not one bit." I lengthen my stride to prove my point.

Laek is light-hearted this morning, almost giddy, despite or maybe because of our all-night train trip. I managed to doze in my seat but I don't think he slept a wink. Laek's high spirits are contagious, and that plus the warm weather, the smell of the sea, and a full day for just the two of us, has filled me with energy.

I turn my head towards the Rock, hoping to catch a glimpse of it beyond the barrier.

Laek covers my eyes playfully. "No peeking! Your first view of Rocher Percé shouldn't be with a polymer wall in the way. Trust me, it'll be worth the wait."

"Speaking of trust, I know how hard it must've been for you to tell your story last night. But it's good for the kids to hear that...history, to try to learn from it."

"Maybe," he says carefully. "I hope so."

"And for me too, to know what you went through. Thank you for trusting me." I put my hand on his shoulder.

"I always have. The things I've kept from you—it's not for lack of trust."

And just like that, I remember how much he still hasn't told me.

"Alright," I say, bringing my arm to my side again. At least it's a start.

We walk in companionable silence through the centre of town. We pass a string of restaurants, craft shops, e-kiosks, and ice cream joints, but surprisingly quickly, the businesses thin out and I feel like I'm in the country. Not long after, we take a left off the main road to climb a modest bluff that leads to some fields of tall grass. I see a small church with a blue steeple; beyond it is a set of benches arranged in a horseshoe shape around a large, white sculpture.

"That's a Northern Gannet," Laek says, pointing to the statue. "A migratory bird."

The road eventually curves towards a small road that leads down to the water. The buildings seem older, dingier. We pass a three-storey structure with a hand-painted sign in front of it that reads: "Le petit Centre d'art-thérapie intergénérationnel." It has a rooftop garden. Right across the street is another building, this one with a more discreet sign that identifies it as an immigrant workers' centre. Beyond these two larger buildings, a few street food vendors and small shops dot the narrow, twisty road.

"Hey, checke ça," Laek says. "A seaweed store! 'Algue pour

tous'. Great name." He presses his face against the glass. "They have all kinds of stuff. Seaweed art, nori soap, even clothing. Whadda you say? We could get you a pair of algae underwear."

"No thanks. We should hurry. The tide safety schedule says to get there by noon."

"That's if you want to watch the tide go out. I'd just as soon arrive when the causeway's dry and most of the tourists are already across it. How 'bout some seaweed ice cream?"

"I'm good, but you go ahead. Just try to make it fast so we're not too late."

After Laek finishes his ice cream, we go down to the water. Our path is sandy in some places, rocky in others. I push the toe of my sneaker against a fist-sized stone, then lean over to pick up one that looks flat enough to skip in the water, but it's not flat; the rock's bulbous bottom was hidden in the sand. Further on is a stretch of large, round boulders, wet and slippery-looking. I'm watching my footing, so don't notice at first that Laek has stopped to look out.

"There," he says, grabbing my arm.

I'd seen both video and static images of the Percé Rock, even a holo or two, but nothing's prepared me for the enormity of its real life, physical presence. It strikes me as incredibly phallic, despite actually being wider than it is tall, causing comparisons to an ocean liner or a beached whale in the tourist literature, yet there's something about the almost aggressive, jutting way it thrusts up from the water that makes me think of a phallus.

Or maybe it's my hyper-awareness of Laek's body next to mine, lean and hard and generating lots of heat, and the images that have been swirling around my head about what we might do together later.

"C'mon," he says. "You want to get closer, yeah?"

"Yes," I tell him. "Yes, I do."

Walking along the beach, I realize I'd underestimated the rock's size, thinking we were closer than we were. Laek walks a parallel course further inland, nimbly climbing up and down the large boulders while the bottom of my sneakers get wet as I step onto a semi-submerged slab of striated grey stone. The Percé Rock is a rich terra cotta with lighter sandstone highlights. Its shape keeps redefining itself as our angle changes. The pierced part that forms a natural arch, big enough to allow boats to sail under it at low tide, can't be seen from this side.

We finally arrive at the causeway, a silty sandbar that rises as it curves towards the rock. It's sprinkled generously with stones, none very beautiful or remarkable, but I lean over and put one in my pocket—a memento of our time here. I imagine myself back in New York, lonely and sad, holding this rock in my hand, then berate myself for indulging in that kind of self-pity. I'm lucky to be here now, and to see Laek and Janie and the kids safe and happy in their new home.

There aren't many tourists—in two months there'll be workers selling tickets and checking wristpads and chips—but now, in late April, we practically have the place to ourselves. Laek runs across the sand spit, anxious to get there, I suppose, but I linger, taking vids and photos, not sure at what angle and distance the shots will be most impressive.

"Hey!" I yell to Laek. He has his arms spread around a portion of the rock face. "Can you turn this way? I want to get some footage." Laek ignores me. Then a couple with a toddler riding in a back carrier cross in front of him, blocking my shot. I give up and walk across the causeway. When I'm close enough for Laek to hear me without shouting, I quip, "I thought you only hugged trees."

LAEK

"Don't be jealous," I respond. "You can have a hug too."

I wrap my arms around him. He hugs me back. Hard. What started as a joke suddenly feels serious. He takes my face in his hands. Kisses me. I let him pull me around the rock. When we're out of sight of the other tourists, he kisses me again. And pulls back.

"What?" I ask, missing the press of his body against mine.

"I'm thinking about the first time I kissed you. You were asleep, and—"

"That sounds a little date-rapey," I say, not above teasing him a little.

"No, no. I mean you were unconscious. It was when you were in the hospital."

"Worse and worse." I'm smiling, but Philip looks horrified. I put him out of his misery. "I'm just messing with you. I wasn't actually asleep. Or unconscious, as you so delicately put it. The morphine had finally kicked in, but I felt your kiss as I was drifting off. I was surprised. But not in a bad way. It made me feel cared for, safe."

"So when you kissed me that last night in Brooklyn, you already knew how I felt. That's how you won that bet!" Philip sounds outraged, but I think it's an act. His next words are quiet. "Did you know all along that I was in love with you? Because Janie said she knew, or at least suspected. She said she could tell by how I looked at you."

"No, I didn't know," I tell him, then examine if this is the whole truth. I did notice that he watched me a lot. But the vibe I got wasn't romantic or sexual. More fraternal. Like he was looking out for me.

"I wanted to tell you before you tried to cross the border," Philip continues. "I wasn't sure if we'd ever see each other again, but I needed you to know, even though you didn't feel the same way."

"What makes you think I didn't feel the same way?" I wrap my arms around his waist.

"For one thing, I bawled like a baby when we parted. You were cool, in control."

"I cried too. Hard enough that I felt like my ribs were breaking all over again."

"But. . . that must have been after I left," Philip says.

"Yeah." I release him, thinking back to the pain of that parting.

"Were you ashamed to cry in front of me?"

I consider, for what seems like the hundredth time in the last twenty-four hours, what truths to tell. At some point in my life, withholding information became second nature to me. Yet I remember a time when truth bubbled out of my mouth like a joyous stream.

"It's true I didn't want to cry in front of you. But not because I was ashamed. I was afraid that hearing me cry would break you."

I watch Philip chew on this. It doesn't go down well.

"There's another reason," I say. "I try to live in the present. For me, the past is a trap, a place filled with pain. And the future's unknown, maybe more of the same. As long as you were with me, I could enjoy your presence. I reckoned I had the whole rest of my life to suffer your absence. Why allow myself to feel that loss before I had to?"

Philip shakes his head. "It's not that what you're saying doesn't make sense. I just don't understand how you do that, make yourself wait until later to be upset. My thoughts race ahead to what's next, dragging my emotions along with them. Like. . . like now. I can't stop thinking about how my time with you is running out. I'm sorry, but it makes me sad."

"We don't know that you'll have to leave. We still might find a way—"

"It seems unlikely. I'd rather not set myself up for disappointment."

The sky is like a bowl of moving clouds. I wait while the ones covering the sun slowly drifts sideways to uncover a crescent of light which grows until the heat on my face warms my whole body. "What if, just this once, you try to imagine it'll all work out?"

Philip hesitates then smiles at me. A fond, tolerant smile. "Alright, I'll try. But then I want you to do something too, something similar."

My back is to the rock and he moves in front of me so that all I can see is him. He takes me by the shoulders, thumbs rubbing back and forth along my collar bones.

"I want you to try to relax," he continues. "To stop looking at everyone like you're evaluating whether they're friend or foe. To stop scanning the environment for the closest exits and hiding spots. I get it; and you may not even be doing this consciously. But. . . well, like Janie said, I watch you a lot and I see how guarded you are, how careful, and it makes me. . . I just want you to feel safe. Let me help you feel safe."

I swallow hard and nod, wanting more than anything to please him, to do as he asks. Maybe, for a short time, I could stop thinking about the airport bombing. Or the students who've suddenly disappeared from my class. Or the parents of little Ariel and Sol at Garderie Mariposa Daycare. Or losing Clara. Or dead birds. Or what Al and Cloutier and even Gabriel are really up to. Well, at least Gabriel turned up and we were able to recall the extraction team.

I lean back against the rock, try to absorb its solidity. It smells like bitter chocolate, like the brownstones in East Brooklyn that burned the night of the rent war. . . no, I won't think of that either. I listen to the high, sharp cries of seabirds rising in counterpoint to the constant low thrumming honks of the gannets. Air currents nuzzle my skin; the sun warms my face, is gone, then back again as bright white clouds fly across a heartbreakingly dark blue sky.

Philip's eyes are a rich brown, the tiniest fleck of orange where the sun lights the side of his face. I focus on his strong, solid presence. His tender protectiveness. His quickening breath as he leans towards me. My breath quickens too. I lift my face to the sun and bare my throat to him.

PHILIP

The full length of Laek's exposed throat is irresistible. I bring my mouth to it, his pulse throbbing against my tongue. I slide my hands under his tank top, thumbs stroking his nipples, fingers gently slipping down his ribs. I grab his hips and pull him tight against me, his hard cock against mine a pleasure so intense it almost hurts. I kiss and touch, my entire focus on his body, almost forgetting the limits and constraints imposed by clothing, place, and other boundaries. After a while, I lose track of my hands and my lips while time itself seems warm and elastic.

LAEK

Eyes closed, I lose myself in physical sensations. A pressure here, a stroke there, the sun on my face, a calloused thumb, a hard limb, the wind buffeting my hair, smooth lips, the solid rock behind me, my own body's rising pleasure and heat. I'm conscious of the cries of birds, the tang of the sea, the slight odour of Philip's sweat combined with the lemon-vanilla smell of the hotel's shampoo.

I hold him tight, my face buried in the crook of his neck. An uneasiness begins to steal into me. I feel it in my chest, a sudden cold. Like the clouds have more permanently aligned themselves between us and the sun, an unforeseen eclipse. But the sun is still there. I feel it on my face. Then I put it together: it's much too quiet.

PHILIP

Laek stiffens in my arms, and I wonder if I've gone too far. His eyes fly open.

LAEK

We're surrounded by water.

PHILIP

I jerk my head around. The whole scene looks nightmarishly wrong, like we were transported to a tiny island in the middle of the ocean. It clicks into place. The tide has come in.

"Come on," I say, quickly making my way around the reinforced rim of the Percé Rock to the part that faces the causeway, but the causeway is gone, a lake in its place, and all the tourists are gone too. Merde, I'd taken note of the quiet and greeted the idea that we might be alone with more relief than concern, but we've stayed too long. The water is rising and it's rising fast. I turn around, expecting to see Laek right behind me, but he isn't. I find him back where I left him, still as a statue.

"What are you doing?" I say. "We need to cross over before the water gets even higher." When he doesn't move, I grab his wrist, tugging him behind me along the perimeter of the stone until we're both facing the mainland.

"Should we take our shoes off or keep them on?" I ask him. "It may help us keep our footing."

Laek doesn't respond. It's like the tide has mesmerized him.

I decide I'd better take control. "Alright, we'll leave them on. Let's go, before it gets too dangerous. Laek?" I say, when he doesn't answer.

"You go ahead," he finally responds. "I'll. . . I'll wait here."

"What do you mean, 'you'll wait here'? It's not safe." Laek doesn't respond. "Can't you swim?" I ask, starting to panic.

"I can swim," he says.

"Alright, good. Then come on. Shit, the tide is really coming in fast."

I reach for his arm, but Laek shrinks back into the rock. Though his voice is even and his face is placid, I realize he's terrified.

"Okay, okay," I say, hands in the air. "How can I help? What do you want me to do?"

"Just go." He speaks matter-of-factly, as though what he was saying were reasonable, trivial even.

"Laek, you can't expect me to leave you here." I try to meet his eyes, but they slide away.

"It's okay," he says. "I'll be fine."

"How will you be fine?" I sound frantic even to my own ears.

"I'm going to climb up. Higher, where the water can't reach."

"Laek, it's a sheer rock face. You can't climb it."

"It'll be fine," he repeats, and as though to prove it, he begins to climb. He manages to pull himself up a couple of feet before sliding down again.

Now I'm really starting to panic. In the few minutes we've been talking, the water has risen high enough that I think it would be dangerous to try to drag him across. He obviously has some kind of phobia, though he said he can swim and I believe him. I get an idea.

"Alright, we'll both climb."

I take a step back on the reinforced perimeter circling the rock and catapult myself up as best I can. I bounce and slip off, bending my knees as I land. I reach down and grab my ankle.

"Shit," I say. "I think I twisted it. Laek, I'm gonna need your help to get back across."

His eyes are going back and forth between the rock and rising waters. If I were to go by his expression, I would think him calm, a little bored even, but his whole body is trembling, as though connected to a low electrical current.

"Please," I say, and then more desperately. "I need you."

After a second of indecision, he flies to my side. I let him pull my right arm around his neck while shoving his left shoulder under my armpit to support me. We leave the platform around the rock where the water is now up to our knees and slide down the slope of the causeway. At this lower point, the water is already chest high. We begin staggering across, step by step, agonizingly slow. It's not so very far. It would be an easy crossing if the water weren't so cold that it's hard to breathe, and if the tide weren't so strong, pushing and pulling at us. And every second the water rises higher.

A wave smashes into me from the left, making me lose my footing on the slippery rocks. Laek holds me upright, solid as a rock himself, but the water is almost to his chin now.

"We should start swimming! It would be easier," I say.

I slide off his shoulder and pray that he wasn't lying about knowing how to swim. With my left arm, I do a modified breaststroke; with my right hand I keep hold of Laek's shirt.

Laek is properly horizontal now, face held high out of the water, doing some kind of doggy paddle.

Gazing across the water to where the shoreline used to be, I fix on an eroded escarpment of rock and stunted vegetation: our goal.

"Kick!" I shout. "Kick as hard as you can!"

I bunch more of Laek's shirt inside my fist and try to take my own advice.

CHAPTER 23
LAEK

High, high, high the tide pushes us and I ride it, pretending to be a seabird, a gannet, flying towards the cliff on the mainland, across the drowned causeway. The Earth spins. I catch hold of it, taking Philip with me. Some kind of protrusion, a rock or root. I cling to it, drenched and shaking, as the tide tries to suck me backwards. I start to go blank.

Philip's hand is against the small of my back. Warmth and safety flow from his palm to my core, anchoring me. The world stills and I still with it, my breath coming in and out.

The next thing I feel is Philip's hand under my rump. Shoving me hard. "Keep climbing," he shouts. "We need to be higher."

I do as he says.

A few minutes later, we're scrambling diagonally along the cliffside. Directly across the water from Rocher Percé. We move north, vaguely parallel to the path we took to get here. Except that path of sand and stones is far below, covered by the raging waters of the bay.

I force myself to turn away. In my mind's eye is a clear

map, a bird's eye view of the area. If we keep going north, we'll come to the end of the bluff. No safe way down to the road. We need to angle further west. Away from the bay, which suits me. I lead. We climb silently, in single file. I focus on the ground beneath my feet, moving carefully. I've stopped shaking. The sun is warm on my neck and shoulders.

"What the fuck was that?" Philip finally asks.

"A perigee tide, I think." My voice is steady. Flat, even to my own ears. "They happen every twenty-eight days. Or a perigean spring tide. Maybe even a blue moon tide. That's—"

"Not my fucking question. What happened to you out there? We could've—"

"But we didn't. We're safe. In fact, I'd appreciate it if you'd let go of my shirt."

Instead of letting go of it, Philip uses his grip on my shirt to tug me towards him, spinning me around to face him. "You promised you'd be honest with me from now on."

I pull away. "I didn't lie. I can swim. Maybe not like you," I say, letting a little temper show. "I grew up in the Midwestern Drylands, not Rockaway Beach. And didn't spend school holidays visiting my grandfather on the island of Puerto Rico, surrounded by water."

"That's a bit redundant, don't you think? On an island, surrounded by water?"

I could laugh at his joke. Take the opportunity he's giving me to sidestep his question. Even pissed off, he's putting my emotional needs ahead of his own, and knowing this makes me reconsider my instinct to shut down on him.

To give myself time, I turn away and bound up the rocky slope. Philip hurries to catch up. When he's close enough, I say, "You're the one who lied."

"What are you talking about?"

"I notice your limp's disappeared. What happened to your twisted ankle?"

"Oh, that." He shrugs, clearly unremorseful. "That ruse was so thin, I was afraid you wouldn't buy it. But you always put the safety of others ahead of your own, so. . . But Laek, seriously," he says, a little more kindly, "Why didn't you mention your fear of water? It might have been nice to know while planning a. . . an activity near water."

We've reached the top of the falaise. I turn and look down on the rising bay, the rock still thrusting out from it. I imagine telling Philip what he thinks he wants to know. In my head, the term "opening the floodgates" keeps repeating itself. I picture creaky wooden doors, old and heavy. Rusty metal deadbolts sliding open with a screech. All that water rushing in.

Because there are emotional floodgates too. And water's not the only thing you can drown in. Pain, terror, guilt, self-loathing. . . that's what I fear is waiting for me on the other side of those gates. On the other side of this conversation. Does Philip really need to see that?

But maybe, in the end, it really is a matter of trust. Trust in his ability to handle it. Trust in my own ability to open up those gates and deal with whatever comes through.

"I wasn't always afraid of the water," I tell him. "It's because of something that happened to me. I'd hoped to spare you some ugly details."

Philip sucks his teeth. "I'm not as emotionally delicate as you seem to think," he says. "Sure, I'm not Janie—nobody's Janie—but I can be there for you too."

"Let's keep going. I. . . I'll tell you what happened. But I need a minute."

I concentrate on breathing. Inhale. Hold. Exhale. Repeat, more slowly. When we've climbed down the bluff to reach the grassy fields, I stare straight ahead and plunge right in.

"I told you about being taken by the Terror Squad. They wanted info. I wouldn't give it. Not even my name. Being a 'domie,' as you called us, I had no surname at birth, and my genetic print wasn't put in the database. I was only fifteen, still too young for a mandatory i-scan. So I was totally off-grid. This. . . frustrated them."

I stop in the middle of the field. Reach down to pull a blade of tall grass. I put it in my mouth and chew. "I was tortured," I finally blurt out. "Waterboarded."

"Dios mío—"

"It's why I'm afraid of water."

"I'm so sorry, Laek. I—"

"I'm not done."

The field ends. We've reached the road. I step onto it, Philip hovering beside me. About two hundred metres ahead of us is a couple holding hands. One points to the sky, the other lifts their head. "I was also raped," I say, continuing to watch them.

I don't want to look at Philip, but I think I need to. To see how this is landing. I shift my eyes to him. To his credit, he doesn't look away. And his expression is far enough from pity or horror or some other emotion I don't want to see that I let out an internal sigh. He takes a step towards me, uncertain. I hold up my hand.

"There's more. Later, after I was released, I. . . I think I killed someone. Doing an action with Al. And I tried to kill myself. Twice. Most recently, not long before we left New York."

"When I visited you in the hospital—" he begins, voice tight with suppressed emotion.

"No. It happened before you came to see me. Before. . . the kiss. The attempt at the hospital was. . . more passive than active. Still, I came close enough that it frightened Janie badly. I hope to live long enough to make it up to her."

"Oh, Laek," he says, and this time his eyes tear up.

A wave of nausea hits me. I retreat from the road, back onto the field. Stumble towards a patch of high grass. My stomach spasms. I retch, dropping to my knees. Nothing comes out. A second spasm and I wrap my arms around my chest. A combination of acid, the remains of my seaweed ice cream and what feels like all my long-withheld memories spewing out of me.

I come back to my body in the present. Philip's rubbing my back. Kneeling behind me in the grass. I'm a little alarmed I didn't hear him climb down the road after me.

"Easy does it," he says when I try to get up. "Just breathe."

I take his advice. When I'm pretty sure I'm done retching, I shake him off and stand, the ghost of his fingers warm against my back. We return to the road together.

"The intersection with main street isn't far from here," I tell Philip.

"Are you okay?" he asks me.

"I will be."

When we reach the intersection, we turn left. The road widens, a broad shoulder on either side filled with tall weeds: their yellow flowers like tiny heads, leaf arms lifted to the sun, stem bodies bending in the wind. After a few more minutes of walking, we come to the outskirts of town and the edge of the polymer tide barrier. Beside it is a flat sign that flashes in warning: "Attention aux grandes marées !" And in a smaller font, "Beware of high tides!" Above is a moving holo image: a stick figure standing still as a wavy, cartoonish waterline rises from the ground to above its head before receding again. I almost laugh, but a secret still weighs me down.

"There's something else I have to tell you, Phil. It's about the bombing."

This time Philip stops in his tracks. I stop with him. Train my eyes on the still far-off buildings in the centre of town.

Imagine them exploding, pieces of wood and chunks of stone flying through the air and striking the polymer barrier.

"I think you might have been its intended victim," I say.

He shakes his head. "That. . . makes no sense. I'm nobody. Not even a real activist."

"But there's something you haven't told me, isn't there? Something related to Al."

Philip stands in the middle of the road, blinking rapidly. I stand beside him. After a moment, he nods. "Yeah, I have things to tell you too. But first, eat this. You'll feel better."

He digs into his side pocket and hands me a small lozenge. It's sticky, the waxy covering half melted into it. I pop it into my mouth. As the covering dissolves on my tongue, the first taste I get is of salt. No surprise. It was in his pocket. While we almost drowned in the sea. The saltiness soon gives way to its true flavour—a cross between a peppermint and a jalapeño pepper. My mouth feels like it's on fire. On an instinct, I bite into it. I'm rewarded with a rich, delicious sweetness that covers my tongue and slips down my throat.

CHAPTER 24
PHILIP

Each of Laek's disclosures is like a blow, the emotional equivalent of a crowbar to the stomach. How should I respond? I need to not screw up, especially after I begged him to tell me his secrets. What I'd like to do is take him in my arms, comfort the scared kid that's still inside him, hurting and alone, but I'm not sure initiating physical contact after he told me he was raped is the best idea. I can't believe he joked about date rape. But that's just his way, one of many strategies he seems to have developed to distance himself from his trauma and pain.

Maybe my reaction's alright because Laek moves close to me on the wide road. I could put my arm around his shoulder. He usually likes that. Instead, I find one of my grandfather's jalapeño mints in my pocket. When I was a kid, everything could be solved with one. Hungry? Jalapeño mint. Stomach ache? Jalapeño mint. Heartache? Have another one.

Laek puts the mint in his mouth without even asking me what it is. His unquestioning trust in me makes something inside my chest constrict and then loosen. I watch his lips pucker, then his eyes water as his mouth opens slightly. Finally, he bites down like the fighter he is and the smile of pleasure that slowly spreads across his face warms me low in the stomach and makes me want to hold him again, though for a different reason this time.

When Laek finishes the mint, he asks me what they are and if I have any more. When I tell him the last of my late grandfather's "legacy" are back in my apartment in Queens, he pats my back, like I'm the one who needs comforting. I put my arm around him. He rests his head on my shoulder for a moment before saying, "Tell me what you've been keeping from me, Phil." So I do, ashamed I've held back this long and for reasons far more trivial than his own.

"I did something foolish. Something you warned me against," I begin. "When we made that plan to get Siri back across the border into Québec, you told me to follow Al's direction but not to trust him, but the truth is, Al did everything he promised. Plus, he was. . . decent to me. He told me I'd done well, that I was good under pressure, calm and competent. I think I let that go to my head. Coming from an obviously powerful man like him—I mean, I told you I thought Al was scary, but he's also the kind of person you want to impress. Do you know what I mean?"

Laek nods grimly.

"Anyway, I didn't worry about it. I had no way to contact him again even if I'd wanted to, but I think my reaction to. . . to his praise affected some decisions I made about a year and a half later." He turns to me. "You remember the legislation nicknamed 'Teacher With a Gun 2?'"

"Sure," Laek responds with a shrug. "But our school was exempt."

"It had been," I tell him. "Not so much because we're an

alternative school, but because of our size. But if you add in the elementary and middle schools. . ."

"But they're separate schools!" Laek argues. "With their own names and budgets."

"Yeah, but everyone knows they're feeder schools for the high school program. Most of those kids end up at our school when they're old enough."

Laek pulls me further onto the shoulder of the road as a group of about a dozen cyclists ranging in age from young kids to seniors zip past us. They're all wearing orange reflective vests with the name "Mouvement syndical pour l'espoir" written in glow-paint. Laek raises his arm in greeting before nodding for me to continue.

"Anyway, last September, we lost our gun exemption. Of course, no one at our school wanted to be the teacher with the gun, so I stepped forward. I didn't think I'd have to go through with it. I thought I might fail the screening, or the legislation would change.

"Well, the legislation stayed, even when a new democratic governor was elected, and I didn't fail. It turns out I have a knack for marksmanship. Not only did I pass all the tests, I. . . I did exceptionally well."

I can't read Laek's face so I'm not sure how he, a pacifist, feels about the fact that I'm good with guns. I'm not sure how I feel either. Ashamed? Proud? Maybe ashamed to be proud.

"During the aptitude tests and training, they used mostly virtual simulations. I did well. I guess all the screen games I played as a kid provided transferable skills. I passed the psych screening too. They decided I was mentally healthy enough to carry a gun at school, to be in charge of defense before the police arrived.

"A week or two later, they told me they had other tests they wanted me to take. They claimed it was advanced training. I didn't know for what. Maybe they wanted to give me two guns, who the hell knows? I did as I was asked—in for a credit, in for two—but this time they used haptics, very deep haptics, and they injected me with something to enhance the reality of the experience. I'd done holo games with deep haptics before and knew what it was like to slip into a simulation. I'm susceptible enough to enjoy sims, really lose myself in them, but this time it was a nightmare.

"In the sim, I was at a school, with a similar layout to our school, in charge of a classroom of kids. There was a shooter. I somehow knew the cops wouldn't arrive until it was too late; I had to take care of the problem.

"I took my gun and prowled the halls. There was screaming, shouting, sounds that could have been gunfire. I knew the shooter could be anywhere. I know now that this scenario doesn't hold together, but it felt very real within the sim.

"I found the shooter. He was in a locked classroom with a bunch of kids at his mercy. I shot him through the glass vestibule of the door. The sim showed me his face. He was very young, much younger than I'd imagined. There was a hole in the middle of his forehead where I'd shot him, blood and glass everywhere. The sim ended. I passed the test."

I'm silent for a moment. We've arrived at the first of the shops and food joints at the edge of downtown, but everything's closed and the streets are quiet, like it's siesta time. The loudest noise is the squish of my waterlogged sneakers as we walk along the road. There are bits of sea glass embedded in the glassphalt and the sun's too-bright reflection off of those shiny parts is making my eyes water. I stop walking.

Laek puts his hands on both of my shoulders, forcing me to face him. "Hey," he says, "You know it wasn't real. You didn't kill anyone." I try to pull away, but my effort is only half-hearted. "It wasn't real," he repeats, holding me in place.

"I know what a simulation is and I know I didn't really kill a child. But what happened was real in the sense that it showed me what I'm capable of. And the worst thing is that I still believe that violence is sometimes the appropriate response. I can't be like you."

"Phil—"

I pull away from him, my emotions swirling. "Mira, it was. . . so hard when you left. I was glad you were in a safer place, but I was also angry that you weren't with me when I needed you. Why did you kiss me the night before you left us all for good? Why would you do that?"

"Why were you so hell-bent on confessing how you felt about me?" he counters calmly.

"Justo. Yeah, that's fair," I say.

"Phil, tell me the rest of what happened. Please."

"Alright." We start walking again. "After the sim where I found out I could kill a child, I was feeling pretty low. I thought about you a lot, about how I couldn't protect you from the cops; I thought about how I can't truly protect our students either. I felt. . . useless. I wanted to try to do something that would make a difference, so when a short time later, Al contacted me again—"

"Fuck," Laek says.

"I know. I should have listened to you." I steal a glance at him, trying to read his expression, worried that he's angry with me. As is often the case, I can't tell.

"What did he make you do?" Laek's voice is gentle, so I relax a little.

"Maybe nothing. Maybe something awful. I don't even know, that's the strange part. He had me do these practicums—that's what he called them. Single-shooter games, some fiendishly complicated, with different layers of reality."

"Did he tell you what they were for?"

"No, but he talked to me about air mines, the ones they've been putting up at unpatrolled borders. And how the president refused to sign the international treaty banning air and space mines even though they kill more civilians than land mines. He also mentioned how hard they are to disarm, that detonating them with drones seems to be the only thing that works, though they're extremely difficult to hit. He led me to believe that these practicums had something to do with that."

Laek's face is carefully blank, but I know he thinks I'm naive.

"My targets were shapes, objects, never people," I say, more to myself than to him. "I was reassured by that, even when I started to get the feeling that maybe these weren't just sims. There's this old sci-fi novel where a kid is tricked into exterminating a supposed enemy race but thinks he's just playing a game. Did you ever read it?"

"No."

"Anyway, one day, after one of Al's practicums, I saw on the news that while I'd been playing, three buildings had been levelled by drones in different parts of the world—factories, supposedly, all empty at the time. There's that, anyway."

I wait to see if Laek will ask me questions, like when and where these explosions happened, but he doesn't. He's neither smiling nor frowning, and his dark grey eyes seem to be looking inward, like he's calculating something. I wonder if he realizes that one of the three buildings that exploded is actually nearby, in Gaspé. He probably read about it when it happened and is working out the timing.

I look around, trying to imagine what that explosion was like and whether it was similar to the airport bombing. Here, even in the centre of Percé, the buildings—mostly white clap-board—seem flimsy to me. A bomb would flatten them. Of course, Gaspé's a much bigger city, the buildings more solid. I decide I want to see it for myself, see where that building was. For now, though, I just keep going with my story.

"I spent a lot of time trying to decide what was really going on, if Al was tricking me or using me or. . . or just testing me. Maybe he was being completely honest about everything. I couldn't figure it out, and in the end, I decided it didn't matter."

"What do you mean? Of course it matters! If he tricked you. . . made you do something you didn't want to do. . ." Laek is agitated, eyes wide, gesticulating—far from his usual calm, cool self. Rather than being concerned by this, I'm reassured. He's upset and unsure and he's showing me that with both his body and his words instead of keeping it bottled up. I smile, grateful to be able to share my own certainty about the conclu-sion I've reached.

"It doesn't matter, Laek, because either way, I don't trust him. So I refused to continue working with him. He was angry and tried to convince me I was wrong in my suspicions, but right or wrong, why have anything to do with someone you can't trust?"

He opens his mouth as though to reply, then closes it. I watch the tension in his body slowly leak away. He blinks, then nods. "That's very wise," he says.

"Are you angry?" I ask.

"Well, you have been holding out on me."

"I'm sorry," I say, a little crestfallen. "I should have told you about all this sooner."

"I'm talking about your grandfather's mints," Laek says. "All these years, you could have been sharing them with me!"

Laek's face is full of mischief, and it lifts a heavy weight from my heart.

"I wasn't sure you'd like them," I confess after a moment. "It's an acquired taste."

"Of course I like them! C'mon," he says, tugging at my hand. He points up the street with his chin. "We're almost there. Time to get these wet clothes off."

CHAPTER 25
LAEK AND PHILIP

LAEK

The friendly, middle-aged woman who worked the front desk this morning is gone. She's been replaced by a younger man whose tag says, "Paden, il/he" and identifies him as the manager. I ask if the room with the king-sized bed is ready yet.

"That room is unavailable," he says. "There is a room with a double bed for you and Madame. We can put in a cot for. . . the other Monsieur in the children's room."

The other monsieur. I replay his tone in my head, wondering if I'm being oversensitive. I prefer to give people the benefit of the doubt, so I try again.

"Are you sure?" I ask, explaining we'd been told that there'd been a mix-up and we could have the room with the king-sized bed later today.

"I am certain," he says without consulting his screen. "It was rented earlier today to a nice couple. I hope you understand—"

"I don't understand," I tell him, suddenly furious. "A

mistake was made on your end. We were promised it'd be corrected. We were out all day. So the previous guests could check out and you could prepare the room. Then you give it to someone else?"

"Laek," Philip says. "It's okay."

"It's not okay. It's really not." My breath is coming hard and fast as every slight, every hurt, every petty injustice I've swallowed turns into angry words climbing out of my mouth. I think of Philip a couple of months from now back in the U.A., alone, possibly in danger, and my hands tighten into fists.

"Do you see this man beside me?" I say. "Do you see how tall he is, how broad? Do you think he'll be comfortable in a double bed with me, and then when Madame is back, with her as well? Do you think that double bed will be comfortable for the three of us?"

The rims of the manager's ears have turned red but he doesn't reply.

"Veuillez nous excuser," Philip says. "We've had a rough day." He grabs my arm, dragging me towards the stairs to our room. Before starting to mount them, he turns back to the manager and adds, "But if you could do something about getting us the room we actually reserved, the one with the big bed, it would be much appreciated."

Halfway up the first flight of stairs, I think of the manager's pink ears and start giggling. By the time the two of us stumble into our room, we're holding each other up, hysterical laughter shaking our bodies. After a minute, Philip subsides, but I can't seem to stop. Though I'm not sure what's so funny. I force myself to quiet. Then imagine Janie coming back and finding out they've rented our room to a "nice couple" and picture what she might say and do to the manager. My hysteria starts all over again.

I go to brush my teeth. Scrub them hard, my tongue too.

Rid my mouth of the taste of vomit. Though the jalapeño mint has mostly done the job.

I look at my reflection closely. Reassure myself that it's a reflection of me. Not mirror me. But I knew that already. Mirror me never hurts this much. But I'm okay with the pain right now. As long as I can feel some pleasure too.

My shirt is pretty much dry but my shorts are still damp at the seams. I take them off and the shirt too and hang them over the shower. I check my reflection again, pure vanity this time. The small hoop in my right ear and the three studs in my left gleam like polished glass. Like the sea has washed them clean.

When I exit the bathroom, Philip says, "We still have almost two hours to ourselves. What would you like to do?"

"What would you like to do?" I counter.

Philip, seated on the wooden chair near the bed, looks up at me, then down at his lap, awkward as a teenager. I decide he does awkward well.

"Do you remember the day I arrived in Montréal?" he asks.

"Kinda hard to forget," I reply.

"I mean later when I got mad and said I hadn't come all the way to Montréal just to. . . to have sex with you."

"Wasn't exactly what you said, but yeah, I remember."

"Well, I lied. I mean, it wasn't the only reason I came but, well, I'd hoped to."

"And now you're ready? You sure three and a half months of foreplay is enough?"

"More like three and a half years in my case, but yeah, I'm ready. If you are, I mean. You've dealt with some. . . bad memories today. I'd understand if you'd rather not—"

I lean over and kiss him to shut him up. Then I straddle him, sliding down into his lap and moving in slow, languid circles there, my tongue in his mouth. His heat, his hardness are palpable through his wet jeans.

"Dios, Laek," he gasps, pulling away from the kiss, but gripping my hips.

I press against him and he wraps his strong arms around me—tight, tighter—bringing me to stillness, and every last bit of tension drains from my body. Philip takes my face in his hands. His thumbs stroke my cheeks. I lean in and brush his lips with my tongue, a feather stroke.

"Yeah, I want you," I say. There's an ease, and effortlessness to my breath as it moves from lungs to throat, from my mouth to his. "Now. And in my life. In our lives. And if that's what you want too, I will walk through fire and water to make it happen."

Philip traces my cheek then my lips with his finger. He smiles, his eyes navigating from tender to playful in one leap.

"You've already walked through water," he says. "I guess that leaves fire."

He stands, lifting me up with him, and pushes me down onto the bed.

PHILIP

I hold Laek close as he dozes. I'm already replaying different moments of our love-making in my mind, storing them in memory against future need, the way a hungry man might hoard food. Laek stirs and I roll onto my back. He climbs on top of me, letting his head rest on my chest. "Mmm, that was nice," he says.

"Yeah? It was. . . it was okay?"

"Perfect," he says.

"Good, good." I wonder if we have time for some more

fooling around before Janie returns—though on second thought, I'd like it if she were here too.

"Hmm. . ." Laek says, his voice soft and lazy.

"What?" I ask, planting a kiss behind his ear.

"Nah, never mind." He snuggles his face into the space between my shoulder and throat.

"What? Tell me what you're thinking," I insist.

He lifts his head. "Okay, but don't take this the wrong way. I was thinking about Janie."

"Oh," I say, relieved. "That's fine, I was thinking about her too."

There's a quick series of knocks on the door, a familiar musical rhythm.

"Come!" Laek calls out, a huge grin on his face.

CHAPTER 26
JANIE, LAEK, PHILIP

JANIE

I walk into our hotel room and take in the scene.

"Oh, thank God," I say. "You finally had sex. But where's our king-sized bed?"

For some reason, Laek and Philip dissolve into hysterical laughter. After the laughter dies down, Laek winks at me, pats the bed beside him, and says, "Care to join us anyway?"

Philip smiles shyly at me, but Laek's candid gaze holds enough sensual heat that I feel myself getting wet. I check the time and see that the kids probably won't be back from their hike for at least forty-five minutes. Not as long as I'd like but I'm not passing this opportunity up. I quickly undress.

LAEK

When, in the middle of everything, Philip nearly falls off the bed, I can't stop myself from erupting into laughter again. I catch hold of him before he hits the floor, but between his weight, the awkward angle, my aching ribs, and the fact that I can't stop laughing, I'm having trouble hauling him up. I don't think I've ever laughed this much in one day, and given the kind of day it's been, I'm not sure that's healthy. But it feels so fucking good.

"Are you going to pull me up or let me fall? The suspense is killing me," Philip says, the perfect straight man in a comedy routine. Janie leans over, wraps her arms around his middle, and helps me pull him back onto the bed with us.

"This bed is too small," Philip states.

"Who are you, Goldilocks?" she says to Philip. "And you," she adds, giving me a severe look. "If you start laughing again, I swear I'm going to stuff a sock in your mouth. Seriously, it's not even funny. I'm considering filing a complaint. It's discrimination against—"

"Tall people?" Philip quips.

"No, throuples," Janie responds.

"Hmm," I murmur as an idea starts to coalesce in my mind. I think about my near mental breakdown at the thought of Janie moving out and the whole painful conversation about who, strategically, should claim a spousal relationship with Philip for immigration purposes. And now, here's Philip falling out of our too-small bed and needing both of us to pull him up. A feeling of clarity hits me so hard it's like I'm experiencing one of Janie's magical signs.

"You're brilliant," I say to her. "We can make a challenge under the Charter. Pierre-Ryan could represent us again."

"Sue the hotel?" Philip asks.

"No," Janie says, in sync with my thoughts. "Sue the government. For discrimination if they won't let us sponsor you—together—for permanent residency. It's an infringement of our rights under the Charte des droits et libertés de la personne. There's all kinds of things we could argue: the right to respect of our private life; the right to be free of discrimination based on sexuality; our entitlement to equality in regard to marriage and civil status. There's already some precedent in family law, but other areas of the law, like immigration, are lagging behind. But we have a good case. We should do this!"

"What do you think, Phil?" I ask.

"I don't know," he says, voice uncertain. "Anyway, Siri and Simon are going to be back any minute. We should shower and change."

Philip needs to get used to new ideas, so I don't let his lack of enthusiasm deflate me. I turn to Janie. She motions with her chin towards the bathroom.

"Okay, I'll take the first shower," I say.

JANIE

Philip watches Laek disappear into the bathroom with a look of naked longing. His face is so easy to read—it's one of the things I love about him. What I don't know is whether the longing he's feeling has to do with the fact that we finally have a hopeful approach for getting him permanent residency or if it's just plain lust.

I'm pretty sure I know what's worrying him, though—Kyla. The last time I raised the idea that he could sue for primary custody, he shut me down, saying he wouldn't do that to Dana. It makes me so angry because he's a hundred times the parent she is. Her main interest in her daughter seems to be to use her as a weapon against Philip.

I decide to approach the question of Kyla's custody through an indirect route.

"I'm thinking about when you and I first made love," I tell him. "I remember how you made sure to mention that you were using contraception. I really appreciated that."

"I've been on the patch since. . . well, since Dana threw me out. I wouldn't want to risk you—or anyone—having an unplanned pregnancy."

"Yeah, the one adult/one child laws have made unplanned pregnancies even more consequential. Hey, if you could have any number of kids, how many would you have?" I ask.

"Kyla is all I need," he responds, a tender smile on his face.

"But what if there were no legal or ethical constraints against having lots of kids? Like if we lived in some kind of utopian world we hadn't overpopulated, polluted, and used up?"

"I guess I'd have a whole bunch of them, in that case." He smiles a goofy smile.

"And your ex? What do you think she would do?" I ask.

"She's not that into kids. Though of course she was thrilled when Kyla was born," he quickly adds.

I must be radiating the skepticism I'm feeling because Philip sits up and swings his legs over the side of the bed, frowning. Loyalty can be a good quality, but I can't help thinking it's wasted on his ex. Plus, in all fairness, she has every right not to be into kids. I get out of bed and find my bag, unzip it, and start going through my clothes. I look up to see Philip watching me, so continue where I left off.

"How about Dana's new partner, would he want to have another kid if he could?"

"What are you getting at?" Philip asks, sounding frustrated.

"Well, they can't have another kid together. Because they already have Kyla and Kyla's stepbrother. Do you think that bothers him? Raising another man's child instead of being allowed to have a second of his own?"

"It wouldn't bother me."

"Of course it wouldn't bother you. You're already like a

second dad to Simon and Siri. Phil, you're an amazing parent and a good person, and I know you want to do the right thing here, especially for Kyla. What if there's a way to make everyone relatively happy?"

"I'm listening," he says, turning to me.

"If we were to have primary custody of Kyla, Dana and her new partner could have another baby if they wanted. And we could sweeten the pot. In Québec, they offer generous child assistance benefits to families. We could offer it to them."

"Dana might see that as bribery and be pissed off."

"I know Dana. If we offer her a small percentage while letting her know the full amount, she'll act insulted, demanding the whole thing for such a sacrifice."

"Maybe," he allows. "But then what would we do?"

"Well, obviously, we give her the whole thing."

Phil pulls at his earlobe. "Well, one thing's for sure, twice-a-week vid calls with my daughter are not enough for me. But I'm worried about rocking the boat."

"Listen, just think about it, okay? I don't want to push—"

My wristpad blips. There's a message from the kids. I scan it. "It's from Simon," I tell Philip. "Something happened when they were hiking down the mountain."

PHILIP

I jump to my feet, heart pounding.

"Where are they? Are they hurt? Were they walking by the shoreline?"

Janie crosses the room and puts her hand on my arm. "They're absolutely fine. They just took an alternate route and ended up somewhere different than expected—a couple of kilometres further away from town. Are you okay?"

"What do you mean?"

"You look like you're having an anxiety attack. I've seen that—it runs in my family. And why are you talking about them walking by the shoreline? They were on the mountain. Even with my shitty sense of direction, I know that Mont Ste-Anne isn't right by the water."

"I'm... I'm not having an anxiety attack," I tell Janie.

By now, my heart has slowed down and the images in my head of Siri and Simon being carried off by the tide have been replaced by them walking down a peaceful mountain trail. For some reason, these images have them hand-in-hand with Kyla, all three of them with angelic expressions on their faces. I simultaneously realize two things. The first is that with all the horsing around and... fooling around, we never told Janie what happened to us today. The second thing I realize is that I don't want to leave Simon and Siri either.

Laek comes out of the shower, unselfconsciously naked, wet, and beautiful.

"Are the kids back yet?" he asks.

"No," Janie answers, "But they're fine."

"Great," Laek says. The tiny wrinkle on his forehead smooths as his brows relax.

"I'm telling them to meet us at the restaurant," Janie says, busy with her wristpad.

"Where are we going?" Laek asks. "Should I dress up?"

"It says 'sophisticated yet family-friendly.' Maybe wear the new turquoise tunic."

"What's the restaurant called?" I ask Janie.

"Le rivage noyé," she says.

"Is that... the Drowned Shore?" I ask. "The restaurant's called The Drowned Shore?"

Laek already has his arms wrapped around his ribs, laughing and hiccuping at the same time, maybe crying too. It's hard to tell. Janie turns to Laek, scowling.

"Sorry, sorry," he says. He grabs a pair of socks from his bag and makes as though to stuff them into his own mouth.

Janie folds her arms and says, "I got the next shower and when I'm out, the two of you will tell me what is so very funny or I will find a blunt instrument and—"

"Don't worry, Janie, we'll tell you everything, I promise. I should warn you, though," I say, my tone sober. "Not all of it— or actually any of it—is funny."

Janie nods, and I have the feeling she already senses this. She's watching Laek, radiating a mixture of fierce love and tender concern. Laek, who's already put on the turquoise shirt Janie told him to wear, has his back to us, and though he can probably feel the weight of her gaze, he doesn't turn. Instead, he carefully folds the clothes from our earlier adventures, as though this is absorbing all of his attention.

"One more thing, Janie," I say. "Yes. Please talk to Pierre-Ryan about your idea—the custody part of it too. I don't need more time to think about it. I know what I want."

CHAPTER 27
SIMON, PHILIP, SIRI

SIMON

Siri and I sit together on a double seat in the mini e-bus for our day trip to Gaspé. Uncle Philip sits across from us. The air inside the bus is cool and smells like tangerines, which is a coincidence because the bus is painted orange. The other passengers are either senior citizens or teenagers who are probably too young to drive. I'm not sure I'll ever get a driver's license. I'd rather bike or ride a tangerine bus.

Siri's still being grumpy so I talk with Uncle Philip. "Too bad Mommy and Daddy couldn't come with us to Île Bonaventure this morning," I say. "I got some footage of the Northern Gannets, though. I can show them tonight, when we get back to Percé."

"I'm sure they'll appreciate that," Uncle Philip says smiling.

"Why do we have to get a new hotel?" I ask. "I liked where we were staying,"

Uncle Philip shifts on his seat like he's not comfortable, even though he has the whole seat to himself. When I'm done growing, I'll probably be as tall as he is but I don't think I'll be as bulky. My muscles will probably be more like Daddy's—strong, but ropey instead of thick.

"It. . . wasn't suited to our needs," Uncle Philip says.

Siri looks up from her wristpad and says, "The bed was too small."

"You could have stayed in our room, Uncle Philip. They gave us three beds."

Siri rolls her eyes at me, like she can't believe how stupid I am.

"I guess you'd prefer to sleep with. . ." I'm about to say "Daddy and Mommy" but change it to "Laek and Janie," which sounds more mature. It's not that I don't realize they probably want to have sex, but they don't have to do it all the time, do they?

"I love hanging out with the two of you," Uncle Philip says. "But yeah, I do like being with your parents, spending. . . adult time with them. About that. . ."

Siri lifts her head up, which tells me I should pay attention too, but Uncle Philip's looking at his hands even though Daddy says you should make eye contact when you're talking to someone, especially if it's important. Just as I'm thinking this, he looks over at us again.

"Um, well, how would you feel if. . . I mean, you know I really love your dad and your mom, and I love the two of you like crazy, like you were my own kids, so we were thinking that I could try to get permission to stay here in Montréal so we could be a family together."

"What about Kyla?" I ask.

"Kyla too, of course. If I were granted permanent residency, I could send for her."

"That would be hyper," I tell him. "I've always wanted a little sister. And having two dads would be great!"

Uncle Philip turns to Siri who shrugs and says, "With Laek as my father, my family couldn't possibly get any weirder."

"That's not exactly the response I'd hoped for." Uncle Philip's voice sounds different—not angry exactly but not in that soft way he usually speaks to us.

"It's not about you!" Siri says, looking at him with wide eyes. "I'd love to have you as my dad. You're great, Uncle Philip. At least you don't keep deep, dark secrets and spy on me and my comrades."

"Laek is a better man than I'll ever be, the finest person I know except for your mom. I will not hear you speak disrespectfully about him." And now he does sound angry.

Siri looks like how I feel when Mommy yells at me, but Uncle Philip didn't yell. He spoke calmly and quietly like he always does. I don't know if I've ever seen him angry before, but maybe he was and I just didn't realize it. I wish I could guess other people's feelings better. Like Aiza's. If I knew she'd be so upset when I didn't want to kiss, I might have reacted differently. Though I know you shouldn't let someone kiss you or anything without consent or just to make them happy. But it's confusing because Aiza being unhappy makes me unhappy too.

"Can I ask you something, Uncle Philip?"

"Of course, mijo. Anything."

"You were Daddy's best friend—"

"I still am."

"Okay, but why. . ." I begin, not sure how to put this exactly. Sometimes when I feel upset or confused about something, it's like the words get too big for my throat. I swallow. "Why isn't that enough? I mean, why do you also need to. . ." I swallow again, but it doesn't help.

"I think I know what you're asking. I'll try to explain." He pulls on his ear then puts his hand in his pocket instead.

"There are a lot of ways of loving someone. In the case of your dad, my body wants to show my love for him too. Maybe you'll understand better someday, when you're older."

"I'm not a baby! I'm almost thirteen!" I say, gripping my seat hard. "Lots of the kids in my class are into sex; they talk about it all the time! Even Aiza." I realize I'm talking too loud and people on the bus are looking at me, so I shut up.

"Simon," Siri says. "Did something happen between you and Aiza?"

I shake my head, not because she's wrong but because I can't talk about it. I look out the window instead. We pass white houses with sloped metallic roofs that are brown or black or sometimes red. The houses are spaced apart now that we're outside the centre of town. It's weird to think of living somewhere without your friends and neighbours right next to you. At night, it makes me feel happy and safe to think of Aiza sleeping just three floors below me, but lately, it's like I live on the Moon and she lives on Earth.

"You know you can tell me anything, Simon," Siri says, switching from French to English. "And Uncle Philip too," she adds, though she doesn't look at him. Her full attention is on me, and it's a good kind of attention, like she wants to help and protect me—like when I was younger and she gave me advice when I was getting bullied.

"Aiza kissed me," I say. "I wasn't expecting it and. . . I didn't like it."

"What did you do?" Siri asks in a calm, normal voice.

"I didn't do anything, but she could tell I wasn't into it. She asked me if I was gay."

"It's okay if you are—" Uncle Philip says.

"I know!" I say. "Why is everyone always telling me that!"

"I get how you feel," Siri says. "Some people think I must be a lesbian because I like sports. People can be really stupid. I'm sure you know it's fine to be whatever you are."

"Yeah," I say. "Only. . ." I glance up at Uncle Philip. He smiles but his eyebrows are smushed together like he's worried. I turn back to Siri. "Only I'm not sure what that is."

"Well, do you have a preference between boys and girls? Or enbies?"

"No. I like them all. But don't want to. . . kiss or have sex with any of them."

Siri almost smiles, then nods. "Okay, so you could be asexual. Ace."

"You don't think it's because I'm immature?" My body feels all tight inside, waiting to hear what she's going to say.

"No, of course not! You've always been yourself. Not immature, just. . . Simon."

I loosen up part way, but I want to be sure. "I still don't know what to think about me and Aiza. I love her. Like. . . like the way I thought Uncle Philip loved Daddy."

"You love Aiza as a friend, a best friend, right?" Siri says.

"Yeah, but also. . . she stands out from everyone. I want to be with her, to watch her, to know what she thinks. It's like there are invisible particles coming out of our brains and hearts that are attracted to each other like magnets and that mix together in the air between us."

This time Siri smiles a big smile. "You know exactly how you feel, Simon. Don't let anyone tell you differently. To me, it sounds like you're asexual but alloromantic. You know what all that means, right?" She lifts her eyebrows.

"Sure. We learned this stuff in school. But it's not the same, hearing definitions and figuring out what the words. . . really feel like. And also, they don't teach us why. Why am I like this? Why can't I be like you and Uncle Philip and Mommy and Daddy? Why do I have to always be weird and different!"

That tight feeling is back, only now, it's not because the words seem too big for my throat but because my emotions do.

"Don't say that, mijo!" Uncle Philip reaches out to me but then lets his arm drop, like all of a sudden he's afraid of touching me without permission. That makes me feel even worse.

"Anyhow, it's not true," Siri says. "Everyone in our family is different. Daddy is pansexual and polyamorous. Mommy only likes sex with guys but is also poly. And Philip's. . ." She turns to him.

"Bisexual," he says, peering around the bus. No one's paying attention to us now, though.

"And then there's me," Siri continues. "I'm not pan or bi like Daddy or Philip, and not poly like Mommy. I can't imagine being in a romantic or sexual relationship with more than one guy at a time. I would feel, I don't know, torn. One's enough for me."

"Hmm, I think I could love more than one person," I tell her. "But right now, I only love Aiza. And she probably hates me," I say, feeling my eyes burn.

"If she's a true friend, she'll accept you as you are," Uncle Philip says.

"Even if I can't give her what she wants?" I say back to him.

"Simon, don't worry," Siri says confidently. "Aiza's crazy about you. She just needs time to figure things out and get used to it. Then everything will be fine again."

"You really think so, Siri?" I ask hopefully.

"Of course! Right, Uncle Philip?"

"Right, mija," he answers.

I don't think I've ever heard him call Siri that before. For some reason, it makes me trust my sister even more.

PHILIP

It's a short walk from the bus stop to the Musée de Gaspé. Siri and Simon walk a few feet ahead of me and it's hard not to think of the distance between us as signifying something. I really screwed up, first by being too harsh with Siri and then by somehow saying all the wrong things to Simon.

We turn off the sidewalk to a winding path that leads to the museum. The path is paved with stones, smooth as marble. On the right side is a low wall. It's about the height of a bannister, decorated with fancy stonework that twirls in geometrically improbable ways.

"Look, Uncle Philip!" Simon points to the twirls. "They're like Möbius strips!"

Simon and Siri leave the path to enter the plaza that fronts the museum.

"Hey, slow down!" I say. Something about the plaza makes me uneasy. It's too open, and the building itself reminds me of a large high school with its square form and tall, glass windows. I start imagining a strategic plan for protecting the space against a shooter.

I blow air out my lips, trying to expel these paranoid thoughts. But then again, Gaspé is where one of the three buildings blown up by a drone was located. Maybe I can find an excuse to walk by the street where the building is—or its ruins.

The kids wait obediently for me by the door. I nod and they scan their wristpads before entering. The ground floor of the museum is also very open, the high ceiling crowned with an oval skylight. Staircases at the four corners lead to separate sections of the museum.

"I read that the museum is four museums in one," I tell them. "History; Architecture and Design; Music; and Hydrology. We're not going to have time to see all of it so let's pick two of the four. What part of the museum are you most interested in, Simon?"

"Architecture and design."

"How about you, Siri?" I ask.

"Music, but don't worry about me. I can go myself," she says.

"I'm not comfortable with that. We're in a strange city. I'd rather we stick together. Anyhow, I'm interested in music too. Let's start there, and then we'll go to the architecture and design museum. D'accord?"

"D'accord," they say in chorus.

I take off diagonally across the broad expanse of the lobby, its ocean teal and foam white-tiled floor like a watery chess board. I concentrate on not making a wrong move.

SIRI

I follow Uncle Philip and Simon from one exhibit booth to the next, not saying much. In the section on gourd instruments, Simon points to something labeled the "Eka-tantri Vina."

"That's from medieval India. It has only one string but two gourds," he reads. "Do you think there'll be faux fish and chips at the museum café?"

One good thing about having a little brother like Simon is not having to worry about awkward pauses in the conversation. Today this is fine since I'd rather not have to make an effort at small talk. I have too much to think about. Like whether and when to confront Daddy and make him tell me who the spy in my group is.

"Look, guitars! Mommy plays guitar. Though she prefers ukuleles," Simon comments.

"Siri, have you ever wanted to learn to play an instrument?" Uncle Philip asks me.

"What? No. I like music but don't have any musical talent, not like you and Mommy. And Simon," I add, trying not to sound jealous. "I can't even sing well. I must have inherited that from Daddy."

"I think you have a nice voice. As for your father, have you ever heard him sing?"

"No, never," I tell him, tired of this conversation. "That's exactly my point."

"Someone can have a reason for not singing that has nothing to do with the quality of their voice. For all we know, he could have a beautiful voice."

I shrug and walk faster. There's no use arguing with someone totally blinded by love.

We pass from the string instruments exhibit through to a long corridor that curves sharply into a U or C-shape. The title at the entranceway reads, "La voix, le premier instrument."

"Weren't drums the first instrument?" Simon asks.

"People were singing even before they were talking," Uncle Philip responds. "I guess the question is whether you consider voice to be an instrument at all."

The wall of the curving corridor is covered by throats and lips in different positions. It looks like they used interactive paint, so I reach out to touch one of the sets of lips. "Ooooo," the lips say in a high airy voice. I touch another set. A whistling sound comes out.

"Hyper!" Simon says. He touches one of the throats. "Arkkk." It sounds like a giant frog.

"This is actually kind of creepy," I say.

"I think it's to show that voice really is an instrument you can play, but. . ." Simon pauses, like he's stuck on a thought. "But what's on the wall isn't our own lips and throats. Can you be your own instrument? I mean, can you instrumentalize yourself?"

"I think you could," Philip says. "Or a part of yourself, at least."

Simon uses both of his hands to strum a set of lips and a throat simultaneously. "Mmmmaah," I hear, a long, extended note in the tenor range.

"I think I have heard Daddy sing," Simon says thoughtfully. "When I was little, he'd put me on a little seat in front of him on his bike and wrap one of his arms around me while he cycled. Sometimes, he'd hum. It wasn't a song, just different notes that sounded happy and sad at the same time—parts of major and minor chords, I guess, though I didn't know those words back then. But even the sad ones sounded happy to me."

Uncle Philip looks away. Were those tears in his eyes? I hope not. I move ahead quickly through the rest of the corridor, which curves all the way around the room before letting us out. I realize now what its shape is meant to be—an ear! One thing I'm not ashamed to have inherited from Daddy is his excellent sense of spatial orientation.

"This way out!" I say.

Simon

In the architecture and design museum, there's a whole room that's just of skylines! They have Manhattan's skyline, of course, with its famous dome that covers downtown, but they even have Brooklyn's. The big clocktower and the Brooklyn Bridge make me feel a little nostalgic.

I move through the room and see holo skylines of Kuala Lumpur, Sydney, Tokyo, Rio de Janeiro, Al-Aḥsā, Paris, Beijing, and Monrovia—which is near where Aiza's family came from.

If I took an image of it and sent it to Aiza, would this make her happy or sad?

"Hey, look at this!" I say to Uncle Philip and Siri. "They have a special exhibit booth on the architecture of Montréal."

Philip walks over, Siri trailing behind him. "How Rooftop Gardens are Changing the Shape of the City," he translates.

"Do you think our co-op will be there?" I ask Siri.

"I don't know. Maybe."

"Aiza and I. . . we were going to propose a new design for our rooftop garden, Uncle Philip. We had this great idea." I sigh and I feel like all of the air has leaked out of my body. "Maybe she'll want to find someone else to do it with."

Uncle Philip puts his hands on my shoulders. He doesn't ask me or hesitate and I'm relieved. It's like things are back to normal between us.

"I said some stupid things before, Simon. Like that Aiza would accept you if she were really your friend. I never meant for you to worry that she wasn't. And when I told you that you'd understand when you were older, I didn't mean that you were too immature now. I meant that we're always learning, no matter our age. Me too. I never would have believed that one day I'd end up in a relationship with my two best friends."

"Uncle Philip?" Siri says. "I'm going to go over there to the model of Gaspé. You and Simon can meet me when you're done talking."

"Uh, sure," he says, and turns back. "So, do you have any questions, Simon?"

"Yeah, just one. If you really think I'm mature, would it be okay if I went by myself to the exhibition on landscape design? I want to ping some images over to Aiza so that we can start planning our presentation to the co-op. I. . . I might even call her."

Uncle Philip opens his mouth then closes it. I can see that

one part of him wants to say yes but his worrying side wants to say no.

"Okay, mijo," he says finally. "But don't go into any other exhibition spaces after that. Siri and I will find you there."

Philip walks quickly over to Siri. I lift my hand to wave to her but she's staring down at the model of Gaspé like she's mesmerized. I didn't know Siri was so interested in urban design.

Siri

When Uncle Philip comes to stand next to me, I've already switched the exhibit to holo view and zoomed in on the area that caught my eye. I lean over to look more closely, and he leans in with me. There's a building that's like a mini version of the one at the border that Gabriel and I staked out. Same strange shape. Same inky black colour. Weirder, bits of it are blinking on and off, like a defective shielding device. And one of the walls reminds me of the one that was closest to the border on that other building; the four points in its corners are flickering, and a fifth blinking light seems to tug the wall into a new shape.

I drag my eyes away from the model to glance at Uncle Philip. He's looking as freaked out as I feel.

"Siri, what do you see? What are you looking at?" he breathes.

"That... that building in the model. The weird one."

"The one across the bay? Off route 198?" he asks.

"Yeah. Why does it look like its shape keeps changing? Do you know?"

He doesn't answer right away. Instead, he backs off a step, like he wants to see it from a different angle. After a moment, he comes back to stand beside me.

"There was an explosion in the building. I think they're showing it as it looks now. The blinking parts may be missing structural elements. Or maybe it shows how it's being rebuilt. Press the star to get more details."

I do what Uncle Philip suggests and see that he's right. It says the building was a factory; that there was an explosion last year and they're rebuilding it to be an artisans' workshop for refugees.

"Siri, why were you staring like that? You looked like you'd seen a fantasma, a ghost."

I don't think I should tell him, but he used the word "fantasma," like what that boy Hector said when I was invisible and trying to help him and his sister. Maybe my mother is right and there's no such thing as coincidence. Just signs the world shows you.

"Why did *you* look so freaked out by it?" I counter.

Philip remains silent for so long I'm afraid he's not going to answer. Then he says, slowly and deliberately, "Because I think I was the one who blew that building up."

Philip

Siri seems weirdly composed, despite what I just said, and a lot older than fifteen going on sixteen. After a moment, she asks, "Is there anything more you can tell me?"

Part of me doesn't want to tell her anything, regrets opening my big mouth to begin with. The other part wants to tell her everything. There's something about the way she asks her question—urgently yet calmly—that makes me believe not only that she can handle it, but that it's essential she know what happened. Wavering between full disclosure and clamming up, I decide to do something in between.

"There were two other buildings that were also blown up, in other parts of the world."

Siri nods, looking thoughtful, almost calculating.

"Do you. . . do you know that building?" I ask her.

As she stands beside me, still as a statue, gripping my right arm—a lefty like her dad—I realize just how much she reminds me of Laek. The next moment, though, she's fully Siri, a tough, smart teenager with her own mind.

"I know a building just like it, at the border," she says. "I saw it, Uncle Philip. Saw kids they've imprisoned there, kids even younger than me. We need to get them out. And then. . ."

"Yes?" I ask.

"And then we should blow that building up too."

CHAPTER 28

LAEK AND SIRI

LAEK

I watch from the entrance of our inn, Le sentier des Émeraudes, as my family leaves for their hike to the falls. Siri's lagging a few metres behind. She stops. Looks over her shoulder towards me. I withdraw into the doorway. She turns back to follow the others.

Slipping out the back door onto the patio, I look out at the garden. There are some daffodils still remaining, orange and purple tulips, blue phlox, giant hostas, wild cornflowers, and immature peonies whose buds look like little fists. To the west are lilacs, not yet in bloom. To the east, the land drops off towards a white shed.

The slap of her sandals on the stone-paved patio causes me to turn. When she doesn't speak, I say, "Le printemps est moins avancé icitte. But even back home," I continue, "the city doesn't smell of lilacs yet. I'm glad I won't miss that."

"Yes, I'm glad you're here now. Salut, Laek."

"Salut, Chloë," I answer, and walk towards her.

Chloë kisses both my cheeks before wrapping me in a hug. "I've missed you," she says.

"I've missed you too. All of us at the school have."

"Even Cloutier?"

"Fuck Cloutier," I answer. "Écoute, did he touch you?"

She hesitates a split second. "Did he touch you?"

"Not really. My arm. My shoulder. Repeatedly. I'm probably oversensitive."

"You're not oversensitive, Laek." She draws me towards a round, metal table worked with fleur-de-lis. I sit. "Let me bring you some iced tea. Or would you rather a beer?"

"I'm good."

"Tea, then."

She goes back inside, returning with a glass pitcher, wet with condensation, and two glasses. She fills both glasses with tea. I take a sip. It's cold and bracing with hints of peachy sunflower. I take a larger gulp.

"Merci bien," I say. "And thanks again for arranging with your aunt to let us stay here."

She takes a sip herself. "She's not my aunt exactly. Elle est la tante de ma blonde."

I nod. "I'm glad things are better between you and Charlotte."

"Getting out of Montréal helped. Charlie is more a country girl."

"But you're a city person. Will you come back? I'm sorry about how. . . intense I was. After Clara's death. My suspicions, the investigations. I know you were struggling too."

"That's not why I didn't come back. Things are good here for me. I'm near family. My girlfriend's happy. I'm doing art therapy with at-risk adolescents."

"At the immigrant workers' centre near Rocher Percé?"

"Ouais, but we may have access to a much larger space in Gaspé soon, in a building they're reconstructing."

I pause. "The building that was damaged in an explosion last year?" I lift my tea and swirl it around in the glass, watching as bits of leaves settle back to the bottom.

"Yes. How did you know?" She tilts her head at me, curiosity mixed with suspicion.

"Philip was in Gaspé with Siri and Simon and saw it on a holo-map."

"Oh." She seems satisfied by the explanation. "And how is your petite famille? Janie, the kids? How is Philip adapting?"

"They're all fine. And Philip—Janie's gonna bring a case for us to sponsor him."

"Oh, Laek, that's wonderful," she says, reaching across the table to take my hand. "Janie est une force de la nature. We all heard what she did for Andressa." Chloë lowers her voice. "I got to meet the girl. She came through here."

"Do you see a lot of kids in precarious situations here?" I keep my tone casual. Move my gaze from a white butterfly hovering near the cornflowers to Chloë's small, round face.

"More than you'd think. That employment program, Programme travail liberté—the one Cloutier and I argued about because I told him it seemed a bit louche? They were sending kids to the regions, though we didn't see many of them at the therapy centre after the first visit. Since the explosion, we're seeing less kids, but the ones we do see are at least coming in regularly."

I nod. "I found out some of the board members of Programme travail liberté have connections to Northern Heritage Guard. Not surprising, with their name. Close enough to *Arbeit macht frei* that you might as well call yourselves nazis and be done with it. Doesn't anyone study history?"

"It's good to have a history teacher among us," Chloë says affectionately.

I decide I like being thought of primarily as a history teacher. I knew talking to Chloë in person would do my heart good. "Cloutier's family may have holdings with the corp that's behind PTL." Before she can react, I continue smoothly: "Was Clara looking into all this?"

She hesitates. "I'm not sure. You know she could be a bit secretive about some of her. . . theories. At least until she had more solid proof."

I know very well because I'm the same way. It happens when you've been dismissed as paranoid or overly suspicious once too often.

"What are you thinking, Laek? Your face looked. . . blank, all of a sudden."

"Mostly about how I miss her. And you," I say, voice catching. "I'm sorry. I don't mean to make you feel bad. I'm glad you did what was needed for your own mental health."

"I know." She touches my cheek. "Maybe you should think about doing the same."

I shake my head. "As an immigrant, I'm lucky to have a job, doing work I love. And I can't give up on the kids. If that means working with Cloutier, I'll do it. If it means taking him down, I'll do that too."

"Bien compris. Like I said, I may have a lead on Clara's files."

"Yes?" I say, glad we've finally arrived at this part of the conversation.

"I need to show you. Come."

Chloë leads me down the hillside to the shed. Unlocks the door. I step inside with her. Her hand touches the wall and the room lights up to reveal a neatly organized storage area with five bicycles lined up on the right side, one of which is missing its pedals. She goes to the one furthest back, blocked by the others, and wheels it over to me.

I drop to my knees, grab hold of the frame and begin to sob.

SIRI

The way I find them is because I hear Daddy crying. I stand by the door of the white shed but don't know what to do. There's something about hearing your parent cry that's scary, like the world is broken in a way that not even they can fix.

I psych myself up, knock once on the door, then pull it open. Daddy's holding onto a bicycle with one hand and wiping his eyes with the other.

"Siri," he says sniffling. "What are you doing here? Is everything okay?"

"Yeah. I decided I didn't want to go to the falls after all.... Are *you* okay?"

"Just a little sad," he says without explaining.

"Salut, Chloë," I say, turning to Daddy's friend.

"Allô Siri. Ça va bien ? T'as tellement grandi, toi !"

I usually don't like it when people tell me I've grown, or worse yet, how beautiful I've become, but I don't mind with Chloë. Maybe it's because she seems so honestly enthusiastic.

"Whose bicycle is that?" I ask her.

"It was Clara's," she says quietly.

Daddy strokes its crossbar as though it were the back of a person needing comforting.

"Then why isn't it all messed up?" I ask, remembering she died in a bike accident.

Daddy's hand goes suddenly still. Chloë opens her mouth then glances at Daddy like she's waiting for some kind of sign. Daddy stays silent. Not only that, his face has no expression at all, so good-fucking-luck finding any answers there.

"Pourquoi il est en bon état?" I repeat when no one says anything. "T'sé, veux dire?"

"Oui," Chloë answers carefully, still looking at Daddy, who nods very slightly. She continues. "It's because it's not the bike she was riding when. . . when she died."

"How do you come to have it?" Daddy asks, all casual-like, but I don't believe it. Sometimes with Daddy, the less emotion in his voice, the more intense he's feeling.

"She gave it to me," Chloë responds. "A few days before the accident. She asked me to keep it safe, that it was full of. . . memories. Memories she wanted to. . . share with others."

"These memories," Daddy asks. "Was she able to share them with you?"

Chloë glances my way, then at Daddy again. The whole thing is frustrating as fuck.

"Écoute, if you want me to leave, just say so. Otherwise," I continue, "I know what you mean by 'memories.' If you found a chip or a mini-flash drive or a holo disquette, just say so. I'm not gonna issue a press release or talk to the fasho police."

For a second, I'm not sure of their reactions, but then Chloë laughs and pats my arm. Daddy doesn't laugh or smile but seems okay with what I said.

"I didn't find anything," Chloë says. "I checked the handle-bars, the seat post, the steering fork—if she hid something, I couldn't find it. I'd come to the conclusion that Clara simply meant that she wanted someone to have her bike and the memories that come with it. But after I talked to you last, I started wondering if I missed something. That's why I wanted you to come and see the bike. I thought that you might also like to keep it."

"I'll check it thoroughly, but you should keep it," Daddy argues. "Clara thought of the bicycle as a vehicle of women's empowerment. The two of us talked a lot about the historical relationship between cycling and feminism."

"It's too big for me—Clara was tall for her generation! And she loved you like a son. Plus, you shared a true passion for cycling."

"I could try to adjust its size for you," Daddy says. "I used to work at a bike shop."

"Even if you moved the seat and handlebars, the frame would still be too big. I have a better idea," Chloë says, looking at me. "Siri, would you like it? You're tall and I think a young woman like you inheriting her beloved *bicyclette* would make Clara very happy."

I turn to Daddy, wondering what to do. Should I say no because he wants Chloë to have it? Or would taking the bike make Daddy happy? As usual, I can't read him at all, and maybe it's time I stopped trying and instead asked myself what I want. It is a really good bike. On the other hand, I prefer my trottinette.

"You don't have to decide now," Daddy says. "You could try it first. Maybe you and I could go on a bike ride. Spend the afternoon together. Chloë could join us."

"I need to get a little work done today." Chloë says. "Besides, I'll be seeing you all for supper later. But feel free to use one of the bikes in the shed, Laek."

She steps forward and hugs Daddy before kissing both his cheeks. She kisses my cheeks too, then tells me to look after my dad, as though I was the adult and he was the child.

Laek

I let Siri take the lead. Watch her pedal confidently. As we bike, I point out things along the route. Siri doesn't say much. Of everyone in the family, Philip included, she plays it closest to the chest. I wish she'd talk to me about her reconnaissance at the border. Or other things. I know Philip mentioned our plans. She's always looked up to him. More than to me, I think. I hope the idea of trying to add him and Kyla to our family pleases her.

A car comes up behind us. Siri holds her ground. The driver speeds around us, reckless and fast. Sending dust and grit flying into our faces. Siri stands on her pedals and digs in even harder, working her anger out physically. Something I do too.

After a long, steady climb, we reach the lip of the rise. We're rewarded with an aerial view of the town of Percé. The blue steeple and bronze bell of the little church. The neat, white houses whose metallic roofs reflect the sunlight. Even the transparent polymer tide barrier adds to the scene with the surreal view it offers of the bay and Rocher Percé. I see Siri glance out at it before bending over her handlebars to race down the steep slope.

I race after her, thrilling in the speed. I can tell Siri feels the same. It's as though, for all our distance, a thin line connects us. Clara's bike is fast, as fast as my own at home, faster than the one I'm riding. It manoeuvres well too, taking the curves gracefully, hugging the pavement. Though I notice a subtle tendency to hitch to the left. I should check the alignment of the handlebars. Or maybe it's just that Siri isn't used to it.

A stone that must have found its way from the shoulder shoots out from beneath Siri's wheel. If that hadn't drawn my eye, I might have missed seeing her back wheel flatten and skid right, the front wheel jerking left. As she struggles to gain control of the bike, I call out, "Turn with the skid!" but it's too late. She's overcorrected and is heading straight for the shoulder. She squeezes her brakes hard to avoid the ditch beyond it. The back of the bike lifts and Siri flies off it, crashing to the ground.

. . .

Siri

The scariest part is before the fall, when I'm fighting to control my bike and know I'm gonna lose the fight. Then I'm airborne, no time to think. My arms instinctively reach out to break my fall. Instead, I land hard on my knees. I've barely lifted myself off the ground before Daddy's beside me, pouring water from his bottle over my cuts and scrapes and tearing his t-shirt into strips to bind up my knees. I sit there, a bit stunned, letting him take care of my injuries.

"Are you alright?" he asks. "I'm so sorry, it's all my fault."

"It's not your fault," I tell him, mentally shaking it off. I feel more shocked than hurt.

"But if I hadn't suggested we go on a bike ride. . ."

Daddy sits facing me, shirtless, with his backpack on his lap. He presses the part of his t-shirt that hasn't been turned into bandages against his face. I think he might be crying again.

"Daddy, stop. I was going too fast, that's all. Not everything is your fault."

"I'm sorry," he says again, wiping his eyes with his shirt before balling it up in his hand. "I don't mean to be so. . . weird. I've been a mess lately. I can't seem to stop leaking my emotions all over the place."

"It's normal to cry when you're sad. And there's nothing weird about being upset that your friend died. What's that?" I ask as he pulls something out of his backpack.

"A patch kit. To fix your tire," he says.

"Was there one in the shed?" I ask, confused. I don't remember seeing Daddy take anything from the shed but the bikes.

"No, I brought it from home. I always carry around a patch kit."

"Even when you don't have your bike with you?"

"Yeah," he answers, like this is totally a thing.

"Okay, I take it back. You are weird," I tell him.

Daddy laughs. He rummages through the kit to remove a tire lever.

"Pass that to me," I say. "I can fix my own flat."

Daddy opens his mouth to object, then changes his mind and hands me the toolkit. I brush at stones and gravel, noticing the small, round impressions they've left on my elbows and arms. I stand, trying to ignore the twinge of pain in my knees. I flip the bike over and use the lever to slowly pull the tire away from the rim. Daddy watches me work while pretending to watch the road behind me. I wonder when I should bring up the spy in my group. I'd planned to ask him who it was when I returned to the inn, but he was with Chloë and upset, so it seemed better to wait. I thought the bike ride would be the perfect opportunity to confront him, but nothing's going as planned.

I pry the last section of the wheel away from the metal rim. Maybe I'm wrong to be so focused on finding out who the liaison with our older comrades is. Because that's how I should think of this person—not as Daddy's spy. Plus, I should really be more concerned with how we're going to get those kids out of that horrible place and shut it down once and for all. Still, I can't help feeling a bit frustrated that Daddy is into all of my business.

"Careful," Daddy says as I tug at the tube to pull it out from the tire.

"It's stuck on something," I say.

I run my fingers between the tire and the tube, hoping to free it. I find the place where it won't come loose. My fingers touch something small and sharp. A piece of glass? I use the glowlight on my wristpad to examine the inside of the tire. Something's sticking out from the tire and piercing the inner tube, just beside the tube valve.

"What is it?" Daddy asks.

I grip the tiny diamond-shaped chip and carefully pull it out from where it's stuck.

"I think I found Clara's memories," I say, holding it up triumphantly.

Daddy reaches for the microchip but I close my hand around it.

"Finders keepers," I say.

"But. . ." Daddy's shoulders slump a little, though he doesn't argue with me.

"I'll tell you what," I say. "I'll trade you. The chip for the answer to a question."

"What's the question?"

"Do we have a deal or not?" After a slight hesitation, Daddy nods. "Okay, who's the sp. . . I mean, who's the person in my group who's been telling you things?"

He crosses his arms. "There's a reason the liaison between our groups is anonymous."

"But some people in my group already know."

"That's true," Daddy admits, letting his arms hang down at his sides again.

"Then I want to know too. Tell me and I'll give you the chip."

"Fine." He sighs. "You may not have met them yet—they're not on the team who interviews and integrates new members. Their name is Robin."

"Robin?" This is the last name I expected to hear. I almost blurt out, *but Robin is my friend*. What I say out loud is, "I thought it would be one of the older comrades."

"Robin's twenty-two. It's true they take a couple of classes at École de la rue, but we have a bunch of students in their twenties."

"Robin goes to your school?" I say, doubly shocked.

Daddy nods, looking a little guilty, which he should be since he never told me that. But then again, neither did Robin. I think back on all the times I visited Robin when they were living on the street, including that last time when I thought that the man with the scarred face had taken Robin's stuff. I felt protective of Robin. And now to find out they're seven years older than me, that they know Daddy and are reporting to him behind my back. . .

"So you know them?" Daddy asks.

"Robin was at the first full meeting I went to," I say, and Daddy nods like that's all there is to it. It seems like Robin didn't even tell Daddy we're friends, that we've known each other for over a year. Is that because our friendship isn't important to them? Or maybe Robin figured it was none of Daddy's business. Maybe it means that our friendship does mean something.

"Hand me the patcher, okay?" I say. "And here's Clara's chip."

Daddy takes the chip from me carefully and hands me the tube repair glue. I use it on the torn part. After it's dry, I put the tube back into the tire and inflate it with the inflation cylinder.

When the bike is ready to ride again, I stand, wincing a little as I straighten my knees. Getting back to the inn is not going to be fun.

"Let's get you on my bike," Daddy says. "I can ride you back."

"But how? We don't want to leave Clara's bike behind. It's a really good bike."

"Don't worry," he says. "I can get us all back."

I sit on Daddy's seat, hands on his waist, as he pedals. He rides one-handed; with his other hand, he holds the handlebar of Clara's bike, rolling it beside us. I don't know how he manages this. I think back to when I was little and first learning to ride. He would hold my handlebars until I could find my own balance. Even when I could pedal on my own, he'd run beside me for hours, to be there in case I fell. It never occurred to me to wonder about the physical strength and dexterity all that took.

"Daddy," I say, about a half a kilometre away from the inn. "I want to walk a little."

We pull off the road. Daddy reaches up to help me, but I climb off the bike myself. My knees are really stinging now but it will be better if I don't let them stiffen up. Plus, I have something I want to say and I'd rather do it on my own two feet.

I take the handlebars of Clara's bike from Daddy so he only needs to push his own. The first few steps are the most painful, but as soon as I'm used to it, I start talking.

"Before, when you asked if I knew Robin. . . the totally honest answer is that I do, not just from the group but from before that. There was a place where they hung out and I'd visit and we'd talk about politics and stuff. I was surprised when they turned up in my group and even more surprised when. . . with what you told me."

Daddy nods, and I feel glad I told him everything. I think about that night in the tent after he and Philip got me back across the border and Daddy told me what happened to him when he was my same age. It must have been hard for him to tell his daughter that kind of thing, and part of me wishes he hadn't. I realize now that he thought it was safer that I know. The truth is, it's not that I wish he didn't tell me, just that those things never happened. To him or to anyone.

"Here," Daddy says, holding the chip out to me. "I want you to take this back."

I keep walking. "You keep it. A deal's a deal."

"You found it and you earned it. Give it to your own group. See if anything you find helps with your investigations. If you want our support with any of the analysis, and once you're ready to share the intel, you know where to find us."

"But Clara was your friend. Your comrade and. . . and colleague."

"Yes. But there's a reason we both chose to work with youth. Take it," he says, and there's an intensity of emotion in his voice that fills me with a weird combination of feelings: pride and embarrassment, but also, determination and hope.

"Alright," I say, taking the chip from his hand. I hold it up to the sun and it makes a mini-rainbow of glittering colours. I smile and stash it in the inner pocket of my shorts. "I guess this means I'm taking the bicycle too."

ACTION THREE: THE SKY

CHAPTER 29
JANIE AND SIMON

JANIE

I poke the sweet potatoes cooking on the stovetop. My fork slides in easily, so I pour them steaming and fragrant into the oversized square blue bowl I've placed on the kitchen counter. It's nice to be home.

Philip looks up from the rice and beans he's cooking. "That's a lot of potatoes!"

"A lot of people are coming," I reply. "Not just from our two buildings but from some of the other co-ops too. I admit I'm surprised that Siri's willing to celebrate her birthday with the community. In the past, she's been pretty resistant to socializing with the Réseau co-ops."

"She probably just wanted to show her independence," Philip says.

"Yeah, she's also having a separate party with her school and baseball friends. I agreed to transfer her some credits so she can choose her own birthday gift this year. I hope she doesn't get herself chipped at one of those places in Pointe-aux-Trembles."

"I'm sure she'll use good sense," Philip says, his tone comfortingly convincing.

I hoist myself onto the counter to reach for the mortar and pestle I use to crush herbs.

"Let me get that for you, shorty," he says.

I reach up to grab the mortar and pestle myself. On my way down, I smack him across the butt with my kitchen towel to remind him where Siri gets her independence. When he holds his hands up in surrender, I hug him to make up for the smack. He gives me a kiss with some tongue, not at all shy. What a difference from before our trip! Though we've been home for a few days, I feel like the three of us are still on a honeymoon.

"I'm glad we went on vacation and that you and Laek got over your. . . thing," I say, recalling how hot the two of them were together in bed last night.

"Me too," he responds, his soft gaze telling me he's also thinking of our lovemaking.

I sigh happily. There's nothing like returning to a job you enjoy after some time off, especially when your family life has simultaneously become even richer and more interesting than before. Excited to wake up, excited to go to bed—I feel so lucky!

"Okay, the pesto sweet potatoes are just about done along with the arroz con habichuelas and the pasta with spicy cashew sauce," I say, consulting the kitchen screen.

"Which leaves the chocolate cake, the empanadillas, the salad, and the chocolate cake."

"You said chocolate cake twice," I tell him. "I guess you'll make the chocolate cake?"

Philip laughs and nods. I tell him I'll start on the salad.

"When are Laek and Siri getting back?" Philip asks,

reaching for the container of flour. "They're both where again?"

"Co-op Villeray Nord. Laek's representing our co-op at the planning meeting for the big demo. I wonder if Cat'll be there —she's the person I met when I got doored. And Siri just happened to be meeting with her 'study group,' in the same building," I say, making air quotes with my fingers. "So they decided to bike together."

"What's the demo about?" Philip asks, plopping a huge quantity of flour into a bowl. A cloud of fine white powder puffs into the air, coating the front of his shirt.

"Oh, you know, the usual potpourri of issues. Environment and food security, intersectional social justice, border-smashing, anti-capitalism and workers' rights—it's for May Day, after all. Simon will want to be with the Peeps. You know the org I mean—"

"Yeah, les Protecteurs de la planète. The one that girl Andressa made famous. Why are you smiling? I don't live under a rock, you know, even if I'm not active like you and Laek."

"I'm just smiling at how seamlessly you've become part of this family. And this community. Also. . . I'll share a bit of intel. Andressa may make an appearance."

"Really? Simon will be thrilled! She's like a hero to him."

"Yeah," I say, lowering my voice. "His spirits could use a lift. Aiza's too. They're both going through emotional growing pains. Hey, thanks for being there for him. It's hard for Simon to talk about certain things. Precocious vocabulary notwithstanding. Speaking of him. . ." I toss some more greens into the bowl and call out, "Simon!"

"What?" he calls back.

"Can you come in here, please? I need your help."

Simon enters the kitchen, dragging his feet. I wish he'd find a way to get over his own "thing" with Aiza. Maybe it's time to give him a nudge.

"I need some more tomatoes from the garden," I tell him. "Some nice ripe ones. By the way, have you and Aiza heard from the rooftop committee yet?"

"They asked us to submit detailed drawings," Simon answers, showing a bit more enthusiasm. "They want an overall visual plan plus some cut-outs of different areas: the winter greenhouse, the summer garden—oh, and the jardin d'enfants."

"Maybe you two could work on it today. I can look at your drawings later."

"That'd be hyper! I have a lot of new ideas. I can tell you all about them."

"Sounds good, sweetie," I say, preparing myself for an hour of detailed descriptions of every passing thought he's had about a new design for the children's garden. I smile anyway. Genuine passion for something useful or creative is something I admire wholeheartedly. Plus, the more time he and Aiza spend together, the more likely they'll work things out.

"Okay, see you later, Mommy. See you later, Uncle Philip."

The two of us wave Simon off. Philip turns back to the stove to pour the pot of melted raw chocolate into the flour mix. He gives it some muscular stirs, batter flying.

Straightening up, he turns to me. "That was well done. With Simon, I mean. What? Why are you smiling again?"

"Your eyebrows are coated with flour. They're like old-man eyebrows. And now there's chocolate on the tip of your nose too."

"Come and lick it off," he says, without missing a beat.

"You're starting to sound just like Laek," I laugh.

SIMON

Grabbing my design screen, I head down to Aiza's apartment. Aiza's dad opens the door.

"Bonjour, Abu Aiza," I say politely.

"Bonjour, Simon," he says. "Are you here about your sister's party? I'm cooking rice bread and peanut soup. Aiza helped her mother make cookies."

"Can Aiza come out with me? I need to talk to her about the roof garden."

"Why don't you come in?" He smiles. "We'll see if she's finished her schoolwork."

I find Aiza sitting at her desk looking at photos on her screen. I think she may have been looking at one of me, but then she twitches her finger to flip to another album. I peer over her shoulder and recognize the photo of the mural at Daddy's school the day we visited. There's also a vid of that kid Pascal who was walking on his hands, and a photo of the photo that Aiza took in Monsieur Cloutier's office.

Aiza's room is very neat: bed made, no clothes on the floor, art supplies stored in labeled crates. She has a new holo on the wall, not a beach or mountain scene like most people prefer but a famous artwork by Salvador Dali. I know that it's called "The Persistence of Memory" because it's one of my favourites, but Mommy and I call it "Floppy Clocks."

"Salut. Are you busy?" I ask. "I thought we could work on the roof garden proposal."

"D'accord," Aiza shrugs, not seeming very happy to see me.

I decide not to ask her if she's mad. I did that already, twice, and each time she said "no" then acted even madder than before. Instead, I decide to tell her how I feel.

"I was at the mobilization committee meeting with my mom yesterday. You're going to the big May Day manif, right?"

"Bien sûr," she says, doodling on her screen. "Practically the whole co-op's going."

"They were talking about all the different parts of the demo. There's a part for families with little kids that has games and stuff, and other parts that'll be less safe—with direct action and maybe arrests. They're planning to have trainings for those. And to set up affinity groups." I take a few steps closer to her. "Do you know what those are?"

"Groups with common interests?" Aiza responds, looking up at me from her screen.

"It's more like. . . My mom told me that it was back in the old days that they started using affinity groups for civil disobedience. It was a way for smaller groups to make quick decisions together in case things rolled differently than planned, and to have each other's backs."

"Are you saying you want to get arrested, Simon?" She screws up her face.

"No, I don't think so. Do they arrest kids in Québec?"

Aiza stands and puts her fists on her hips. "They tried to arrest Andressa!"

"That's true," I say, remembering that Mommy told me they'd put her in detention before trying to deport her. Aiza looks brave and stubborn and it makes me like her even more.

"But if I were going to get arrested," I continue, "I'd want to get arrested with you. I want to march with you for our planet and all its animals. I want to make decisions with you and do art with you and design sustainable roof gardens with you. I want to look out for you and for you to look out for me." Aiza is staring at me and I can't read her expression exactly, except that her face looks soft now, not angry, so I keep going. "So what I'm asking is. . . Aiza, will you be my affinity group? Even though I don't like kissing, I really like you."

I wait for Aiza to answer me, my heart beating hard. What if she says no?

"Oui," she finally says. "I would like to be in your affinity group."

"That's good."

"Just good?"

She smiles in a crooked way, so I know she's teasing me, but she's right. The word "good" isn't good enough. "That great!" I say instead. "No, wait. That's phenomenal! That's—"

"That's enough," she laughs. "So what do you want to do now?"

"My maman needs some tomatoes from the greenhouse. Want to come?"

"C'est parfait! We need to go up to the rooftop anyway, to plan our new drawings."

We leave the apartment in a hurry, each grabbing a cookie from Aiza's mom on the way out. When we get upstairs, I tell Aiza I want to check on the pigeons who live in the pigeonnier near the connection to our sister building's roof.

"I'll take images of the summer garden area!" She walks to the other side of the roof.

On the way to the pigeon coop, I walk through the greenhouse. The air is warm and wet and smells green. There are rows of seedlings being fed by tubes of water from our rain barrels. I go to where the tomato plants are and pick a big red one and a purple one that's almost too ripe. We have lots and lots of tomatoes—more of them than anything, except maybe cannabis.

At the pigeon coop, I check to see if any of the pigeons have messages. None of them are wearing little chip carriers. I lean over the coop and try to coo like a pigeon. I reach out my arm and the one I call Blue perches on my wrist.

I wave to Aiza who's taking images on the far side of the

roof. She waves back. I look up at the sky. I don't see any pigeons flying to us with messages from another co-op. I do see something moving across the sky, though—something that catches a ray of sunlight and flashes it back into my eyes. At first, it's just a speck, but it's moving in our direction, very fast. As it gets closer, I see it's round and maybe made of metal.

"Aiza!" I call out, pointing to the sky.

She looks up and sees it too. As it gets closer, she points her wrist screen at it, I guess to take some footage. She looks from the sky to her wrist screen and back again. Even though we're standing far apart, I can tell that she's frowning. That's how well I know her face.

"Simon!" she shouts. "We should go back inside!"

"Why?" I shout back.

The thing is very close to us now. I wonder if it's a tiny spaceship or something.

"I think it's a drone!" she says.

I squint at it. It's small and shiny and doesn't look anything like the drones I saw flying over Manhattan when I was little, which were grey and kind of scary-looking. This one is like a ball of metal lace with coloured blinkies. It's actually kind of pretty. I move forward a few steps to get a better look, Blue still perched on my wrist. The drone stops and makes a beeping sound. I'm still standing there, mesmerized, when fire starts pouring out of it.

CHAPTER 30
SIRI AND LAEK

SIRI

The room in the sub-basement where I'm sitting with my comrades is like a small white cube. Soft plasti-foam covers the walls and floor, adjusting to our shapes and muffling our sounds. Ari and Ali are making out in the corner and the rest of the group is working at screens or joking around. It's grey-boxed, secure and comfortable, but I'm feeling claustrophobic. Or maybe just impatient. We've been here for, like, an hour and I still don't know if there's anything useful on Clara's microchip.

Comrade X has given us general info on what he's found there so far: hundreds of names, events, seemingly random records of numbered corporations from the Registre des entreprises du Québec, and other long lists. He's sitting cross-legged in his torn, black jumpsuit peering bare-eyed through an ocular holo-viewer. He twirls his right index finger in the air—more than seems normal if what he's trying to do is bring the image into focus. Maybe those wraparound glasses he usually wears really are prescription.

"Tu ressembles à un pirate queer, Comrade X," Anaïs teases him.

Comrade X looks up and frowns before going back to his chip reading. I'm beginning to see why Anaïs and M.M. tease him like that—he's so serious all the time!

"Did you find anything useful?" I finally ask, unable to hide my impatience.

"Yeah," he says. "If you want to open a museum on rad organizing."

Gabriel, sitting as far away from me as possible in this little boxy room, snorts his laughter. I swallow an angry response and continue to ignore him. He and I, neither of us members of the intel committee, are here by invitation, a kind of reward for the info we brought in from our reconnaissance mission.

The problem is that it's starting to look like Clara's memories were just that: histories, stories, descriptions of past events, and long lists of people, some who haven't been active for years or are even dead. Not that I've had a chance to look at any of it myself.

"Maybe it's coded," I blurt out. "Maybe it only seems like lists and stuff."

"Comrade X is aware that information may be coded," Wakanda, a comrade I haven't met before, says. He sits between M.M. and Comrade X, looking fierce but calm, and his dark eyes seem to take everything in. "Try to be patient, Dandelion."

"*Dandelion* doesn't know how to be patient," Gabriel says.

I imagine myself punching Gabriel in the face but decide this wouldn't make me feel better. I look around the room, feeling a wave of love for my comrades, and make myself be calm and patient like Wakanda. I wonder where Robin is. I wish they were in this room instead of Gabriel, but it's Gabriel who's here and I have to admit that he adds to our group too. He's reliable, brave, and strong. He's capable of acting selflessly at least sometimes and. . . yeah, I owe him an apology for what happened during our mission.

"Gabriel," I say, moving towards him. "I want to thank you for what you did during our action," I tell him, careful not to get specific. I think everyone in the room already knows the details of our reconnaissance mission, but it's good practice not to break discipline.

"You acted right away when you were worried about my safety. Though I think I would have been okay anyway," I add, truthfully. "But I acted. . . impulsively. It ended up putting you in danger. I'm very sorry, and you're right, I do need to work on being more patient. And. . . well, I hope you'll forgive me."

Gabriel pounds his fist against the squishy floor, and it sinks in without making a sound. "You think that's enough?" he says through clenched teeth. "Los guardias almost fucking had me because of you! You think I'm gonna just forgive you because you say 'sorry'?"

I crawl back to my place next to Anaïs and draw my knees up to my chest, trying to preserve the little shelter of calm I built before. I take a breath, choosing my words carefully.

"No, I don't think that. I said what I said because it's true and I owe it to you and to the group to say it. All I can do is try my best, and when I mess up, apologize and hope to do better next time. You're free to forgive me or not. That's on you."

Gabriel scowls and turns away from me. He doesn't leave the cube and neither do I. After a moment, I feel Anaïs's hand on my back, and when I turn, Anaïs is giving me a proud smile.

There's a warm little bubble inside my chest. Anaïs's approval is only a part of it. There's something about doing what you think is right, consequences aside, that makes you calm and happy. And being surrounded by a group of people—Gabriel included—who are also trying to do what's right gives me a sense of belonging and well-being. It's almost enough to keep my impatience in check. Almost.

"Dandelion, get over here," Comrade X finally say. "Maybe you can find something interesting for us." He hands me the ocular patch.

I take it before he can change his mind and place it over my eye. Everything is blurry. Twirling the finger of my left hand forward only makes it worse, so I twirl it backwards until the text focuses.

Each file is represented by an icon of a paper book. I've seen more real paper books than most kids my age since my dad's a history teacher and my mom's addicted to reading, but I get why Comrade X was thinking about museums.

I choose the first book. I start by reading carefully. Then I decide to skim. After a while, the excitement of getting to look at this secret microchip starts to fade under the weight of all those long lists and blocks of text. I decide to try to get a general shape of things instead. It's not the usual vertical organization of files, subfiles and sub-subfiles. Instead it's organized like an actual book with chapters and intros and conclusions. The text of the intros seem awkward—grammatically correct but not making a lot of sense. Some kind of crypto puzzle?

"What about a book code?" I say, remembering this from old spy novels I read on Mommy's novel screen.

"What's a book code?" Ali asks.

"It's an antiquated way of coding a communication," Comrade X answers. "From before computers. People would use a book they both had as a way of decoding a secret message."

"Why would someone use that these days with all the digital options?" Ari asks.

They all turn to me. "I don't know. Because Clara was old? Because she loved books?"

"There are advantages to book codes," Comrade X answers. "Even if the message gets hacked or stolen, it's almost impossible to decode. Anyhow, even if this were a book code, we'd have to know not only which book but which edition of the book for it to work."

I decide to keep going through the info. I focus on the last file, which is probably the most recent. It has chapter headings, each written in a fancy font and followed by a micro-image. I bring it into hyper focus and make out a star, a tree, a moon, an ocean wave, and. . .

"There's a picture of hands making patterns out of string. I bet that means something."

Under the "string chapter" are lists of names. I think it's interesting how Québec names are different than Brooklyn names, not just different kinds of names—like Tremblay, Gagnon, Bélanger, instead of Brown, Rodriguez, or Cohen— but also, there seem to be less names in total in Québec. In the file, I notice there's a Lapointe on the list, like my friend Amina, and a Cloutier, like Daddy's boss, though the prénom on the list is Marc, not Stephan.

There's another list of names following it that seem at first to be more like New York names—lots of Latine names, for instance, and non-European ones, but then I see that there are a bunch of typical Québecois names too. . . like Bourque. "Patricia Bourque" I read, and I think of Pascal Bourque, the boy who I saw at the building, just before the guards came and Gabriel shouted and led them away from me.

Next to the list of names is info about some numbered corps. That's hyper boring so I flip to the last list. It has just three names. I don't recognize the first two, but the third one —a single name only, no surname—makes my heartbeat spike. "Laek" it says and then I remember what Pascal Bourque said to me: *Tell my teacher. Laek. Don't know his last name.*

Shit. I never told Daddy about him.

"Are you all right?" Anaïs asks.

My face is hot, and I realize I'm breathing hard. I tear the transparent patch from my eye. How could I have forgotten? At first, I was too worried about Gabriel and then too angry about who I thought of as Daddy's spy in our group. Later, with the excitement around Clara's chip and my bike accident, it just slipped my mind.

"I messed up, and I think. . . I think we need help."

"What kind of help?" Wakanda asks. "What are you proposing?"

"That we call in our older comrades. That we call in. . . Ocean."

LAEK

"But shouldn't we know what the real target of the demo is?"

Robert, a newcomer to the group, says these words in an even, persuasive voice. Underneath, I sense a tone of falseness. Am I being paranoid?

I gaze around the room. It's windowless but painted a bright yellow. Mismatched chairs, stools, cushions, and leaning posts sit in a circle. Though large enough to hold our group of thirty-eight people comfortably, the space is small enough that I can hear the murmuring of some of our group's usual worriers. I catch the eye of the animatrice. She nods her head in assent.

"There is no real target," I say. "There are multiple targets. Like always." Also, we still don't have enough intel to ensure the safety of an action against the factory—the target Robert may be hinting at. Let alone guarantee that it will be shut down for good.

"But there's a special one, right?" Robert persists. A target that's more. . . strategic?"

I remain silent. Jabur, sitting right beside me, says, "I don't wish to know about anything more strategic than how many sandwiches we will need to feed everyone on the bus ride home."

"And how much cannabis to put in your medical bag for those of us who get nauseous on high-speed e-buses," a comrade adds.

The last two comments are greeted with appreciative chuckles. The next person from the speakers' list asks about logistics concerning the Vélorution bikes we'll be taking with us.

"I worry that the city will notice the missing bikes," a comrade says.

Cat, a new friend of Janie's, makes a tapping motion in the air with her right index finger to indicate she has a direct answer to that question.

"I'm leading a crew of Vélorution employees and volunteer bike mechanics. We'll be using bikes that are out of commission for serious repairs. We'll fix them to supplement the bikes some members will be taking out on all-day rentals. So everything's copacetic."

"Well, I hope those employees aren't putting their jobs at risk." Robert has taken advantage of our detour from the speakers' list to slip himself into the queue again. "Or that other unnecessary risks are being taken, like that special target I was talking about...."

I stop listening. I'd like to trust the group, and this new person, Robert, as well. To not wonder why, at the last meeting, Robert was taking the opposite position, pushing for actions that were riskier. I decide not to engage for the moment. I arrange my face in a neutral expression. Distract myself with daydreams of last night. My face between Janie's breasts. Philip's hands gripping my hips. My lips taste the soft skin of Janie's stomach. Move further down as Philip—

"Laek?" Cat says. The image dissolves as I give her my full attention. "There's an intra-web message from your family," she says. "Maybe about your daughter's party? You can take it in the community kitchen."

I follow her out. Feel the eyes on my back.

"What is it?" I ask her, knowing this isn't about Siri's birthday.

"I don't know," she answers, "But you can't complain about the timing."

She takes me through the kitchen and down a ramp. Through the underground passage that leads to the greybox room. Outside is one of Siri's comrades. The techie from Abitibi who calls himself X. Who's visually impaired and developed his own assistive device. And is only twenty-one but looks older.

Cat and I bump fists. As soon as she's out of earshot, I say, "Comrade X."

"You're. . . you're Ocean?"

I nod, used to surprise at my appearance. "Is everything alright?"

"Fine. You just don't look like Dandelion's dad. Or anyone's dad."

"Dandelion," I repeat, smiling at the name.

"Suis-moi," he says, squaring his shoulders. I follow him into the greybox.

My gaze sweeps the room, searching for Robin, who missed our last rendez-vous. My chest constricts, followed by a painful twinge in my ribs. I focus on the young comrades who are in the room, most of whom I recognize from other actions. I've attended solidarity planning meetings with two of them—Wakanda and M.M. And there's Gabriel. Showing me his back.

"We'd like you to take a look at the chip data," X says. "There's a possibility that some information might be coded, but we don't recognize the code."

"Or maybe there's just something we're not grasping," says the Acadian kid with the long, brown braids who sometimes goes by Marichette and sometimes by Anaïs.

Siri walks up to me, a look of uncertainty on her face. She hands me an ocular patch.

"That's okay," I say. "I have my own."

I take a tiny, round case from my boot and remove the lens from it. Spit onto its surface and pop it into my eye.

"DNA-linked lenses, right?" X says.

I nod once and reach my hand out for the chip. Place it in the reader.

My heart squeezes as images of books come up. Just like Clara. I blink once, twice. Navigate text and images with both eye and finger motions. Double the speed and scan it all again. They're right. There's a code here. A book code. But there's information on the surface level too. I decide to start there.

"Daddy. . . Ocean. I saw your name in the last file. The section with the string picture."

"Fan sheng," I say absently, and when that gets me a lot of blank looks, I say, "Cat's cradle. That's what the picture is of. An ancient game."

I scroll down to the end. See my name next to the other two. My back against the corner, I sink slowly to the ground and cover my face.

There's a hand on each of my shoulders. One belongs to Ali

and the other to Marichette/Anaïs. Siri's planted herself right in front of me. Looking fierce and protective.

"What is it?" she asks. "What's it mean?"

"Nothing," I tell her. "Nothing. . . strategic. They're. . . the other two names are of Clara's kids. One's dead, the other estranged."

I watch as understanding dawns on Siri's face. That Clara listed me in this document as though I were her own child.

I push myself back to a standing position. Resume scanning the chip.

"There's something else you need to know," Siri says. "One of the kids in the factory yard. His name is Pascal. Pascal Bourque. He asked me to get a message to you."

I don't ask why this is the first time I'm hearing this. I continue scanning the lists.

"And I found the name Bourque on the list too. But not Pascal."

"It's him," I tell her, my eyes finding the name.

"But it says Patricia," Siri argues.

"Deadname," I reply. Marichette/Anaïs gasps.

"How did—" Siri begins.

"Pascal changed his name when he ran away to Montréal. The birth records list his deadname. Those are the records the scumbags who have him must be using. I recognize some other names too. Former students at École de la rue. Or kids who just came through the Centre to crash. And then disappeared."

Everyone is on their feet now.

"We have to get him out of there. Sans délai," M.M. says.

"All of them," Wakanda adds.

"We're already working on it." No one objects when I pocket the chip. "I'll be in touch."

Siri checks with her comrades before following me out. We climb the stairs. Go out the back exit near the kitchen. Past the compost heaps to the bicycle parking. Cat's there waiting for us. A messenger pigeon perched on her wrist. Her face tight with anger. Or fear.

"There's been a firebombing. At least six co-ops in the collectivity have been hit. Le Point, Little Burgundy, St-Michel, the Exes, Rosemont. . . and Griffintown," she finishes.

"We need to get home," I say, blood feeling like ice in my veins.

I turn to Siri, but she's already unlocking her bike.

CHAPTER 31
SIMON, JANIE, PHILIP, SIRI

SIMON

There's a line of fire between me and Aiza, and everything smells like burning and like skunk. I look up at the sky to try to watch the pigeons I sent out with messages, but I can hardly see anything through the smoke.

"Simon, it's not safe on the roof! Faut qu'on s'en aille !"

"I can't leave until all the pigeons are safe," I tell her. "Go! Fly away!" I shout, but I can't speak pigeon language so the three in the coop just huddle closer together, and Blue hangs onto my shoulder even tighter with her claws. "You should go down and get help," I tell Aiza.

"I'm not leaving you up here alone! We're. . . we're an affinity group."

"But we can have different jobs. I need to save the pigeons, and you need to save the roof garden." Aiza puts her hands on her hips and glares at me. "Okay, fine," I say. "I'll escape down the gardening chute, I promise. I just want to try one more time to get the other pigeons to fly the coop." I can't help smiling at my jeu de mot even though I'm really nervous.

"D'accord. On se retrouve en bas. In the ruelle behind the building."

Aiza takes off for the stairs on her side of the fire line and I turn back to the pigeons.

I wave my arms and shout, "Caw, caw, caw!" With my loose black t-shirt and tight green jeans, I'm hoping I look like a falcon or a big, scary crow, but the pigeons just stare at me. Even Blue only shuffles back and forth on my shoulder. I take off my baseball cap and try waving it; when they still won't budge I reach into the coop to grab the smallest one. "Ouch!" One of them pecked me! I drop my hat and suck on my knuckle, which hurts a little, but I'm not angry. I know they're just scared. Maybe those three pigeons are a family, like Mommy and Daddy and Philip, and shouldn't be separated. I try to think of what to do.

The fire's even bigger now—a tall wall of flame dividing the roof in half. It's making my eyes tear and I'm beginning to feel a little dizzy. I pull my arm out of my t-shirt and shift Blue onto my now-bare shoulder so I can pull the t-shirt off. I move towards the three pigeons, the t-shirt covering my hands. I try to hypnotize them with my eyes, then I drop the shirt over the three scrunched-together birds and quickly scoop them up. Blue startles into the air and lands on my head, her toe-claws holding onto my hair. I press the other three birds gently against my bare chest, run to the garden chute, and slide down feet first. Blue hangs on, flapping her wings the whole way down.

I land hard on my butt and let go of the three pigeons wrapped in my shirt. They make some grunting sounds and half fly, half run down the alleyway. I take Blue off my head, put my t-shirt back on, and look around for Aiza. She's not down yet, but that makes sense since she was going to get help and knows not to use the elevator.

It feels like someone's behind me, so I turn, thinking it might be Aiza—but no. The person behind me is big. They're standing sideways, watching me and the street at the same time. Then they turn their head and my heart jumps. It's the two-faced person!

I pick up Blue and cuddle her to my chest. She's cooing, unafraid, and this helps calm me down. The first time I saw this person, when we were spying on Siri, their face took me by surprise. This time they look less scary. Is this because they're more familiar now? Maybe it's because their face looks half-burned and I just escaped a fire.

I take a step towards them and Blue startles, flapping her wings hard and landing on my head again. The person stumbles backwards and their two hands turn into fists.

"You're Laek's son, aren't you?" they say in a low, hoarse voice.

I start to feel scared again.

JANIE

Pressing the rim of the ceramic mug against the last of the rolled-out dough, I manage to squeeze out three more circles. Philip puts a teaspoon of his spicy vegetable mixture in the centre of each one; I fold and press the edges together to create a last trio of empanadillas, ready to fry. Glancing over at the waiting bowl of salad, I feel a twinge of uneasiness.

"I wonder what's taking Simon so long," Philip says, brows pinched with worry.

"I did expect him back by now, with Aiza if they've made up, and definitely with those tomatoes. Simon takes food very seriously. But maybe I'm being a little neurotic," I say, not wanting to make Philip more anxious than he already is.

Philip frowns and puts down the sponge he'd been using to wipe the counter. "You have good instincts. I'll go up to the roof and see if he's there."

After Philip leaves, I use a pair of metal tongs to turn the frying empanadillas and am surprised to see that they're barely golden brown. From the smell, I would've guessed they were more well done. I pick up my knife, thinking I might cut up some green onion for the salad, but first I check the time. It's just past noon. I don't expect Laek for at least another hour and Siri even later since she has baseball practice after her "study group."

I try to force calm into my uneasy stomach. The desire to know where all my family members are at any given moment is an unhealthy compulsion. To be fair, Laek's given me ample opportunity for legitimate concern about the safety of my loved ones, and Philip's right: I do have good instincts, which only makes it harder to know when my worries are reasonable and when they're the result of an anxiety disorder.

And poor Philip—he's even worse than I am.

PHILIP

I smell the smoke as soon as I near the roof. At first, I think someone's barbecuing, maybe for Siri's party tonight, but it doesn't smell very appetizing. What it smells like is fifty giant blunts; in other words, like the concrete courtyard behind the high school where Laek and I taught together in Brooklyn. I hope that Simon and Aiza aren't smoking weed at their age.

Once on the roof, the smell is even stronger, but my brain has trouble making sense of what it's seeing. There's no one up here lighting a joint; instead, the plants themselves are on fire.

I remember some vid footage my grandfather showed me when the government fire-bombed the farming cooperative, Soberanía Alimentaria Boricua, claiming they were harbouring so-called border terrorists. This fire is like that only small-scale, and what's burning aren't crops on a farm but cannabis plants on a roof garden.

"Simon!" I shout! "Mijo, are you up here?"

A narrow, rectangular swath of flaming plants forms a fiery border between me and the other part of the roof. The flames shoot up into the sky, making it hard to see past it. What if Simon is there, helpless, even unconscious? To my left, the flames stretch almost to the parapet. I go right, where the fire is less dense, cover my face, and run through the flames.

I emerge on the other side into a hazy, grey world. Coughing and eyes tearing, I call, "Simon!" My heart is thudding but my head feels stuffed with cotton. Where our roof meets the roof of the adjoining building, there's a tall, raised barrier that hadn't been there before and that reminds me of the polymer tide barrier in Percé. It's cutting off access to the adjacent roof and trapping the smoke on this side. Some kind of automatic fire wall to protect the building next door? If Simon came up here, he'd be trapped.

Moving forward, away from the burning plants, I continue to search for him. I see a square structure—the pigeon coop, I think. My heart lurches as I notice a dark shape on the ground next to it. I get down on my hands and knees and crawl towards it. It's Simon's cap. "Simon, where are you?" My voice sounds hoarse from coughing and from all the smoke I've inhaled. I crawl inside the coop but no Simon and no pigeons either. I crawl out and run to the edge of the street side of the roof. I peer over the side, fearing to see Simon's crumpled body. People are beginning to pour out of the building. I can't distinguish anyone.

A wave of dizziness hits me and I drop to my knees. I don't know if it's all the weed smoke or just vertigo. I try to slow down my breathing but find myself hyperventilating, so I crawl away from the ledge and closer to the fire.

Glancing at the line of flaming plants, I think about returning to Janie without having found Simon. I just can't. And I can't look for him on the adjacent roof either since it's blocked off by that weird-looking fire wall. I don't know what to do.

I lie down. The air is cooler and slightly less smoky closer to the ground. Maybe this will help me think more clearly. To avoid a panic attack, I take long, slow breaths. After a while, it feels like my heart is starting to slow down too. Though I still feel dizzy, it's a nicer kind of dizzy: mellow, like after I've had three or four beers. I decide that Simon is probably safe, maybe downstairs in Aiza's family's apartment working on their proposal for redesigning the roof garden. It's going to need it after this fire. I chuckle to myself, though I'm not sure this is actually funny. Well, better to laugh than to cry, my grandmother always did say.

I remember that old Bob Marley song she used to sing: "Three Little Birds." I start singing it to myself, deciding that maybe I don't need to worry so much. Yes, the cannabis crop is on fire, but nothing else seems to be catching. I mean, all that soil on top of the roof must make it pretty fire resistant. Laek's gonna be upset, with all that weed burnt to the ground, but next year, if they let me stay, I can help him replant it. Kyla can help too. Okay, maybe not with the cannabis plants but with the kids' garden.

Yeah, I'm not gonna worry about a thing. Everything's gonna be all right. Yeah, every little thing. . .

JANIE

After adding more cucumbers to the salad, I hear a rap on the front door.

"Did you forget your keys?" I call out, thinking Philip's back, hopefully with Simon.

I pull open the door and see Aiza, all by herself.

"We were on the roof and a. . . a drone came!" she says, practically jumping up and down in agitation. "It set some plants on fire! And the alarm and sprinkler system didn't turn on!"

"Oh my God. Where's Simon?" I ask as I press my palm against the panic button inside the front door. My handprint scans and I hear the rising scale of the general alarm begin.

"He was saving the pigeons but promised to go down the chute. What should we do?"

"I need to go to the roof. Philip's up there looking for Simon. Go downstairs to apartment 13D. They're the fire marshals this rotation and have the portable extinguishers."

"I went there first. No one was there."

"Okay, then go find your parents instead."

"D'accord! And after, we should meet Simon in the ruelle, near the chute!"

I'm already at the door to the stairs leading up to the roof when I realize I'm still carrying my chopping knife. I hesitate, but rather than returning to the apartment, I slide it carefully under my belt and reach for the stairwell door. There's some resistance when I push it; then the mechanical assist kicks in, compensating for the effect of air pressurization in the fire stairwell. I'm relieved to see that at least some of our emergency systems are still online, though this makes the emergency feel more real. I pound up the stairs, shove open the door to the roof and am greeted by a wave of heat and smoke.

"Philip!" I shout, craning my neck, but all I can see is a row of burning plants exactly where our cannabis crop used to be. I move closer to the flames and spy Philip on the other side. I cough and cough again, feeling like I just took several consecutive hits off of an enormous bong. "Philip!" I call out again. I think I hear him singing.

PHILIP

"Philip! Where are you? Are you alright?" Janie's voice calls.

"Every little thing's gonna be alright," I sing back.

"What are you doing?" she shouts.

"Lying on the ground," I answer, feeling calm and peaceful. "I was looking for Simon."

"Aiza said he went down the chute. You need to do that too!"

"What do you want me to shoot? Laek once asked me to shoot something too." I smile, remembering how I hit that 9G tower for him and that he was pleased with me.

"Okay, you're not making any sense. I'm coming in after you."

I sit up, curious about what's going to happen next. Janie emerges from the fiery plants. She runs towards me, her beautiful reddish curls like a halo of flames around her face.

"Janie," I say, filled with amazement. "Are you some kind of a superhero?"

"Philip, what the fuck?" She stops to cough. "Can't you see the building's on fire!"

"It's just the cannabis plants. The building's fine."

Janie takes a long, wheezy breath, then starts coughing again. "I think it's giving me asthma," she says. "Maybe it's toxic. Did you see the drone? Aiza said there was a drone!"

She pulls on my arm, trying to get me up.

"That's not going to work," I tell her. "I'm too big and you're too small." I pull her into my arms instead. "Stay down here with me. Don't worry about a thing."

"The weed is affecting your brain!" she says, squirming out of my arms and coughing.

"It's gonna be alright," I tell her, a feeling of wellbeing washing over me.

"They're out to get us," she says, tugging on my hands. "We have to save ourselves. The drones may come back, this time to kill us."

"Janie, I need to tell you something. Back in Percé, Laek said that if I wanted to stay here and become part of the family, he'd walk through fire and water to make it happen." Suddenly that moment is like a fiercely bright point of light, brighter than the fire on the roof.

"And I'll kill anyone who tries to hurt you," Janie replies, sounding ferocious.

"But don't you see? It's one of your signs, Janie! Laek walked through water in Percé, and now you walked through fire."

"Then let me save you," she says, and stands up, and this time when she reaches down and tugs on my hands, I end up standing too.

We go down the chute, Janie first and me just behind her. When we hit the ground, she pulls a knife out from her belt.

SIRI

One second, there are flames on top of our building, and the next second, the flames are gone and a peach-coloured vapour cloud is floating into the air. I'm pedalling behind Daddy, who dismounts his bike while it's still moving like he's one of the acrobats at Cirque Vélo. Aiza waves and motions us to follow her.

We push through the crowd of people. A bunch of them try to talk to Daddy, but we keep moving until we get to the ruelle behind our building. Aiza runs over to Simon, who has a pigeon on his head for some reason, and takes his hand. I guess they're not fighting anymore.

I see Mommy and Uncle Philip by the chute that runs from the roof garden. Philip has soot smeared on his cheek and his eyes are glassy and red like he's stoned. Mommy's also red-eyed—were they smoking together?—and looks deranged in her bare feet and with a big messy cloud of hair around her face. Not to mention that kitchen knife in her hand.

"Step away from the child," she orders, pointing the blade at someone near Simon.

I'm so focused on Mommy and her knife that it takes me a minute to recognize that person as the dude with the messed-up face, the one I saw near Robin's stuff that day back when I was first interviewed by Jeune Vanguard!

"Every little thing's gonna be alright," Philip says in a slow, sing-song voice.

"Someone tell me what's going on. Fast," Daddy says, his eyes never leaving the dude.

"Are you. . . Laek?" the dude says. "Please, tell her to put the knife down."

"No one tells her what to do. Least of all me. Who are you? What are you doing here while our home is under attack?"

"I didn't do anything. I swear! I came to warn you."

"Simon, Aiza—to me." The two of them rush over to stand next to Daddy. "Did this person hurt you?" Daddy asks, his eyes still fixed on the dude.

"No, Papa. They didn't touch me. Or Blue. But I think. . . I think I might know them."

Simon turns to Aiza and the two of them exchange a look. She whips out her screen and quickly scrolls through some flat photos, Simon peering over her shoulder.

"Yes, I think it's him," Aiza says, pressing her finger against the screen.

"Who?" Daddy says sharply.

Simon and Aiza get down on hands and knees, and Simon uses a stylo to draw on top of the photo, then Aiza takes the stylo out of his hand and does some quick sketching too. Simon watches her work, nodding his head. This all takes maybe twenty seconds, but it feels longer.

Aiza hands the screen to Daddy. He glances at it before giving it back to her.

"You draw well." Daddy's voice is gentle.

"I've seen burn scars. I can draw them." Aiza presses her lips together, looking unhappy.

"It's a photo of a photo, n'est-ce pas, Aiza?"

"Oui. I took it on career day, that day we visited École de la rue with you. It was on Monsieur Cloutier's desk. Simon thought it was of him when he was younger. Mais tu vois? I added the burn scars to one side of his face after Simon made him look older."

"What's your name?" Daddy asks the dude, not gently at all. "Answer me now."

"Marc. Marc—"

"Cloutier, yes?" Daddy says.

Marc Cloutier! I saw that name on one of Clara's lists.

"Cloutier? Are you related to Laek's asshole boss?" Mommy asks, pointing her knife. "First he makes Laek cut his hair, and now he sends you to burn our cannabis garden."

"I swear, it wasn't him who sent me," the dude says nervously. "I came about Robin."

"What about Robin?" I ask, my voice almost drowned out by the sirens.

"They're missing. I think they're in trouble."

"They. . . he did ask for you, Papa," Simon says. "He wanted to know if I was your son."

"And whose son are you?" Daddy asks the dude.

Marc doesn't respond, but his face goes all still and hard.

"I'd like to talk to him alone," Daddy says.

"No! I should be there too!" I insist. "Robin. . . Robin's my friend."

"Siri, someone clearheaded needs to check out the scene now that the fire is out." He points his chin towards Mommy. "And Janie and Philip are not their usual selves."

Maybe it's how he called them by their names as though I were his peer, instead of saying "your mother and Uncle Philip," or maybe it's just that he's right. I watch Uncle Philip sway back and forth, like he's singing to himself, and next to him, Mommy holds her knife like she desperately wants to do something with it other than chop vegetables. I let out a sigh. The adult thing to do is go upstairs with them and make sure everyone is safe. And after that, I'll check the roof for clues.

"Fine, but you have to promise to tell me everything he tells you."

Daddy gives me a quick, sharp nod and I turn to Uncle Philip. It's weird how pot affects people differently. In a situation like this, I would have expected him to be anxious and stressed, or paranoid like Mommy, but instead he seems happy and relaxed.

"Uncle Philip," I say, "You should smoke more often. It agrees with you."

I turn to Mommy and take the knife out of her hand.

"And you," I say. "You should never go near weed again."

I turn to wave goodbye to Daddy, but he and the dude are already gone.

CHAPTER 32
LAEK

I make him walk ahead of me. We go down to the canal. Water puts me on edge, but I need my edge for this conversation.

"Talk," I say when we've reached Bassin Peel. I force myself to gaze past the crowds of people. To focus on the water. It's flat and motionless. Almost black. I ignore the rainbow of bike paths that arc across the canal, though they usually make me smile. Stare instead at the highway bridge, half-deconstructed. Like a giant knife sliced off the mid-section.

"Where do you want me to begin?" he asks.

"With Robin. How do you know them?"

"We're friends, and they're missing." I look at him. "We're lovers," he amends.

I grab his arm and make him face me. "Get this straight. You want my help, you answer my questions truthfully and exactly. Clear?"

"Fine," he says, pulling his arm from my grasp.

"How long?" I ask, resuming our walk along the canal. People with dogs, kids on grav boards, couples holding hands —they all keep their distance. Like they can sense the discord.

"We've been seeing each other for about three months."

"Not that, I don't give a fuck," I snap at him. "How long has Robin been missing?"

"Oh. I'm not certain. We had an argument. I thought they were still angry. But Robin doesn't hold grudges and it's been more than a week since I heard from them. I don't know how many days were because of the argument and how many because... they're in trouble."

"And you're sure they're missing?" I ask, though I'm convinced of this myself.

"Yes," he says and looks over at me, clearly waiting for my response. I ignore him and pick up the pace in order to think it through.

The last time I communicated with Robin was the day we left for Percé, so eight days ago. They were agitated about the Gabriel affair. Wanted an extraction team sent out right away. When Gabriel turned up on his own, I relaxed. Waited to report once my family was asleep on the train since we'd agreed not to send a team for twenty-four hours anyway. Robin didn't respond, but I hadn't worried at first.

I stop to glance at the new factory buildings across the water. A suspicion takes shape in my mind. "Does your father know about you and Robin?"

He shrugs.

"Does that mean you don't know or don't care if your queer-phobic, fash-leaning, control-freak of a father knows you're fucking an enby radical activist?"

He turns to face me. "Why do you despise me? What have I done to you?"

I'm about to say that finding him suspiciously lurking in the back alley with my twelve-year-old son, my partner pointing a knife at him, and my home in flames doesn't exactly inspire trust, but an instinct tells me to let the deeper truth slip out.

"Because you look like him."

"Look like. . . my father?" he asks with wide eyes. I nod. "C'est trop drôle!"

He begins to laugh. There's a hysterical edge to it. People stare. We both ignore them.

When he's wiping tears from his good eye and all that's left of his laughter is ragged breathing, I lead him to a bench on the far side of the path from the water. We both sit, and I wait for him to speak.

"You're not going to ask me what's so funny?" he asks.

"I figure you'll tell me."

"You're a cold one. Bon. What's funny is that my father despises me exactly because I *don't* look like him. Not anymore. He blames me for my accident, for ruining his hopes for me. He said that because of my foolishness, I'd turned myself into a monster."

I examine him carefully. His face, the unscarred half, is easy to read. Something else he has in common with his father. But where the father's expression speaks anger and arrogance, the son's is full of vulnerability and pain. My heart softens towards him.

"The kids," I say. "They recognized you despite your scars. From the photo your father keeps on his desk. From university maybe?"

"He still keeps that photo of me? It's from cégep, from right before. . . what happened."

I want to skip over this, to get to the part that will help me to find Robin. But maybe he needs to tell me this before he trusts me with the rest.

"What did happen? If you're willing to share your story. . ."

He shifts on the bench. "You remember the third wave student movement?"

"We haven't lived here that long. But I read about it. When you finally won the right to a free education up through university. And funding for a network of Indigenous colleges and universities. Political and social history interests me."

"Robin told me you teach history."

"What else did they tell you?" I lean back casually against the bench. Like the question were only of mild interest. But I'm listening carefully.

"To come to you if anything ever happened to them."

I nod, satisfied. "So you were involved in the student movement?" I prompt.

"No, but there was this kid in my school who was really enthusiastic. And me, I was enthusiastic about this kid. I'm not a political person. My upbringing, I suppose."

I nod again, though he's confused supporting the status quo with being apolitical.

"I was a late-comer to the action," he continues, staring at his hands. "I determined to make myself indispensable to the coordination team, which happened to include this student. A strike was called demanding access to all basic services—education, fully holistic healthcare, water—and a complete dismantling of the energy monopolies in favour of community control and the environment. There were blockades by the Indigenous students and their allies. There'd been threats of violence against us, so I decided to take on the role of my friend's unofficial bodyguard. I was strong, knew how to fight. My father made sure of that.

"Not that he appreciated how I was using these skills. My father had only contempt for the protestors, calling them whiners, parasites, infants. It made me furious and even more content with my rebellion. My father was very controlling, especially of me."

He pauses, fixing his gaze on the sign for Farine Five Roses Bar across the canal. After a moment, he continues. "They'd under-estimated our numbers. When the SCSVM arrived—"

"That's the SPVM," I correct. "Back then, they were still just the cops. They were renamed after the riots. And the reallocation of municipal funding."

"I guess you really are a history teacher."

I don't react. Just wait for the rest of the story.

"The police tried to control the crowd, to keep us from our goal: the headquarters of Trans-EnerQ Patrimoine. We planned to draw attention to our issues with a picket, then present our demands, preferably in front of major media streams, but the mainstream media didn't arrive. The riot police were sent in and immediately attacked with sonic grenades. My friend kept pushing to the front anyway, so I followed.

"A group of us managed to make it through the police lines. Then we realized our error. The government or Trans-EnerQ— I don't know which—had hired private security. We were surrounded, the police behind us and the private security in front of and on either side of us."

"They kettled you," I said.

"Is that what it's called? That was my first and last manif. Anyway, that's when they moved in and pepper sprayed us with hose guns. They sprayed so much, we were enveloped in a cloud of orange mist. My eyes were burning, my nose; I could hardly see or breathe."

He touches the scarred side of his face.

"I stumbled forward, looking for a way out, looking for my friend. I panicked. I may have shouted. That's when one of the private security officers shot me with a stun phaser. I thought I was burning before, but now. . ."

I put my hand on his shoulder. "I understand. I've had phaser weapons used on me too."

He shrugs my hand off, turning to me for the first time since he began his story.

"You don't understand," he says. "I was literally on fire. The propellant they'd used to douse us with the pepper spray was flammable. When it came into contact with the electric charge from the stun phaser, it ignited."

Part of me is horrified. Another part wants to ask about the type of propellant they used. Methane, butane, nitrous oxide? But I don't ask.

"That's why I came to your building today. Not just because of Robin. I. . . I learned what had been planned, about the firebombings. I couldn't just sit by."

"Who was behind it?" I ask.

"No one was meant to be hurt," he answers.

"Fire can't be reliably controlled."

"You think I don't know that?" He springs to his feet and begins to walk west, towards les Écluses St-Gabriel. I follow him.

"I'm sorry," I say, when we're side by side. "Will you. . . will you tell me more?"

After a moment he continues. "After my recovery, I didn't go back to school. I had trouble finding work, keeping it. I sometimes get. . . angry, and when I lose my *sang-froid*, let's just say that my frightening appearance is not helpful."

I've already noticed how he monitors the people around him. To see who's staring, maybe. Most people will glance at him, turn away quickly, then catch a second look.

"Around six months ago, my father told me about a position. I usually try to stay away from my father's business connections, but I was tired of going from job to job. The company in question was interested in expanding their share of the market in the cannabis trade."

"The cannabis trade," I repeat. I glance at him and when he won't meet my eye, a sick hunch slides towards certainty. Our co-op and the other co-ops who'd had drone visits, all had one thing in common. A healthy trade in cannabis. Offering low, off-grid prices.

"You're saying the firebombings were. . . it was a business decision?"

He nods.

All that speculating over which far right group might have been behind it. Only to learn it may have been simply capitalism! I want to laugh. Or throw up. It's time to finish this conversation. To get what I need from Stephan Cloutier's son and go home.

"I need you to tell me everything you know about this company—starting with their directors and main shareholders. As well as the other companies in your father's portfolio."

"What does this have to do with finding Robin?" he asks, sounded frustrated.

"Have you heard of Northern Heritage Guard? Programme travail liberté?"

"My father was once a member of The Guard. And Robin mentioned PTL. It's a youth employment program, *n'est-ce pas?*"

We've arrived at les Écluses St-Gabriel. Mark stops to watch the water enter the lock and raise the small boat waiting inside. I force myself to watch with him, though the rising water level makes me nauseous.

"More like a human trafficking cartel that targets street kids," I say, once the boat continues on its way. "And teenagers whose parents have been deported. I think they have Robin in one of their microchip factories."

"Where? How do you know this?"

"We've been investigating them. And Robin's been involved in that work."

"I've had differences with my father, but I can't believe he'd support that kind of thing."

"He's been referring kids from École de la rue to PTL. Kids who are now missing."

"Homeless youth often disappear." He folds his arms over his chest. I sense a door slam.

"Okay. I understand your skepticism. Even though you've had issues with him, he's your father. I'm sure the things he's done. . . he had your best interests at heart, right?"

He searches my expression, maybe looking for irony. I keep my face blank.

"Écoute," I say, calculating that a little backtracking could move us faster to my goal right now. "I was wondering. What ever happened to your friend? The one from the student movement."

He walks away from me and mounts the small footbridge that stretches across the canal. I follow. He stops when he's halfway across. I stand beside him.

"I never heard from them again," he finally says. "I imagine that one look at my new face was enough to see that the fun was over." He laughs; it's a bitter sound.

"But if you never saw your friend again, how did they see your face?"

"I mean my father was the only one to visit me. The kid disappeared." He shrugs.

"Did it occur to you that your father may've kept them away?"

He leans against the metal railing of the bridge and gazes

down into the canal's waters, as though searching its depths. He sighs and shakes his head.

"My college friend was a militant—brave enough to go up against the government, powerful corporations, the police— yet somehow not brave enough to stand up to my father?"

So, yes; it had occurred to him. But I'm surprised to see where he's placed the blame. Then again, if I'm reading things right, his own father has done something similar: blamed his son and the left-wing activists he hung out with for his injuries rather than the cops who actually hurt him. And Marc is still keeping company with activists.

"I care about Robin. A lot," he says, as though reading my thoughts.

I nod and wait. I won't push him.

"What was your father like?" he asks me.

It's not a question I expected. I lean over the rail as he had done and gaze into the water. I think about telling him I didn't have a father. Which is true. Or that I had two. Which is also true. I think about the man who sired me. Charismatic, a leader. A megalomaniac. Cold and indifferent to me. I think about Al. Also a leader, also charismatic. But he cared for me, taught me important things. Made me love him. Before betraying me.

"Marc," I finally say. "Your father was wrong about turning yourself into a monster. You're not a monster. You know that. But our fathers. . . well, maybe they're not monsters either. But they've done monstrous things. What should we, their children, do?"

He searches my face for a long moment. "Alright," he finally says. "I. . . I'll do my best to find the corporate files, and to bring you anything else that might help."

"Merci."

"In return, you must do everything you can to find Robin, to bring them back safely."

I nod. He extends his hand and we shake, as though we've made a business deal. But I think he knows I would have done what he asked anyway.

CHAPTER 33
PHILIP, LAEK, SIRI, JANIE, SIMON

PHILIP

I wake without coughing for the first time since those pendejos fire-bombed the roof garden a week ago. It's early morning, and I'm alone. No, not alone. I see Laek, quiet and immobile, on the floor at the foot of the bed, doing some kind of impossible isometric exercise. If I hadn't been sleeping propped up to ease my breathing, I wouldn't have noticed him.

He wears a pair of tan briefs and nothing else. My eyes hungrily follow the lines and curves of his slim, smooth body, corded with muscle on his arms and calves. Laek's head turns in my direction and I close my eyes, embarrassed at the idea of being caught gaping like that.

After a few moments, I open one eye, wondering what he's doing. My heart jumps a little and I quickly shut my eye again. Laek crept up on me somehow and is sitting on the floor right beside the bed, staring up at me. He's not smiling, and it's creepy.

I try to keep my breathing long and steady, like I'm still

asleep. I don't know why I'm doing this, so after a few moments, I open my eyes. He's still sitting in the same position.

"What. . . what are you doing?"

"Waiting for you to quit pretending to be asleep," he replies.

"But why are you frozen like a statue? You haven't moved a muscle in at least—"

"It's been less than three minutes, Phil. I can hold my *breath* for longer than that."

Delivered cold, that last remark cuts like a razor, especially when I think about which of Laek's life experiences have made it so he knows precisely how long he can hold his breath.

"You should get up, get dressed." Standing in one fluid movement, he reaches for his clothes, neatly folded on the wooden trunk at the foot of the bed. "Janie's been gone an hour already," he adds. "I thought you would go with her. Join the band for the manif."

I swing my legs over the side of the bed and fill my lungs. Still no cough. "I don't know the other band members. I wouldn't want to impose."

"A marching band can always use more drummers."

Laek punctuates this observation with a sharp tug of his pants leg which he then tucks into his calf-high metal-toed boots. The pants are black and seem lightweight but strong—not a uniform exactly but very. . . functional-looking.

I shrug and dig a pair of cargo shorts out of the dresser I share with Laek.

"Will you go with Simon, then?" he pursues, "to the eco-youth contingent of the march?"

"Isn't he going with Aiza and her parents?" I rummage around for a pair of clean socks.

"Another adult is always useful. To keep the kids out of trouble."

"You can't be seriously worried about those two getting into trouble. I don't think I've ever met kids that age as cautious and obedient."

"Did you know that Simon and Aiza had met Marc Cloutier before? They were following Siri. Spying on her. Cloutier was guarding the entrance to her group's meeting place."

"No, I didn't know that. But still. . . Laek, are you angry with me about something?"

"Why would I be angry?" He fingers one of the articles of clothing on the trunk.

"I don't know. For getting stoned on the roof? For being a bit useless?"

"It's not your fault our cannabis crop was firebombed."

"If you're not angry, why are you trying to pawn me off on Janie or Simon?" When he doesn't answer I ask, "Which contingent of the demo do you plan to join?"

"I have something I need to do first. We'll meet up at the border march later on."

"Can't I go with you? I can watch your back."

"I don't need anyone to watch my back."

"But I—"

"No. You'll only slow me down."

Laek turns away from me, reaching for the article of clothing he'd pushed aside earlier. It's an undervest of some kind. He puts it on. The material is a matte black with a texture that looks almost rubbery—probably a new synth. He fastens it across his chest with velcro.

When he turns back to face me, I say, "That was unkind."

He looks down but not quickly enough for me to miss the bright tears that prick his eyes.

"Laek," I say, reaching for him, but he backs away.

"No. Just. . . don't. I have to do this alone."

I drop my arms. "Why, because it's dangerous?"

"Please, Phil. I couldn't bear it if something happened to you."

"And how do you think I'll feel if something happens to you? And Janie, how will she feel? Mira, Laek, we've talked about this!"

"Janie knows what I'm doing today. She understands."

I put on my shorts. "So you think Janie can understand but not me."

"Look, it's not the same. Janie and I are activists before everything. We've both been taking risks for things like this for a long time."

"I believe the same things you do. Just because I'm not what you'd call an activist. . ."

Laek turns away to reach for his remaining clothing: a black, hooded t-shirt and a pair of silvery, fingerless gloves. He wraps a black scarf around his face. Only his eyes show, like he's wearing a balaclava, and once again they're staring at me, steely grey and unwavering.

"Okay," I say, trying for humour. "It's true I don't have the gear, but couldn't I just borrow some of your clothes?"

Even behind the scarf, I can see that he can't help but smile back.

"Ah, Phil." He unwinds the scarf and ties it loosely around his throat instead. "There isn't anyone I'd rather have at my back." The corners of his lips curve a little, but his face quickly regains its serious expression. "I've thought a lot about this, though. And about my conversation with Marc Cloutier. You know how he got those scars? Following a lover to a demonstration he wasn't prepared for and didn't necessarily believe in."

"I told you. I just don't have the right clothes." This time

Laek doesn't smile. He's a stubborn one, but he's about to learn who's more stubborn. "That Cloutier character. . . even through my stoned haze I could tell he's a half-grown daddy's boy, looking for a little action. That's not me. I'm not an experienced activist like you or Janie, but I can take care of myself."

"I know," Laek says.

"Good. Let me help, then. I know I can be of use, and I think you know it too. Otherwise, we wouldn't be having this conversation. You'd be long gone."

Laek gives me his deadpan stare for a few more seconds before finally nodding.

"Alright," he says. "You could help with something. Some intel. About that building in Gaspé. You know the building I mean?"

I nod, not sure I like where this is going.

"If you were familiar with that building's layout, that could be very useful."

"Because you're planning something for the building at the border."

A look of surprise ruffles his face for a split second before it returns to its previous smooth mask.

"We believe the two buildings have a similar design, yes," he says. "Though the one on the border is much bigger."

"I've never seen either building IRL, but I saw the one in Gaspé in VR and know its general shape and layout from the holo-print. I'm not like Simon or Aiza, though; my drawing skills are just about nil. I could try to describe what I remember in words, though."

"Even that could help."

"Going with you would help more. I could tell you everything I know on the bike ride over. I assume that's how you're planning to get there."

Laek presses his lips together, unhappy, but then he seems to shake it off. He shrugs and give me a half-grin. "Yeah, well, you won't have the breath to tell me anything. Not if you're gonna keep up."

I smile, knowing I've won.

"Wait," he says. "I have two conditions. One, you do everything I say without hesitation. And two, you actually use some of my gear."

"Agreed," I say quickly, before he changes his mind.

He pulls off his t-shirt, then unfastens the undershirt and tosses it to me. "Put this on."

"What is it?"

"A protective garment."

"Don't you think you should be the one wearing it? I mean, your ribs—"

"Philip. You literally just gave me your word."

"Okay, fine."

Laek squats to root around in the trunk at the foot of the bed while I put on the undervest. It's as light as it looks and, luckily, very stretchy. I wasn't sure I'd be able to close it over my broader chest and thicker waist. It does have a rubbery feel to it, but it's also kind of silky against my skin and, all in all, surprisingly comfortable.

"Wear a shirt over it," Laek tells me. "Preferably dark. And here, take this."

He hands me a mask which I stuff into the pocket of my shorts, then I dig through my t-shirts, finally finding one that's black. It was a gift from Simon, his love of wordplay evident in the quote stamped in white lettering on the front:

LE MOMENT OÙ YOU BEGIN TO DREAM
DANS LES DEUX LANGUES SIMULTANEOUSLY

"You don't own a plain black t-shirt?" Laek asks, shaking his head at me, but his smile is gentle and open and full of sweetness. I follow him out of the bedroom, and things feel easy and natural between us. When we leave the apartment a few moments later, without even thinking about it, I reach out to him....

LAEK

... and I catch his outstretched hand in my own.

It grounds me. The strength of his grip recalls a muscle memory. Lying in the hospital, him squeezing my hand. Me, squeezing back. When the pain of my crushed ribs was too much, I lived in the rhythm of our wordless exchange, back and forth and back and forth.

We release hands when we get to our bikes. I attach both paniers to my rack instead of having him carry one. For balance, I explain, and he accepts this partial truth. My heart lightens as it always does when I mount my bike.

It's not my habit to revisit decisions already made. I try to live in the present. Moving from one moment to the next. Only later looking at the invisible lines that create continuity, that end up looking like inevitability.

And I know that allowing Phil to accompany me on this action is the ethically correct choice. He's an adult. Strong and competent. A teacher who, like me, would do anything to help his students. Or kids who could be his students. Intellectually, I realize that my fear for him, for all those I care about, deserves no greater consideration than theirs for me. But it's hard to escape the voice inside my head. The one that continues to insist that my life is worth less than theirs.

Once we cross the Canal into Pointe-Sainte-Charles, I slow.

Let Philip pass me. We glide onto the part of the "Bicycle Bob Bike Lane" that leads to the pont Champlain. When we get to the target, I must be done with uncertainty, but here on the protected bike path, I indulge in my fear that I've made a mistake—the kind of mistake that could end with Philip broken under a pile of rubble. Like what almost happened at the airport. Or with him on a plane or prison bus, cuffed, on the other side of the cruel border that kept us apart these last three years. I feel my chest constrict.

"Will this route take us onto the Estacade?" Philip asks, peering at me over his shoulder. "Because if so, I should start talking before it gets so buggy I can't safely open my mouth."

"When were you ever on the Estacade?"

"I wasn't. But I've read every Montréal-area tourist *fiche* I could find as well as a series of mystery novels set here. It's amazing how much good information you can get from fiction!"

"You're really something, you know that?" My sadness dissipates like a bad dream. I increase my speed and slip ahead of him.

"Am I slowing you down?" he asks.

"Nah. But this way you can quit turning around when you want to talk to me. Plowing headlong into something would be a bad way to start our adventure."

"Our adventure, huh?"

"Come closer, Phil. Right beside my back wheel. Now tell me about that building."

When he's done reporting everything he can recall, I make him repeat it. Question small details. Sharpen vague descriptions. Then take it from the top again. I'm impressed by his patience. Especially since I know he has his own questions.

As Phil predicted, this close to dawn, the Estacade is thick with gnats and mosquitos. I release the handlebars to wind a scarf around my face. Philip twitches and spits. I pass him the scarf instead. While he struggles to tie it around his nose and mouth one-handed, I gaze at the river. The St-Laurent is green, flecked with white. To the left of us is a bird sanctuary, a sandy finger in the distance. Simon would enjoy this ride.

After a time, we turn right onto Le petit chemin du fleuve. The river opens up before us. Dizzyingly vast. We pedal on a long spit of land that feels as narrow as a balancing beam. Land that will probably be swallowed up by the St-Laurent within five summers.

All that water around us makes my breath short. I force myself to look straight ahead. At the landmass that starts out as Québec and, if you continue, ends up in the United America. I imagine our target in the distance, at the juncture of the border. A holo image of the building spins in my mind. A mélange of Phil's dry rendering of structural elements and the more fantastical intel I got from Siri's group of a four-dimensional polygon. Where one side kept changing shape. It has the head-feel of an Escher painting, impossible yet coherent.

At last, we come to the end of Le petit chemin. My shoulders loosen the moment my wheels touch the mainland. We ride along the river. The path, thick with weeds on either side. Almost hiding the entrance to the small park a kilometre down the road. A gate arm is blocking the way inside. We slip around it on our bikes.

The park is deserted, poorly maintained. Filled with old-tech transponders. I take us on a south-easterly path that spills us out onto the main road. It's busier than I imagined, cars speeding by, raising dust. The shoulder is wide, though. Room enough for two cyclists, side by side. I motion Philip to ride beside me. His unposed questions hang in the air between us.

"Laek, can I ask. . ." He lowers his voice. "Are we going to blow up the building?"

"There are kids inside that building. What do you think?"

"After we get them out? Otherwise, what's to keep those bastards from doing it again?"

"What's to keep them from building another monstrosity to enslave and exploit other kids?" I counter. "You think blowing up one building's gonna change that?"

"When we taught together in New York, I watched you turn yourself inside out to help just one kid graduate and avoid mandatory military, or to hide just one family from the immigration cops. Did that change anything?" He raises his eyebrows.

"It did for those kids, those families," I say, though in dark moments, I fear it was all for nothing, that the oppression I managed to escape has crushed those students I left behind.

"But the same can be said for destroying an evil place like this. I respect that you're a pacifist, but eliminating something evil can help make things better."

"Only if we build something good to replace it." I release my handlebars to cross my arms over my chest, using my lower body alone to guide the bike.

"Sometimes things grow better on scorched earth."

"Like our roof garden?"

This last comment silences him. I feel guilty.

"Listen, Phil. You're not wrong. And just to be clear, I'm not judging others. I believe in a diversity of tactics. Plus, destruction of property isn't the same as violence against living creatures. But in my experience, it's almost impossible to ensure that taking down a target doesn't inadvertently cause physical injury." I flash back to a complex in the Midwestern Drylands. To a person who wasn't supposed to be there. To knives flashing in the darkness.

"I get that," Phil says. "But people are being hurt anyway, right now, and sometimes violence is. . . if not necessary, the morally correct thing to do to avoid greater harm."

"Maybe I'd just rather concentrate my own efforts on building rather than destroying."

"With those steel-toed boots?" he asks, nodding towards them.

"They can be handy for kicking doors down. Look, I'd love to jump ahead to a near-future world where we've succeeded in liberating those kids from that sweatshop prison. To figure out what's next. But for now, kicking down doors is what we should be concentrating on."

"Alright," Philip says after a moment, his patient and practical nature reasserting itself. We bump fists. The talk has settled us both. Solidified our solidarity, despite small differences in philosophy. It's also made me hungry for action. I accelerate. . .

SIRI

... on my trottinette, anxious to get to the meeting place.

My left knee is still sore from the bike accident in Percé, but it's the hangover that's slowing me down. Each time my trottinette goes over a bump or crack in the pavement, the jolt bounces painfully in my head. Maybe it wasn't such a good idea to mix beer and Free Ungava cloudberry gin, or to keep drinking even after the room started spinning, but you only turn sixteen once, and after the firebombing and the news that Robin's missing, it felt good to let go.

I'm taking a peek at the new tattoo on my left shoulder—a baseball diamond that glitters on all four corners—when I hear Gabriel's garbled voice, "Ooska tu ...v... Seeree?"

"J'arrive dans cinq minutes," I subvocalize back. "Non,

quatre," I say, remembering a shortcut through parc des Faubourgs.

"Drrr… pêche-toi!" he says.

I tell him that I'm already hurrying. Fucking Gabriel. And he says *I* have no patience.

When I get there, the buses that will take our comrades in this sector to the border for the manif have already arrived. They're parked not far from métro Papineau, just under the pont Jacques-Cartier overpass. Gabriel is slouching against a huge grey stone pylon, vaping, his eyes on the metal girders criss-crossing the underside of the bridge. Beside him are Oiseau Noir, Harriet, Anaïs, Em Goldman, QS, Myriam, and Wakanda, along with some other comrades I don't know. All of them seem tense, even Gabriel, though he's trying to look relaxed. I know him, though, and he only vapes when he's wired.

I lean my trottinette against the opposite pylon and grab my sports bag, going through its contents in my head: a breathing mask, my black face scarf, a spray bottle of liquid antacid mixed with water for if we get tear-gassed by the cops, bandages, anti-bacterial cream, and tubes of skin sealant. My batting helmet and bat are also in the bag, from practice yesterday afternoon. Where are my sunglasses? I try to rub my eyes and realize I'm wearing them. How is it so bright out? I feel like someone's shining a searchlight into my brain.

Gritting my teeth, I fist bump everyone before asking for a status update.

"Oiseau Noir spotted a group of boneheads a few blocks away," Em says.

"How many of them?" I ask, squinting into the distance.

"About a dozen. Carrying hockey sticks and shock sticks." Em cracks xir knuckles.

"Why didn't our intel say they'd be armed?" Oiseau Noir complains.

"They also underestimated their numbers," Wakanda says.

"Doesn't matter. We can take'm," Gabriel says.

"Where are the bus drivers?" I ask.

"They went for coffee," Wakanda says. "Still fifty-two minutes before departure."

"Les manifestants arrivent dans une demi-heure," Anaïs adds.

I picture Simon and Aiza, excited to take the bus to the border with the other protesters. They'll probably be wearing ridiculous costumes and giggling, armed with pâtisseries—innocent and totally vulnerable.

Wakanda looks west along Ste-Catherine. Harriet and QS are also monitoring that direction, towards rue Dorion and the métro. Myriam and Gabriel face south, though you can't see much past the wide white building with the big cymbal-shaped transponder on top.

I turn east to watch for anyone arriving via De Lorimier. Suddenly, I hear QS yell, "Incoming!" I spin around to see Gabriel, Harriet, and Wakanda take off to intercept a tall, dark-haired person who's carrying a baseball bat and coming out of the alley to our right.

"Wait!" I take off after them, but my comrades have surrounded xir and grabbed the bat.

"Careful!" I hear Maneesh say. "You're spilling my coffee!"

"Let xir go!" I shout.

"Siri, finally!" Maneesh says when I'm a few steps away.

"You know this. . . person?" Gabriel says.

"Gabriel, right? Don't you recognize me?" Maneesh says. "You went to our high school."

"Oh. Yeah. We can let. . . them go. They—I mean xe—isn't

a threat." Gabriel says this like not being a threat is an insult instead of something good.

"Maneesh, what are you doing here?" I ask.

"I came to bring you your bat. You left it at my place last night."

Gabriel smirks.

"It was my birthday," I explain, glancing at Gabriel. "My party was cancelled after the drone thing. So I went out with some friends last night and ended up having a more informal party and then crashing with Maneesh." I don't know why I feel like I need to explain anything to him. I turn back to Maneesh. "Anyway, I have my bat. That one's for your little brother. I told you that."

"I guess I forgot," Maneesh says. I grab the bat from Gabriel and give it back to Maneesh. Wakanda and Harriet wander back to the buses. Gabriel sticks around, looking from me to Maneesh, like we're a puzzle he's solving.

"I thought. . . I thought I might stay," Maneesh says, giving Gabriel the side-eye. "I mean, I want to go to the demo too. My grandparents were immigrants, and borders suck. And we're destroying the planet. Obviously. And. . . well, I don't know why you had to get here so early, but I figured it must be for something important. Maybe I can help."

"No you can't," Gabriel says with a disdainful look on his face, and even though I kind of planned on saying the same thing, his response pisses me off.

Before I have time to argue, I hear Harriet yell, "Incoming!" again, and I run to take my place among my comrades. Maneesh follows me. The group coming towards us looks like a lot more than the dozen people Em noticed earlier, and almost all of them have sticks in their hands. I fumble with my bag, trying to unzip it. I succeed, my hands first finding the batting helmet.

"You should run, but if you're gonna stick around, put this on!" I tell Maneesh.

I feel the adrenaline shooting through my veins. It clears my headache and makes my vision sharp. Standing shoulder to shoulder with my comrades, I'm calm and ready for anything.

I grab my...

JANIE

... instrument, feeling focused and confident. I'm standing in a circle with the other members of the Insurrection Band. With the precision of well-practiced choreography, we transform our circle into a line, swinging our instruments left, and stand shoulder to shoulder, ready to serve as a screen for the comrades behind us, closer to the road, who prepare the escape vehicles for our siblings at the border.

The vehicles behind us include tandem bicycles of various sizes including triples, quads, and quints; box bikes and freight tricycles; flatbed e-vehicles for transporting Vélorution bikes, decorated and repurposed as though for a parade float; and most important of all, our mariposas being readied for their special cargo, on their way to the purple tent.

Our instruments are our weapons, tuned and polished, loaded with songs and ready for action. Remembering that nightmarish day in lower Manhattan when an anarchist marching band saved Laek's life, my determination flares even brighter. I will pay it forward. ¡Adelante! The music is meant to distract our enemies, and if we're lucky, it will also contest, inspire and transform, appealing not only to the intellect but to the heart and soul—for, at its best, isn't that what art does?

Our bodies can be instrumentalized too. ¡No pasarán! We'll dance in the revolution, our diverse bodies breaking patterns, dancing not just in pairs but in triples or bigger ensembles, long lines of us connecting from point to point to point. We'll show them our joy, but first—

"Earth to Janie," Zende says, tapping me lightly on the head.

"Oh, shit. Désolée!"

I must be nervous to have slipped into auto-narration of my life in real time. I take a deep breath, letting it out in a long, sustained note on my wind synthesizer, the beginning of the first song of our moving-line set.

Zende answers with a rousing measure of syncopated drumbeats, which are echoed by the three other drummers who could make it today. I think about Philip, wondering if I can convince him to join us next time. He has a hell of a lot of musical talent, and not just as a drummer. I let my mind wander again, imagining myself dancing with Laek and Philip, Laek's movements full of beauty and grace, Philip's adorably awkward but solid and grounded as he sings along with his strong bass.

I feel my mouth curl into a smile, then spy the group of cops approaching us from the main road across from the parking lot. What the fuck are city cops doing here this early?

"Woop-woop!" I play on my synthesizer, sounding a warning.

The trombones answer with the opening notes of KRS-One's "Sound of da police."

"Woop-woop!" we all chant back, to show we got the message.

"Pas un bon signe," whispers one of the band members.

"Yeah, they're either anticipating trouble or planning to make some," says another.

"Qui est le responsable ici?" the lead cop demands, blue-uniformed chest puffed out.

"No one's in charge, we're anarchists," says our hurdy-gurdy player to some laughter.

The cop, unsmiling, asks to see our street performer's license. Ariel, who's usually the one to deal with the police, explains that we're not street performers in the sense that the law intends, that we don't ask for money or contributions, that we're merely practicing and enjoying the open air while getting ready for the demonstration.

Meanwhile, the comrades preparing the vehicles behind us have had the chance to camouflage them. They make a big show of bringing out their bigger-than-life-sized puppets and organizing their paints and craft supplies.

"Et eux?" another cop asks, indicating those working behind us.

"Ils travaillent avec les marionettes. A show for the kids."

And indeed, the Neo Bread and Puppet Circus have set their marionettes in motion. A puppet resembling the President-and-Chief of the United America rides a papier-mâché elephant; she's chased by a puppet in a faux beavertail hat who represents the president of Can-Telecom Public Partnership. I turn back to the cops. *And who's pulling your strings?* I want to say.

Zende, our conductor for today's events, raises both his arms, and all of us come to attention. At almost two meters tall, Zende is easy to see. We wait for him to signal a song. He gives us a lopsided grin then throws his head back, locs flying, and stares up into the sky. We break into "Murmuration," our most challenging performance in terms of choreography, paying tribute to the capacity of starlings to evade and confuse predators by flying in constantly changing, complex patterns.

This is an apt metaphor for how we hope to stymie the government and our enemies today through our complex and ever-moving set of objectives for the manif. I think of Laek's mission to break into that sweatshop some kilometres west of us, praying that Philip is with him; of Siri and her group still in Montréal protecting our buses; of the border actions and the mariposas; and of Andressa and the Peeps. I picture Simon and Aiza and all their other young comrades who, dressed as endangered species, will present a detailed list of recommendations for immediate protective measures for the Earth and its inhabitants.

I wonder about Simon's costume. Like Aiza, he designed and created it by himself and wouldn't let any of the adults see it ahead of time. Will he dress as a black panther, the animal of his childhood obsession? For some reason, I don't think so.

At the manif, there will be cougars and otters, snakes and frogs, caribou and whales, turtles, elephants and bears. But most especially, I think, as I act my part in a starling's murmuration, there will be all kinds of birds. . .

SIMON

". . . spreading our wings and flying from our coops and co-ops. And we'll all meet at the border for the big May Day manif! A May Day 'mayday,' which is from the French term, 'm'aidez,' because the animals are in trouble, and so are we, and we need to aid each other," I tell Aiza's parents as we show off our costumes in their living room.

"Very good speech, Simon," Aiza's mother says.

"Êtes-vous des pigeons?" Aiza's dad asks.

"We're doves," Aiza explains. "But doves are from the same family as pigeons."

"Are pigeons and doves endangered?" Aiza's mom asks. "Mais il y en a beaucoup!"

"Some are," I tell them. "Carrier pigeons are completely

extinct, and turtle doves are endangered in Europe. And, of course, our coop's pigeons were en danger just last week!"

"C'était courageux, how you saved our co-op's pigeons," Aiza's mother says, smiling at me. "Were you not afraid, being so near to the fire?"

"I was mostly afraid the pigeons would be hurt." Just thinking about it makes me upset. Aiza brushes her wingtip against mine and I feel better.

"On y va," Aiza's father says. "We must hurry or the buses will leave without us."

"D'accord, Abu Aiza," I say. I turn to Aiza. "Let's go down the stairs. There may not be enough room for our wings in the elevator." Plus, I love to jump down each half-flight. I bet that the wings will make it feel even more like I'm flying!

We beat Aiza's parents outside, then the four of us fast-walk down the street. We're supposed to be there in thirty-six minutes. I calculate that the ride on the métro will take us twenty-four minutes, so we need to hurry since our station is almost a kilometre away, and then there's still going up and down the stairs and walking from métro Papineau to where the buses are parked. I can't wait to show Siri my costume! She said she'd be there early for guard duty, though it's hard to imagine how someone could steal one of our buses.

I hop in the air and flap my wings like a pigeon would, just to see how it feels.

"Aiza, do you think our contingent's affinity groups will be organized by species?"

"Maybe by phylum. Or by taxon."

"I was kind of joking," I tell her.

"I know," she says laughing. "So was I."

I notice that Aiza isn't leaping in the air like me, though she does flap her wings ever so often like she's testing to see if they're working alright.

"Do you think I'm being immature, trying to hop around like a real pigeon?" I ask.

"No, you're just trying to get into character. Like an actor. And I'm glad that you get excited about things. Some people in our class, they pretend like nothing fazes them. They think it's mature to be above it all, but I think it's just apathetic."

"And being apathetic is pathetic!" we both say together. It's our favourite Peeps' chant.

I can't wait to see the rest of the Peeps in costume. I can picture it in my head, a zillion types of animals, all demanding that the government and big corporations stop putting profits ahead of the Earth and its living creatures. Then I imagine real animals joining the manif, or at least those who live in the city, like pigeons and squirrels and racoons and skunks. . . skunks especially, spraying the police and people in suits who decide their fates without caring about them. Now I really am thinking like a little kid, but I love the images in my head. Maybe I'll invent a screen game like that.

"Aiza, when you were little, did you ever play screen games?"

"Of course! Which ones did you play?"

"My favourite was called Animal Rescue," I tell her. "My parents would get mad at me, my mom especially, because I played it all the time, even in the middle of the night."

"I don't know that one. Tell me about it."

We're on rue Notre-Dame now. We pass a Vélorution free bike stand. I count how many bikes there are—only twenty-four left, the empty spaces looking like missing teeth. I wonder how to explain Animal Rescue to Aiza and what it meant to me.

"It's about saving animals, which I guess is obvious from its name. The rescue missions were based on real-life situations involving species that were actually endangered. When stuff in the world changed, the parameters of the game changed too."

"That sounds hyper!"

"Yeah. I did lots of research and came up with action plans, like huge projects to repair eco-systems, or transporting entire animal populations to other zones. I thought I was really helping. IRL, I mean. I knew the animals were only sims but I thought they. . . like they represented real-life animals, and that all the people who played the game were together helping to change things in the actual world. I was pretty silly, I guess." I shrug, feeling embarrassed.

"I don't think that's silly. Lots of kids think sims are real. And even if your actions didn't have a direct effect in the real world, it was. . . comment dire. . . to practice. Practice for today, even. The things you learned in the sim probably helped when we met with the other Peeps to decide what demands to make at the manif. N'est-ce pas?" She raises her eyebrows.

"C'est vrai," I answer, feeling happier. "Did you have silly ideas when you were little?"

"Évidemment que oui! When I was younger, I wanted to fly. Not on a rocket but with my own wings. Like a butterfly. And now we do have wings!"

"They're not very aerodynamic, though." I shrug with them.

"No," she says, giggling. "But that reminds me. There's something I've been wanting to talk to you about without my parents around." Aiza glances behind her. Her parents are half a block behind us. "At the planning meeting last night, I overheard a conversation about mariposas."

"About how they're endangered?" I walk a little faster so Aiza doesn't have to worry about her parents hearing us.

"No, not that. They mentioned a rescue over the border *using* mariposas!"

"How could you use a butterfly to rescue someone? They're too little."

"At first I thought they meant someone dressed as a butterfly, or a giant marionette butterfly from the Bread and Puppet cirque, but that doesn't make sense either."

She's right. "Maybe 'mariposa' is a code for something. Butterflies are used as a symbol for the Erase Borders movement. Or maybe a mariposa is some kind of new weapon or. . ."

". . . a vehicle," she says. "I heard them talking about a team flying *in* it, and how teenagers are more lightweight so they can rescue more people that way."

"We're lightweight," I say.

"And I've always wanted to fly...." Aiza responds with a big grin.

". . . and I've always wanted to do a rescue mission."

"So maybe we can combine the two. . ."

". . .and do a butterfly rescue!" I say.

"Aiza! Simon!" Aiza's dad shouts. "You are getting too far ahead!"

We slow down to wait for them.

Aiza lowers her voice. "We'll need to make a plan. In the bus, we'll sit in the back with the other kids. My parents always sit in the front."

"And we can speak in Babble. So our communication will be secure."

But I'm not really worried about talking in front of the other Peeps and activists. We'll be safe with them, on one of the buses that. . .

SIRI

... it's our responsibility to guard. They'll soon be filled with our comrades, including seniors, kids, disabled folx, other vulnerable community members who are ready to put them-selves on the line for social justice. I'm picturing Simon and Aiza and her parents, hoping they don't arrive early, when Wakanda shouts, "Close ranks!"

There's sweat in my armpits and on the palms of my hands. I grip my bat so hard I can feel the skin stretching across my knuckles, so I balance it across my shoulder to make myself relax, remembering how I'd swung at that curve ball yesterday, the one I hit over the fence.

Only this isn't a game, and it's people—not baseballs—I may have to swing at.

Em says xe'll be right back and the rest of us form a solid line, spreading out two arms' lengths from the comrade next to us. Maneesh is a few metres behind us in the lot under the bridge, standing with xir back against a bus.

"What's going to happen?" xe shouts.

"We're gonna break some fash heads," Gabriel shouts back, fists clenched.

"Maybe you didn't notice, but they have weapons," Maneesh shouts back.

"And so do we!" Em reappears with some banners, and for a second, I think xe means that we're armed with words and ideas, but then xe detaches the poles from the holo boards and hands them out to Wakanda, Myriam, and Oiseau Noir, keeping one for xirself.

"I can call the police. There was a police officer at the coffee shop. A bus driver too. Was that your bus driver?" Maneesh is talking really fast, like xe does when xe's nervous.

"They're Thunder Union," Anaïs says. "They have friends on the police force."

"Fucking pitufos," Gabriel mutters, adjusting the black kerchief tied around his face.

The boneheads are now just across the street from us, and

though my heart is beating hyper fast in my chest, now that they're here, I feel calmer, more focused. They're close enough that I can see their smirks, the same smirks that were on the faces of the bullies I tried to protect Simon from in Brooklyn, the same smirks that all bullies have when they think you're weaker than they are and that they can hurt you without anything happening to them. Well, they may outnumber us, they may have more weapons, but they're gonna learn that we fight back.

There's not a lot of street traffic, but for now, a string of cars and motos driving east on Ste-Catherine is keeping our two groups apart. As they wait, some of the boneheads slap their sticks against their palms; others toss the rocks they're carrying from one hand to the other, like they're advertising their weapons to us.

"I still think we should call the police," Maneesh repeats nervously.

"Stop talking," I say. "Please, Maneesh, just get behind the buses."

The traffic is clearing the intersection and for a stretched-out moment, I wonder if anything's really gonna happen; then one of the boneheads pulls their arm back to throw something, and Gabriel springs towards them. A tall dude wearing green fatigue shorts cuts Gabriel off. I look up to see something roundish flying in the air towards us.

Instinct takes over. I lift the bat off of my shoulder, step forward, and swing. I hit it squarely. It's not a rock but a small silvery disk that looks a little like a hockey puck but isn't. There's a cracking sound as it ricochets off my bat and soars back at our attackers in a low arc, trailing a tail of smoke. I hear a dull thump followed by a cry as it hits the person who threw it in the middle of their chest. They're knocked backwards right onto their butt.

All hell breaks loose. The boneheads cross the street in one big mass, sticks raised and the smirks wiped off their faces. All around me are shouts and curses and the clack of sticks hitting sticks. A buzzing sound like an angry wasp is followed by a scream and Oiseau Noir is down, his pole on the ground and his hands under his armpits. I run towards his attacker, bat raised. There's a weird odour, like how it might smell if the cleaning supplies they use at our school were set on fire. A shock stick discharge?

I aim at the attacker's weapon, not feeling okay about bashing someone over the head, but change my motion at the last minute, realizing that my bat might conduct electricity. I smack the attacker on the wrists instead with an undercut that makes the shock stick fly out of their hands. Myriam stoops down to grab it from the ground where it's fallen, then picks up Oiseau Noir's stick too. Oiseau Noir takes the opportunity to retreat, looking shaky. I see Maneesh dart out and lead Oiseau Noir behind the buses.

In the vacant lot beside the buses, Gabriel and the tall bonehead in fatigue shorts are having a fistfight. Wakanda is there too, wrestling with a bald dude in a tight army green t-shirt. As they roll around, dust puffs up into the air from the dry, packed dirt of the empty lot. I notice a second bonehead sneaking up on Wakanda with a lifted hockey stick. Before I can get there, Harriet jumps up and grabs hold of it. Two other boneheads come running to attack her. I trip one of them with my bat and hit the other one on the arm, harder than I'd hit the person who'd shock-sticked Oiseau Noir.

I pivot one way, then the other, trying to figure out where I'm most needed. I've never been in a group fight before. It's overwhelming, like playing basketball with ten different balls, everyone trying to score and steal at once, only what they're trying to score are hits and punches.

"Dandelion!" Em yells, and I duck, the shock stick that was aimed at my head barely missing me. I back off a few paces, thinking I need to pay more attention to my own situation, but it's hard to lose the habit of taking in the whole field. Plus, watching Em, an experienced dancer and fighter, has shown me how to time my moves against a shock stick.

I dart forward, poking at my attacker with my bat, then quickly retreat when they trigger the charge on their stick. As soon as the stick's zap has completely discharged, I hit it hard with my bat. They manage to hold onto it, but the tip is broken, which I'm pretty sure means the shock part won't work anymore. Plus it's shorter now, so it will be pretty ineffective against my bat. I see the bonehead make the same calculation and run off.

Most of us are not doing so well. QS is still fighting but has a bloody nose. One of the comrades I don't know has their arms wrapped around their ribs and the comrade next to them is trying to fight two people at once. Anaïs is pinned against one of the pylons, struggling with a big dude wearing a vest that looks like it's made of real leather. Gross. I move in that direction, but Anaïs manages a kick to the balls that sends the dude to his knees.

I look around for Gabriel and that's when I see another group coming towards us from the east, carrying baseball bats. They're a little under two blocks away, close enough for me to see that most of them are wearing caps and matching t-shirts but not to read what they say. Les Soldats du loup dress like that, as though they're some kind of sports team. We didn't get any info that they were coming in from Chicoutimi, but our intel hasn't been perfect so far.

I don't have time to think about them because I suddenly catch a glimpse of Gabriel behind the pylon closest to

De Lorimier. One of the boneheads is holding him from behind while the other two are taking turns punching him.

I run over, and this time don't hesitate to use my bat against them. I start with the one who's punching Gabriel and hit them hard across the shoulders. They arch their back and let out an "oomph" sound, stumbling backwards. The second bonehead turns to face me. I aim low, for the knees. They cry out and fall to the ground. The person holding Gabriel releases him. Gabriel doesn't even wipe the blood off his face before spinning around and punching them hard in the stomach then kicking them in the face. The first one I hit runs off, leaving their friend on the ground, still groaning in pain. Someone else has to come and drag them away.

I let my bat sag to the ground, feeling a little sick to my stomach. Then I sense a movement above me. I try to dodge out of the way, but I'm hit on the cheek with the blade of a hockey stick. The pain stuns me for a second, but I manage to lift my bat to block the next swing. The blow is so hard that I can feel the vibration all the way to my shoulder joints. The bonehead lifts the stick again and I retreat, holding my bat with two hands like a sword. The muscles in my arm ache and my bat feels very heavy; I'm not sure how long I'll be able to keep dodging and blocking the longer, lighter hockey stick. But I won't run.

The third blow sends me to the ground, and even though I manage to block it, I won't be able to lift my bat in time for the next one. "Siri!" Gabriel yells, but he'll be too late; the hockey stick is already on its way down towards me. I curl into a ball, arms wrapped around my head.

Next thing I know, I hear a grunt and the hockey stick falls to the ground with a clack just next to me. My attacker is bent over, holding their wrist, and two people with raised baseball bats are standing on either side of them. "Décrisse! Get the fuck out of here!" one of the two says, and my attacker takes off. I realize that I recognize the voice. What's she doing here?

I get to my feet slowly and look around. The group with the bats arrived while I was busy getting smacked around. And they're not Soldats du loup, they're not boneheads at all; they're actual baseball players! I see some of my own teammates from L'Exposition swarming the area under the bridge and chasing off the boneheads, helped by players wearing the pink and lime green jerseys of The Phoenix and others whose t-shirts have the logo of Les Gros Bats.

"Tu vas avoir un pas pire bleu!" Nasrin says, pointing to my cheek.

I put my hand on the bruise. "It won't keep me from striking you out next week." I grin, which makes my face hurt, but I can't help smiling watching those assholes getting chased away by baseball players from three different teams! At the same time, I am so totally confused.

"Qu'est-ce que vous faites ici? I mean, how did you know—"

"It's all you talked about last night when you were shit-faced drunk." Maneesh has come out from behind the bus now, nodding at Nasrin who smiles back shyly.

"What did I say?" I ask, worried I'd broken confidentiality.

"Pas grand-chose," Nasrin replies. "Just how you had to guard the buses."

"And we could tell you were worried there might be trouble," my teammate August says, adding, "Fucking fascists." August's freckles stand out against his pale skin, and I can't tell if he's angry or, like me, kind of freaked out about what just went down.

My comrades have gathered around us and everyone is bumping fists and laughing.

I have this sudden, weird thought about my party last

night and how anxious I was about whether my baseball friends, my friends from school, and my comrades from Jeune Vanguard would get along. It's like I'm looking back on the thoughts of a different, younger person who was too immature to see past surface differences to all the ways people can connect. I watch Maneesh and Nasrin sneak looks at each other. Are they flirting?

A few minutes later, after everyone but August—who's decided to join us for the manif—has gone, Gabriel says, "I can't believe that fucking *baseball players* saved our asses."

"I guess you never heard of the Christie Pits riot," I tell him.

I know I sound smug, but I am the daughter of a history teacher, after all.

Gabriel opens his mouth to ask a question, but Em says, "Just look it up."

"Also, to be precise, it was actually Siri who saved *your* ass," Maneesh says.

Gabriel glances at me and I try out one of the smiles I've seen my dad give, sweet and confident at the same time. He blinks and then smiles back, like he can't help himself.

"C'mon, let's clean this shit up," QS says. "The bus drivers are coming back. And some of our people are starting to arrive."

We pick up the rocks and broken sticks. The rocks, we put between the pylons; the remains of the sticks and the things that look like pucks are gathered together for Wakanda to give to Comrade X for analysis. Gabriel and I work side by side, and for once, there's not all this tension and hostility crackling between us.

After everything's been cleaned up, and the bus drivers are ready, we begin letting the first of the demonstrators inside the buses. I look up the street and finally see Simon and Aiza hurrying along Ste-Catherine, followed by her parents.

I run to them and wrap my arms around Simon, feeling an enormous wave of relief.

"Careful of my feathers!" he says, hugging me back awkwardly with his wings.

"You two look great!" I say, and actually mean it.

"You look messed up," Simon tells me. "Did you get drunk last night and fall down?"

"I did drink but—"

"You shouldn't have done that right before the big manif. There are all kinds of different big plans and plots and stuff going on. We need to be alert!"

"You're right, I should have been more alert," I say, feeling big-hearted, but I can't resist adding, "And what are your big plans? Flying over the manif and pooping on our enemies?"

"Ha ha, that's a good one," he says.

Aiza is watching me with that careful way she has. I can tell she has some more realistic suspicions about the bruise on my face.

We board the bus with Aiza's parents. Simon and Aiza find some seats in the back and ask me to sit with them. Glancing around the bus filled with my comrades, neighbours, and friends, I'm glad to not have to choose between them. Aiza's parents claim a seat near the front and help distribute water and pastries while the usual safety announcements are made. A comrade with first aid training starts circulating to check on those of us who were injured; someone hands me an ice pack.

After the bus has pulled away, Aiza and Simon say a few words to each other in that weird language they made up. Then they switch back to their usual Franglais.

"On a un plan, but..." Aiza says.

"C'est un plan secret. Top secret," Simon finishes.

"Can we ask your advice?" they both ask at once.

"Sure," I tell them.

Simon holds his screen out to Aiza and she uses her finger to draw a butterfly...

PHILIP

... whose wings are a gorgeous violet-blue outlined in black. I watch it flutter off in the direction of the building I'm hoping we'll later blow up and feel a twinge of anxiety. For the butterfly? For the kids? And where the fuck is Laek already? He left our cover in the woods to do some reconnaissance and said he'd be back in a few minutes. It feels like hours.

"What are you thinking about?"

I jerk my head around, startled by Laek's voice just behind me. I'd been watching the road, visible through the trees, expecting him to return from that direction, but somehow he snuck up on me again.

"A... about the kids in the building. What's our plan?"

"I was thinking. A few may manage to escape during the action. Someone should stay outside. To guide them to safety." Laek's watching the building, not me, as he says this.

"And you're thinking that someone should be me?" I say. Laek nods carefully. "Well, think again," I tell him. "How can I watch your back if you're in there and I'm out here?"

"Your focus ought to be on the kids. Not on my back."

"Their chances of getting out will be better if we work together, and any strays will find their way. Meanwhile, you'll have another pair of fists, if need be."

"Our strategy is stealth, not violence."

And sometimes the best strategy is not to respond. I cross my arms over my chest and wait. After a moment, Laek begins to silently make his way forward through the trees towards the road. I follow him, trying to match his swift, careful movements.

When we're almost at the edge of the tree-line, Laek squats down. I squat down with him. We're hidden from view by how the land slopes down from the embankment as well as by the thick undergrowth. He pulls two items from his boot: a tiny, flat greybox and a knife—the one I gave him before he left New York. He lifts the blade to his wrist and I flash back to that time in the hospital, when he joked/not joked about using it to slit his throat.

Laek makes a small, precise slit in his wrist, right through that tattoo he has of a double strand of barbed wire. A trickle of blood runs down his arm in the approximate shape of a question mark. My biceps tense as I fight the urge to grab the knife out of his hand. He puts it aside and my muscles unclench. He inserts a diamond-shaped chip into the slit he made in his wrist, then cleans and seals the wound using a spray he fishes out of one of his many pockets. Taking up the knife again, he says, "Your wrist, Philip."

I swallow. I'm not particularly scared of pain but seeing Laek cut himself has already made me a little queasy.

"Alright," I say, closing my eyes and extending my arm. I feel him remove the wrist band he insisted I wear, and brace myself. Nothing happens. After a moment, I take a peek and see him using the tip of the knife to insert something into a recess in the band. Our eyes meet and the corner of his lips quirk. He hands me the wrist band and I put it on again.

"I thought you were going to cut me." I'm surprised that I sound disappointed.

"We can become blood brothers another time." The quirk blossoms into a wide grin.

"But what did you do?" I ask.

"My chip is shadow-web. DNA activated. It'll get us in. For you, I inserted a tapper. With your wristguard, I'm the only one who can pinpoint or signal you. Feel that?"

"Yeah," I say, flexing my wrist against a light pressure.

"And now?" This time I watch Laek clench his fist twice in succession.

"Two taps."

"Perfect. If we get separated, one tap means all clear. Two means stay put. And if I give you three taps, you get the hell out of there. As quickly and as silently as you can. Got it?"

"I got it," I say, anxious from all this waiting. I pat my pocket, assuring myself that my chain of worry-rings is there, but I don't reach for them. "When do we start?"

"It's already started. Earlier, we introduced malware into their system. They're using some of the same vendors as the building in Gaspé. We found a zero-day vulnerability through one of them and exploited it. As soon as they detect the malware, they'll have no choice but to hit the kill switch. With their security system compromised, we'll slip in undetected."

"How will we know when. . . that happens?"

"Watch the building," he tells me.

I do, but it's a full five minutes before anything happens, and even then, I'm not sure what I'm seeing. The building we've been watching seemed rectangular, a bit longer than it was wide, but maybe I was mistaken because the building I'm now seeing is longer and more irregular, and has somehow stretched itself across the border. I blink my eyes. The outline seems to flicker; a wing appears on the east side as though it spontaneously grew there.

Laek bursts from the trees and flies across the road. I follow him at a sprint, crouching to take up less space. He's heading directly towards the previously invisible eastern wing.

He flattens himself against the building's outer wall. His hand snakes out to try the door. There's no knob, so he simply pushes against it. When it doesn't budge, he stands in front of it and sketches some shapes into the air. Whatever holographic he's manipulating, I can't see with the wristguard in place, blocking access to my chip. After a moment, he presses the wrist he cut against the door, then pushes again. The door opens with a small click, and we go inside.

The first thing I notice is a wall of holo-screens. Most of them are dead, black and silent; some are flickering. Two show a row of binary code backlit in green, but the numbers on one of them seem to be coalescing, taking some purposeful shape.

On the opposite wall a few yards away is a row of cots. They include restraints at foot, waist, and shoulder height, and attached biometric monitors. My brain is wondering what they're for but my body has already connected the dots, producing a shot of fury-laced adrenaline that makes my face hot. Laek, however, seems calm, his expression smooth and unreadable. He lifts his wrist and waves it around, presumably taking some footage, then pulls a lump of some greyish, clay-like substance out of another of his pockets and starts spreading it on strategic-seeming locations on the screens, the metal restraints, and the cots themselves. It's only when he turns back to the holo-screens that I notice the tightness in his jaw muscles.

"We may have to blow something up, after all," he murmurs. Before I can frame a reply, he continues, "What do you make of the screens?"

I turn back to them. "They're trying to restart the security programs. The one to the far left has nearly completed the cycle. Maybe we should. . ."

I stop myself, noticing the screen in question go black like the others.

"Good," Laek says. "We fucked them up again."

Something occurs to me. "Do we have help on the outside?"

"Of course! You play too many single shooter games, mon

chum." He grins, and I think that this is when I love him most —confident, joyful, teasing, and with an intimate smile, just for me. "Yeah, there's a tech support team. Including a certain young hacktivist. A comrade of. . ." The smile slides from Laek's face. "Time to move."

We approach an interior door that connects to the rest of the building. Laek presses his ear to its metal surface, then shrugs and turns the three deadbolts. The locks are obviously not meant to keep the people in this room from leaving but rather to keep those outside—the young workers, presumably —from wandering in.

Laek opens the door a crack, peers outside, then gestures me to follow. We walk along an empty hallway lit at regular intervals by glowlights giving off an oily, yellowish illumination. The hallway terminates at a short set of metal stairs; to our right and our left are corridors leading in opposite directions. At the bend in the left corridor is a holo in the shape of a green arrow pointing up; the right corridor has one pointing down.

Laek rejects both corridors in favour of the metal stairs in the middle leading a half-level down. The stairs are wet, like there's been a flood. My foot slips a little as I climb down. Laek, despite his heavy, metal-tipped boots, descends with soundless agility, like a cat.

It's dark at the bottom of the stairs, the only illumination a reddish light pulsing from above. I'm reminded of the scene at the airport, the day I arrived and a bomb went off. I suppose this is a similar type of emergency lighting, but the sensory memory makes me edgy.

The next door has neither knob nor deadbolts. Laek once again traces some pattern with his hands. A whir and the door retracts into the wall. The space beyond is vast and empty. Before I can observe much else, the door begins to slide closed once again. Laek grabs my arm and leaps inside, pulling me along with him.

Although not as dark as the corridor, the room is nevertheless dim, which surprises me. Based on its size, the long rows of worktables, and equipment that resembles the images I've seen of neuro chip fabricators, this is clearly the factory floor. Even young workers with their sharp eyes would need more light to complete the intricate tasks demanded of them. Then I notice that there are actually plenty of lights—or the remains of them—strewn all over the tables and floors, and that the lights, like most of the equipment in the room, have been smashed up.

"No bombs needed here." Laek sounds pleased. "The kids have taken matters into their own. . ." He trails off, turning his head sharply towards the far end of the room. I follow his gaze and see a slight figure dart across the threshold of an alcove, maybe a storage area; a couple of other faces quickly pull back out of view. I start to move in that direction but am brought up short by the double tap against my wrist and Laek's whispered warning: "Don't move. There's a rat. Not the natural kind."

I freeze, heart pounding, my own eyes finding the chipmunk-sized mechanism as it drags its segmented, metal tail across the threshold of the entranceway where the kid had been.

"Al taught me about that kind of rat. And how they bite," I say in a low voice.

"I'll distract it. So you can get to the kids. But tread carefully."

Before I can voice a concern, Laek begins cartwheeling across the room. The rat freezes, its four red, mechanical eyes spinning as its facial recognition software attempts to get a fix on Laek's head. I use the time to inch my way down the length of the room, back pressed against the wall. The kids keep poking their heads out to see what's happening, risking the rat's attention, and this is all taking too long. I use the most direct route, darting across the open floor. The rat stops, pivots in my direction; Laek claps his hands, the noise like thunder in the cavernous space, and the rat pivots again and streaks across the room after Laek.

I want to follow Laek's instructions, to offer the kids what protection I can, but I'm imagining the metallic rat flying at his neck, its sharp, triangular teeth clamping down and sending an electrical charge through his body. Instinct takes over. I grab my chain of worry-rings from my pocket and fling it at the thing. The rings clunk against the wall and the rat stops, spinning on its circular base. I sprint towards it, as fast as I've ever run, and grab it by its tail. I smash it against the wall, once, twice, and again for good measure, until all I'm holding is a jointed metal tail trailing wires that resemble obscenely long antennae.

Laek is at my side in an instant. For a moment, I think he's going to chew me out. Instead, he says, "Well done," and squeezes my shoulder. I flush with pleasure. Then he adds, "But they'll soon pinpoint where the last signal was. So we gotta move."

He jogs over to the kids, and I pick up my rings and jog after him. The alcove is roomier than it looked from the outside. A group of about thirty teenagers are inside, pressed into the corner, ranging in age from maybe fourteen to eighteen. One teenager breaks off from the group—I think they're the one we saw run across the threshold—and throws themself at Laek.

"Je savais que tu nous trouverais! I just knew it!" they say in a muffled cry.

Laek hugs the kid tightly, then asks, "Where are the others?"

"Some of us escaped—during the. . . the panne d'électric-ité. We were headed for the roof. Mia and her brother and Nizar are probably already there. We had a plan. To wreck the factory. To escape, to jump if we had to. But les salauds locked the second shift into the salle de travail and sent the rat to guard us before they left. And they locked down the dorm where the younger kids sleep. About ten kids are stuck down there. Robin from our school went to try to help. Did you send them?"

Laek looks pained. "No, Robin came on their own. Écoute: I need you to go with Philip. He'll bring you all up to the roof. Will you help him, Pascal?"

Pascal nods.

"Philip, take him and the others up to the roof. When you're there, remove your wristband. Use the special message app to ping Janie. Keep it short, then put the band back on."

"What do I tell her?"

"To send the mariposas to you. Ping me at the same time so I can pass the message on to the support team."

"Okay, and where will you be?" I motion to the kids to line up behind me.

"I'll join you. As soon as I get the rest of the kids. But don't wait for me."

Following Laek, I lead the kids through the empty, wrecked factory floor through the door where we entered. Once outside, we go in opposite directions, Laek to the stair-well leading down and us towards the door with the up-pointing arrow. The group following me is about the same size as my last high school class, and for a second, I feel like a teacher again, but on some kind of dystopian field trip. The kids are unnervingly quieter than a group of teenagers ought to be, the only talk from a long-haired kid who whispers in Spanish to hurry. Pascal is holding the hand of a smaller child whose eyes are so wide with fear that you mostly see the whites.

We climb to the top floor. The stairwell ends at a plain metal door. From the floor plan of the building in Gaspé, I can guess at what's beyond it: a wide, windowless space with a ladder leading to the roof, a second set of stairs on the opposite side leading back down.

Or maybe I'll find classrooms, their doors bearing shattered glass transoms, blood seeping over their thresholds.

Pascal taps my shoulder. I lift my palm in a halting gesture and put my finger to my lips before cracking the door open. The way seems clear, and the ladder is where I guessed it would be, ending at a hatch to the roof. We file into the room and the kids begin to climb the ladder, one by one. They seem more anxious now, this close to our goal. There's some jostling, so I raise my arm again. The next instant, I hear the sound of boots racing up the opposite staircase.

A guard emerges from the stairwell with what looks like a phaser projectile weapon in hand. I spread my arms, trying to protect the kids behind me, but one of them has already made a break for it. The guard swings their weapon towards the child, and I shout, "No!"

The guard fires.

The child's hands go to their chest and they collapse with a scream, twitching, a wet stain spreading from their crotch. There's a low whine in my ears and everything is tinted red. All at once, I'm standing a little less than arm's length from the guard, fists clenched, though I don't remember moving. A roundhouse punch to the side of the head sends them to the ground. I stomp on the hand holding the weapon and kick it away, following up with a series of hard kicks to their side until the guard stops trying to move.

"Montez! ¡Suben!" I shout at the kids as a second guard

emerges from the stairs, similarly armed. The kids start scrambling up as fast as they can.

The second guard immediately levels their weapon at me and I twist my body to the right, away from their shooting hand, but not fast enough. There's an agonizing pain in my left bicep as my muscles spasm, but something like momentum keeps me moving forward. I grab at the guard's shoulders, their gun now flush against my chest. I hear a dull pop and wait for the pain. Instead, my chest is encompassed by a growing warmth, like the way your butt feels sitting in one of those chaises chauffantes they have here at cafés during winter. The guard's eyes go wide. Another pop and the heat increases before cooling down again.

I don't understand what happened, but I tighten my grip on the guard's shoulders, jab my knee into their stomach, then smack the back of their head against the wall a couple of times. They slump to the ground.

All the kids have climbed up to the roof except Pascal, who stands looking at his poor friend lying in a pool of their own urine. The kid seems groggy and disoriented but is no longer moaning. I signal Pascal to climb up before gently lifting the child and carrying them up the ladder, their head on my shoulder. The smell of their urine-soaked pants makes my eyes tear; at least, that's what I tell myself.

Two of the older kids stand on either side of the entrance to the roof with improvised weapons—one holds a shoe and the other something that looks like a scrap of metal shingle. The other kids sit against the parapet, making themselves as small and unnoticeable as possible.

"Stay down," I tell them. "I'm going to get us some help."

I lower the kid I'm carrying—who seems alert now—onto their own two feet.

"Are you alright?" I ask. They nod, eyes downcast. "Do

you. . . do you ever wear dresses or tunics? Because my t-shirt is long enough to go past your knees." They nod again.

I remove my t-shirt. "Here." I also hand them the scarf Laek gave me on the bike ride here. "Take this too. You can use it to clean up a bit."

I turn my back so they can change, and remove the wrist guard to send that message to Janie. As I do this, I'm thinking about all the gear Laek gave me to wear for this rescue: the wristguard, the scarf, and the sleeveless vest I'm wearing made of that weird rubbery material. *It's a protective garment,* I remember him saying. I touch it where the phaser weapon was pressed against my chest and I realize what it's meant to protect against: electronic weapons.

Then I think of Laek with no protective vest, and his own, younger, group of kids locked up somewhere downstairs, the direction from which the two armed guards had arrived.

"Stay here," I say to the kids. "Four of you guard the trap door. Take turns. The rest of you, watch the sky. . ."

JANIE

... for the new-gen solar mariposas that will soon float across the border like the butterflies they're named for. The first time I saw them was above the practice fields on Île Bizard preparing for today's rescue operation. Their rainbow colours dotting the heavens reminded me of the parachutists I saw the day we crossed the border into Québec by bicycle more than three years ago. Back then, I was looking for signs. And here I am, still watching for signs and trying to keep my family safe.

"Ow, Mommy! Stop holding my hand so tight," Siri complains.

"Sorry." I glance again at the bruise on her cheek. Another

couple of inches and it could have been her eye. "You sure you don't want some more ice? That must hurt."

"Not as much as my hand does. I think you crushed my bones," she says.

I bring her knuckles to my lips and kiss them. "Sorry. All better?"

"Franchement, Mommy," she grumbles, but doesn't pull her hand from my grip.

Simon and Aiza are on my other side, craning their necks for the puppeteers' tent. They told me they wanted to consult with them about something, and when I asked them what, they said it was an "artist thing." That, the conspiratorial glances, and the whispered conversation between them are more than enough to tell me that something's up.

"How was the press conference?" I ask.

"C'était hyper!" Aiza answers. "We did a die-in—"

"And then we came back to life," Simon adds. "Pour parler de mesures de mitigation."

"And ecological solutions," Aiza concludes.

"Do you practice finishing each other's sentences?" Siri asks in that half-annoyed, half affectionate tone she uses with her brother. "You sound like an old married couple."

"We're an affinity group!" they both answer simultaneously.

We arrive at the exhibition they're calling "Jouer avec les frontières/Playing with Borders." The artists constructed it right beside Haskell Free 2: the children's library and multimedia performance space that straddles the border. Supposedly, that fucking evil factory west of us also spreads across the border, except that the part of the structure that's in the U. A. is said to be invisible from the Québec side. Urban myth? Who knows. Maybe Laek does, I think with a pang of worry. I wonder how he's doing, and once again, pray that Philip is with him.

"Okay, this actually is hyper," Siri says.

She's right. There are tetherball, volleyball, and badminton courts, with kids smacking spheres of various sizes back and forth over the border; there's a whole line of younger children going up and down on transnational seesaws; teenagers, some on Québecois soil and some in the U.A., are playing tug of war, with winners declared the moment someone's foot touches the border; there's even a balance beam audaciously placed right on top of the invisible line.

The municipal cops haven't intervened but there are an absurd number of them, watching these children playing like they're watching the unfolding of a plot to overthrow the world order. I hope they are.

"The puppeteers should be just past here," I tell Simon, motioning to a stretch of circus tents in rainbow colours. "Do you want to check out the exhibit first? It's interactive; we're allowed to use the equipment."

Simon shakes his head and runs off. Aiza, whose parents have, unlike us, managed to teach their child manners, says, "Non, merci," before catching up to him. From behind, the two of them look like twins—tall and slim and in identical dove costumes that cover them from head to toe. Perfect, since the idea was to wear costumes that hide your identity.

I'm looking for the group of activists that will be accompanying Andressa, wondering what type of animal disguises they'll be wearing. And wondering if our performances, exhibits, and actions will divert the cops enough for her to lead the cross-continental solar punk relay without getting arrested or deported, while also allowing the group of young refugees from across the border whom we're protecting to disappear into the crowd. With hundreds of kids and teenagers dressed up as animals, faces covered by beaks and snouts and muzzles, this plan may actually work.

A sudden pulsating heat against my wrist makes me slip my hand from Siri's to check my messages. Laek? I think, heart pounding. The ping came through that special app he installed, so I take out my decryptor, ready in my pocket. I move a few steps away from my daughter, pressing the decryptor against my wristpad. A message appears:

Laek says to send the mariposas to the roof.

"What is it?" Siri asks. "Is it from Daddy?"

I pocket the decryptor and the message dissolves.

"No, from Uncle Philip, but go find Simon and meet me at the first aid tent. Quick!"

Siri takes off at a sprint in the direction of the circus tents, where Simon and Aiza were headed. I jog to the first aid tent—big and white and with four red insignias: a crescent moon, a six-pointed star, a cross, and a wheel. Just behind it, a bit closer to the border, is an even larger tent whose roof is adorned with purple stars.

I look up to see Siri running towards me. Simon and Aiza are not with her.

"I couldn't find them," she says, a little out of breath, "But one of the puppeteers said they'd invited them to do guerrilla theatre with some other teenagers." She points in the direction of the tents beyond the first aid station. "That's where they're getting ready for the big act."

"Okay, listen," I say. "I need to help Daddy and Philip with something. Once you find Simon and Aiza, do me a favour and stay with them."

"But where are you going? If Daddy needs help, I should be the one. I know that building. I surveilled it, I—"

"You've risked yourself enough," I tell her, anxious to get going. "Promise me you'll find your brother so I can worry about one less thing. You've done your job. Now it's my turn."

"But Mommy, that's how I feel. That you and Daddy have done your job and that it's my turn, my generation's turn."

I'm thinking how glad I am that Siri hasn't lost the Brooklyn custom of referring to her parents as "Mommy" and "Daddy" right through adulthood. Yet, how differently the word resonates at different points in the parent-child relationship. One day, if I live long enough, "Mommy" will refer to that small, frail person talking in exaggerated detail about past adventures but who can't remember what she said two minutes ago. But for now, Siri's still my child to protect as much as I can, even if she's taller and stronger than I am.

"My work's not quite done yet. Please, Siri, find your brother. Stay with him, but don't tell him what we're up to. He's a worrier."

"Okay, but. . . you'll be back soon, right?" For a moment, her bravado slips just enough that I can see she's worried too.

"It'll be okay, sweetheart. I even promise to try not to get lost on the way."

She laughs and then, with a final wave, starts walking towards the green tent. I take off for the one with the stars. I've already decided that, not only will I see to it that they send the mariposas, but I'm going to be on one of them myself. If all goes well, this will be my second roof rescue in a week. I think of Laek, willing him to...

LAEK

... hang on. Janie's voice in my head. As though she knows what I'm thinking. I want to ignore those words. Throwing myself down the stairs would distract the guards one flight below our position, maybe win enough time for this last group of kids to make it to the roof. There's a memory that's insistent, though. Janie by my hospital bed in New York, face twisted with anger and grief. Demanding that I hang on.

So instead I yell to Robin and the group of kids to hurry. Then I grab the child who's stumbling with panic and fatigue, and carry them up the stairs. We make it to the top landing ahead of the guards. Once we're inside the door, I put my back against it.

We're in a rectangular space. On the perpendicular wall, a ladder to the roof. The first few kids hurry through the roof hatch. The rest are in a tight line, waiting their turn. On the wall opposite me is another door. It leads to the down stairwell. At the threshold is a downed guard. Chest moving, so unconscious rather than dead. They always work in pairs, so where's the partner? And if we did our homework right, there'll be a third pair in the building, patrolling. By now, looking for us too. Unless. . .

I spare a thought for Philip. No. I must assume he's safe. On one of the mariposas, looking after the first group of kids.

The door concusses against my back. I manage to hold it closed. Their second attempt cracks it open a finger's width. I push it closed again. The next attempt will succeed, I think. So I step aside when I hear them make a running start. With no resistance, the first guard flies across the threshold, smacking into the opposite wall; the second, I help to the ground by hooking the metal toe of my boot around their ankle.

The smaller guard pulls a weapon. I duck behind the stairwell door and the phaser dart bounces off it. The big guard lunges for me, stunner in hand. I go low and we grapple. The guard manages to press the stunner against my side. An intense burning sensation, then my whole body seizes. I find myself face down on the ground. The taste of metal in my mouth. The guard kicks me onto my back. I stare up at a square face, red with fury.

"Who are you working with?" Another kick to the ribs. "Answer me!"

The guard speaks in English. With a mid-United America drylander accent. I go cold inside. Remain silent as I fit some pieces together. When the next kick comes, I let a cry of pain escape my lips. "J'comprends pas!" I moan. My lips are wet with slobber. Or blood.

By now, all but two of the kids have made it to the roof. Robin is hurrying them, glancing back and forth between the roof hatch and me. Clearly torn.

Go, just go, I think at them.

"Drylander" notices the kids too and flips priorities. Starts moving towards the ladder. I push myself from the ground. The other guard shoots me with the projectile phaser. It's like a million wasps are stinging me, inside and out. I still manage to wrap my arms around Drylander's legs. I'm rewarded with another hard kick in the ribs. When I don't let go, Drylander uses the stunner again. This time I blank out.

I'm flying fast through a dark sky, bodiless, surrounded by ethereal, multi-coloured butterflies of magenta, umber, cerulean, tangerine, other colours I can't name. Like they're more ideas than colours. With that thought, sensation floods back into me, and most of that sensation is pain. The smaller guard is dragging me away from the foot of the ladder. Drylander batters uselessly at the roof hatch. Robin and the kids are gone, the hatch barred behind them. Safe, or at least safer.

Drylander climbs down the ladder. No questions this time, just a series of kicks to my ribs, hip, head. My mind separates from my body again. I idly wonder if they'll decide to beat me to death, and it's the mildness of this curiosity that frightens me out of my dissociation.

My pain returns along with my other senses. I hear sounds from the stairwell. A single set of pounding, echoing steps. The partner of the unconscious guard? Whoever it is, they're large. An intuition, or sense of familiarity, accelerates my heartbeat. *Philip*, I think, as he bursts into the room. Our eyes meet and his expression show a mix of emotions: anguish, guilt, then both eclipsed by fury. It burns through the last of my torpor and I roll away to avoid the next kick.

Philip is between me and the guards in an instant. He grabs the smaller one first. Flings them hard against the wall. They fall to the ground, cradling an arm. Philip turns to Drylander, who takes out a projectile phaser and shoots. The dart hits Philip in the chest, but the vest I gave him absorbs the electrical charge. He brushes the dart away like a bear would a mosquito.

A thousand questions form in my head. The first, nonsensically, is: what happened to Philip's t-shirt? More importantly, what went down in this room before?

Philip and Drylander begin trading blows. I pull myself to my feet. My legs tremble but support me. I move towards the two guards slumped against the back wall—one conscious, one unconscious—while keeping my eye on the fight between Philip and Drylander, a fight Philip seems to be winning. I'm also aware of the exits: the hatch to the roof, the doors to the two stairwells on either side of the room. We need to make our escape.

I begin with the guard who's conscious. Use a greybox bag to cover their hands and midway up their arm. The guard cries out from the pain of their injury as I bind their wrists.

"Sorry, I'm sorry," I say, but I can't risk the possibility that they call for reinforcements.

I drag the guard into the stairwell by their feet, tie their ankles to a railing.

"Keep your injured arm elevated," I say. "It'll hurt less. I'll call for medical help. As soon as we're out of the building."

"They'll catch you," the guard says, face betraying confusion. "You know that, right?"

I return for the unconscious guard. Drag that one more gently towards the stairwell. Philip has just landed a blow to the chin that nearly knocks Drylander off his feet. I bring the unconscious guard outside. As soon as I'm back in the room, I use my chip to fuse the lock closed. One less door to defend.

Philip's nose is bleeding, but Drylander is staggering, out of breath, trying to retreat. Philip's next punch is to the stomach; then he grabs the guard in a bear hug.

"Enough," I say. "We have to get out of here."

Philip continues to squeeze; Drylander's knees buckle.

"Right now!" I grab Philip by the shoulders. Shake him once.

Philip lets go and the guard falls to the ground, panting. I move to the exit, but it's too late. There's the sound of a double set of pounding steps in the stairwell. The third pair of guards. Approaching the door, the one I didn't block. Before I can even take a defensive position, the door flies open. But no one runs in.

"Down! Mask!" I yell. I have no mask; no scarf either, so I take a deep breath and throw myself to the ground. Bury my face in my arms.

There's a sound like a firecracker on the fourth of July, followed by a hiss. I peek out through my folded arms to see Philip, maskless, moving towards me. He wraps his body around mine. Trying to protect me, but from the wrong type of bomb. *Put on the mask I gave you!* I want to shout, but I need to hold my breath. Already, the room has begun to fill with smoke.

I raise my head as Philip starts coughing. Two guards are entering the room cautiously. Pressure masked. Projectile stunners drawn. One moves towards Drylander, who's coughing and gasping for breath.

"Give me your mask," Drylander demands of the shorter of the two new guards.

"But—"

"Give it to me!" Drylander repeats in a hoarse roar. "I'm your superior!"

"Yes, sir," the taller guard responds, ripping the mask off their partner's face to give to Drylander. The now-maskless guard, coughing, stumbles towards the door.

"There are two injured guards in the stairwell! But you'll have to go around." The words tumble out of my mouth without forethought, but by this time I've found Philip's mask. While I press it against his face, I'm shot with a phaser dart. I feel my back arch, then nothing.

I awake to the sound of Philip's snores. *Is it morning?* I wonder, disoriented. I reach for him but my hand touches the cold, hard floor and I remember where I am. My muscles ache and there's something snugly covering my nose and mouth. The mask.

My eyes fly open as I come to full awareness. Not snores. Wheezes. Drylander is kneeling on Philip's chest. His wide grin is obvious even behind the mask.

"Like how it feels, big man? Not so tough now, are you?" he says, bearing down harder.

There's only one other guard in the room. The one who said "Yes, sir" and tore the mask from their partner's face. 'Yes-sir' guard stands at the foot of the ladder to the roof holding a phaser gun. Philip wheezes again. I sit up. Yes-sir guard turns, points the gun at me. I go still.

"S'il vous plaît, let him breathe!" I say, not bothering to hide the fear in my voice.

Drylander says, "Watch that one carefully. He can't be trusted to stay down."

"Yes, sir."

Are these the only two words this guard can say?

Philip wheezes again, his struggles weaker.

"Please! You need to do something. He's killing him!" I lock eyes with Yes-sir, still hoping for some show of humanity. No response, so I turn to Drylander. "We gotta get out of here. Before the bombs go off. You can take me with you. I can tell you things. He. . ." I move my eyes to Philip, pinned to the ground, gasping. "He doesn't know anything. But if you kill him, I'll never tell you a thing. I swear. I'll take every bit of intel I have to the grave."

Drylander's only response is to tell Philip to stop resisting. Philip coughs. A weak, staccato sound. His arms drop to the ground.

My muscles clench, desperately searching for some kind of opening. But Yes-sir has me in the gun's sights, seeming more than happy to shoot again. I want to lunge at them anyway, pull the guard off Philip, protect him with my own body. I know I won't make it, but I'd rather be unconscious—dead— than watch Drylander crush the life out of him.

A sudden shaft of light across Yes-sir's eyes. The guard looks up, squinting, as the roof hatch scrapes open. A beautiful, perfect pair of legs hangs down, and before the guard can bring up the gun, Janie drops onto their head.

Drylander clambers to his feet, pulls out his own weapon. His eyes widen as he catches sight of Janie. Surprise or recognition? In a millisecond, I'm in front of him. He's gazing upwards at Janie. Yes, recognition. I strike. A hard, vicious blow to the throat. A cracking sound and he collapses. Like a marionette whose strings have been cut.

Even as he's falling, I'm pivoting. The other guard, standing now, has recovered the gun. I aim a blow to the solar plexus. Another two to the side of the head. The guard drops.

I turn to Philip and Janie. Both stare back at me with the same look of shock.

"Put the mask on, Philip." I toss my mask to him.

"I'm okay," Philip says, in an uncertain voice. With the pressure off of his chest and the roof hatch letting in fresh air, he's wheezing less. But his right nostril is clogged with blood.

"Just for once, do what I ask." My voice sounds cold.

I turn away from both of them. Bend down. Check Yes-sir's pulse. Pull back their eyelids. Symmetrical pupils, not dilated. Good. I turn to the guard whose larynx I crushed.

"Is he. . . is he dead?" Philip asks.

"Not yet," I say, without looking up. Rapid pulse. Shallow breathing. How long until swelling or a collapsed windpipe cuts off the air to his lungs? Or he chokes on his own blood?

"What should we do?" Janie asks. "How can I help?"

I want to tell her to take Philip and leave. To run as far as they can from this scene. And especially, from me.

"Make Philip put his mask on," I say instead, and to my horror, I realize I'm crying. How will I do what needs be done when all I want is take out my knife and cut my hand off?

"Dearheart." The tenderness in Janie's voice makes me ache. And as though there were a psychic line connecting our minds, she takes my offending fist in her own hand and kisses the bottom of my palm gently. I swallow hard as she turns it over and kisses each bruised knuckle, until my fingers loose, one by one. A huge wave is cresting inside my chest and I'm fighting it so hard I begin to tremble.

Philip reaches for me. "I'm sorry. I'm so sorry." The rawness of his voice makes me cry even harder; I can't even speak to tell him that none of this is his fault. He pulls me into his arms and then Janie too and we stand there many seconds longer than we can spare and an infinite number of seconds shorter than I'd like.

I pull away first. Force myself to speak our options out loud.

"Option one: we leave him," I begin. "He would almost certainly die."

"He tried to kill me," Philip says. "After beating the crap out of you."

"And he's the one who. . . at the airport with Andressa—" Janie adds.

"I know," I tell her. "But I don't think I can."

Janie nods slowly, frowning.

"Option two is we take him out with us. But the thing is, doing that could put us in danger. All three of us, I think."

"Then what?" Janie asks.

"There's a third option. We can walk the corridor. Bring him to the other side."

"I don't understand," Philip says.

"He means the long passageway. The one that supposedly runs all the way to the border. It's real, then. But why do that?" Janie asks. "What's the advantage?"

"We'd be sending a message. That we've ID'd him. They won't send him back with his cover blown. And. . ." I meet Janie's eyes briefly. "They'll be monitoring the passage. It's a zone frontière. A no-man's-land. They won't come across, but if they value him, he'll get medical help. Maybe quickly enough to save his life." *And I won't have killed him.* "But we'd have to hurry. There's just enough time."

"Before what?" Philip asks. "We really are blowing up the building, aren't we?"

"Not the building. Just two cancerous parts of it. The long passageway to the U.A. And the room with the biometric monitors and the. . . cots. It's already in motion."

"So that greyish clay you were spreading. . . Laek, mira. There's something I need to tell you." Philip looks guilty but determined. "I locked a guard into that room. He'd hurt one of the kids. I wanted him to feel what it was like to be powerless. As far as I'm concerned, we can leave him there, but I don't want you to have anything more on your conscience."

The missing guard. Everyone finally accounted for. I'm filled with a sense of inevitability that resembles relief. Our course is set. The choices made.

"On y va," I say.

We use up six minutes and twenty-four seconds moving the guard from the room with the cots to the factory floor and securing him there. After that, all three of us are running. Running on the moving walkway to the border, to the invisible line. Philip carries the guard I call 'Yes-sir' over his shoulder, while Janie and I carry Drylander between us. His gasps and wheezes remind me eerily of Philip's from before. Every few minutes I peer over my shoulder, but nothing pursues us. Nothing but a sense of déjà vu.

It doesn't take long to reach the other end of the passageway. There's a threshold where the moving walkway terminates. A door—metal, no knob—exactly where I expect it. We need to get the two injured guards inside, safe from the blast, and us back to the main building before the explosives detonate. We have a little time but the door is barred and my codes don't work.

"Maybe it's a regular lock. I mean, not a smart lock—just some kind of latch," Janie says.

Philip eases the guard he's carrying to the ground, out of the way. Puts his shoulder to the door and shoves. Janie and I do the same. I get the idea of using the moving walkway for momentum. I back up a few metres for a running start, then jump, twisting and bringing knees to chest before letting my legs kick out at the door. I end up in a heap on the ground. The door still shut and the pain from my various injuries screaming in protest.

"Let me support you on one side," Philip says. "This way you can kick a few times in a row with those metal-tipped boots of yours without ending up on your ass."

"And I got your other side," Janie says.

The two of them wrap their arms around me, Janie around the waist and Philip around my shoulders. I hold on to them and kick out hard, thinking of all the kids who've been hurt in this place and places like it. The door budges a little. I kick out again, picturing the guard, knees on Philip's chest, sadistically smiling as Philip fought for every breath.

"Again!" Janie cries. My legs explode against the door a third time as I recall how the guard punched Janie in the stomach, back when she organized that action for Andressa.

"Keep going! You're almost there!" Philip says, so I kick out a fourth time, this time for myself, for all the damage I've taken resisting illegitimate authority and fucked up institutions, struggling against people who get off on power and repression.

And then I kick out one last time, just for the joy of kicking, and that's when the door flies open...

SIMON

... and once the door is open, we walk right in.

The inside of the tent is filled with teenagers who seem around Siri's age or older, maybe even some young grownups.

Nobody notices that we're only twelve because we're both tall for our age, and plus, we're wearing costumes that cover our faces. Still, I'm a little nervous that we'll get in trouble. I wish Siri were with us.

"C'est dommage que Siri ne soit pas ici avec nous," Aiza says.

"I was just thinking the same thing. But only people dressed as non-human animals are allowed inside the tent. Anyhow, Siri wanted to wait for my papa et maman and Uncle Philip. She got a message they were on their way back."

I look up at the tent roof. The sun is shining through the purple stars we saw from the outside, making a star-shaped portal of violet light, like in a fantasy screen game. I stand under one and it makes me think of Daddy's special fireplace that helps take away depression, because the star-shaped light is making me feel happier. I didn't notice from the outside, but the purple stars on the tent roof are set up like constellations, and as each star lights up another one of our comrades, it's like together we're constellations too.

We follow the crowd. I'm realizing that the tent isn't actually our destination, that it's a passageway to somewhere else. Towards the back of the tent, there are five doors, and each animal person is being sent through one of them.

When we get there, one of the organizers tells us, "Birds go to door five."

"Hey, we were right, Aiza! They *are* sorting us by animal species!"

She nods with her dove-shaped head, which makes me laugh.

"Look Simon! The mariposas!" Aiza pulls me through portal five with her.

Outside of the tent, we stand around with the other bird people on the dusty ground. If I could read minds like Mommy sometimes can, I'd say that everyone is thinking about how they can't wait to be in the sky, flying. Above us is a tarp that looks like purplish see-through aluminum foil, and it's very hot underneath. The mariposa is right in front of us and the only word I can think of to describe it is "majestic." It has a long passenger area that looks like a giant caterpillar and huge, beautiful, wings with a million colours. The wings are decorated with spots and stripes like real butterflies have but using the same shiny material as the stars on the tent.

Around us are demonstrators dressed as bright red cardinals with their big head crests, parrots in different pastel colours, a long-beaked hummingbird, and some other birds that seem kind of made up. There are also a bunch of crows, their feathers so black and shiny that they look like they have oil on them. The shortest crow takes off their headpiece and my heart starts beating faster.

"It's Andressa!" I shout-whisper to Aiza.

"Chut," she whispers back. "Don't call attention to her. Or to us."

I follow Aiza's example and try to look casual, but I can't help feeling excited. Even though Mommy has taught me that social justice is won by movements and groups, not by individuals, I can't help feeling that Andressa is a real, live superhero.

"Do you think we'll get to ride with her?" I ask Aiza as we move forward with the others towards the mariposa. And then my excitement turns to disappointment because Andressa hands her bird's head to someone who's around the same size as her and trades it for a wolverine head. Andressa completes her transformation from bird to wolverine by slipping thick, furry arms over her skinny hairless ones and adding huge wolverine paws with claws to the furry arms. She looks fierce, and I decide that it's right for her to have different animal personas.

A few minutes later we're boarding the mariposa and then I'm too busy attaching all the safety straps to think about anything else. And like a second later, whoosh! We're flying!

When I was little, I used to envy Mommy because she got to fly in a plane as a kid, before all the airport bombings, but this is so much better! We're not in a big metal machine with roaring, polluting engines but out in the fresh air, powered by sun and wind, and there's no room inside me for disappointment or fear or jealousy or anything bad.

"Look down!" Aiza says.

Below us is the white tent with the purple constellations, the first aid tent with the red symbols, and there's the green one where we spoke to the puppeteers! I can even see the puppets, which look much smaller from up here. And the people look smaller too, almost like dolls.

"C'est comme une simulation!" I say. "Or a screen game! Or a bas-relief holo map!"

"Only it isn't. It's real, Simon."

"Really real," I agree.

I look out at all the demonstrators, and I think of constellations again because they're making different patterns together. I try to see if I can find anyone I know.

When I'm almost ready to give up, I finally spot, on the very edge of the crowd, three people riding in on two bicycles. Someone with straight brown hair carrying a bag—maybe a baseball bag!—runs to meet them. They get off the bicycles and I see that one of them is really tall and has curly brown hair and another one is much shorter and has curly reddish hair, and in between the tall curly haired person and the short curly haired person is a medium-tall, straight-haired person dressed in black who's jumping up and down and shouting and waving at us and that's when I'm sure it's them, it's my family, because no one else in the world except my Daddy can jump so high and look so excited, as though it were him who was flying in the air.

"Salut! Salut! Salut!" I shout, and Aiza shouts with me. "It's us! We're flying!"

Then all of us start waving and shouting, but the mariposa takes us up higher and soon the people on the ground are too far away for me to tell one from another anymore. We go even higher and the border station looks like a tiny little toy and I realize that I can see not just Québec but the United America. I try to figure out where one country ends and the other begins, but I can't. The line is invisible, and even though this is something Daddy explained to me when I was just a little kid, seeing it from up here makes me think hard about things: like how something can be invisible and still be real and powerful.

Then I think again about people as constellations, about my family and Aiza and the co-op and the network and the Peeps and all the animals and plants, and I realize there are other types of invisible lines—lines that connect us instead of divide us. But which lines are stronger? I think believing in something can make it more powerful. Maybe it's up to us to decide which invisible things to believe in.

EPILOGUE

PHILIP

"Papi, take one!" Kyla thrusts a plate of what she calls her choco-banana special cookies towards me with a mischievous gleam in her eyes. Simon, standing behind her near the kitchen table, offers an indulgent shrug, and even though a mischievous expression accompanied by an indulgent one almost always spells trouble, of course I grab the largest cookie on the plate and bite right into it.

My mouth is on fire, like I've just sucked on one of my grandfather's jalapeño mints.

"Mmm, delicioso," I say, my eyes tearing. Kyla, who even at seven is hard to fool, is laughing at me. "Seriously, mija. You should serve them tonight at our community welcome party. Everyone will want the recipe."

She doesn't react as I expect—with a giggle or a conspiratorial smile. Instead, she frowns, blinking as though close to tears.

Simon puts his hand on her shoulder. "What's the matter

Kyla? You look sad. Or worried. If it's about the cookies, lots of people love spicy chocolate, and everyone else will think it's a funny joke. But if you want, we could make a sign just in case —like a content warning."

"Okay," she sniffles, "but. . . what if people don't like *me*? What if they don't want me to live here?"

"Oh mija, everyone will love you." I reach down to lift her into my arms, holding her close. She presses her face into my shoulder and I rock her a little until I feel her body relax. When she finally lifts her head and begins to squirm, I place her on her feet again and scooch down in front of her, placing myself so that eye contact is easy. "We're all so, so happy that you're living with us."

"That's for sure!" Simon chimes in. "I've wanted a little sister since, like, forever!"

"You know, Kyla, it was hard to convince your Mama to let you come, but she did it for you. She knew you'd be better off living here." I say this although it's a generous take on Dana's mixed motivations. "I will always be grateful to her for that," I add, and that part is true.

"Don't feel bad if you like it better here," Simon adds thoughtfully. "That doesn't mean you don't love your mama and stepdad, and your baby brother, of course."

I find myself surprised at his insight, though I shouldn't be. Simon's always been a smart, sensitive kid, and his people skills have skyrocketed since he took it upon himself to help Kyla integrate into her new family and home.

"I'll tell you what," I say. "Remember how you said you wanted to make a picture book for your baby brother's birthday? What if you did a little recipe book, with all your favourite dishes? Simon could help with the illustrations and I can help you translate it."

"Into Spanish *and* French," she says, both her enthusiasm and her willfulness back.

"Yes, of course," I agree.

"Can we start now, Simon?" she asks.

He nods his head and Kyla claps her hands in delight, leaving me with a plate of what might be the sweetest and spiciest cookies in the world. Sweet and spicy: a good way to describe my new life, too.

Before I moved to Montréal, my happiest memory was of Kyla's birth. Now that memory stands side-by-side with the one where Janie, Laek, Siri, and Simon stood before a judge and testified about how much they loved me and what an integral part of their family I was. With Pierre-Ryan's hand on my shoulder, I listened to the judge affirm our relationships. Kyla arrived in Montréal one week later. That day was frightening as well as exciting because even though Janie's brother drove her to the border, she was forced to walk across it alone.

I've been thinking about my life, about what's next. I have the mental space to do that now. With a fiery-haired partner whose temper's even worse than mine, and a sweet-natured one who can hit harder than I can, I'm feeling strangely calm.

Going from being alone with occasional time with my daughter to being a member of an active, six-person family has, ironically, also made me calmer. This community is starting to feel like family as well, which adds to my sense of security. With my anxiety a few notches lower, I'm beginning to see how I can best contribute. The answer is as a parent and educator. I'm also a protector, though I wonder if this trait is the result of living in a society where caring for children means constantly having to worry about threats to their safety and well-being. Maybe in a society that's healthier and kinder, a teacher could concentrate on teaching.

I've begun to work on a plan to create a network of alternative schools for the kids in our community. I'll start by presenting it to our own co-op then to the Réseau des coopératives. If we're ever going to change this society, to see more solidarity and less oppression, education will be a crucial element. That's where I mean to make my stand.

SIMON

One of the best things about Uncle Philip getting to stay with us forever is that now I have a little sister. I'm also glad I'm not the youngest anymore. Kyla thinks it's hyper too. With her mom and stepdad, she always had to take care of her baby brother. She loves it when Siri and I take care of her instead. I think she likes all the attention.

It's weird, but the other thing I've learned from having a little sister is that polyamory makes sense. Of course, it's great to have three parents in the family, but some people say that having more than one partner is disloyal or means that you love your first partner less. It's obvious that this isn't true just from seeing how much Mommy and Daddy love each other at the same time that they love Uncle Philip. But on top of this, I know from my own experience too. I definitely don't love Siri any less just because I have another sister. In fact, I think I love and appreciate her even more.

When Aiza and I grow up, if we decide to be a family together, we can invite others into the family too. For instance, there are things that Aiza likes that I don't—such as sex and dancing—and things that I like that she doesn't— such as basketball and cooking. And it's true what Daddy once told me. Love isn't like fossil fuel or clean water, a scarce resource that we're in danger of using up. Just the opposite! The more people you love, the more love there is in the world.

SIRI

For now, I've decided not to get a wrist chip after all. I'd been looking forward to getting chipped when I turned sixteen, but as usual, my birthday was full of drama and surprises.

Some of the surprises were horrible—like the drone strike on our roof garden—but some of the surprises were good. Like how the community party being cancelled led to me inviting a few of my comrades from Jeune Vanguard to celebrate my birthday with my school and baseball friends. Not only did members of my team and of rival teams end up rescuing me and my Jeune Vanguard comrades, but now there's a budding romance between Maneesh and Nasrin.

Speaking of romance, it's weird, but I'm getting this vibe that Gabriel is looking at me in that way again. He's actually being nice to me, which is a good change of pace, but I'm feeling cautious. When it comes to Gabriel, my emotions have always been extreme: I either have a huge crush on him or can't stand him.

I have to admit that Gabriel does seem to want to change. He was the one who suggested that I wait a little while before deciding whether to get a wrist chip. "I know I teased you about your parents not letting you get chipped, but you shouldn't do something just to rebel against them. Just like you shouldn't *not* get chipped just because your parents are against it."

I was kind of impressed by how reasonable and mature this advice was, and also insightful, because I do sometimes think too much in binaries. Rebel or conform. My militant friends and my non-militant friends. Hating Gabriel or being in love with him. I'm beginning to realize that I can be like my parents and also be my own person. I can find things in common with all different kinds of people. And maybe I can also see Gabriel as both problematic and admirable, to acknowledge his strengths and his faults.

Part of refusing a binary is realizing that life can be complicated, and accepting that helps you to understand things better. Plus, complexity—in both people and the world—is way more interesting.

LAEK

Lying between Janie and Philip on the new king-sized bed that pretty much fills up our small bedroom and feeling just as safe as it's possible for me to feel, I decide to do my best to give detailed answers to every one of Philip's questions.

"It's your penance," Philip tells me, "for telling that sadistic guard I didn't know anything. How about you start by telling me who he was."

"An agent from the U. A.," I say.

"It was his accent that tipped you off, right?" Janie says.

"Among other things," I reply.

"I noticed it too, but wasn't sure," Janie says, then directs her comments to Philip, on the other side of me. "Though Laek's from the Midwestern Drylands, he can mask his accent."

Philip nods at Janie, then turns his attention back to me. "What about your ex-boss, Cloutier? How much did he know?"

"He knew he was sending those kids somewhere bad. Why else was his company paid so much per head? Between Marc Cloutier and the info from Clara's decoded chip, we were able to document it. So yeah, he was aware at a minimum that he was selling vulnerable kids into forced labour. And who knows what else." I go cold, thinking about the room with the cots. "Was Cloutier in on every detail? Maybe, maybe not. I don't think he would have cared," I finish.

"Do you still think he had something to do with Clara's death?" Janie asks. "I know you had someone look into it and they didn't find a connection. But you still seemed. . . unsure."

"When Clara died, I needed someone to blame. Cloutier was the perfect candidate. He'd benefited from her death, was into all kinds of shit. When our own people confirmed that Clara was probably just the victim of some run-of-the-mill asshole hogging the road and driving carelessly, I didn't want to accept it. It's why Chloë stopped talking to me for a while. She couldn't deal with how obsessed I was with blaming Cloutier."

"And what do you believe now?" Janie asks.

I shrug. "In the banality of evil, I suppose. And that life isn't like a murder mystery, all the clues lining up at the end."

Janie takes my hand and squeezes it.

"Okay," Philip says. "Now: the airport bombing. How did you really know?"

I close my eyes briefly, wanting to take my time before answering this one. I replay the events of that morning in my head for the umpteenth time, hoping this time to find certainty.

"Like I said, it was mostly instinct. At the time, I couldn't have described every clue I had, and if I could've, it would have been foreknowledge, and everything would have gone down differently. But thinking back on it now, there were things I noticed. Things I can name."

"Then go ahead, name them," Philip says.

"There was the kiosk worker. Their puzzled look after receiving a message. How they quickly left the area. The faint odour I recognized from having spent time near explosives."

"And that communication you got before we left for the airport," Janie says. Her words drop like a rock onto my chest.

"Yes," I admit.

I know I need to say more. I could tell them exactly what the message said. I still remember every chilling word. But it wouldn't mean the same thing to them as it did to me. Communication doesn't work that way. You bring in as much as you take out.

"Was it Al?" Janie speaks gently, with none of her usual anger about him.

"No. And yes. Another old comrade. But I knew where the message originated. I was asked to recall the action I did. At the complex in the Midwestern Drylands. And the rewards of fidelity. Along with the consequences of the opposite."

"And?" Philip asks, speaking gruffly to hide his anxiety.

"The message included geometrical figures relating to a building. And a formula. For four points on the same geometric plane. And how the introduction of a fifth point brings instability. Volatility. Do you understand?" I ask, looking from one to the other. When neither of them responds, I try to explain. "Planes. Volatility. Four then five. Punishments for infidelity. That morning when Phil arrived, it suddenly seemed horribly clear. I. . . I know it sounds crazy."

Philip looks troubled and confused, but Janie smiles and shakes her head.

"It's not crazy, what you thought," she says. "But it's an easy problem to solve. Just make the five points collinear."

"Collinear?" Philip asks.

"You know. On the same line. That way, the geometric plane can pass through all five points. Also, we're not five points anymore, we're six, with Kyla."

Philip blinks a few times. Then his muscles relax, as though letting go of a tightly held burden. "Well, I'm not much of a mathematician," he says with his usual self-effacement. "But I guess the important thing is that we got through it together and now, here we all are."

"Here we are," Janie repeats, a slow smile spreading between her two rosy cheeks.

I wait. Look from Janie to Philip, ready to answer any other questions they have. But there are no questions. After a moment, Janie puts her hand on my thigh. Squeezes. On the other side of me, Philip gently pushes the hair from my eyes. My haircut has grown out. I'm ready for a new one. Or maybe I'll let my hair get long. I don't need to worry about that anymore.

I kiss both sets of lips.

"Enough talk," I say. "It's time for some action."

JANIE

"So now that we've made the world safe from enforced monogamy, what's our next défi?" Pierre-Ryan jokes, leaning in the doorway of my office.

"Hmm, maybe birth certificates," I answer seriously. "There needs to be more flexibility on who gets listed as parents."

P.R. grins at me. "Et puis, after that?"

"Name changes, obviously. You shouldn't have to jump through so many hoops, especially to change your first name. After that we should take on patriarchy," I continue, getting up from my desk to pace. "All hierarchy, actually. There are so many laws that date from feudalism or spring from other outmoded ideas. Including capitalism, of course. Worker-owned cooperatives should be the norm. And we should replace money with barter, or a rational, non-exploitative economic system that doesn't externalize costs like the environment, health and safety, and the lives of living creatures. And of course, first we kill all the landlords!" I declare, raising my fist.

"I thought the quote was to kill all the lawyers," P.R. responds.

"Land*lords!* Even the name is an outrage. What gives them the right to be lord of the land? Land that other people are living on! Property is purely a legal construct and—"

"Janie, we have that meeting in a few minutes—"

"And once we've conquered capitalism and hierarchy, then racism, colonialism, nationalism, ageism, ableism, sexism, genderism, speciesism. . . well, all the other evil isms, really, can't be far behind."

"Are you done?" he asks, smiling.

"Nope, I'm just warming up."

ACKNOWLEDGMENTS

My first thanks goes to Ursula K. Le Guin, whose work showed me the potential of speculative fiction as a tool of positive social change.

As always, I am extremely grateful to the members of my writing groups who read early versions of this novel, chapter by chapter, and offered me invaluable feedback and encouragement. I would also like to personally thank my beta readers: Joel Miller, Jessica Patterson, Keiran Gibbs, Margaret Sankey, Maya Merrick, Duff McCourt, and Émilie Laramée—who also verified my French (though any errors that may have slipped through are my own.) A special thank you to Chris DiRaddo who helped me to understand why people were asking about a sequel to Cycling to Asylum.

My enormous gratitude to H. Givens, whose insights as a sensitivity reader were worth so much more than than the amount I paid them for their work.

Mille mercis to Flame Arrow Publishing's Dave Dufour, who believed in this project, and to editor Célia Chalfoun who is not only brilliant but kind.

Je tiens à remercier tout particulièrement HK de HK & les Saltimbanks pour la chanson "On lâche rien," album Citoyen du monde (2011). J'utilise cette chanson merveilleuse et féroce dans mon histoire avec l'aimable autorisation de l'artiste.

Last but far from least, love and thanks to my family—

Glenn, Mara, and Josh—who have accompanied me on this journey from the start, and continue to provide inspiration and support.

ABOUT THE AUTHOR

Credit: Rachel Karp

Su J Sokol is a social rights activist and a writer of speculative and interstitial fiction. Xe is the author of three novels: *Cycling to Asylum*, which was long-listed for the Sunburst Award for Excellence in Canadian Literature of the Fantastic; *Run J Run*; and *Zee*, a finalist for the Janet Savage Blachford Prize for Children's and Young Adult Literature. Su's short fiction and essays have appeared in various magazines and anthologies. Originally from Brooklyn where xe worked as a housing rights lawyer, Sokol has made xyr home in Montréal/Tiohtià:ke since 2004.